ARKHANGELSK

ARKHANG

ELIZABETH H. BO

HOUSE
PANTHER
PUBLISHING

ARCHIVE #10456

LAST RECORDED LOG BEFORE SEPARATION
DAY 227, COLONY YEAR 22

LOGGED BY: EVGENIA TYMKIV
B. SHIP YEAR 190
D. COLONY YEAR 32 (EST.)

DIRECTIVE 17 GOVERNMENT USE ONLY
SCHOLARLY ACCESS FORBIDDEN

The planet looks so beautiful from up here. Bright white, peaceful, the mountains scattered little dots.

And that massive scar, that pit in the middle of the mountain range. Our new home.

My new home. Without Niki.

We should've just stolen the munitions in the first place. But we asked for them, knowing they'd refuse, and then they knew we were coming. And Niki…Niki said "It's my idea. I have to go."

So now I have to go on without Niki.

Not just Niki, of course. Alex and Tara. Meehra. Tamar. David. They didn't think those bastards in the city would hurt them. They thought we were all on the same side. I guess we know now, don't we?

I was meant to drop the power core next week, but there's snow blowing through from the other side of the planet, and even without a windstorm I'm not sure the engines will give me fine enough control in-atmosphere. I've practiced it on the simulator, and I get it into the pit about sixty percent of the time. I get it in undamaged about forty percent of the time, but Connor says we can coat it in more ice if it splits.

Which is just shoving the problem into next year, but Connor's sure the city will come around, and we'll move back there and be one big happy family.

After Niki? I don't want to be their family. I sure as hell won't break bread with them. Which means I need to get the core down in one piece.

I understand it now, how the Old World destroyed itself. I understand how they could keep killing each other, even knowing they were tearing it all down, destroying the future. Because I would, if I could. I would tear them down. I know we're the end of it all, the last of everything. I know if we die that's the end of humanity, any dusty fingerprints we leave behind waiting to be discovered by the next quasi-intelligent species to wander into our stars.

But if I had the chance to take my revenge, I'd do it. Over and over and over again.

I always thought survival mattered to me. Turns out it was only Niki.

Anyway. *Arkhangelsk* is officially decommissioned, as of now. Random Aliens of the Future: please know that humanity was a horror show and we're best left undone. For all the gods, even out here on this icy world we can't keep from killing each other. Let us die. Let us die. Let us die.

INVASION

CHAPTER ONE

Irina and I are running late again.

We should be traveling under the ice for safety, down the main spoke from the Hub to the Eastern Arc of the Inner Rim; instead we've climbed to the surface to save time, crossing the courtyard in the sunshine. Despite the bright skies I can feel the wind through my protective suit, and by the time I reach the airlock I'll be chilled through. But Irina, dressed as always in fleece pants, white knit top, and boots too big for her eight-year-old feet, doesn't feel the cold.

Irina can never resist unfiltered daylight, and even facing our grim errand she's half-running, half-dancing, skipping over the intaglio etched into the icy ground. The inlay is changed after every storm and thaw, but the weather's been clear now for twenty-six sunsets, and so frigid the sparse foot traffic hasn't yet damaged the design. I'm glad. Sometimes the carvings in the courtyard are abstract, but this time they're animals: fish and mammals and sinuous reptiles, Irina's favorites. I like the animals.

There are no animals in Novayarkha.

The etchings grow sparse before we reach the Eastern Arc staircase. Irina leaps over a wise-eyed buffalo, following me down the stairs and waiting as I turn the wheel on the airlock. Her eyes on me are black and huge, but apart from that she doesn't look like me at all. She has yellow hair and frost-colored skin and a smile that used to keep me warm.

I give the wheel a final tug, and the *thunk* of the hydraulic release vibrates through the soles of my boots. The door falls open into my hand, sluggish. Like so many things in Novayarkha, it needs to be fixed, but even when we have the materials we never have the time. I pull the door closed behind me, and as I spread my arms and wait for the decontamination cycle to complete, Irina stands on her toes to peer through the exterior window. There's nothing to see besides the long, shadowed staircase arcing thirty meters up to a sliver of azure sky.

I pull off my protective clothing and enter the decon chamber; when the airlock's green light appears, I peel the oxygen seal off my nose and mouth and push the inner door release. Lauren's front door stands directly opposite, across the wide hallway: a prestigious location, with easy access to both the surface and the main passage to the Hub. The house itself is three luxurious rooms wide, lit by the extra-large solar tubes that adorn every Inner Rim residence. For two, it was opulence; now that Lauren's alone, it's become nothing more than empty space she has to fill.

Beside me, Irina slips her fingers into mine, and I ring the doorbell.

More than a full minute passes before Lauren answers the intercom. "Who is it?"

She sounds tired, disoriented; for a moment I wonder if I've misremembered the time. "It's Anya Savelova."

There's a brief pause before she says "Of course."

She's forgotten. Whether that's a result of the illness or stress, I don't know, but it's not typical for anyone in Novayarkha to forget an appointment with the city's head peace officer.

A moment later the lock clicks free, and I drop Irina's fingers as the inner door opens.

When I ran into Lauren last week in the Hub kitchens, she

looked animated, almost healthy. Now she's grown small, the deep circles around her albino-translucent eyes muddy gray, and she presses her palm against the doorframe, shifting her weight from foot to foot. The illness takes people at different speeds, but in Lauren the pace is accelerating.

She doesn't smile when she sees me, but moves stiffly away from the door as I step into the bright front room. The space is over-warm, and I wonder for a moment about the ventilation system, but it's not the air that's left the stale taste at the back of my throat.

All around the room, Tamara is everywhere: a bas-relief of her as an infant, her head elongated from her natural birth; charcoal sketches focusing on her nose, her jawbone, her eyebrows; bust after bust showing her features blooming from childhood to elegant young womanhood. Expert work, much of it recent. There's no other decoration, nothing else beyond the sparse furnishings. Lauren's always been outgoing, productive, well-loved; she could have every luxury the city offers. Instead, everything is Tamara.

Tamara inherited her mother's beauty, but inverted: dark and warm-skinned where Lauren is colorless. Lauren's Selection was a surprise to some, but it stands to reason her rare expression of the variegated legacy of the Old World would be a variant we'd want to preserve. Tamara didn't get her mother's pigmentless skin, but she carries her genes.

Carried. She's a loss, and of late we've had too many losses.

Lauren braces one hand against the wall, stepping carefully until she reaches the stone hospitality stove in the corner. The room doesn't require a stove—the Eastern Arc sits squarely over the ore processing vents—but Lauren spreads her palms above the warm surface, and I catch a tremble in her hands. "I'm sorry, Anya," she says. "I fell asleep again. It's…difficult, these days." She flexes her fingers one last time above the heat, then turns to me. "I need to know if my daughter is dead."

There's no other possibility. We don't lose many in Novayarkha, but the ones whose bodies we never discover are just as gone as those we find frozen in the snow, or broken at the bottom of the quarry. "I checked the security records." It's an empty offering, but an expected one. "We haven't had any breaches."

Lauren's response is predictable. "They're getting in somehow."

With every disappearance, the family makes this argument. But the Exiles aren't subtle. They don't sneak. Tunnels under the city would require blasting; they could never dig in stealth. They storm our walls out in the open, take only what we don't fight to keep, and leave again. In all the years I've searched for the missing, I've never found evidence the Exiles are kidnappers, or even particularly creative thieves.

And yet it's the story, what people believe. It's what we tell our children: don't play outside, or the Exiles will take you. I feel the same dread as anyone when I think of them. They're our existential enemy, the opposite of us, anarchic and disruptive and selfish.

They didn't take Tamara. But I understand why Lauren needs to believe they did.

"I'll check again," I tell her, even though there's nothing to check. "You said you have her diary?"

Lauren pushes herself off the wall and shuffles toward the couch. I stand close, in case she needs help, but she doesn't ask, and I don't offer. Leaning over she pushes on a panel inset into the stone coffee table; it slides aside noiselessly, revealing an old electronic tablet. I hadn't known any of them were in private hands anymore.

Lauren hands me the tablet, and I touch the screen. "NO ACCESS" it reads, in low-res lettering, and to myself I curse. Fingerprinted, or maybe even retina-printed. I don't know enough about the old tech to be able to tell which, but it won't be easy to get into it. All I say to Lauren is "Thank you."

She slides the panel back into place and turns back to me, not quite meeting my eyes. "Tamara's young," she says. "I remember youth. Whatever she says in there—unless it's going to help us find out where she is, I don't need to know."

Preserving the victim's innocence: they all do that, too. With all of the vast illogic that goes into being a survivor, this is the part that makes sense to me. They'll never have more of their loved one than they have in this moment. They'll cling to an image that was never fully realized, and slowly excise impurity and imperfection until they are left with a sweet-natured, smooth-edged ghost to keep them company.

I could tell Lauren jagged edges are better, that they take longer to blunt and to fade. She wouldn't believe me.

By the time I disengage from Lauren, I am more than twenty minutes late to the governor's office, and I must wait until Yulia decides to acknowledge me.

She sits at the desk, her back to the monitors displaying the camera feeds from the surface, and I study the silver-gray top of her head as she writes in her tight, precise hand. The graphite stylus in her fingers is trembling, just a little; I briefly abandon my post to fill up her glass at the utility sink in the corner. Angry with me or not, she's almost certainly been pushing too hard again.

"Thank you, Anya," she says when I set the glass down by her hand, but she doesn't invite me to sit in my customary chair.

Eventually she lays down the stylus and looks up. My guess was right: she's exhausted, her typically gold-tan skin waxy and almost green, as if she's bruised all over. She's smiling, but her tawny eyes, usually full of good humor, betray mild annoyance. "We have talked about this, Officer Savelova."

I've learned to answer no unasked questions when talking with Yulia. "Yes, Governor."

Her eyebrows creep up. She's a small woman, her head barely at my shoulder when we're both standing, but her slim form conveys an authority earned in her thirty years as our city's leader. "Then perhaps," she says, "you could explain why you've missed half our meeting pursuing something you *know* will have no satisfactory resolution."

I swallow my first response. No matter my schedule, I wouldn't have denied a mother's plea for help, and after all our years together this is a thing Yulia should know about me.

"Loss isn't so easy for someone like Lauren," I say instead.

"It's not so easy for any of us." But Yulia's voice has softened; she knows grief as well as I do. "Your kindness speaks well of you, Anya. But you know we owe too much to the living to spend ourselves on the dead."

"Yes, Governor."

Lecture completed, she sits back. "You may take six sunsets to cater to Lauren's speculations. No more than that, and all investigation must be on your own time. I will not tolerate further lateness."

I'll be expected to repay her generosity in the future, but for now she only gestures, at last, at the chair.

We spend the next half hour going through the block reports. Most of the items are mundane—public arguments, noise complaints, property disputes—but there's been an increase in vandalism and fighting, the sort that's often concomitant with sudden death. We've never been a people who discuss our losses, and grief suppressed, I've found, often comes out sideways. Most of the vandals are Tamara's friends, but after Yulia's earlier concession I choose not to point that out.

We're reviewing the supervised work schedules when a voice comes from beyond the office's rear door.

"—wouldn't have thought it'd have such a strong—Oh! Anya." Doctor Halvorsen catches my eye as the door swings shut behind her. "I'm sorry, I thought you'd be finished by now."

I check the time—five minutes over. "My apologies. We started late."

"I'm glad to hear that. I thought I'd forgotten how to read the clock." She smiles at me, bright and guileless. "I was surprised to miss you at the ceremony earlier."

Doctor Halvorsen is our oldest citizen, at eighty-three nearly twenty years older than Yulia, and a full thirty years older than me. She's been present at every birth in Novayarkha, natural or incubated, and for those of us born of incubators, she's the first parent we know. Her age alone gives her authority, but it's her status as Mother that keeps me from pointing out to her that I never attend the monthly Remembrance ceremony, and she knows why. "I was attending to other duties," I tell her, and I almost sound civil.

Her lips thin in anticipation of delivering a rebuke; but Yulia's on my side this time. "Leave the girl alone, Magda," she snaps. "Remembrance isn't mandatory, and I'm not about to make anyone stand in that dark, cramped crypt if they don't wish to."

Doctor Halvorsen recovers effortlessly. "Of course not. It's only that I find it such a comfort, honoring those who've come before us."

I don't believe she's being deliberately cruel, but the morning has frayed me, and I get to my feet. "Do you need anything else from me, Governor?"

"Not today, Officer Savelova." Behind Yulia, Doctor Halvorsen loiters by the big monitors, her face lit by the images of the sun-brightened snow. "Thank you for your time."

It's a sound from Doctor Halvorsen that stops me from leaving: a wordless interjection, fear or excitement I can't tell. She's staring at the center screen, and she isn't looking at the expanse of snow-covered ice, or the distant granite mountains. Instead she's looking into the sky, above where our yellow star sinks toward the horizon. Between Doctor Halvorsen and the screen, Irina stands on her toes, bracing her fingers against the wall and staring along with the old woman.

"There it is again!" Doctor Halvorsen exclaims. "Just like yesterday. I told you, Yulia."

Slowly, with more effort than Doctor Halvorsen notices, Yulia pushes herself to her feet and joins her friend, studying the pre-sunset sky. After a moment her eyebrows twitch together, and she turns away. "There's nothing there, Magda," she says. "There wasn't anything there yesterday, either. It's your old eyes, staring at the sun too long."

"Hmph." Doctor Halvorsen looks away. "My eyes are better than yours. And my mind obviously a good deal more open."

"Your mind is a chasm, that is certain."

Irina drops back on to her heels and returns to my side. I'm always an intruder when Yulia and Doctor Halvorsen begin to bicker, and it's past time for us to go. I meet Yulia's eyes briefly, and she nods her dismissal; I don't bother taking my leave of Doctor Halvorsen. With half an hour left before first dark, I should have time to talk to Tamara's friends before the quarry shuts down.

The exterior quarry path isn't carved, but Irina spins and jumps anyway, restless and manic. This is my favorite time of day in Novayarkha, when the sky deepens from azure to violet, and the sun turns bloody orange before sinking below the icy horizon.

Today I can't think about the sunset at all.

"Irina," I ask, as we reach the outskirts of the quarry, "did you see something?"

Irina stills, and looks at me with her sober dark eyes. She nods.

"I saw something, too." And we cross the courtyard in the indigo dusk.

CHAPTER TWO

Irina swings on the rails of the tram as we speed along the Western Arc. It's two hours into first dark, nearly dinner time, but even after my long afternoon at the quarry I'm not hungry. I was tempted to walk outside again, cutting across an anterior courtyard, but Costa lives in the farthest arc of the Outer Rim, and I'd've had to wear a quarry suit to make the trip in the lethal cold. Instead I choose safety and let Irina pounce and jump, her mood unfettered.

At the end of the tram line we head up a narrow secondary spoke to the far western tip of the city. As a teacher, Costa can live wherever he chooses, and he chooses this place. It's away from nearly everyone else, and thanks to its proximity to the prison, generally quiet. I wish I'd had the foresight to take the house before he did.

When I ring he unlocks the door without asking who it is, and Irina runs inside ahead of me. Costa is sitting at the desk with his back to me, bent over a stack of thin slates. He waves me in without turning around. "Get the door," he says. "The heat never keeps up on nights like this." He makes a mark on a slate, then puts his stylus down, turning. "Fair evening, Anya," he says, and smiles.

Irina heads to the back wall, where Costa's mounted a massive piece of polished slate that's currently covered in mathematical equations. She reaches up as high as she can and starts tracing the symbols with her fingers. I count the slates in the stack before him; I get to twenty before I stop. "You're busy."

"I am," he agrees. "Which means I'm thrilled to be interrupted." He gets up and heads into his small corner kitchen. "I'm having supper. Stay?"

I nod. He's not much of a cook, Costa, but he's one of the few people I can spend time with who doesn't insist on constant conversation. I settle into a chair at his kitchen counter while he pulls packs of dried stew from a cabinet. "Since I know you didn't come for the food," he asks, "what's up?"

Wordlessly, I pull Tamara's diary from my pocket, laying it on the counter. Out of the corner of my eye, Irina, distracted from the alluring order of mathematics, pauses her tracing of Costa's equations.

He puts the dried stew down, all the light in his eyes disappearing. "Oh," he says.

"It's locked," I explain, although he already knows why I've brought it to him. "I don't want to damage it."

He stares at it for another moment. "After dinner, yes?"

I pocket the tablet, and in a few minutes he's himself again.

Usually we sit in silence, Costa and I, two oddities keeping each other company. Costa's oddity is tolerated more than mine. He's never entered a marriage or a child-rearing group, but somehow no one seems to remark on this. The popular theory is that he's suffering some brand of unrequited love, and has chosen to teach because he has no one with whom to build a family. The theory gains credence every year, when a few newly-grown former students approach him with romance in mind; he has cultivated an effective blend of well-timed obtuseness and gentle, unambiguous refusal.

But Costa pines for no one. The truth is both simpler and less conventional: he likes being alone, and always has. There aren't many of us like this. He's accepted because he's charming and open in front of other people, but I've never been such an actor. I should hate him out of envy, if nothing else, but he's the closest thing to family I have, after Irina.

Tonight, as we eat, I tell him about Doctor Halvorsen's vision, and my own speculation about what it might have been. Irina glares at me: I'm hedging my bets. I set down my spoon. "The thing is, I don't think it was eye strain. Not both of us, not at the same time. And she said she'd seen it before."

"You agree with the old bat, then? That it's aliens?" Costa's teasing me, and when I scowl, he laughs. "It's probably just an asteroid, An, and it's hardly the first. You used to see them all the time at the quarry, remember?"

My quarry duties are thirty years behind me, but I remember well enough squinting into the sunshine during a break from excavation, afterimages dotting the stone before me. "I never saw the same thing two days in a row."

"Even assuming Halvorsen wasn't spinning tall tales," he says, "which she might have been, you know, given how much she likes to scare the children—this planet captures all sorts of rubbish in orbit. Most of it's too small for us to see, but if it contains a lot of metallic ore, it's going to catch the sun now and then." He knows his handwaving isn't comforting, and he grows more serious. "Whatever it is," he assures me, "the observatory will have a handle on it. And if it was dangerous, we'd all have been alerted already. We're not going to be pulverized by space junk. Not tonight, at least."

When Costa and I were three years old, an asteroid hit. The impact was hundreds of kilometers away from Novayarkha, but there were tremors, and people feared for the stability of the permafrost. My memories of it are scant, and filled in by later accounts; but I remember the adults, the ones who were looking after us, betraying more fear than I'm sure they intended. It was my first taste of impermanence, of the fleeting nature of everything I knew.

After dinner I pull out the tablet again. Food seems to have made Costa curious enough to get past the morbid truth behind the object. "I didn't think any of these were privately owned," he says, turning it over in his hands.

"Lauren tells me Tamara came home with it when she started at the radio station, but she wouldn't say where it came from."

"Not keyed as stolen?"

I shake my head. "Tamara's listed as the legal owner, but there's no transfer data, so there's no alert on file. No ownership history, either. And it's locked with a fingerprint, not a code."

Costa gives me a shrewd look. "Not a lot of people who could have managed that."

With a fine-edged palette knife, Costa separates the screen from its backing, and begins to pry off parts that aren't welded together. When he extracts the memory chip—a wafer-thin rectangle the length of my thumb—he takes it to a memory reader we both know he's not supposed to have. He sets the chip in a prefitted tray, and the tiny screen lights up with blocks of hexadecimal numbers.

Costa can read hex as easily as the nursery poetry we are all taught as children. After a moment, he lets out a "Hah!" but I don't think he's amused.

Irina turns to look at us from the blackboard, where she's been tracing equations again. I lean over his shoulder; his machine has translated for us:

FUCK OFF MOM.

Preemptive hostility, even with a fingerprint lock. "What about the rest?"

"Encrypted," he says. "And no data before eight months ago. Lauren doesn't know when she got it?"

"I don't think they talked to each other that often," I tell him. It feels churlish, repeating a fact that has turned into such regret for a grieving mother. "How bad is the encryption?"

"Simple text, most of it," he says. "As far as I can tell. But there are dead spots on the drive; some of it's going to be lost. I'll submit the job to the central cryptographic system. As long as she hasn't used private keys, I should have what's readable in an hour or so."

"And if she has?"

His lips tighten. "Then we're talking about days. Longer if I can't get enough of a slice of machine time. Keep your fingers crossed she wasn't that paranoid."

I don't say aloud what we're both thinking: whatever happened to Tamara, a little excess paranoia might have been a wise thing. "You kept in touch with her after she graduated, didn't you?"

"A little," he admits. "She'd ask advice about what she could do besides the quarry. They all do that for a while, so I didn't think much of it. But when the radio station position became available, she asked if I could recommend a vocal coach."

An anomaly, of sorts; Tamara was not known for lacking confidence, but neither was she lazy. And she had, in fact, learned well; her news broadcasts had become increasingly popular. "Who did she end up working with?"

"Lev, I think," he says. At my look of surprise, he grins. "I recommended Viktor to her. I figured he knew the job at least, but she thought his delivery was dull. She's not wrong, and at least Lev has a nice speaking voice." He makes the same connection I have. "You think Lev gave her the tablet?"

Lev is head of the observatory, and as such has served on Yulia's council with me for nearly ten years now. He would have access to hardware, registered and unregistered, but a tablet seems like an oddly personal gift. "I'll ask him after dinner," I say. "If they're that close…he may have a better idea of what she was up to lately."

I'd prefer Lev know nothing. He's quiet enough by nature to make him difficult to know, but he's always been kind to me, even when I have not made it easy.

Costa is watching me closely. "You really think something's happened to her, don't you?" he asks. "You really believe she's not lost to the ice."

It's a euphemism, that phrase. We love the sunlight here in Novayarkha; all our buildings are designed to let it in, all our activities scheduled to give us as much brightness as our outdoor gear can grant us. It's inevitable that occasionally people wander too far, lose sight of the flat plain of the city, get disoriented by the white-out snow squalls that can form without warning. We find them days or weeks later, and we inter what remains in our crypt. Suicides are less common: nineteen in the thirty years I've been a peace officer. Even here, despair sometimes wins, no matter our efforts to counter it.

And then there are those we never find.

There has been a slow increase in the unaccountably missing over the last several years, and despite knowing they're lost to us, despite knowing some, at least, are simply taking more care about where they choose to end their own pain, I won't abandon them. On fine days when I am free, I wander with Irina across the tundra surrounding the city, swinging a wider arc than is safe, hoping to come across some fragment of the missing. Twenty-one in thirty years, twelve just in the last five, and they are somewhere.

That I will never find them is acceptable; that I should stop looking is not.

"If Tamara was a wanderer," I concede, "it's the most likely explanation. But Lauren doesn't believe it. And we haven't had squalls for twelve sunsets. Do you really think she could so easily lose her way?"

He nods, accepting without agreement. Costa is much more like Yulia in his thinking; he believes I'll find nothing. But he knows me, and he knows why I need to give Tamara every chance I can.

I've never been able to save anyone; my work so often begins when the danger is long past. But answers mean something. And I would, if I can, give Tamara's mother something to bury.

she thought I was good at that. The tablet was so she could record between sessions, and we could go over her work together."

"You must have believed her sincere, to give her such a generous gift."

My criticism is implicit. Tamara, bright and vivacious and favored, was never known as a diligent student. "When she first made the request," he says, "I was skeptical, yes. She and all her friends in the quarry..." He trails off, knowing I'm aware of the block disruptions, the noise complaints, the sorts of disturbances often attributed to the young and aimless. "But once I spoke with her, I did believe her." He meets my eyes, his expression direct, honest. "She seemed determined, as if she had some sort of personal mission."

"Perhaps she just wanted to get away from the stone."

"Perhaps." But he doesn't agree with me. "It's only an impression. But I think...for some reason, this was important to her."

"She never said why?"

He shakes his head; of course she didn't. He'd have already told me if she had.

"Why did you strip the ownership history?"

"I didn't." His gaze shift away from mine. There's truth in his voice, but something else as well. "There are— I know we're supposed to inventory our hardware, Anya." He looks back, his expression full of apology and appeal. "Do you know how long out of date our parts list is? I started in the observatory fifteen years ago, and it wasn't up to date then." I must look confused, because he sighs. "The tablet came from the parts closet," he tells me. "It's never had a history, not as long as we've had it. There's at least one more like it in there, along with an oxygen cleanser, three surface decontaminators, and a handful of circuit boards in microcloth."

"So when there's an audit," I press, "you lie to Khristen."

"We all lie a little bit," he says. "Can you tell me you have no contraband of your own?"

I think of Costa's memory reader, and a mass of cobbled-together transmitter components I've had stashed under my sink for a dozen years. "Nothing I have has been owned by someone who vanished," I point out. "It's a valuable gift, Lev, and a personal one. You understand why I need to ask."

It takes him a moment to catch on, and when I see the shock on his face I'm overcome with relief. "No, Anya. Tamara was—there was nothing romantic between us."

"Her idea, or yours?" When his lips thin, I reach out a hand to him. "Lev. We are all vulnerable to beauty, and she was more than old enough to choose for herself."

He takes a breath, and pulls dignity over himself like a shroud. "I won't say I wasn't fond of her," he tells me. "I knew the gift was...injudicious. But I harbored no hopes, Anya. Apart from her age, I knew she was already involved."

This is news. Lauren has been adamant that Tamara was on her own. "Was it serious?"

At that, he looks away again, but I don't think his embarrassment is for himself. Preserving her innocence again. "For him, yes. For her...it was always hard to tell."

"Him who, Lev?"

He looks at me squarely, innocently. "Rolf Eldaroff."

And I know the ice did not take Tamara.

Five years ago, Oksana Reikova, newly graduated from Costa's school and beginning a rotation with Doctor Halvorsen's nurses, left for her morning break and was never seen again. She'd been seeing Rolf Eldaroff for some time, continuing a relationship that had begun when they were teens, and when I interviewed him he was angry and evasive. Distress might have accounted for his behavior, but it was only because of Yulia's directive to move on from an unsolvable case that I didn't go back to speak with him again. Murder, after all, is passionate, visible; vanishing is a solitary act.

At twenty-five, Rolf is older than Tamara, and completed his quarry rotation before applying to work in the observatory. He's been there a full year. He would have seen every time Tamara met Lev for a lesson, watched the two of them together, Lev full of quiet kindness, Tamara wanting to learn—and maybe more.

Would he have been jealous?

"When is Rolf's shift?" I ask Lev.

"He's on now, for another forty minutes."

Lev tells me Rolf works the orbital monitors. A dull job, with too much opportunity for mischief; better suited to someone older, less fractious, but a necessary step for those hoping to make a career at the observatory. I find him on the second level, brooding over a radar schematic, a much-erased slate propped up next to it with row after row of scrawled numbers.

"What are you looking for?" I ask.

He jumps. "Oh! Officer." He fumbles for his coffee cup as he turns toward me.

"I didn't mean to startle you." I stay on my feet. I'm tall, but Rolf is taller, and I prefer being able to look down on him for now. "What are you looking for?"

"Asteroids," he tells me. I've kept my tone relaxed, but he's gripping his coffee cup like a climbing rope. "Comets we can see from further away, but it's hard to find asteroids ahead of time unless they're large enough to disrupt the orbits of the other planets in our system."

It's not at all the reason I'm here, but I can't resist the question. "Do you ever find any?"

"Now and again. Usually, though, they're small, and they fly past, or burn up in the atmosphere. If they hit, they almost never cause more than a mild tremor." He sets the coffee cup down, opening his hand with undue care. "Is there something I can do for you, officer?"

He must know. It's been three days, and there are no secrets in Novayarkha, not for long.

"Rolf," I ask, "when did you last see Tamara?"

I am utterly unprepared when he bursts into tears.

"He's confessed?" Aleksey asks over the phone.

"Not precisely," I reply. "He says they took a walk, and he fell asleep." It's a painfully outlandish story, and I half expect Aleksey to laugh.

Aleksey has been my assistant for ten years, and I wish I liked him better. He's always respected my methods, including my frequent need for solitude, which even Yulia still doesn't understand. He listens, and does as he's told most of the time, and he feels like an ally even when I'm not sure he is one. But there's always been something studied about him that's kept me cautious, more than just his unseemly excitement when uncovering the truth behind tragedy.

Professionally we balance each other well enough, but even he knows we will never be friends.

"What were you planning on doing this evening?" I ask.

"Just following up on the Outer Rim noise complaints."

It's in his voice: the eagerness. I was the same when I was his age, so certain I was making a difference, that intimidating people was imperative and right and would lead them back to the path of good citizenship. I'm too old now, and I fight an irrational surge of envy for Lauren and her creeping illness. I'm long past the point where I believe I'm leaving behind anything good.

"I need you to come here to officially arrest him," I tell Aleksey, "and settle him into a cell. Take his statement, but that's all. I mean it, Aleksey. I won't risk a nonsensical confession. We need to find her."

He grumbles his assent and hangs up, and I shake off irritation. Aleksey should have more wisdom. If we frighten Rolf too much—if we hurt him—he'll tell us anything, true or false, and we'll never have Tamara's body back, never mind real evidence of what was done to her. It's a given Rolf's life will be lived out in prison, but if he can tell us why he did this, if we can understand what's gone wrong with him, we may avoid raising more children to do the same.

Back with Rolf, I finally sit. It costs neither of us anything, now, to pretend to be friends, to talk over the sad incident of him murdering the woman he loved. "Tell me again." He'll hear those words later, and not as kindly; but I want him to have at least one clean chance to volunteer the truth.

His eyes fill, and he looks away from me, sniffing. "She wanted to take a walk."

"Outside?"

"She said—she thinks it's ridiculous, how much time we all spend inside. She says the illness will take us all anyway, so why not enjoy our youth when we have it?"

Strange, for a woman who so determinedly fled the quarry; but it's not a radical perspective. "What did you wear?"

He shifts, and for the first time looks genuinely guilty. "She had Lilith borrow some quarry suits."

Lilith, Tamara's closest friend, said nothing of quarry suits when I interviewed her. "So if I check," I say, still relaxed, "I'll find two suits missing from the quarry."

"She left hers behind," he tells me, "and I returned them both when I got back." He looks young, younger than he did five years ago. "Why would she do this?"

"You're saying that she took off her suit—out there on the ice—and left it with you?"

He nods.

"Why didn't you tell anyone?" It's difficult, now, not to telegraph my incredulity.

"I thought she was playing a prank on me. I thought she had her regular suit on underneath. I thought she left the quarry suit and walked back here. It wasn't until the next day I found out she didn't."

It was always hard to tell if she was serious, Lev had said. "Was she prone to that sort of prank?"

"People bore her. Sometimes she can be...unkind. She doesn't mean to hurt anyone." As if intent excuses all.

"Why didn't you tell anyone when you realized she was missing?"

And at that, his eyes fill again, and he stares at me, lost and vulnerable and suddenly, appropriately, afraid. "I kept hoping she would come home."

The anger arrives at last, but I swallow it. Instead I reach out and pat his arm gently. "We're going to have to talk to you officially, Rolf." To his credit he doesn't beg. "The more you can tell us, the faster you recall the details, the easier it'll be."

I don't say *stop lying.* I don't scream and rail at him in front of his worried colleagues. I wish I had the equanimity to conjure Irina in this crowd, to let her howl at the mad injustice of every bit of this.

Aleksey arrives, and Rolf stands. From time to time we've needed reinforcements for arrests, but Rolf is neither a runner nor a fighter. Aleksey won't need to intimidate; the absurdity of the lie will break Rolf down, and then I'll have a place to begin my search for whatever's left of Tamara.

I have to tell Lauren. Perhaps that's the duty I should have delegated to Aleksey.

Rolf is pulling on his coat, still looking dazed; Aleksey stands next to him, impatient. Aleksey isn't a particularly big man, but he's meatier than Rolf, more physical, and Rolf feels it. I open my mouth to tell Aleksey to give him space, but there's a commotion behind me, and I hear Rolf's name.

I turn to see Lev and the others gathered around Rolf's terminal, most chattering with what sounds like excitement; but Lev is frowning, and Isolde, the youngest, has a closed expression that looks disconcertingly like terror.

Lev comes over to us, ignoring me entirely. "How long have you been monitoring that recurring anomaly?" he asks Rolf, and every hair on my body stands on end.

"Which one?" Rolf glances at the clock, and his expression clears. "Oh, that. It's nothing. I'm guessing it's something that broke up further out in the system, and is streaming by in pieces. It—"

Uncharacteristically, Lev curses. "You damn fool," he snaps. "It's in orbit."

Rolf frowns, and for a moment he's no longer my prisoner, but another irritated scientist. "Don't be ridiculous," he says. "It's irregular. If our gravity had captured it, the appearances and the position would be consistent."

"Not if it's manipulating its location."

"But that's—" Rolf gapes. "How can it possibly move on its own?"

"It can't," Lev tells him. "Unless it's artificial."

I wait for the joke that doesn't arrive, and then my reality opens into a vast darkness and I can't look at any of them anymore.

CHAPTER FOUR

"IT'S NOT ALIEN," YULIA SAYS.

Lev, Dmitri and I are standing in her living room, in her small home down the main spoke from the Hub. Yulia is seated on the couch, relaxed, holding court. At Dmitri's recommendation there's a guard on her front door, and out in the Inner Rim hallway I can hear the murmur of a crowd. She'll need to speak soon; I've already had to dispatch Aleksey and my junior officers to dispel crowds along the spokes. People are terrified.

I'm one of them.

"The Exiles, then." Dmitri, who's been the city's civil defense chief for forty years, is also terrified, but he shrouds his fear in belligerence. Once, a century before the oldest of us was born, *civil defense* meant preparation for any possible external invasion, and in fact Dmitri has developed an efficient, streamlined strategy for dealing with the Exiles. But like the rest of us, he has no experience with anything like this.

"It's not the Exiles," Lev says. His tone is patient, but he paces the room, all nervous energy. "We monitor seismic as well as everything else, and there's no way—even if they'd been able to find the materials—that object launched from our surface."

"You think it's Old World." I make myself say it before my fear silences me completely.

Yulia gives me a satisfied nod and sits forward, quickly and with purpose. Putting on a show of good health. Since she and Dmitri were children she's insisted she would outlast him, and now that it seems she won't, she won't concede even the smallest weakness. "Look," she says to us, pointing at the monitor in front of her. "The shape of it? The lettering? Do you really think an alien is going to have the same aesthetics we do? Do you think they'll have an alphabet?"

The image is blurry, and I can't make out any lettering, but she's right about the shape. We've all seen the few surviving exterior images of our old ship—sixteen still pictures and one twelve-second video—and all children study the design drawings kept in the archive. This object has enough similarities: a cylindrical fuselage within a single spoked wheel where our ship had three; mirror symmetry along a central axis; cones on one narrow end, suggesting ventilation or exhaust. It doesn't belong hanging in our sky, but I don't find it outlandish to think it's of human construction.

There were those who left the Old World before us, never to be heard from again. There were those who tried, and who never made it off the ground, destroyed by enemies, poor construction, or bad luck. There must also have been some fleeing after us—we couldn't have been the last to make it out before it all ended.

"Will there be people?" I ask.

Yulia waves off the idea. "We were five thousand, and cramped in a much larger ship. The size of this—it might hold a hundred people, perhaps two hundred if they carry no cargo."

Our ship had carried far more than our ancestors on its two-hundred-year journey. "They'd've gone mad in such a small space," I realize. "Even as few as a hundred."

"Unmanned, then?" Lev suggests.

Yulia nods. "That's the logical assumption."

"But unmanned for what purpose?" I ask. The Old World, in its ancient times, sent probes to the stars, but they were slow, slower than even the most primitive early lightspeed rockets. I can't do the math in my head, but they couldn't have made it this far, not even after all this time. And the pictures I've seen of those antiquated probes look nothing like this object.

"Maybe they're looking for us," Dmitri says, unmollified.

"Then why haven't they contacted us?" Yulia's question stumps him, and she relaxes a little. "If they wanted to attack, Dmitri, they would have done so by now. And if they wanted to speak to us, it would be the same. The Old World is long dead. This is a drone, or some leftover piece of a probe sent long ago, before the Fall." She stands, and I resist the urge to give her my arm. "I will speak with our people."

Dmitri opens the door for her, and the murmurs in the hallway stop. She steps forward and smiles, and although the crowd's anxiety doesn't vanish outright, a ripple of calm follows in her wake.

All along the Rim and down the wide main spoke Yulia passes the gathered crowd, her stride easy, her smile sincere. Every now and then she lays a hand on the head of a child, even stopping to offer a few words of greeting, and I see the fear in their faces abate. That's always been Yulia's greatest power: if she's not frightened, they're not frightened. I walk next to her, and as we approach the Hub I begin to see the strain in the corners of her eyes. I understand the need to keep up appearances, but surely that's of no utility if she exhausts herself to death while we still need her.

In the Hub the crowd gathers around her, but she uses the main speaker system anyway, and her voice reaches throughout the city, transmitted via the embedded antennas out into the observatory and the quarry, across the tundra's thin air. "You've all heard about the orbiting object," she says. "I've met with my council, and I want to assure you: our city is safe."

A collective sigh of relief fills the air.

"Our conclusion at this time is that it is an unmanned probe of some kind, launched from the Old World shortly after we ourselves left. We deduce this from its size and its topology, and the fact that it has neither threatened nor contacted us in any way."

"Is it armed?" someone shouts from the crowd.

Yulia, usually impatient with interruptions, is unfazed. "That's one of the questions we're working to answer. But once again, I assure you: we've seen no evidence of threat at this point. I understand you're afraid," she says, as the crowd begins to murmur again. "But we don't believe there's anything to fear. We'll continue to observe and gather data, and anything we find will be made immediately public. If you have questions, address them to your block mayor. We are in this together," she concludes, "and together we are strong."

Together we are strong. The crowd echoes the phrase. I wonder, not for the first time, where it came from, and if there's any substantive truth to it.

As the crowd dissipates, Dmitri heads off with his staff to review the Exile raid procedures, and Lev retreats to the observatory. Yulia and I return to her office, where she takes her customary place at her desk; behind her, the screens monitoring the surface are darkening with second sunset.

I can't stay silent. "You're going to work *now?*" She would have been up earlier than usual, preparing for the Remembrance ceremony. On an ordinary day, she'd be long asleep.

She fixes me with a look I know: *Do not treat me as if I'm weak.* "I'd like to be here when the questions come in." She smiles, still deliberately relaxed. "Can you imagine the kinds of things we're going to hear from the Third Block?"

The Third Block has always been full of conspiracy theorists, positing everything from historical records manipulation to government mind control, but for the first time in my life I don't find them amusing. "Yulia," I begin.

"I see you've arrested Rolf."

It takes me a moment to register the change of subject. I don't want to talk about Rolf, to be distracted from the enormity of what's happening. "He was with Tamara when she disappeared," I say. "Aleksey is taking his statement."

Her look is not entirely disapproving; I've limited the use of resources enough, it seems. "Then we should be able to deal with him soon." Yulia has always favored swift, public justice, tempered with as much mercy as the crime permits. There will be little mercy available for a killer. "I hope this helps you to understand, Anya. All those other cases, the ones you won't let go of—when they're not lost to the ice, they're like this. One damaged person. Personal. Specific. Our safety here is precarious, always. You need to focus on the living, on the crimes we can mitigate, the offenders we can cure. It's not just personnel limitations, it's *your* time, specifically. I need your energy for what's tangible and changeable, because otherwise you'll run yourself into the ground, and I need you. Now more than I ever have."

It's deflection, this argument, every time, and I wonder if she's bringing it up because she thinks I'm afraid. "You know I cannot become governor, Yulia."

"Why not?" She spreads her fingers, palms up. "You're smart and thoughtful and dedicated to justice. And I have great faith you would set your emotions aside were the good of our people at stake."

After all these years, Yulia can't mistake me for a stoic. "They won't follow me. They don't like me."

"You think they like me?"

"I think they love you."

She pushes herself to her feet, leaning heavily on the desk, and I understand suddenly what it's meant, all these months, that she's shown her weakness only to me. "They love me because I have been consistent and decisive and just. You'll be all those things, Anya."

"Lev and Dmitri will destroy the council before they see me at its head. They'll never agree for me."

She waves a dismissive hand. "Lev is a scientist. He doesn't care, as long as you listen to him yammer at you. And Dmitri will do as he's told. He has no desire to be in charge, and he agrees with you more often than me already."

"He does not."

Her lips twitch in a brief smile. "Perhaps not. But he respects your intelligence and your observations. He'll learn to listen."

She's eroding me, as always. "What about law enforcement?"

At that, Yulia looks surprised. "That's why I gave you Aleksey."

When I was young, I gave up the quarry job I loved because Yulia appealed to my sense of duty. All these years later, I feel that same pull of loyalty, that same sense that I should trust her over myself. But I cannot, in my most fluid imaginings, see Aleksey in my job. And whatever Yulia says, I am still too much that young woman she took in off the stone.

"I'll think about it," I concede, as I always do when she's exhausted my arguments. It's as close as I can get to agreement without lying to her.

Yulia accepts that the skirmish is over for the day. "That's all I can ask." And then, with wonder in her voice: "It is something, isn't it? To see a ship from the Old World after all this time?"

I have no label for the feeling. It's wonderful, terrifying, hateful, hopeful all at once. I wish deeply for the days to roll back, to live in a time where I've never seen that strangely familiar ship. "That they should be able to launch a drone..." I think back to my childhood lessons. "It seems impossible, given how it was when we left."

"Humans persevere," she says, and smiles. "Maybe that's the message we should take from this. Despite everything they did to themselves, despite their ultimate destruction, they managed a last gasp before they died. We did not take all of their strength away with us."

It's a strange thought. We've been so careful, from the start, guarding our resources, balancing our numbers. We tend to one another as carefully as we tend to ourselves, treating our community as an organism all its own. All of the mistakes of humanity heeded and reversed. All of those mistakes brought back to us in the blurry image of an Old World drone ship, dutifully orbiting our frozen planet.

"It unsettles you, still," she observes.

"It's a coincidence, don't you think? There's a great deal of space, and for it to find us..."

"You think Dmitri may be right. That it's looking for us."

"I think we must consider that."

She lowers herself into her chair again. "I have considered it," she admits reluctantly, and I wonder why she said nothing in front of the others. "But there's something else you forget. Everything we've done here—burying the hull, the ice insulation, the lower levels and the tunnels—all the infrastructure that protects us from the radiation also makes us invisible from orbit. If this Old World drone is looking for us, it'll find only ice, and possibly some slight infrared variance. Even weapons would not be as effective a defense as the climate."

I take my leave of her, mildly relieved and entirely exhausted. Instead of going home to sleep, though, Irina and I head for the Inner Rim where I began my day. I should find Lauren before the rumors reach her, before she learns Aleksey is holding Rolf for Tamara's murder. Neither drones nor aliens will change her child's fate, and I owe it to her to tell her the truth face to face.

I stop at one of the spoke's wide surface monitors and take in the darkening sky, the sun setting for the second time today. The image is crisp and perfect, but it's an image nonetheless, transmitted from thirty meters above my head. I turn my back on it; Irina won't look at all, and she drifts in and out of my peripheral vision as I convince myself we're safe.

We've burrowed into the ice, buried ourselves like a mythical city. If the Old World drone came closer, it might be able to see people in the quarry or crossing the courtyard, but from its distance, Yulia is right: all its instruments will find is ice and more ice. We are as undetectable as if we had never come here at all.

I'm almost at Lauren's door before Irina stops, frozen, her dark eyes wide and frightened, and all the security I felt moments ago dissolves into uncertainty and terror.

"The radio." I turn and run back toward Yulia's office.

NZKO *HYPATIA*
FTL FIELD TRANSITION REPORT
================================
BATTERY CAPACITY: 5% CHARGING
SUBLIGHT FUEL CAPACITY: 90% DOWN 4%

CREW COMPLEMENT: 29% NO CHANGE
FTL SYSTEM STATUS: NOMINAL/OFFLINE
================================

FTL FIELD TRANSITION COMPLETE

RECIP: National Earth Space Organization, Vostochny
REPORTER: Loineau, Madeleine, Cmdr. NZKO *Hypatia*
Mission year 40, day 72

What the fuck, Vostochny? Is this some kind of a joke?

RECIP: National Earth Space Organization, Vostochny
REPORTER: Loineau, Madeleine, Cmdr. NZKO *Hypatia*
Mission year 40, day 73

The Colonel says I should apologize for my last dispatch.

He says our original mission data probably included information on this planetary system, and it's part of what we lost in the accident. He says you wouldn't have dropped us in the middle of a place cluttered with massive pieces of rock, each with its own little gravity field, without having a strategy to deal with them.

He says I shouldn't swear in mission dispatches. I told him to fuck off.

Of course, he's probably right. We probably had data about this star system. We probably had all the details on orbital trajectories and star composition, and all kinds of plans for orienting the transceiver in a way that gives us a clear field. Maybe we even had an alternate location, in case this system turned out to be too problematic for us to work with. We might have had lots of things before that asteroid took a bite out of us, but we will never know.

And now we're here, dealing with potentially insurmountable gravitational and electromagnetic interference, and all this time and everything we've lost might have been for nothing.

Sorry, Vostochny. I shouldn't write these things when I'm angry. But—forty years, and there's a good possibility it's all been futile. So forgive me if I curse you and all your descendants into whatever your personal Inferno looks like. After all, it's not like you can fire me for it.

RECIP: National Earth Space Organization, Vostochny
REPORTER: Loineau, Madeleine, Cmdr. NZKO *Hypatia*
Mission year 40, day 75

Kano wants to blow up a planet.

I feel I should mention he has been soundly outvoted on this. Qara says we're stocked to shatter asteroids, and doesn't think we've got enough ordnance to take out a whole planet, even a small one. The Colonel has pointed out that even if we *can* get to the core with a spike nuke, it's pretty certain the blast will turn it into a pack of fragments in the same damn orbit, and it'll still be big enough to mess up the proper encapsulation of a light-plus communications field. Ratana and Seung want us to step back and redo the math, to see if there's a way we can adapt the field generator design to work around the problem.

Léon, always the reliable pessimist, just flat-out hates spike nukes, and I'm pretty much in agreement there. Nukes make a hell of a mess, did you know that? The manual says they're designed for "precision, contained destruction," which is a pack of words that lose all meaning when you try to use them together. The truth of physics is this: once stuff starts to fly apart, you're on your own.

I think *Hypatia* has been hit by enough big chunks of rock, don't you?

The planet in question is this icy rock close to the star. It's *massive*. Well, not by your standards. Not like Jupiter, or even Earth. But massive enough to destabilize the transceiver field. Divya's studying the orbitals to see if we could throw enough big rocks at it to change the orbit, which would take a lot longer than blowing it the hell up, but might be more predictable. Kano's disappointed, but the rest of us are much happier with the idea of torquing it a little rather than blasting it into rubble. We'll be gathering more data as we get closer, and within a few days we should be able to know if Divya's strategy is worth a try.

Meantime, I have to find a way to reassure Kano he'll still get some fun out of this. I've asked Hina to pick a couple of asteroids she thinks might yield us some useful alloys, and I'll let Kano take the ECV out to blow them up. Morale is everything at times like this, right?

RECIP: National Earth Space Organization, Vostochny
REPORTER: Loineau, Madeleine, Cmdr. NZKO *Hypatia*
Mission year 40, day 76

The good news is Divya says Ice Planet's orbit isn't that eccentric, and it spins without much of a wobble. Pretty stable little satellite, actually, if you don't mind radiation and a poisonous atmosphere.

The bad news is it's in almost the worst possible place.

The *worst* possible place would be running right through the middle of our transceiver location. We've got enough clearance to build the structure, although Seung's still trying to figure out how to enhance the proximity detectors. (That wasn't even a part of the original architecture. No offense, Vostochny, but your design lacked some foresight.)

Sanity has prevailed, at least for now, and Qara's suggesting if her fling-some-asteroids idea proves unviable, we could survey the surface to see if it's worth mining for materials to accommodate a redesign. We may be able to do the survey from space, although with all that ice, it's a good bet we'll have to head on down there and do it up close.

It may surprise you to learn nobody is excited about that idea. We are not, on the whole, excited by planets at all.

You structured this whole mission believing we'd be motivated by the vanishingly small possibility we'll live long enough to make it back to Earth and see a sunset again. But the thing is...I don't remember sunsets, not real ones. None of us do—well, the Colonel might, but he hasn't talked about Earth for fifteen years. Hell, Hina's never seen a sunset at all, except in all those damn movies you sent with us. You probably think the reason we're still doing this, sacrificing our whole lives, childhood to adulthood to old age to death, is because you're holding out the slim chance of some grand reward at the end. But that's not it at all.

On my more cynical days, I'd tell you it's just inertia, that we've had this single-minded purpose for so long we find ourselves unable to turn away from it. But I think it's different than that. This isn't some reflexive conditioned rat-response. We stick with this because we remember our crewmates, the family we lost when that asteroid hit. A lot of them, unlike us, were volunteers who went to you and said *Yes, take my whole life and the lives of my children so we can build this communications system and open up the galaxy to humanity.* Which may look like a stupid decision in hindsight, but it was theirs, and they died for it. Who the hell would we be if we didn't try to finish the job for them?

Which is my philosophical way of saying nobody is looking forward to leaving this ship and standing on that planet. (It's also possible Kano's afraid of flying the tiny ECV in a huge gravity field, but don't tell him I said so.) The whole idea feels weird and alien and wrong, and I'm finding myself warming to the spike nuke idea, however unviable.

Hina says the asteroids are disappointing, by the way. The usual iron and magnesium, with some precious metals here and there. A fair amount of sulphide ore, which is kind of interesting from a mineralogical perspective; but there's nothing here we can use, unless we need ballast. I think Hina's getting bored again. Maybe I'll make her fly the damn ECV.

RECIP: National Earth Space Organization, Vostochny
REPORTER: Loineau, Madeleine, Cmdr. NZKO *Hypatia*
Mission year 40, day 78

Today we picked up a radio broadcast.
A radio broadcast.
I'm beginning to think this isn't a joke after all.

RECIP: National Earth Space Organization, Vostochny
REPORTER: Loineau, Madeleine, Cmdr. NZKO *Hypatia*
Mission year 40, day 79

Here's what we know:

1. The radio broadcast is not alien. It's in Russian. Old Russian, probably pre-Plague, Hina says, but definitely Russian.

2. It's a weather report. And a tea report. Here's the transcription, in total:

—morning blasting. That should give our art community something to work with! And remember, the show starts at first sunset, so make sure you have an early lunch. And now, weather. Novayarka[?] is cold today, a frigid minus sixty-five, and we can expect this to last another two dozen sunsets, keeping our raid risk very low. We have no storm systems closing, and nothing but clear skies. Good times for ice carving and for getting the children outside. After the dinner hour, we will have tea distribution. Halvorsen[?] tells this station that this harvest is robust and smooth, and will make up for the disappointing nature of the last. In crime news, the disruptions in the inner spokes[?] are—

I've attached the original audio. You should listen to this. It's a performance. The broadcaster sounds like a young woman, and her reading is cheerful and clearly enunciated. She's an *entertainer*.

Okay, that last part's a guess. But it's just like the rubbish we see in all those videos we've got. She's talking like a host, a presenter. An actor.

3. It's coming from the planet. The Colonel confirmed it.

4. There are *dozens* of broadcasts, maybe more. The tea report had the strongest signal, but we picked up weaker ones over other frequencies: music, recipes, even one on mineralogy. And one where this woman with a wavery, old voice was reading children's stories, and damned if a couple of them weren't variants on the stories we told to Hina.

These people are from Earth.

They have to be from one of those massive evac ships that took off a few centuries back, but holy hell, Vostochny, to think that they took root here is mind-boggling. This is an ugly little planet. I mean, yes, the gravity isn't too bad—a touch stronger than Earth's, but the Colonel says physiologically they would have adapted pretty easily—and although it's fucking cold at night, it's not so cold that heavy-duty environmental equipment wouldn't protect you. But the atmosphere is thin, with too little oxygen and way too much CO_2, and the magnetosphere isn't strong enough to keep the surface radiation level anything better than slow-burn deadly. Those old ships had decent radiation protections, but keeping that operational in a stationary habitat, never mind all the power systems…even Léon, who knows more about starship architecture than any of us, is impressed on the face of it. We're all pretty much in agreement that whoever these people are, they should never have survived.

But there's a bigger mystery here, at least to me, and I haven't said anything to the others because this whole situation is overwhelming and it's too soon to remind them that transceiver-wise we're still kind of fucked.

Why are we here, Vostochny? Why are we here in *this place*?

Hypatia isn't any help on this. She doesn't have any data on why you chose this particular location for the transceiver, at least not in any of the surviving data stores. I mean, really, this is a big fucking galaxy, never mind how little of it we can cover with the technology we have. There's a lot of room out here. But first a star system, and then a radio signal? I'm superstitious as hell, Vostochny—we all are, at this point—but I'm not completely insane. If both *Hypatia* and an ancient evac ship took this route, I refuse to believe it's a coincidence.

They came to this place for a reason. You sent us to this place for a reason. Same reason? What the hell could that be? Do you have any idea how pissed off I am that I can't get an answer from you?

We're going to settle into a counter-orbit tomorrow and see if we can take some closer readings of the surface. We need to be careful. Hina's worried we'll scare them, and so am I. She's worried out of compassion, though. I'm worried because I don't know what kind of weapons they might have, and right now I'm feeling pretty fucking vulnerable in our battered little ship.

By your Deities, Vostochny. *There are people down there.*

RECIP: National Earth Space Organization, Vostochny
REPORTER: Loineau, Madeleine, Cmdr. NZKO *Hypatia*
Mission year 40, day 82

So, I think I know who they are, and you'll think I'm out of my mind.

We've listened to the news for three days. The woman's been replaced by some deep-voiced dullard, but it's the same sort of news: weather forecast, community events, crime stats. They fight a lot down there, I guess, but they never talk about damage so it's hard to get a sense of how bad it is, or even how many people are involved. And I'm sitting here conscious that I'm interpreting everything I hear through my own narrow experiences, when these people are descendants of a chaotic culture that's been taught to me as ancient history...but really, between recipes and Grandma's bedtime stories, it's hard to think of them as all that different from us.

They call the town Novayarkha. I thought New York at first, but there weren't many ships out of North America, and I don't think they'd have been speaking Russian.

And then I thought about some of the ships nobody's really sure existed, the big permaculture leviathans, and wondered if it was an eliding of Nova Arkha. New Arkha. *Arkhangelsk.*

I know, I know. Of all of them, *Arkhangelsk* is most likely to be a myth. Some albatross of a generation ship intended to carry people and genetic material off Earth, away from the impurity and violence and general human-driven nastiness, to start over out here in space and avoid all the historical human mistakes. Bunch of pacifist cultists who never got off the ground, right?

But if they got away, if they did survive...*Arkhangelsk* was built to carry five thousand, and another hundred thousand genetic samples, along with what passed for sophisticated incubation systems at the time. They wouldn't even have needed to depend on their human population to reproduce. There were genetically modified plants and protein synthesizers and air cycling units and drug manufacturing equipment and flexible radiation shielding and everything you could possibly imagine. With all of that? When I manage to convince myself I'm not spinning some romantic fantasy I'll ask Léon, but that seems like enough to survive on a planet's surface, even a planet as unrelentingly hostile as this one.

I want it to be true. Don't you? Everything we've heard about that era—the disease and destruction and hopelessness and horrific loss of life—wouldn't it be something if some of those people really and truly got away, and made it this far?

But you already know, I'm sure. Because this is why we're here, too. It has to be. God, this is frustrating. Fucking time dilation. If we finish this transceiver—if we can even figure out how to make it work, and right now it looks like we can't, since we sure as hell aren't planning on nuking the planet anymore—I'm going to hold every fucking dispatch I've written hostage until you explain to us what the fuck this mission is really about.

Excuse me. I have to go apologize to the Colonel again.

RECIP: National Earth Space Organization, Vostochny
REPORTER: Loineau, Madeleine, Cmdr. NZKO *Hypatia*
Mission year 40, day 84

They've gone silent.

We thought, at first, we'd had some kind of malfunction, but it's just FM radio. There's not enough that can go wrong on our end. It's not a weak signal, something we could pick up if it had a better boost. It's static. Dead air.

They've stopped broadcasting. Either something's happened to them, or they know we're here.

Now what?

CHAPTER FIVE

"YOU'VE ALREADY SAID ROLF LIED TO YOU," YULIA POINTS OUT, ENTIRELY unconcerned. "Surely different tactics are called for."

With Yulia's contagious aplomb the only thing keeping the peace since the sighting, this is almost certainly the wrong moment for me to pick a fight. But the monitors behind her desk, dark despite the hour, are a disproportionate irritant. I hadn't realized how much I counted on them to track the time of day. We're all on edge, with the external monitors shut down and everyone forbidden to go to the surface. I'm not the only one claustrophobic and tense, and I suppose that's why Yulia's not losing her temper.

I was with Lauren, holding the hand of yet another parent hearing the worst news her life could bring, when Aleksey called to ask permission to use "different tactics" with Rolf. My refusal was terse but unambiguous, and I fully expected him to sulk theatrically and argue with me later.

I did not expect him to circumvent my authority and complain to Yulia.

"Why is it," I ask, "that for Aleksey *different tactics* always means violence?"

Yulia's looking at me through half-closed eyes. "You weren't always so opposed to such tactics, as I recall," she says smoothly.

I was young, and doing as I'd been taught, and it was Yulia

herself who'd changed me. She had been a newly appointed governor, popular with the people in part for her advocacy of non-violent peacekeeping and limits on Original Law. My own conversion grew out of her conviction, and my need to understand where my own lines were drawn. "And the reason I became opposed to them—twenty-five years ago, Yulia, when I was far younger than Aleksey—is because *they do not work*." Her lips thin, but I'm not finished. "Aleksey's not suited to be a peace officer," I say bluntly. "Torture elicits nothing but fear and lies. There is no rule of law that can stand in the face of violence."

I'm quoting her own argument, but her teeth clench, and for one instant of madness I wish for her to shout at me, to spill out all of her doubts and regrets, to open the door for me to do the same.

But there's a reason Yulia is governor and I am not. Her flash of temper dissipates, and the look she gives me is weary and resigned and not without sympathy. "Your heart is why you've been so good at your work for so long," she says, and my own anger collapses into a small coal in the pit of my stomach. "You're right; we must be cautious, for the sake of everyone involved. But given all the inconsistencies in his testimony—are you disputing Rolf's guilt?"

They're two different issues, and now is not the time. "No, Yulia." And then I breathe out the heat of the coal, just a little. "But it's not enough, not for Lauren, not for any of us. And not to take away his freedom."

There's a hardness in her stare that keeps me wary, but she's still an old woman who's ill and tired and frightened like everyone else. Eventually her eyes drop closed. "Verify the details without Rolf, as much as you can. But I don't want this to drag out, Anya. Be quick. No more than fourteen or fifteen sunsets. Tamara is a great loss, and people need to be able to move forward."

I swallow an instinctive apology. "Thank you, Governor."

A door closes in the next room, and Doctor Halvorsen's voice drifts in. "Every time," she's saying, and she sounds as exhausted as Yulia looks, "it's not easy. But I've finished, Governor. I just need you to—" She enters the room, a small box tucked under one arm, and meets my eyes. "We do keep stumbling over each other, don't we, Anya?" But she's not needling me this time; instead, she looks worn and weary, very nearly her age. "I don't suppose you'd be able to leave us alone for a bit."

"'Of course. We were finished, I believe." I meet Yulia's eyes, and she nods, and for now we pretend there'll be no fallout from our conversation.

But when I turn to bid Doctor Halvorsen farewell, I look more closely at the box she carries: tiny and nondescript, the same as hundreds I've seen, only smaller, and the last of my anger is doused by a wave of grief.

When we lose an incubator growth, Doctor Halvorsen always analyzes the remains. Sometimes, she says, the cell division goes awry; sometimes, no matter what one does, there is no reason, and it isn't an issue of bad environment or bad genes. But those misfires we usually lose very early, when they're still far too small to warrant the miniature casket cradled under Doctor Halvorsen's arm.

Silence is impossible. "Is there something I can do to help?"

Yulia meets Doctor Halvorsen's eyes, and they communicate something I don't understand. "I don't think so, Anya," Yulia says, her voice all kindness. "But I do need you to keep what you've seen here to yourself."

Our population has always waxed and waned, each drop of a year or two followed by a plentiful run of healthy children, but our people have a long memory, and we are not foolish enough to assume a problem addressed once is solved. In my early teen years, we began a drought that lasted nearly a decade; we leaned heavily on the incubators and the wider selection of genetic material we can use with them to keep our numbers in a safe range. By the time I began as a peace officer, years of worry were banished with a large, robust generation, born naturally, like Irina. The last several years have been thinner, although not catastrophically, not yet. Yulia's tapped some Selected to have second children, which limits our diversity, but works as a temporary measure. Mostly we've leaned on the incubators more than usual, but the more years I see the more difficult it becomes not to notice the age of our hardware. Spare parts are hard to find; breakdowns are becoming more common.

And sometimes when the incubators break down, they're already in use.

"Perhaps we can have our discussion later, Magda," Yulia says, and I remember how well she knows me.

"Of course." Doctor Halvorsen gives me an uncharacteristically sympathetic smile before retreating through Yulia's back door. Despite her briskly callous nature, she'll look after that barely-grown vestige of hope, and will see it properly buried. The ashes of our dead are kept in the crypt in respectful, organized stacks, safe under the gardens and the medical center and the ore processing equipment.

Irina is in there, somewhere, and for a moment I can't see anything.

"How many incubators does that leave us?" I ask Yulia.

"Seventy-three operational," she says. Her voice is all compassion, our disagreement forgotten, and I blink until I can see her again. "We've been running them too frequently, I expect; that's why we've been having outages. We'll re-establish a balance."

Yulia is always positive, unconcerned, at least where others can hear; but even Doctor Halvorsen recognizes the incubators will all wear out eventually. Despite our planet's rich mineral deposits, our attempts at manufacturing replacement parts have been uneven and unpredictable, leaving us to scavenge our already limited supply. Yulia's right; as hideous a loss as Tamara is, we're fighting far worse than an unsolved murder. Neither Rolf's confession nor Yulia's optimism will save us from entropy.

But then Doctor Halvorsen's footsteps approach again, this

time heavier, faster. She's running when she bursts into the room, still clutching the coffin, and all composure has vanished from her deeply lined face. "Yulia," she says, breathless, "turn on the radio."

Yulia frowns in familiar irritation, even as my grief fragments into shards of ice. "Whatever for?" she snaps. "Nobody's broadcasting."

It's all over Doctor Halvorsen's face: *We* aren't broadcasting. But someone is.

My hand is oddly distant from me, shaking as I reach for the office radio. The knob is smooth and cool, vibrating just a little from the passive current entering the device. I turn it on.

The signal is broken by static, fading in and out. But it's a voice, and it's not a voice I know, and although the words are familiar, some are lost to her strange pronunciation.

"*...first of many, if all* [unintelligible].*We would like to* [unintelligible] *before then. Please respond. Message repeats: This is the* [unintelligible]. *We have arrived from Earth to* [untranslatable]. *We will be the first of many, if all succeeds. We would like to communicate before then. Please respond.*"

The message loops, and somewhere in the distance Yulia argues with Doctor Halvorsen, but I am frozen, hands at my sides, staring at the radio. I don't notice when they fall silent.

Through the fog, another hand reaches out: Yulia's. She snaps the radio off, and puts her fingers on my arm, looking up at me. "Anya, it's a recording," she tells me, and I wonder why that matters. "It's just the same message, over and over."

As I look back at her, my head abruptly clears, and Irina sidles up to me, oddly composed, staring at me expectantly.

And I say, "Then perhaps we should answer them."

CHAPTER SIX

"CONTACT ALL THE BLOCK MAYORS." I HAVE TO SHOUT INTO YULIA'S office phone. "If they ask for reinforcements, pull Ioseph and Tove off the metals lab, and get Vassiliya off the prison desk."

Aleksey's reply is inaudible over Dmitri's yelling.

Ten minutes after the broadcast, picked up on every radio in the city, shock has given way to pandemonium. Doctor Halvorsen has retreated to her clinic to look after her handful of resident patients, but her handwringing has been taken up by Lev and Dmitri, both of whom seem entirely incapable of thinking before they speak. Lev is spinning nightmares of alien fleets and doomsday weapons, echoing the gossip circulating through the crowd gathering in the Hub.

Dmitri, as is his habit, just yells. He yells as if it'll give him more control, as if proclaiming outrage will change what's unfolding in front of all of us. Yulia's right about him: he doesn't have the temperament for any of this. None of us, no matter how brave, are adept at dealing with terror.

"You can't be seriously considering speaking to them!" he shouts again.

Yulia glares at him, the hollows under her eyes stark against her waxy skin. "Would you rather hide in the ice for the rest of your life, Dmitri?" she says acidly. "Because I would not."

She's more aggravated than afraid, and it calms my nerves. I turn back to the phone. "Pull reinforcements for them even if they don't ask," I tell Aleksey. "And let me know if things start getting out of hand."

"On my way," Aleksey says crisply, and disconnects. Whatever my reservations about his interrogation methods, he's better at handling widespread panic than anyone I'm dealing with in this room, and I'm counting on that. Even suspending safety surveillance for the duration of this crisis, I haven't got enough officers to effectively monitor or maintain a peacekeeping presence in all four blocks at once.

I've already spoken to Costa at the school. "We're all right here, I think," he told me. "The older children are putting on a front for the younger ones. We've had a few tears, but for the most part everyone's just...waiting."

With far more patience than Dmitri, it seems.

"We are *defenseless*," he's saying to Yulia. His voice is quieter, but it's in his eyes: he needs to believe we can assert some level of control.

"We're not defenseless," Yulia says. She sits back, and despite all the unwanted witnesses, I fetch her some water. "Your people have their handguns, and we still have the others we've reconditioned. Anya, how many energy weapons do we have locked up?"

My fingers around her water glass are beginning to shake again. So much easier when I can give orders to others. "Twenty-four." I set the glass before her, keeping my face a mask; but Yulia knows how I feel about energy weapons.

We don't, in truth, have frequent need even for the handguns, which fire standard projectiles. It's tradition, like the uniforms Dmitri's people still wear. But decades ago, after two of our horticulturalists were killed in an Exile attack, Yulia resurrected the plasma-based weapons that had been in storage for sixty years. Fortunately most of them were irreparable, but we managed to refurbish a small but deadly arsenal. It's been at my insistence that they've been locked away instead of distributed to Dmitri's staff, or even my own.

Yulia believes they deter simply by existing, but she can't counter my argument: they were designed for use in vacuum, and inside the risk of thermal bloom is too great. Our ancestors built us an architecturally sound habitat, but it's too easy for us to forget how precarious all this is.

"Get them all out," she says wearily to Dmitri, and takes a long drink of water without looking at me. "Make sure they can still do what they're supposed to do. Outside," she finishes, meeting my eyes at last; this is the best concession I can hope for. Dmitri nods, and flees.

Yulia is still looking at me.

"What are you going to say to them?" I ask.

She runs a hand over her face. "I'm going to tell them we're armed, but that if they leave us alone, we'll leave them alone."

"But—" The idea of threatening them into retreat is appealing, but I can't make myself believe it'll work. "They've said they're the first of many. Shouldn't we find out what they're doing here?"

"The first *if* they're successful," she points out. "They said that, too. Perhaps they won't be."

"But until we know what it is they're trying to do—"

"You know where they're from, Anya." There's a sharpness in her words, the tone I was expecting earlier when I pushed back about Aleksey. "You know what we left behind. Do you really think it's worth the risk?"

At this point, all the risks look alike to me. "The Old World may have changed."

"Indeed. And what if it's changed for the worse? We are so fragile, Anya. You saw that earlier. I'm to let strangers in, undermine us, jeopardize all progress we're working to make?"

I have no retort to that. "How will you answer them?"

She folds her hands and straightens her back. "I'll use the same frequency," she says. "And I will make sure the whole city tunes in. It's their fate as much as it is yours and mine."

Which wasn't what I was asking, but she knows that, too.

Yulia's voice is as strong and measured as I've ever heard it.

"Unidentified probe, this is Yulia Orlova, Governor of Novayarkha. We have received your message. Please discontinue transmission. No further communication on your part is required."

Almost immediately, the repeating message stops, but Yulia does not relax. If the message isn't automated, surely there will be more, no matter what our request.

A few minutes later, the reply comes through—the same voice as before, only less rehearsed. "Governor Orlova." The voice is pitched higher than Yulia's, steady but less measured. Maybe even friendly. "I'm Captain Madeleine Loineau of the starship *Hypatia*."

Hypatia. Greek or Roman, perhaps; ancient beyond my learning. They honor their past, then, these people from the Old World. But which part of it?

"And of course," the voice went on, "if it's your choice, we will leave you alone." Her accent is uneven; half the words are pronounced strangely, but she's careful when she speaks, trying to make sure she's understood. "But we won't be the last ship to come here. We don't have any control over that. We feel—" Her words speed up, and I lose a number of them before she regroups. "We can give you information on what is coming," she concludes.

Yulia lets the radio sit idle as she thinks. Whether or not these people are dangerous matters less than whether or not there are more coming, whether we have to learn, sooner rather than later, how they wish to change us. "Can it hurt," I suggest, "to hear what they have to say?"

"If they're being honest? Perhaps not. But if they're lying?" She shakes her head. "The consequences of this choice, Anya. Do

I risk our present to learn of our future? Do I open us up to cultural destruction, to attack?"

"If they could attack us they surely would have done so already."

"That is a theory," she says harshly. "And we can't know."

"We can't know either way, Yulia."

She swears quietly, a thing she doesn't do, and turns the transmitter back on. "You may relay your information, Captain Loineau," she says, and waits.

The pause is longer this time, and my palms grow damp. It's nearly ten minutes before Captain Loineau responds.

"We think it would be easier if we came to see you," she says, and my heart begins to race.

"We are armed," Yulia warns. "We will not submit to an attack."

"Not an attack," Captain Loineau tells her. "Three of us. Myself, our navigator, and a linguist."

"Why do you need a linguist?"

A brief pause before she answers. "Our languages are the same, but time may have skewed some word usage. One of my crew has studied your era, and can help us—" I lose the end of her phrase again, but it doesn't matter this time.

Yulia thinks for a moment. "Only three of you?"

"Only three."

"How is this possible?"

Another pause at this, and then: "We have a small ship that we use for external work. It's capable of landing on your planet's surface."

"And you will come unarmed."

"If that's your condition, yes."

Yulia mutes the transmitter. "Anya?" For the first time I can remember, there's doubt in her voice.

People. People from Earth. People who have not spent their whole lives huddled under the ice. Despite my persistent terror, I'd say anything to make Yulia agree.

"We have weapons," I point out. "We can greet them with armed guards."

"And if they show up armed? Or with more than three?"

"Then we shoot them."

She holds my gaze. Yulia worries I would hesitate, perhaps beyond the point of usefulness, to shoot anyone with our ancient guns. But I would shoot to save her life, and possibly even my own, and I look back at her calmly as she studies my face. Eventually, she turns the radio on again.

"You may send your three," she tells Captain Loineau. "If you send more than three, we will defend ourselves. If you come with weapons, we will defend ourselves. If you are hostile in any way, we will defend ourselves. Do you understand?"

"Yes." I don't know anything of this Captain Loineau, but I think she sounds relieved. "We will come down in—" more lost words—"see you in about three hours. Loineau out."

As Yulia leans back in her office chair there are murmurs and shouts from the hallway. She arches a tired eyebrow at me. "It's not going to be so easy to reassure them this time."

I'm not sure how you reassure people who are about to play host to the first visitors they've ever had.

CHAPTER SEVEN

THE WIND IS STIFF, THE COLD SEEPING UNDER MY PROTECTIVE GEAR, BUT that's not why I'm shaking. Looking up into the clear, mid-first-light sky, I'm not at all sure what I'm hoping for.

They're overdue by nearly twenty minutes now. *Hypatia*'s orbit has taken them over the horizon, and I wonder if we'll hear the landing ship before we see it. Our video archives aren't extensive; even the short clip of our own ship doesn't show it in flight. But there are a few videos of different ships, ships designed for atmosphere: small, graceful, bird-like structures, white and clean, cutting through clouds with the faint rumble of fuel-burning engines. Perhaps *Hypatia*'s landing ship will be like that, gliding gracefully down onto the ice, settling before us like a fine-boned sparrow to disgorge its passengers.

Centuries since we left the Old World. Will they even look like us?

At last the hum of the ship's engine penetrates our thin atmosphere: a low growl, like a comminution grinder, that takes my aging ears a moment to triangulate. It's nothing but a dark speck in the sky, too far away to make out much of a shape at all. As it grows closer something folds out from its sides: wings, reaching out from a spherical base to spread parallel to the ground. It lurches dramatically before stabilizing, and I glance at the others, wondering if we're standing too close to the landing zone after all.

Aleksey is in the Hub, attending Yulia. I've brought Dmitri's assistant Katerina, and two of my junior officers, Sofia and Ioseph. They're ten years younger than Aleksey, but they're level-headed enough, and they stand confidently with guns at their hips as if they carry them every day. Katerina's the only one carrying an energy weapon, and although it's substantially more dangerous than the handgun she usually trains with, she too radiates a calm authority.

Yulia agreed to let me remain unarmed, the ambassador. It's been six years since I've trained with a weapon. I've never had to use force for security, never had to do more than threaten incarceration. Any posturing I did with a gun would be utterly unconvincing, and she knows it.

The landing ship grows larger and louder, and eventually slows and then stills, hovering in front of us, its engine drowning out all other sound. There's a mechanical whine over the low growl, and as the winged sphere slowly drops downward, the pitch lowers. As the ship's belly touches the ice, legs flip outward from its curved surface. They haven't landed quite evenly; the ship rolls and slides before it stops. My officers are miraculously still, but Katerina flinches, the only nerves she's betrayed all day.

The engines shut off, and we're left with the familiar quiet of the ice, an alien ship before us.

It's not white or clean. It's dark gray, made up of at least three different metals. There are dents on it, and what looks like scorching. One of the wings is at a slight angle to the other, as if it's been struck by something heavy. This ship is not a bird but a stone, rough-hewn and graceless like something blasted from the quarry, battered by a history I can't imagine.

There's a sound of hydraulics, quieter and cleaner than our own but still familiar, and a narrow section of the sphere unfolds into a staircase.

The people from the Old World step out.

They're all in descendants of our quarry suits, lighter and granite-grey instead of orange. Covered, all three faces look much the same: amorphous features visible through the glare of the hard helmets. But even so I can make out eyes, noses, skin in shades of brown and beige. The centuries have not made the people of the Old World inhuman.

As they walk down the stairs, differences among them become clear. The one in the lead is tall, and slimmer than the one who follows, who's nearly bursting out of the suit. The third has a distinctly quicker step and is several centimeters shorter than the others. They all move with care—trying to look non-threatening, or simply adjusting to our strange environment.

They are born of a world I will never see. But they are familiar enough, and the worst of my fears subside behind curiosity. I signal my team to stay where they are, and step forward.

"I am Officer Anya Savelova." Somehow my voice doesn't shake. "I'm here to take you to Governor Orlova."

We haven't given them our shortwave frequency, and in the thin atmosphere it's possible they can't hear me at all. But the first of them, the tall slim one, takes a step toward me, staggering just a little.

"How do you do." I recognize the voice before she introduces herself. "I'm Madeleine Loineau."

She holds out her hand, palm to the inside. A familiar greeting as well. We shake, my glove insulating me from any sensation beyond pressure. She drops my hand and turns to the others.

"This is Kano Yudin," she says, gesturing first at the thick person, "and Hina Tadeshi."

I shake hands. We have no Yudins, but the phonemes in the name are familiar. Hina has a grip that belies her size, and through her helmet I catch a brief flash of teeth. She's smiling at me, and my stomach lurches.

"The walk is short." My people haven't moved, and I have to

gesture again before they fall into step behind the strangers. I walk next to Captain Loineau, watching her feet. She's more sure every step, and I want to ask her what it's like on her ship, how all of this is different. I want to know why her landing ship doesn't look like the ones I've seen in pictures, why she chose these two people to come with her, why they're here at all.

We take them down the stairs and through the Outer Rim airlock, and the strangers follow me in, my people at the rear. If the guns have frightened Captain Loineau, she doesn't let on in any way I recognize. The decontamination room provokes the slightest of hesitations; Captain Loineau glances at the back of her glove, which hosts a thin display: a dosimeter. She gives an easy shrug of approval, and they follow me into Phase One.

I stretch out my arms for the decon spray, and the strangers follow suit; when the sequence completes, I pull off the suit and add it to the automated deep decon bin. "Your suits will be cleaned and ready for you to use by the time you leave," I assure them.

Together, the three of them tug off their gloves, then unclasp their helmets and remove them.

They are familiar and unfamiliar all at once.

Kano Yudin looks much like Viktor Gregarin and the Yatovich cousins, his eyes heavy-lidded, the planes of his face nearly flat apart from his wide nose. His skin is a warm limonite brown, his hair black and enviably thick, and there's a curiosity in his dark eyes, a light that I'd call amusement if I saw it in one of us. Hina Tadeshi resembles Damian and Lilith, although somehow finer and more detailed, her features delicate where theirs are bold. Her complexion is paler than mine—not snowy like Irina's, but sandstone touched with sun, smooth around her lips and eyes. Her eyes, like Kano's, are nearly black, sitting close to the surface of her face, and she's younger than he is, maybe as young as Tamara. Despite her earlier smile her expression is guarded, but there's curiosity there as well.

Captain Loineau shakes her head when she pulls off the helmet, and tangles of loose curls, like Irina's but deep brown instead of yellow, fall into her eyes. If she were one of us I'd suspect her of being my genetic sister: her skin, like mine, is golden tan, but her dark eyes are far lovelier, deep-set and crowned by heavy, graceful eyebrows. Her nose is substantial, rounded and wide, and her mouth turns upward, as if she spends a lot of time smiling. That as much as anything will set her apart from us. She looks at me, and her expression is that of both her crew members combined: intelligence, amusement, and frank curiosity.

She studies my face as if we've met somewhere before.

There's one thing about all of them that is utterly alien: all three of them, with all of their varied skin tones, have about them the warm glow of well-fed vitality. Whatever sustains them on their ship they have in abundance, and I'm abruptly conscious of our worn clothes and tired faces.

Kano says something quick and unintelligible to Captain Loineau, but all she does is shoot him an irritable look. "I'm sure it's fine," she says, and when she looks away, Kano and Hina exchange a glance behind her. There's an odd informality about it all, an irreverence that feels inappropriate. I proceed into the next decon phase, leaving them to change.

They join me on the other side, all three of them smaller without their elaborate suits. Their clothes are unusual not in fabric—the cloth has a familiar weave and drape, despite clearly having more synthetic in the blend—but in color. Instead of our earthy browns and grays, they have trousers in shades of blue and deep green, pigments we can't produce in any practical volume, and shirts as white as new snow. I wonder at the resources on their small ship that permit them such valuable colors for ordinary clothes.

My assistants emerge behind us, and I nod at Sofia, who heads into the Outer Rim hallway. "There are crowds," I tell the strangers. "Say nothing to them. You're safe traveling with us, but I'm not sure how everyone will behave. If you become nervous, just let us know."

Hina and Kano glance at each other again, and this time Captain Loineau catches the look. But she ignores it, and gives me a gracious smile. "I'm sure we'll be quite all right," she says, and before I realize I'm doing it I smile back.

Katerina precedes us, and Ioseph brings up the rear as the three strangers move with me into the corridor.

The people are waiting.

They stand along the Rim walls, huddled together, some of them with their arms around children. That should be a good sign—if they're allowing the children out at all, they must have some confidence in their safety—but it's impossible not to see it as hypocrisy. Their eyes are not friendly, and there are frequent murmurs as we walk by. I keep my eyes fixed on Sofia and Katerina before us, channeling Yulia to show the crowd nothing but calm.

Captain Loineau isn't helping her cause. She's looking around at all the people and up at the walls and ceiling, her eyes taking in the ice-filled solar tubes and every Outer Rim front door. She looks like a child out in the sun for the first time, like Irina used to look every time the etchings in the courtyard changed. I wonder, then, how long their trip from the Old World has taken them. Hina is young, but not a child; they might have left as long ago as five years, even more.

As we round the Western Arc to reach the main spoke to the Hub, Captain Loineau is meeting people's eyes and nodding, smiling as Hina smiled at me. She's persisting in the face of no response at all. It's not foolish of her to attempt rapport, but she's come to us defenseless. We had no need of guns; it would be easy enough to shove her through an airlock door, leaving her to the slow suffocation of the surface.

Captain Loineau, helpless as a baby just released from an incubator, betrays no sense of danger, here among the very people she has terrified.

The crowd in front of Yulia's office parts as we approach. Captain Loineau stops nodding at people and instead looks up at the spire atop the interior building. It hasn't occurred to me before that it might be impressive, or even unusual, but Captain Loineau's mouth drops open, and she makes a sound of amazement. Kano speaks, and this time I understand him: "You're acting like a tourist, Maddie," he says, but there's fondness in his voice.

Captain Loineau ignores him.

As we get to Yulia's door, Sofia and Katerina flank the entrance. As agreed, I knock on the door, and wait for Yulia's acknowledgement.

But it's Dmitri who opens the door, and past him Yulia's sitting at her desk, hands folded, Aleksey standing rigidly behind her like a personal bodyguard. This is too authoritarian for my taste, too threatening. There's nothing dangerous about these strangers.

Somewhere along the length of the Western Arc, I stopped being afraid.

CHAPTER EIGHT

I HAVEN'T EATEN A MEAL WITH SO MANY PEOPLE IN MORE THAN TWENTY years.

The round table Yulia uses for our council meetings is covered in dishes: bowls of grains and noodles, a massive plate of Doctor Halvorsen's beets and onions, a sandstone basket full of fresh bread. Katerina is inside, by the door, and Sofia and Ioseph are keeping the crowd occupied in the Hub. I can hear Ioseph through the wall, his deep voice relaxed; so far the mood outside seems nothing but curious.

Throughout the meal I keep one ear on Ioseph's tone.

Seated between Dmitri and Aleksey I have a clear view of Yulia and the three strangers. Kano and Hina eat very little, sipping water and gingerly sampling some vegetables, but Captain Loineau tries everything, including the sweet barley liquor Yulia likes to put in her tea. After one sip the captain's eyes water, and Kano says something to her, fast and irreverent. "Oh," she says to him, briefly hoarse, "I think this'll take care of everything." He laughs, and she grins at him, and Hina looks vaguely embarrassed, and they feel like a family. Irina is next to me, trying to take in every detail and nuance, and she can't take her eyes off them.

We learn during the meal that *Hypatia* grows fresh food in hydroponic gardens not dissimilar to ours, although Captain

Loineau insists our beets are better. We learn their gravity is variable, dependent on the spin of the wheel that looks so much like the rings of our own Rims. We learn they keep no animals, and apart from growing some crystalline minerals and complex medicinal compounds, they're constrained by the supplies they carried when they left the Old World.

Earth. That's what Captain Loineau calls it, and it's a flat, mundane word divorced from history.

Conversation is kept light and insignificant until the main courses are done, and then Yulia leans back, hands relaxed on the arms of her chair. "Now, Captain Loineau," she says, convening her meeting. "Perhaps you can tell us when you and your ship will be leaving."

Captain Loineau's expression is equally bland and guarded. She holds a bread roll between her fingers. Despite her appetite for the rest of our food the roll has succumbed mostly to fidgeting, and there are crumbs all over her plate. "Our mission is not very flexible, I'm afraid," she says, and I don't know if the conciliatory tone is instinct or artifice. "We're here to build a communications station. We can't leave until it's finished."

Yulia's eyebrows twitch almost imperceptibly. "You may surely build it elsewhere."

At this, Captain Loineau looks down at her fingers, placing the mauled roll down on her plate as if she's just discovered it. "I wish we could," she says. "But that's not how it works. Earth will be looking for transmissions coming from this location. If we build it too far away, they won't be looking for it, and none of it will work."

"What is it exactly you're building, Captain?" Lev asks. "Surely not radio, not out here."

Captain Loineau's brief laugh relieves none of the caution in her expression. "Goodness, no. If radio were at all useful at this distance—"

"You'd have found us long ago." This Yulia says mildly, without expanding on the implication.

Captain Loineau only nods. "We were sent here to build a faster-than-light communications satellite."

"An ansible," Lev clarifies.

"If you like."

He frowns in thought. "I understand you've developed different technologies than we have." I marvel for a moment at his ability to imply we've developed anything at all. "But—back when we left the Old World, the problem with faster-than-light communications wasn't bandwidth. It was distance. You'd have to build a field big enough to carry a starship, and even then you'd hit the same battery restrictions you would on a mechanical drive."

"I'm not one of the tech people," Captain Loineau tells him, "but as I understand it, about thirty years before we left Earth, they came out with a narrow-band field design. We still need the physical transceiver, but the field itself is small and efficient. Although they're not that sure of distances a lot greater than this."

"So they figured out the compression." Lev leans forward, engaged, dropping any pretense of asking rehearsed questions. "What are they using as a transport medium? Did they adapt the starship drives? Did you—"

Yulia reaches out and puts a hand on his arm, and he falls silent, looking away from Captain Loineau and sitting back again. Kano and Hina exchange a look I recognize: they're surprised. They thought we were primitive, backward. They thought we would be some kind of living time machine, a screencap of an ancient world they didn't know anymore.

Odd, how we thought the same of them.

"If you don't mind me bringing up more practical considerations," Yulia says dryly, "what is to keep you from telling Earth—" the word sticks a little in her throat—"that you're building in a different place?"

At that, Kano says something too quickly for me to understand, and Hina's hand on his arm silences him as easily as Yulia's did

Lev. "Slow down," she says to him, with less of an accent than the others. She looks at Yulia as if they're equals, and reflexively I tense. "Any message we send to Earth using conventional means, Governor, will take close to a hundred years to get there. We don't have the technology to ask them to accommodate the situation."

"The time dilation. Of course." Yulia frowns, and for once asks the question that's foremost in my own mind. "How long have you been away from your home, Captain Loineau?"

"Forty years," she says.

Forty years.

Forty years ago I was thirteen years old, and Irina didn't exist. Forty years is an age ago and another universe.

"But—" Yulia's also wrestling with the number. "How can you know *their* plans have not changed?"

Captain Loineau looks at her steadily. "We can't."

"Yours is a very chancy mission," Dmitri remarks, and he's right but that's not what I'm thinking.

I'm thinking that Hina, who at the very most, if she ages slowly, is thirty, could not possibly have been born anywhere other than on that ship in our orbit.

"Even at the best of times," Captain Loineau is saying, "our odds of success have been low. The reason I wanted to come down here, Governor, was to let you know what's going to happen. Whatever my own feelings, I cannot grant you veto power over our mission. I can only tell you what will happen if, as we hope, we succeed."

She's warning us. She's warning us that more strangers are coming. Perhaps not in my lifetime, but soon.

I want to know when. I want to know how long. I want to know what they'll bring with them. I want to know if they'll turn us into something unrecognizable.

I should be afraid of all of it. I should.

Yulia has tensed, head to toe, but *decisive* and *impulsive* are two different things, and Yulia's always been the former. "How long will it take you to build this station?"

Captain Loineau relaxes, just a little, and I find myself with a strange impulse to warn her. "Based on our current plans, about a year."

"You're aware we haven't the resources to help you."

"Of course." Captain Loineau looks surprised at the question. "We didn't expect to find you here. We've no need to disturb you at all."

As if they've not already disturbed us.

Yulia remains tense, but in her eyes there's careful calculation. "Thank you for your honesty, Captain Loineau." She pushes her chair back and gets to her feet. The rest of us rise automatically. "You understand, we must discuss what you have told us."

"Of course." Captain Loineau smiles again, her habitual deflection. "And thank you for allowing us into your home. It's been a privilege for us, seeing what you have here."

The Hub is the most elaborate area we have, and Yulia's office is well-furnished, but it's average, utilitarian, designed for use and not beauty. Irina looks around the room for me, trying to see the space with a stranger's eyes.

They are shaking hands farewell, and I send Katerina out to tell Sofia and Ioseph we're leaving. When I turn back, Aleksey's talking to Hina, her small-boned hand between both of his; like Lev, she's a blusher, and she's very red under Aleksey's gaze. I try to get his attention, but he ignores me.

Captain Loineau is less subtle. I catch her eye just before she looks over at Aleksey and her crewmate. "Hina," she says, her voice gentle, "we need to go."

Hina's color deepens, and she extricates her fingers from Aleksey's and joins her companions by the door.

The crowd's conversations fade into silence when we enter the hallway, but there's been a change in mood: where earlier children were pulled close, now they're left to stand on their own, and one or two people actually return Captain Loineau's tenacious smile. Yulia's welcomed the strangers, and they haven't harmed anyone; they're safe now, acceptable.

They're diligent in the airlock, securing their helmets and gloves, checking each other when they're finished. That level of caution would be necessary out in space, without even thin air to breathe. I suppose they haven't considered that here it's the cold that's the greater worry, at least for the short walk to their landing ship.

Katerina moves toward the outer airlock door, and before I can convince myself I'm being foolish I say, "I'll take them."

She gives me a disapproving look, thinking like a security officer: three of them, one of me. If they want to hurt me, it'll be easy—as easy as it would have been for us to hurt them while they were inside. Before we reach their small ship Katerina will have reported me to Dmitri. Yulia will be angry and have words with me, but as long as the strangers leave, she'll forgive my impulsiveness.

Under the rapidly darkening sky, I escort the strangers back to their ship, Irina walking with us. She keeps looking up at Captain Loineau, face now concealed behind her faceplate. Yulia didn't ask enough questions, didn't show enough curiosity about any of it, and I long to stop out here on the ice, to demand Captain Loineau paint me a picture of her crew, her ship, the Old World as it was when she left it, hundreds of years after all we've ever known.

"We noticed," Captain Loineau says, her stride unhurried, "that you only use the lower radio frequencies to broadcast."

"We use the higher ones for localized communications." That's not entirely true, of course. Yulia has emergency frequencies tied to each of her council members, kept secret from the town. The number of times she's used them is small. She's never used mine at all. "We have antennas leading to the surface, but the lower frequencies travel through the ice better, so that's what we use for anything city-wide."

"So if we want to communicate with you, we should use the same frequency we used before."

"That makes sense."

We're nearing their ship, its bulk sitting awkwardly on the ice, the door still open. Captain Loineau stops before it, surveying the sphere as if she's checking for damage. Hina and Kano climb the stairs, arguing about something, once again speaking too quickly for me to understand, their words half-swallowed by the thin air.

"It just occurs to me," Captain Loineau says, eventually, "that at some point someone may want to talk to us without the whole city listening in."

"Yulia believes in transparency." But my stomach is fluttering; I don't think that's what she means.

She keeps surveying her ship. "Maybe it's just that after all these years out in space, I've learned to believe in contingency plans." She turns toward me, the glare from the ice obscuring her face.

It may not be a question, of course. She may not be thinking the way I'm thinking at all. But I take a leap of faith nonetheless. "For confidentiality, something over 105 would probably work best."

And I'm not wrong. "Let's say 107.9, then. We'll monitor both. Just in case." She turns and walks around the wing to the staircase. "It's been...astonishing, Officer Savelova." And she stops, and this time there's no glare on the helmet, and I can see her dark eyes focusing on mine. "I hope we'll get a chance to talk again."

She turns and climbs in, and I step back as the door closes after her and the engines start. There's a great roar, and the ship kicks up a cloud of snow as it blasts off the ground. The pilot, who seems to have regrouped since the landing, turns the ship with confidence and angles it toward the sky.

Irina and I watch and watch until it becomes too small for us to see anymore.

RECIP: National Earth Space Organization, Vostochny
REPORTER: Loineau, Madeleine, Cmdr. NZKO *Hypatia*
Mission year 40, day 90

Sorry for the delayed update, Vostochny, but I had to stave off
a mutiny.

We never should've let Hina talk first. She was so composed
when we were down there, but back home the whole story came
out of her like some explosive lab experiment, everything scram-
bled together in a big out-of-order mess. Kano kept having to correct her, and I'm still not sure she made any real sense.

I stayed out of it, because I was processing the experience. Still
am, to be honest.

All those people, Vostochny.

Hundreds, in the hallways alone. All those different faces,
young and old and in between—not people from the movies, but
real people. Real people that I don't know, haven't grown up with,
haven't been confined with on this ship for forty years.

And about a third of them are visibly ill.

I'm not going to make a definitive diagnosis without actual
data, Vostochny, but my best guess is cancer, and with a fair
amount of variety. I saw everything from hollow eyes that might

have been sleeplessness to people too emaciated to stand on their own. There were even some amputations here and there—cleanly done, from what I could see, so their medical science seems to be holding up all right—and at least one woman I'm pretty sure was blind. Kano suspects the power core they're sitting on, that somehow the containment is starting to give after all these centuries, but the radiation readings in there weren't all that elevated, especially once we got to Orlova's office. I think it's those suits of theirs—with those soft seals and all the wear and tear they couldn't be rated more than three or four hours on that planet's surface, and I'm guessing even then they're insufficient for regular use. Their magnetosphere buys them something, but not enough. Without it those suits would be as bad as wearing nothing at all.

They're not *all* sick, of course. Cancer's creative that way. They had a lot of children for one thing, and I suppose they'd need them. Officer Savelova looked healthy, although like the rest of them she's frighteningly thin. But one of the men—Lev, the one who knew all the comms stuff—seemed to get tired awfully easily, and Governor Orlova looked decidedly gray. Despite the rich food, the curious children, those gorgeous ice carvings—paradise this place is not.

What's interesting is that outside of the cancer they're doing surprisingly well. We exchanged viral profiles before we went down, and I expected to have to stay in our environmental suits to keep from infecting them. But they're immune to just about everything, which suggests some kind of large-scale inoculation program; we were at much more risk than they were. Even after mainlining antivirals, I'll be monitoring the hell out of everybody for a while.

I feel like I spent too much time in a hot bath, and I'm soaking wet and disoriented, and I don't even have the energy to reach for a towel. I don't quite know what just happened to me.

Which is probably why I didn't anticipate how the others were going to react.

As soon as Hina was finished, Divya asked, "When do the rest of us go down?" and they all started talking. And because I'm a coward, I let Kano be the one to stomp on their excitement.

"You don't," he told them, and broke the news that we'd promised Orlova we'd leave the colony alone.

"But that isn't *fair*," Seung said, as if fairness ever made a fucking difference. "We've come all this way. You can't just leave us up here."

He looked at me when he said this, like I was his mother instead of the same fucking age, and I wanted to say *Fuck you, Seung, none of this was my idea* but I guess it was, Vostochny, so instead I said "I think we need to give them a little time."

"And then what?" He crossed his arms, just like Kano, and glared at me. "We wait for them to invite us for a picnic?"

So, what the hell, I confessed I'd told Officer Savelova she should dodge the old woman and call us herself, and they all gaped at me. Especially Kano and Hina.

"You told us," Hina said, "to follow the rules. Why do *you* get to decide when that changes?"

Léon spoke up and said it was because I was Captain, and reminded them they'd all decided that together, and since they'd voted they had to live with the results. I let them argue for a while, because between you and me, Vostochny, I did kind of fuck up.

"Look," I said at last. "It may have been stupid." Kano opened his mouth again, and I glared him into silence. "But didn't you notice? How she watched everything? Where we sat, what we ate, who we talked to?" Hina blushed at that, but she looked a little less pissed off at me.

"She's the *police*," Kano said. "It's her job."

"With all those armed security people in there?"

"Which is another thing," he insisted. "They've got *guns*, Maddie. We've got fuck-all." He looked around at the others. "This isn't some pack of colorful characters from of some old movie.

These people are *afraid* of us, and any of you who forget what humans do when we're scared can go study some remedial history for a while."

But Seung wasn't backing off. "We're stuck here for a *year*," he said. "We're supposed to just ignore them?"

And then Qara, who'd been quiet for this whole argument, gave us a reminder. "We're not stuck here for anything. Without dealing with that planet, the transceiver is DOA."

That ruined the party and the mutiny all at once.

Léon, Seung, and Ratana started arguing over design issues, and I slipped away to let the smart people do their work. I don't know if they remember, but I do: twenty years ago, when half our building supplies got blasted into powder, the three of them spent four days without sleeping redesigning the system to work with what we had left. I'll grant you the problem we were solving wasn't a badly-placed planet, but they know what they're doing. If there's an answer, they'll find it, and if there isn't? We have time. We pretty much have all the time there is.

RECIP: National Earth Space Organization, Vostochny
REPORTER: Loineau, Madeleine, Cmdr. NZKO *Hypatia*
Supplemental

"You shouldn't have done that without telling us, Maddie."

I was halfway down the spoke to my quarters, still mostly weightless, and I hadn't heard Kano closing in on me and I just about jumped across the whole damn ship. "*Fuck,*" I snapped. "Don't *do* that. Not after the day I've had."

"*Fuck* your day." Oh, he was mad. "You put us in danger. Did you see that plasma weapon?"

Okay. On that one, he had a point. But dammit, Vostochny, I was tired, and I never have been good at letting Kano win. "I saw *one* energy weapon, and a couple of projectile handguns."

"Oh, I'm sorry, I didn't think there was an acceptable quantity of *shit that could drop us in our tracks.*"

"They were *scared*, Kano." I turned away from him and kept going, grabbing the ladder as the gravity got stronger. "We're, I don't know, aliens from beyond the stars or something."

"I was scared, too," he told me, hanging on to the rung beside me. "But I didn't pack a spike nuke in my pocket."

"Of course you didn't. That would've killed us along with them."

He put his free hand on my arm, stopping me, and when I turned to him I focused on looking annoyed and not at all like it's already occurred to me more than once that I might have indeed done something monumentally stupid. But Kano, fucking Kano, wasn't mad anymore. He was *afraid*. "Why'd you do it, Mads?"

Here's the thing, Vostochny: I know it doesn't make any sense at all. These people are from a completely different culture. Earth was...not at its best when their ancestors left. Even with the few records that survived, we know most of the evac ships that took off back then were built by radical political factions or wealthy families. One of the reasons *Arkhangelsk* was always considered a myth was because they were different: they were a science expedition that took anyone who was willing to swear an oath of peace, or some such bullshit, although seriously, that one plasma thing could have taken out the ECV and roasted a big chunk of that tundra of theirs, so I'm thinking *peace*, at least, was the mythical bit.

But I shook her hand, Vostochny. And while we were getting our footing—and yes, it was weird walking in gravity that high—she slowed down for us. Didn't say anything, just took smaller steps, waved at her people to back off, let us acclimate. And she warned us about the scary staring people, and told us she'd protect us if she had to.

She looks like me. I mean, not *really*—she's older, and her hair is nearly black, and it's got silver streaks going through it and she wears it longer so the curls cover the back of her neck. And she's shorter, and she's thin as a rail like the rest of them. But she has my heavy eyebrows and square face, and her skin's a little darker than mine but has the same gold undertone.

And when she walked us back to the ECV without the others—and their weapons—I felt like she wanted to say something. Like she wanted to know about us. So I gave her a way to find out.

I know, I know. I'm projecting.

Kano and I lowered ourselves hand over hand. "We gave you

this fucking captain gig because you're supposed to be the logical one," he said, and at that point I don't think he was so afraid anymore.

"That's not true. You gave me this fucking captain gig because I was the one who stood up and did stuff when nobody else would."

"Like expecting good intentions from the head cop in a group of cultists."

"They're not cultists," I corrected. "They're *descendants* of cultists."

We hit the wheel and walked up the hallway into my room, and I went straight to my bed, dropping onto the mattress. Instead of hospitably disappearing, Kano sat on my desk. "We're going to need to watch Hina, you know."

Kano's older than all of us but the Colonel, and he's always been overprotective. In this case, though, I can't disagree with him.

With all the objections I have about how this mission came to be, Vostochny, I know in some ways you did your best. There were supposed to be children. There were supposed to be a couple of generations, staggered, all genetically unrelated. You thought about sex and reproduction and plain old ordinary companionship. You didn't think most of us would be killed halfway through the mission. You didn't think we'd lose most of our children, too.

You didn't think our hearts would be broken.

Hina's our only child. We've all been her parents. The Colonel more than most, yes; but she's our little girl, and we see her like that, and that keeps her separate. For ourselves...we do all right. We entertain each other. Ratana and Léon are mostly monogamous, but even they'll leave the door open if someone's looking for company. I almost never get the urge anymore, and if that's my nature or living in space for so long, it doesn't matter. I'm happy enough. The point is we all love each other, and we take care of each other.

But Hina's left out of all that, as she should be, and she doesn't see us like that, either. She knows all there is to know, thanks to teaching and medicine and video, and she's twenty-five and an adult. In a way, it hasn't been my business for years.

When I was in Novayarkha, walking through those hallways under the eyes of all those people who were terrified of us, I kept coming back to one thing: *there are so many young people.* Yes, they've clearly got some difficulties with illness, but there are *nine* of us up here, and I saw at least three hundred of them. And I don't think that's all there are.

That kid in the governor's office, the police officer. A little polished for my taste, but he looked at Hina and he saw a woman, not a child. And she looked at him, and saw a man and not a parent. (I guess she likes men. I never thought to wonder before.)

I've always known, Vostochny, that we'd be asking Hina to shoulder an unforgivable burden. That she'd be piloting *Hypatia* home for us, and that most likely she'd be watching all of us die along the way. But I never really *felt* that until today. And...I don't think I know how to ask her to do that anymore.

"Unless you want to lock her up," I said, "we're going to have to find a way to get to know them better. And that means making friends."

"You think your police officer is going to contact you?" he asked.

I managed enough energy to prop myself up on an elbow. "Look," I told him. "I don't know how this is going to go. Maybe we'll get nothing but full dark from Orlova and her crew. Maybe we won't. But since when is uncertainty new to us? Hell, here we are, where we were headed, and we can't even say for sure we can build the station anyway. One day at a time, Kano. Or one minute, if we have to."

He let out a puff of laughter. "So long as we look after each other first. Okay, Maddie?"

"Of course."

I wonder now, Vostochny. What did he think I'd say to that?

CHAPTER NINE

Whether or not I should confess my conversation with Captain Loineau to Yulia becomes moot as soon as I'm back through the Hub airlock. Dmitri greets me there, stern and paternal, lecturing me about my personal safety. I manage a glare at Katerina, staunchly at attention behind him; she doesn't meet my eyes. But I'm unable to muster much anger at either of them. There's a thrum of worry and fear under Dmitri's words, reminding me that we're all going to react to this disruption differently. Dmitri's not wrong: I'm too trusting, and my promise to be more careful in the future is mostly sincere.

Before I can ask for Dmitri's impressions of the strangers, Katerina interrupts with a whisper in his ear, and he disappears to debrief his security people. And I've taken only three steps down the corridor before I get two calls at once: one from Costa, looking for a calming presence in his classroom, and another from Mathilda Pedersen, mayor of the Third Block, concerned that public arguments there are becoming heated.

For one moment I consider sending Aleksey to Mathilda and taking comfort in the children, but Aleksey's never been one to use words to keep the peace. And words are what's needed right now.

When I arrive at the Third Block, nearly all the residents are standing in the corridor watching Mathilda and Anatole Smirovski shout at each other about whether or not *Hypatia* is an Old World cover for an alien invasion. In truth, it's a far more mundane idea than I'd anticipated, and I'm comfortable standing aside for a while, listening. Some in the crowd see me and step back from the argument; at their looks I only nod, letting them know I'm here to quiet the situation. I let Anatole and Mathilda go on for a few minutes, watching the crowd bubble with unreleased energy, before I break in.

"I ate with them." They all turn wary eyes on me. They'll never trust me not to arrest anyone, but they know I'm neither credulous nor a liar. "Do you think another species would be able to drink Yulia's liquor, never mind manage politeness over Jenna Viktorova's wheat noodles?"

Mathilda's lips tighten; she's never been able to let go of a theory, no matter how mad. "They might be able to fake it," she says. "They might be able to fool us in all kinds of ways."

"And what sense does it make to invade us by sending three unarmed people to sit in Yulia's office?" Practicality will be no comfort to Mathilda, but not everyone in the Third Block has turned their backs on reason. "They are *human*, Mathilda, just like we are."

"They're no less dangerous than aliens," Anatole puts in; but he's comforting Mathilda, conceding enough of her point for her to save face. "We'll need to be just as cautious. More so, because it'll be easier for them to fit in."

I leave them discussing how to defend their homes against future strangers, how to be polite but secure. It's only later that I realize they're assuming there *will* be future strangers, regardless of what Yulia's said.

And that I've been assuming the same, all along.

I'm busy throughout first dark, tackling everything from a fistfight in the Hub to arresting four people for shouting and threats and having Vassiliya lock them in a holding cell to cool down. I see all the myriad reactions: fear, which is dominant; anger at the threat to all we've built here; a smug superiority that the strangers, even with their warm planet and their technology, have traveled no further than we did two hundred years ago.

But there's curiosity hand-in-hand with the anxiety, and I choose Captain Loineau's reaction to Yulia's liquor as the story I repeat, making her strange and familiar all at once. Some even laugh in sympathy at the tale.

Things grow quiet close to second sunrise, and Irina tags the cobblestones next to me as I walk through the Hub toward Yulia's office. Physically I'm exhausted; but my mind is spinning, and I long to retreat into my own house to allow my thoughts to settle. I feel full to bursting, as if I've drunk too much tea, something I can't identify threatening to erupt out of me. Some of it is fear, as paranoid and unreasonable as Mathilda Pedersen's; but my mind keeps returning to Captain Loineau's voice, casual and easygoing, offering me a glimpse of some bright unknown. Fear I am used to, can process and dismiss. My longing for the brightness is nearly unbearable.

My mood turns to stone when I see Doctor Halvorsen approaching me from Yulia's closed office door.

"Is she all right?" I ask.

Doctor Halvorsen frowns, puzzlement in her furrowed face. "Of course she is," she tells me, as if I'm a student asking a foolish question. "But you've missed her. She's gone home for the evening." She straightens a little, nearly as tall as I am. "Doctor's orders."

I dislike postponing confrontation, but somehow I still feel relief. "Thank you, Doctor Halvorsen," I tell her sincerely. "Was her afternoon difficult?"

I turn and fall into step with the doctor, heading away from Yulia's office back up the main spoke. "She fielded a lot of questions," she tells me. "So many people. And of course she didn't want them to see how fatigued she was."

We're both well aware Yulia's spirit will never let her take enough rest.

"Are things quieter?" she asks. "Aleksey was saying there were riots."

"That's an exaggeration," I assure her, although I suppose that depends on her definition. "I only had to break up one fight; the others petered out on their own." I glance over at her; her concern seems sincere. "The Third Block is deciding whether they're more worried about Old World corruption or aliens in disguise. We'll need to keep an eye on them."

"Hmph." Her disapproval is palpable. "They're alien enough just as they are."

I wonder how she'd feel if I told her she sounded like Anatole Smirovski.

We walk in an almost companionable silence, encountering few people on our way to the tram, despite the relatively early hour. Generally people wander after dinner, but today they've all retreated, to what thoughts I can only guess. We've none of us lived through anything like this, never thought there was even a chance.

Doctor Halvorsen clears her throat. "While I have you, Anya, dear…" Her tone is odd, both hesitant and disapproving. "I need to have a word about Aleksey."

"What has he done now?" I ask, before I remember Aleksey and Doctor Halvorsen are usually on the same side.

But if she notices my presumption of guilt, she ignores it. "I appreciate his desire to help people, of course, but his timing was… unfortunate." I say nothing, and with a sigh she gives up her secret. "He had a rather pointed argument with Yulia."

"*Today?*" For one moment, Doctor Halvorsen and I are of one mind. "What in the skies could have possessed him?"

"Well." She coughs a little. "I don't think it was the skies."

I remember, then, Hina's small hand in Aleksey's fingers, him holding on just a little too long. My irritation with Aleksey eases, but my confusion remains. "I can't believe he doesn't understand the best way to see Hina again is to give Yulia time to work out a strategy."

She smiles, then. "He's young, our Aleksey," she tells me, as if he were not a man in his thirties. "I understand his passions clouding his judgement. But if you could speak to him, Anya, and see that he doesn't bring the subject up again." At my raised eyebrow, she explains. "He was advocating asking the strangers for their DNA."

My annoyance returns full-force.

"I can't argue with his intent," Doctor Halvorsen allows. "But he knows how careful we need to be, and we've got no behavioral data on these people at all. No way to verify anything they'd tell us, even if they agreed to it. And without understanding what's happened on the Old World since we left?" She shakes her head. "We can't let that happen. The wrong trait in their genome could destroy us in a generation."

But she's reminded me, and she's a doctor after all, our expert on these matters. "What do you suppose they use for incubators up there?"

She looks surprised. "Who knows? They're only forty years from home, after all. Perhaps they don't need any."

The thought that Hina might be a natural-born child is as unsettling as anything I know about them. "They'd have to have something," I argue. "It can't be a particularly pleasant environment for pregnancy. There's more radiation up there than there is here."

But Doctor Halvorsen has told me everything she plans to tell me tonight. "How they solved the problem isn't relevant," she says. "We have our own methods, and despite intermittent wobbles, we manage very nicely. What's important is that Aleksey lets it lie. He can have whatever fantasies he chooses, but I can't have Yulia upset like that. Can you give him that message, Anya?"

All the things I wish to say. "Of course," I tell her. "I won't allow him to disturb her again."

Satisfied, she smiles again, relieving me of the need to continue our temporary kinship. "Are you taking the tram, Anya? You must have had a very long day."

Solitude feels abruptly critical. "No, thank you. I could use a walk." I bid her goodnight, and wait for her tram to glide around the arc out of sight.

The solar tubes are showing the odd, backlit blue-gray that hits before second sunrise, and I let Irina emerge to pace restlessly again. We head out through the main spoke airlock, and walk across the secondary courtyard toward the Inner Rim. The choice isn't a wise one. It'll be twenty minutes more before the sun rises enough to shift the thermostat toward something less hazardous. But I'm bundled up, and I walk briskly, letting Irina run ahead of me to keep my mind on my destination.

Aleksey's insistence on arguing with Yulia is unfortunate, but she hasn't retained power without being pragmatic. DNA may not be our problem, but Yulia knows full well that we've been struggling to maintain the delicate incubators. She'll be considering how to ask the strangers for help without exposing our weaknesses, without acknowledging that we have nothing to offer them in return. She won't be looking forward to being friendly with them, but she'll manage the necessary charm once she's confident of her cause, whatever she decides that will be.

What I do between now and then will be in aid of the same cause.

The sky has grown lilac and the worst of the bitter cold has eased by the time we get home. I warm my fingers over the utility stove, palms down. My solar tubes reveal little of the second sunrise light, leaving the room to be lit by strips of narrow yellow-white bulbs, reflecting the spectrum of a sun I've never seen.

Captain Loineau was born under that sun. It woke her in the

mornings and touched her skin, those wild curls. She's lived its rhythms, however long ago, watching it rise and set only once in a day.

My radio transmitter is stashed haphazardly under the sink, and I have to clear it of a substantial layer of dust. It's deceptively small, built with dials rather than touch controls—manufactured here, in Novayarkha, from a patchwork of new copper wire and electronics centuries old. I power it up and wait for it to short out; it doesn't.

I set the tuner to 107.9. Irina is looking up at me, her eyes sober.

"I should tell Yulia all of it."

She waits.

"I am an old fool."

When I turn on the transmitter, Irina is smiling.

RECIP: National Earth Space Organization, Vostochny
REPORTER: Loineau, Madeleine, Cmdr. NZKO *Hypatia*
Supplemental

"I'm sorry to wake you, Maddie," said the Colonel, "but the radio is asking for you."

The Colonel's artificial voice is pleasant enough, although it lacks some subtlety. More specifically: it's cheerful. All the time. I've grown to rely on the involuntary optimism it inserts into our days, but I know he's got some ambivalent feelings about it. He was a pretty upbeat person pre-disaster, but I think it says something that he still prefers the display when we're all in the same room.

The Colonel never wakes me up for anything unless it's important. And there was only one important call I could possibly be getting in the middle of the night.

"How much range have we got?" I asked, climbing out of bed.

"You've got another twenty-five minutes before we hit radio blackout."

Twenty-five minutes. Not much time for international diplomacy.

I switched my room communicator to the radio, and a static-clouded voice came over the line. "Captain Loineau? Are you there?"

She pronounces my name strangely. Kano tells me my name's hard to pronounce because it's French, and I'm a descendant of old imperialists and I deserve every terrible thing that's happened to me. He usually says that when I've beaten him at handball and he's too winded to get off the floor. "I'm here," I replied. "Is this Officer Savelova?"

I didn't really have to ask. She has a distinctive voice, mid-tone and warm, full of musical vowels. Nicer than how Hina pronounces old Russian. "Yes."

I waited for her to say more before I realized I'd probably guessed right: she wasn't supposed to be calling me, and she was worried Orlova would yell at her. I'd half expected the radio signal to be from that stiff old woman, railing at me for being a subversive influence on their city.

It's early days yet, of course.

"Is there something I can do for you, Officer Savelova?"

There were several seconds of static, and then: "I have questions."

That made two of us. "What is it you'd like to know?"

"I'm not sure—" She broke off, and I swear, Vostochny, she sounded embarrassed. "There is a great deal. And I fear we have not represented ourselves in a way that will incline you to tell me very much."

"I think it's safe to say this is a strange situation for all of us," I tried. "If it helps at all, I've got a few questions myself."

"Of course," she said, and do you know, I think she was surprised. "Perhaps—I'll try to answer your questions, Captain Loineau, but I hope you'll understand if I have to decline some of them."

I guess we all have secrets to keep. "Why don't you go first?"

There was another long pause, and I started to think most of our twenty-five minutes was going to be eaten up by her dithering. "How is it humanity did not die out?"

She sounded genuinely incredulous, and I realized, as I frantically paged in the history I'd largely ignored while I was being schooled, that I didn't have a good answer for her. "The period when the evac ships left Earth isn't my specific area of study." I don't know why I couldn't just tell her I was ignorant. "But as far as I know, we survived the way we always do."

"How is that?"

"Dumb luck."

She made a sound, and I had to listen for a second before I realized she was laughing. She swallowed it quickly. "I'm sorry. But please understand...of everything you've brought here, this is the most difficult thing for us all to absorb. All our lives, we've been told the Old World is dead, we're all that's left, and we must unify and fight to survive or there'll be nothing after us."

"Is it so bad, being taught that way?" I asked her.

This time I couldn't be sure if she was hesitating, or carefully considering how much she wanted me to know. "I don't think it's good for anyone," she said eventually, "to live under the shadow of so much despair."

Well, hell, Vostochny. I wasn't going to argue with her on that one.

"My turn?" I asked.

"Of course."

"Are you *Arkhangelsk*?"

When she said, "We are," I felt absurdly pleased with myself. But when she asked how I knew and I mentioned our archives, she said, "You have written history?" and there was such longing in her voice I wanted to wrap up our data stores and give them to her like a birthday gift.

"We've got archives that cover the years after your ancestors left. But I'm sure you must keep history of your own."

"Yes. But that's *our* history. It's your turn for a question, Captain Loineau."

That fucking title. "I wish you'd call me Maddie," I said.

"Maddie." Her accent made my name sound more formal than *Captain*. "I'm Anya."

I wish she could have seen me grinning at her. "Anya. How many of you are there?"

This time she didn't hesitate. "I don't think I ought to tell you that."

"You're afraid of us."

"Of course we are." Surprised again. "A week ago, the most shocking thing that could happen here was murder."

I think murder's a whole lot more shocking than we are, actually. But I didn't push that one. "What are you afraid of?" I asked instead.

There was a briefer silence this time, and I figured we were finally getting somewhere. "I am afraid that everything I live and breathe and feel and love every day is going to change."

Oh. Is that all? "Surely things always change."

"Here? Not often. Can you—what's it like now? Earth?"

She said *Earth* like it was a magic spell, like she wasn't sure if it was going to grant her wishes or turn her into a toad. "I haven't been there for a long time," I said. "But I can tell you a little about what it was like when we left."

I described to her what we have in our videos: the sunshine, blue sky uncut by clouds; rain falling in sheets onto acre after acre of solar collectors; organized squares of emerald farmland; wildfires that rage, unchecked, close to the equator. I told her stories from our books and our movies, tales of romance and adventure; and I told her of music, so unlike what we heard on her radio, and so much the same.

It's as alien to me as it is to her. What does it say about me that I desperately wanted her to believe it was beautiful?

"There's so much," she said at last, and her voice sounded odd and thick. "So different from what we left behind."

I asked her the second biggest question I've had since we found them. "What do they tell you about that?"

"They tell us the Old World was dying," she said. "That there were storms, hot and cold, that most of the cities had fallen into riot and ruin, hundreds and thousands freezing in the winters and dying of heat stroke in the summers. That people had stopped caring for each other, were looking only to themselves, and disease and violence spread like dry snow in a night breeze. That the culture was irredeemably corrupt. That there was no hope when we fled."

They were close, weren't they, Vostochny?

"I expect that's about right," I told her. "Except people stopped dying after a while, and started rebuilding."

"And eventually built *Hypatia*."

Well, that was the most shorthand history lesson I've ever given. "Yes."

"How old were you when you left Earth?"

I was young. I was a different person. "Eight years old."

"And how is it that an eight-year-old found a place on your mission?"

I don't replay those memories much, Vostochny. I don't really know, anymore, how many of them are real, and how many are reconstructed, or conflated with the memories of the others. I sat back in my chair, and started to tell her things I shouldn't. "It was the same for most of us who were little when this started: our families needed something, and the government offered it in trade for us. I remember…" I swallowed. "I remember a baby, too small. Sick. Coughing a lot. And a woman, maybe my mother, crying. I remember a man, and a hug, and someone telling me to be a good girl."

Another long pause. "Maddie. That is barbaric."

Barbaric.

We don't think of it that way, here on *Hypatia*. We were children, except for Hina and the Colonel. We didn't have choices. And the people who took us were compassionate, and the crew on *Hypatia* was mostly kind. I see it in the movies and documentaries you provided us, and the news broadcasts and histories: there are so many awful ways to raise children. In a sense we've been lucky.

But it *was* barbaric. Bargaining with a family too poor to keep an infant alive, making them choose between a sick baby and a healthy eight-year-old. And maybe it wasn't like that; maybe we were all unwanted. Maybe we were kids whose families couldn't be bothered. But I've seen what's left of the records, Vostochny. We're all smart, smarter than average. We'd all, by the time we were chosen, shown aptitudes. *You targeted us*, and our families, and you found out what you'd have to offer them so they couldn't turn you down.

I don't remember that baby's name. I will always hate you for that.

"It *is* barbaric," I admitted. "But we're here now. And we've built a family from it all."

"How many are you?"

I wanted her to know. "I don't think I ought to tell you that," I said instead, and she laughed again, and then it was all right. "Fewer than I saw when we were in Novayarkha, at least. We can't hurt you."

A small lie. About the size of a spike nuke.

She made a sound of consideration. "That's something we think about, of course. But it's not the biggest worry. All my life... the Old World tore itself apart, we've been told. To think that they might someday talk to us, the way I'm talking to you—you're alien enough, you and your friends."

"That's funny. Kano tells me I look like you."

"You do. But you move so differently, all of you. And don't think it's just the gravity. Where are you all from, originally?"

"The Siberian Plains," I told her. "There's a fair mix of ethnicities there." Or were, when we left. "My people are mostly Eastern Russian—Slavs and Mongols, although there's the odd Caucasian a bunch of generations back. Kano's mostly Thai Phuan, and Hina's ancestors all came over from Japan, when it got flooded."

"Do you have other children?" she asked.

She sounded so curious, so eager, so *hopeful*. And I should have hedged, but instead I said, "Not anymore."

And again, that stretch of uninterrupted static. "I'm sorry, Maddie."

There was something in her voice, something more than sympathy, and I remembered the faces down there, how many had sallow skin and sunken eyes, even the little ones. I thought of Governor Orlova, sharp-tongued and guarded, and how her hands shook when she picked up her glass.

We lost all of our children but Hina in a single moment, crossing from faster-than-light to normal space, one misplaced piece of rock ripping away twenty-two people and half our ship. Instant. Painless, perhaps; or at least not prolonged pain. But in that moment they returned to the dust from whence we all came, and the rest of us were wounded, doomed to spend the rest of our lives as patched-over cripples, just like our ship.

Anya would have watched dozens of people—maybe hundreds—die from lingering illnesses. In discomfort, agony, fully aware of what awaited them. She'll probably die that way someday, and she knows it. And *she* was offering *me* comfort.

I said, "It was a long time ago."

"People here say, sometimes, that we need to let go of our grief and move on," she told me. "I've often thought that was foolishness. Loss destroys, and there's no way to proceed as if you still had the same resources you did before. If there's any hope of rebuilding your life, you need to acknowledge you're building on top of something fundamentally different."

I'm sure, Vostochny, that the room got blurry then for no reason at all. "The Colonel says we carry them with us."

"Your Colonel is very wise."

She could have asked me who he was. She could have wheedled all kinds of secrets out of me at that point. "It's just," I said, "it's not enough, is it? Acknowledging that we carry them."

"No," she agreed. And there was weight in that word. "But carrying them is not a choice. Learning to live while we do it—that's the decision we must make."

How did I end up talking philosophy with a woman who thinks we're here to corrupt everything she loves?

"Maddie," she asked, the hesitation back, "how long has it been since you've spoken to Earth?"

No offense, Vostochny, but I've long since stopped having the numbers at my fingertips. "Our time? Thirty-five years. Their time? Maybe...I want to say sixty years, but it might be as many as a hundred."

"They may be as strange to you as they are to us."

Will you be strange, Vostochny? I've been talking at you for so long, I can't believe you will. "Or they may be as much the same as you and I."

She laughed again. Strange, that this woman with such watchful eyes should be so ready to laugh. "That will be my hope," she told me, and sobered. "It's a part of us, what we know about our past. Even recognizing that humans survived after we left is going to be difficult for a lot of people."

"I promised your governor we'd let you alone, and I meant it."

"But when your communicator is completed, that's going to change."

Will you leave them be if they ask you to? If *we* ask you to? Will you let them stay insulated and separate, with all of their illness and bad history? "Probably, yes," I agreed. "If only because contact will be available. I can't believe all of your people would refuse it if it's offered."

"Oh, they won't. The young people in particular. Which isn't to say they'll come to love any of you, but they're curious."

"So are you, I think."

"Not everyone considers that to be a strength of mine."

I'm betting *not everyone* meant the old woman. "I've always preferred knowledge to ignorance," I told her. "Even if your choice is not to change...it's a false choice if you don't understand what's on the other side of it."

I checked the clock; our time was running out. "We're moving out of range, Anya. Can we talk again?"

There was no pause this time. "I would like that very much, Maddie." But the connection held, just for a moment, and right when I thought we'd lose it, she said: "Maddie. If we needed you, would you help us?"

Which is an impossible question without qualifiers, right? I mean, what does she want help with? Disseminating propaganda? Building lasers so they can shoot us out of the sky? What the hell can we give them, with our crippled ship and barely enough parts to build a transceiver that isn't even going to work?

"Of course we would," I told her, and we moved out of range.

With everything I should be taking from this day, Vostochny, I know I shouldn't be hopeful. These people are inbred and insular, and they don't want anything to do with us. I should be focusing on my promise to leave them alone. But...we've *been* alone. All of us. For too long. My family is everything to me, but I want more than eight people in my life. I want more than the rest of my days filled by the same souls. It's not that I'm dissatisfied with them, or I'd change them, although Kano could be a hell of a lot less sarcastic.

It's that I want *more*.

ARCHIVE #9451

DRAFT SETTLEMENT PROPOSAL
SHIP YEAR 172

LOGGED BY: JARI SAARINEN
B. SHIP YEAR 151
D. COLONY YEAR 32

DIRECTIVE 17 GOVERNMENT USE ONLY
SCHOLARLY ACCESS FORBIDDEN

*****
DRAFT
*****

Proposal for staged dismantling of the carrier *Arkhangelsk* in preparation for settlement on planet 87-99-C.

Note: Proposal is for informational purposes only. No public access or comment.

Stage One: Location

The ideal settlement placement will be a flat, open area no less than 8 km^2. Permafrost must be deep and well-established to ensure long-term stability.

Mining requirements and environmental limitations dictate we must locate near a substantial stone deposit.

Risk factors: We won't be close enough to the planet to determine an appropriate settlement location for another 22 years. At that point our engine issues might limit our options.

Proposed mitigation: Determine what materials would be needed to place the settlement in a non-ideal landscape.

Stage Two: Excavation

The main power core will need to be placed beneath the settlement itself. This will require a deep central excavation, with a tiered surrounding structure.

This presents us with the conflicting problems of requiring explosives to achieve the necessary depth while also needing precision in setting a foundation for the habitat area. We propose a single deep detonation, with areas surrounding the power core location filled in with native materials, including ice as necessary.

Risk factors: The explosion may expose substrate that will render the location unstable. Much of our ordnance has been in storage for well over a century; we've no good way to test if it works.

Proposed mitigation: Do not dismantle or disconnect the main power core before the excavation and staging are complete. Fallback will be to remain on *Arkhangelsk*.

Stage Three: Construction and Migration

The laboratory and recreational ring will be placed first. Construction crews will travel in shifts to and from *Arkhangelsk* and establish the ring as a viable habitat.

Once the ring is environmentally sound, the main power core will be disengaged from *Arkhangelsk* and placed in the center of the ring, then covered and insulated. *Arkhangelsk*'s systems will be shifted to the secondary power core.

As surface food production increases, individuals will transfer to the planet and begin preparation for the main habitat ring.

The habitat ring will be disengaged and placed once the remaining shipboard population drops below 350, the number that can be housed safely in the fuselage.

Risk factors:

1.   Damage to the power core during transfer is a real possibility, and neither the settlement nor all of *Arkhangelsk*'s rings can operate entirely on the secondary core. Some core damage can be minimized with insulation, but that's a temporary fix at best.

2.   Food production has worked well for us for over 150 years. We have no reason to believe transferring our systems to the planet's surface will change that; however, if our food production becomes compromised, the settlement will never be viable.

3.   A number of people on the crew have expressed the desire to remain in flight, and not establish a settlement at all. While most of the individuals in question do not have criminal backgrounds, it's worth noting that anonymity, threats, and convenient accidents have historically been employed by *Arkhangelsk* dissidents.

Proposed mitigation:

1.   Construct a flight simulator, and populate it with detailed planetary data as we near 87-99-C. Train multiple crew members on atmospheric flight and placement of the power core.

2.   Increase current food yield and preservation. Stockpile at least 20 years of non-perishable food by the time we reach 87-99-C.

3.   Monitor all known dissidents. Maintain up-to-date lists of activities and comrades. Reinstate Original Law, and make it clear that any sabotage of the settlement plan will result in swift justice and the harshest possible legal penalties.

ASSIMILATION

.

CHAPTER TEN

Irina waits at the top of the stairs, her face turned toward the waxing glow of first sunrise, while I repair the prison airlock.

We have five lifetime residents in our prison, and one of them, Aanika Koskinen, has the habit of trying, now and again, to take a stroll in the sunshine without a suit. Mercifully she's not adept with hardware, and Vassiliya noticed the tamper alarm before Aanika was able to do more than damage the hydraulics on the airlock door. Why she chose today I can only guess—her attachment to reality has always been tenuous, and I can't believe she understands what's happened over the last two sunsets. But Vassiliya, although competent at her clerical duties, is a persistently unimaginative person, and she's always been unnerved by Aanika's breezy delusions. She seemed palpably relieved to call me in for a mundane door repair.

Aanika's infirm mind likely saved her life twenty-five years ago. Yulia broke the old tradition of Original Law, sparing Aanika from the vengeful justice of the family of the woman she murdered, which would likely have been a death sentence. Nearly two decades before that, when I was just nine years old, I witnessed Karl Yasnikoff, convicted of beating his closest friend to death in a drunken rage, publicly bludgeoned by the matriarchs of the dead man's family. I remember Costa gripping my hand, whispering that

I didn't need to watch; but he was wrong. I needed to know what we did to the guilty, where our limits were.

There was significant public outcry over Yulia's breaking of tradition over Aanika's sentencing. And yet today, with the victim's family long dead, nobody speaks of Aanika at all, unless I am called to repair something she's broken.

It's a death, too, of sorts: being lost from memory. But I'm not at all certain, had she taken family from me, I'd find it sufficient.

When the airlock seal is holding again I climb the stairs to stand next to Irina. She's looking over the plain to the north, squinting into the sun, and for a moment I let the still morning take my senses. The tundra is flat for nearly five kilometers, and then there are the mountains, huge even from this distance. My hair is confined under my hood, but Irina's blows all around her head, up and down and sideways, like a living thing, and as the wind pushes against the soft hood I feel an echo of it against my skin, achingly cold.

I don't know how old this rock is, if it was always covered in ice, if it was ever green and warm, or if it's destined to be so in the future. We've never studied this planet beyond blasting great holes below us, hoping to find livelihood in the stone, but I don't think all of the spectral color winding through the quarry is a reflection of the sky.

"There's too much to do to stay out here," I say aloud. I head down the stairs again, my descent taking longer than it should, looking over my shoulder as Irina lingers.

Inside the airlock I take my time pulling off my protective gear, composing my expression to hide my mood. Where most of the city is anxious, I'm full of an optimism I haven't felt in decades, and it seems rude to be so palpably buoyant in the face of everyone else's fear. Most people pay little attention to me, but those who'd notice would be unlikely to find my optimism a comfort.

It's foolish, my hopefulness. I know what the strangers are. It's a sign of my own short-sightedness that I feel as if I've found the sun after weeks of heavy snow.

All those exotic words Maddie said to me: *grass* and *wildfires* and *oceans*. And *Slavs* and *Mongols* and *Thai Phuan* and *Japan*. After *Hypatia* moved out of range, I searched our archives and found long lists of ethnicities, people who look like me and Costa and Yulia and Maddie, sometimes clumped geographically in homogeneous cities, sometimes in mélanges that make us seem monochrome as deep-quarried slate. I saw still images, people with Hina's fine and expressive features, with Kano's smooth skin and quirky lips. And still more variation: populations that are taller or fatter, complexions all dark or all light; seafarers and astronauts and farmers and technologists and all of those together. Somewhere during my education I must have seen these images, as my teachers sketched for us the doomed history of the planet we fled, but at the time I never thought of them as having anything to do with me at all.

The Old World was big, so much bigger than our icy home, and there were *people*, all over, even after the wars and the disease, even after millions upon millions had died. They were different from us, and the same, and they were *everywhere*.

No. Not *were*. *Are*.

Aleksey botched his argument with Yulia, but he's not wrong. *Hypatia* will be followed by other ships. One way or another, we're going to have to deal with change—not just in our genome, but in our culture. Yulia will resist, but even she must understand the inevitability of what's happening, the need to form a strategy that will preserve our strengths and our resources in the face of forces we can't control.

New. Everything will be new.

I'll need to talk to Maddie again, to find out when she thinks these other ships may arrive. We may have years. We may have decades. We may have the rest of my life, and nothing but hope that the generations after me will make the right choices. Most social changes creak and groan in slow discomfort, like sheet ice; but they're changes all the same. More reason to begin as soon as we can.

In my reverie I very nearly skip examining the prisoner visitor log as I'm leaving, but what I see there drops me unpleasantly back into reality. There's only one reason Aleksey would visit the prison outside of his assigned hours without clearing it first with me.

And here I had thought Yulia and I had an understanding.

"Did Aleksey say why he was here?"

My tone is harsher than it needs to be, but Vassiliya's too used to me to be bothered. "He didn't say anything," she says. When I don't respond she has the wisdom to straighten, meeting my eyes. "I assumed he was just asking questions. I didn't monitor the room."

"Do so next time." I head through the locked passage to the cells. It's unfair of me to be annoyed with Vassiliya. Aleksey's precise and draconian when it comes to interpreting the rules. He feels entitled to any confession at any cost, while I need Rolf clearheaded to knit together the meager fragments of hard evidence I've been able to find.

Aleksey's insistence on his rules over mine may cost me answers.

Our prison takes up a small arc of the far end of the Outer Rim, repurposing the quarters of *Arkhangelsk*'s environmental maintenance crew. We've removed the doors to each individual room, so there's nowhere for anyone to hide; but the solar tubes are kept as clear as the ones in the Inner Rim, letting in as much natural light as possible. In keeping the prison a place of quiet, of peace, Yulia backs me up without question. Neither she nor I are sentimental about crime; violence requires segregation, and irredeemable violence requires that segregation be permanent. But no crime necessitates cruelty.

Rolf is in the cell on the end, a corner room just a little smaller than the others, used only for short-term holding. When he's convicted, we'll move him to a bigger, brighter room, and I'll indulge his living preferences within the confines of the law.

"Rolf?"

He's sitting in a chair in one dark corner, and he starts at my voice, turning his head toward me, eyes unfocused. There's darkness around his right eye—blood or bruise, I can't tell. I scan the small room: no dishes anywhere.

"When did you last eat?" I ask him.

He blinks as if he's just woken. "I don't know."

"Will you eat if I have something brought?"

Hesitantly, he nods, and I radio Vassiliya, and then Maria Kalyagin, Doctor Halvorsen's senior assistant. Rolf doesn't look up when Vassiliya arrives with the food, Maria at her heels, but when I set down the tray in front of his chair, his head turns a little.

"I'd like the doctor to examine you," I tell him, "if you'll allow it."

At that Rolf looks up sharply, but when he sees Maria his whole body relaxes. He unfolds himself from the chair, slowly and stiffly, and turns to the tray, nodding his agreement.

Maria gives him as thorough a physical as she can while he devours soy loaf and herbs. Not the best of our recipes, but it's freshly made, and the tea Vassiliya brought with it is dark and smoky. Maria's careful fingers probe around Rolf's eye as she cleans away dried blood with disinfectant; when she's finished, she asks him to track her finger with his eyes. He does this without interrupting his methodical chewing.

"Did you black out?" Maria asks him, and when he shakes his head, she sits back. "I don't think you have a concussion," she says, "but if you start throwing up, or feeling like you're becoming clumsy, have Vassiliya call medical right away." She puts a hand on his arm, and his eyes shift to hers, suspicious; but all she does is smile at him. "It'll take a few days," she says, "but you'll feel better."

Rolf says nothing, but his eyes stay on her while she packs up her equipment and leaves. I take her chair, and I wait for Rolf to finish his meal.

"I'll have Vassiliya take you to shower in a little while, if you'd like," I tell him. "And she can get you a proper change of clothes."

His eyes narrow. "Why?"

"Why not?" I counter, and I keep my expression neutral in the face of his hostility. Eventually he looks away, and puts down his fork.

"Thank you for the food," he says stiffly. Whether it's ingrained manners or sarcasm I can't tell.

I want to reassure him that he shouldn't have been starved, that what's happened to him is improper and won't continue. But those are internal matters for me to handle, and not to be discussed with a prisoner, no matter how angry I am. I wonder, then, how Maddie handles criminals on her ship, if their Old World rules are more like Aleksey's than mine.

"I know you've already answered some questions," I say, and I push aside my anger when he flinches. "I have a few of my own, if you'll talk to me."

He makes a sound like a cough that I realize is laughter. "What could I possibly say to you that would make a difference?"

"You know my reputation." I want him to remember I'm not like Aleksey, that I have not been since before he was born. "I don't like things that don't make sense. I want to understand what happened, and why."

"You're asking the wrong person." The anger has leached from his voice, leaving it flat, expressionless.

"Who's the right person?"

"Tamara."

I let her name sit in the room with us for a few moments, undisturbed. "I don't have her to talk to," I tell him, as if his response were reasonable. "But you did know her. Better than most, I'm led to believe."

That choked laugh again. "You've been talking with Lilith, haven't you?"

Lilith has been consistently outspoken and eloquent on the subject of Rolf's malice.

"Lilith isn't worth Tamara's old oxygen fittings. None of them are. They knew it, and she knew it. Not that any of it matters."

"Why doesn't it matter?"

I expect him to say *Because she's dead* or *Because they're fools* but instead he says "Nothing matters here. It never has. I'd expect you, of all people, to know that, Officer Savelova."

He meets my eyes at last, and I'm hit, abruptly, with the impact of a strong personality, a visceral sexuality that's built entirely on the physical. I feel a tingle under my skin, a subliminal warning; I'm fit enough, but I have few pretensions to self-defense. Rolf is not a large man, but he's larger than I am, strong from working with the stone for years, and I'm aware that I've chosen a chair far away from the door and Vassiliya would be unlikely to arrive in time to prevent him from doing me harm.

And he sees it, Rolf does: as easily as I see the threat, he sees my fear, and for an instant the balance in the room is very different.

But he's worn down, and perhaps too young to know how to wield what he has, and his eyes drop and after a moment I forget how it felt to be pinned to the chair. "Is that what Tamara thought, too?" I ask.

"It's how we all think." He's talking into the floor now. "There's nothing here. There's now, this moment, and nothing else. All we have to look forward to are the little boxes you put us in. Work in the quarry. Contribute your DNA, but never even know if you're Selected."

Rolf's complaint, then, not Tamara's.

"Raise children, or teach, because only children matter. They're the future, not you; you only exist to keep the momentum going, and nobody needs *you*, what you have, what you are."

I've heard that grievance before, and it saddens me, every time, to think someone can see life through such a narrow lens. "Wasn't she fond of the radio station?"

His lips narrow. "That's not what it's about."

I press him. "She had some skill. That lovely voice, and her delivery, even of the driest news, was always dynamic. Everyone was remarking on it. Perhaps that was difficult for you."

Rather than becoming defensive, he takes the question seriously. "I thought it was helpful," he said. "I thought it would make her happier, give her something to focus on with her mother getting sick. She'd been sad, lately, and there seemed nothing I could do for her."

"How long had she been sad?"

He blinks, once. "Six months? Maybe longer."

Before Lauren was diagnosed, before she showed any symptoms at all. He's still implying melancholia.

"But I think it just made it more obvious what was ahead of her," he went on. "She'd take care of her mother for a year, or maybe five or ten if Lauren's got some strength, and then it'll be her, sick and infirm with someone hovering and waiting for her to die, and she'll have had no life at all."

What sort of life is it if we can't spend all the time possible with the people we love? "You could have helped her," I pointed out.

His eyes return to mine, and this time all I see is a simple appeal, like a child who doesn't understand the way of the world. "I wanted to," he says, and he's so convincing. "I wanted to be her partner, help her with Lauren so she could have the radio station and whatever else she wanted."

"You'd have raised a child with her?" I ask.

"Tamara didn't want children," he says, as if I should have known that. "She never has. Even if she'd been Selected, she'd have turned them down. She believes children should be wanted, always, or having them is cruel."

My mind shies away from life without Irina—colorless, unbearable. Intellectually, I understand wishing to remain childless. But as Lauren's daughter, a recessive herself, it's almost certain Tamara would have been Selected, and heavily pressured. I wonder, for a moment, how she would have responded, this confident young woman just beginning to enjoy her celebrity, and I still can't get to suicide.

"Why do you think," I ask at last, "she would have taken her own life?"

And Rolf surprises me again. "I don't think she did. I think—" He breaks off and looks away again, perhaps aware he's been talking too openly. "I think she only meant to take a walk," he says at last. "Maybe to stay away a day, or even two. But you know what it's like in the dark."

"You think she got lost on the ice."

"Yes."

I am tired, all of a sudden, and my heart is gone from this. "Why would she take a quarry suit, only to leave it? Why would she leave you and walk away?"

His lips tighten, and he looks young again, miserable, a child clinging futilely to a stubborn lie. "I don't know," he says at last.

After all the work he's done to manufacture a narrative, here is where it all falls to pieces. I straighten in the chair, and then stand. "Thank you, Rolf." The conversation was useless, all of it, like Tamara's death; but there's no reason not to be polite. "I appreciate your insight." I resist the urge to say how much it will comfort her mother; nothing will comfort her mother, and if Rolf had any consideration for such things he wouldn't be sitting where he was.

I stop at the desk, where Vassiliya is paging through the visitor reports, trying desperately to avoid my eyes. I don't care if she looks at me or not. "Rolf is to have three meals a day," I tell her. "Twice the amount you brought earlier."

She looks up at that. "He won't eat that much."

"I don't care." If there's one thing we have bountifully in Novayarkha, it's soy loaf. "Three meals a day, even if he doesn't take a bite. I will be checking, Vassiliya."

Her lips tighten. "Yes, Officer Savelova."

"And the next time Aleksey chooses to visit Rolf, you are to contact me immediately. No matter where I am."

"It's part of his job to check on the prisoners."

"And it's part of your job," I tell her sharply, "to do as you're told." It's laziness, not insubordination, behind Vassiliya's objection, but her reasons aren't relevant. "Aleksey works for me. You will tell me when he arrives here, and you will see that Rolf has food and proper care at all times. We're not animals."

I stalk off, remembering none of the animals I learned of in school would abandon their own to starve.

CHAPTER ELEVEN

YULIA LISTENS PATIENTLY TO MY ACCOUNT OF ROLF'S CONDITION.

"I'm beginning to think you may be right about Aleksey, Anya," she tells me when I've finished.

She's looking away from me, leaning back in her chair as I stand on the other side of her desk. It's not enough, not really, but it's more of a concession than I expected of her. Lev reported she'd had a good night's sleep, but her fingers are trembling again, and I wonder, a little, if she's only giving in to end the conversation.

I would feel some guilt, had Aleksey's transgressions not been so serious.

"He was given too much deference during his youth, I expect," she says. "We coddle our children too much." Her eyes close. "You may discipline him as you see fit. Suspend him if you must, although perhaps defer that, given the current circumstances." She takes an uncharacteristically deep breath; despite her improved color she's still anemic and fragile. "Give him to Dmitri for a few days. He needs to learn restraint."

I'm not at all certain Dmitri is the one to teach Aleksey restraint, but I take the support as given. "Yes, Governor," I say. Her eyes stay closed, and the last of my annoyance dissipates. Risking her outrage, I ask, "Is there something I can get for you, Governor?"

She waves a hand at me, and her fingers are so thin. "You're very kind, Anya, but I'm all right for the moment." She opens her eyes, and favors me with a bleak smile. "Frustrating these days. I'm so often exhausted, and yet I can't sleep, not well. My mind...I have too much to get done, you see. And whatever Aleksey may think, there are no shortcuts."

"He is prone to speaking at the wrong times, Governor," I tell her, but she hears something in my voice, and her gaze sharpens.

"You've heard about the argument."

"Doctor Halvorsen told me."

Her face betrays a flash of irritation with her old friend. "There was a time in our history when conversations with medical professionals were confidential," she says. "I suppose you concur, that we can somehow pick and choose which pieces of toxicity we take from these strangers."

Which is a different assessment of the conversation than I heard from Doctor Halvorsen. "I don't think it's possible to fine-tune human interactions," I tell her.

Her eyebrows go up, and she straightens a little in her chair. "Really? I'd have bet on you agreeing with him, Anya. I think you liked those people."

That I agree with Aleksey on anything threatens to bring my annoyance to the fore again. "Does liking imply agreement?"

At that she smiles, and looks more alert. "Tell me why it doesn't."

Rushing a reply would be a mistake. "I don't like many people," I tell her honestly. "When I do...I'm aware of bias, and I try to respond accordingly."

"You think it makes you easier on them."

"It makes me harder. The consequences are so much greater if I trust them without reason." And yet I can't think, just now, of anyone I liked who turned out to be traitorous.

She's looking at me as if something about me is new. "So tell me, Anya," she says. "What do you think? Do you think we should continue speaking with these people? Do you think we should host them again?"

After so many years, I cannot lie to her. "I do."

"Why?"

Such intensity in Yulia's pale copper eyes. "They're coming, Governor." It's so hard to keep my voice neutral. "Others from the Old World are coming. Even if *Hypatia* doesn't succeed in their quest, others will follow them. They may already be on the way."

"So you would bow to inevitability?"

Her tone's turned sharp, but that's not quite what I mean. "*Hypatia* wants our friendship," I tell her. "Or at least not our active antipathy. If we take the initiative here, now…we may make them our friends. Even our allies."

She shakes her head. "It's corrupting, Anya. Even simple contact. And Aleksey—do you share his bias? Do you think we should be taking their DNA, and damn the consequences?"

"Not their DNA, Governor." That's not an argument anyone will win with Yulia, at least not yet. "But…there are things they may have to share that might be of equal benefit." When she's silent, I continue. "How old do you think Hina is?"

"Twenty. Twenty-five."

"They've been traveling for forty years, Yulia."

"And?"

"She was born on board."

"You think that's so difficult?" She waves a hand at me. "Women have been having babies for millennia, Anya. Space isn't going to stop them."

She's still not seeing it. "Their ship is small. It's a contained habitat. Captain Loineau said it—they have nothing they didn't bring with them, apart from their food. They have *medical* equipment, Yulia. Better than ours." I think of that tiny coffin under Doctor Halvorsen's arm. "They're centuries ahead of us. And surely—technology alone isn't toxic."

"It wouldn't be technology alone, would it?" But I can see the calculation on her face: she's thinking, not just of the incubators, but of all our medical processes, all the medicines we manufacture slowly and painstakingly, all the progress of which *Hypatia* might have knowledge.

"It might be," I suggest. "If we're careful."

She watches me while she considers, and I wonder what it is I've betrayed that's made her look so closely. "Very well," she says at length, and pins me again with a glare. "We are to be rigid about this, Anya. There must be rules, and they must be followed absolutely. The strangers are to go nowhere without my personal approval, and they are never to be unsupervised. They are not to interact with the general population, except in ways that are required for us to make use of their assistance. And if they can't help us, then we'll send them away and never contact them again. Is this absolutely clear?"

"Absolutely, Governor." At this point, I'll promise her anything.

She leans back in her chair. "I'll also say," she continues, her tone softened, "that if this goes wrong, I'll bear the blame alone. You're right, Anya. Technology, at least, should be neutral. We should be able to resist their corruption. If we fail…well. If we fail, it's better now than later, don't you think?"

"I think we won't fail."

This time, when she smiles, I believe we're friends again.

"Starship *Hypatia*," Yulia says into the radio. "This is Governor Orlova. I would like to speak with you."

She's chosen a different radio frequency—one that's been long reserved for seasonal horticultural updates. As far as I know, nobody in the city has ever cared to listen in, at least outside of drying season, and we're forty sunsets away from any kind of useful crop. That Yulia would keep her inquiry secret suggests she's far less certain of her decision than she's represented to me.

Maddie responds in less than ten minutes. "Governor Orlova." She sounds polite, neutral, careful. "What can we do for you?"

"You told me yesterday," Yulia says, "that you would leave us alone if we desired. Today I find myself wondering—if we had questions for you, would you answer them?"

"I'll answer anything I can, Governor."

Of course we would, she'd said, when I asked if she'd help us.

"We have some equipment that we'd like to repair, but we're unable to do so with the materials we have on hand. Would you be willing to share your knowledge with us?" Yulia's tone is as polite and formal as always, but her eyes are deeply unhappy.

There is a pause. "Our own equipment is old as well," Maddie says, "but of course we'll help if it's possible. Depending on your needs, we may even have some spare parts you could use. What is it you'd need to repair?"

"It'd be easier to explain face to face," Yulia says smoothly. "I could show you the schematic diagrams we have."

Maddie's reply is long in coming; I suppose she must be conversing with her crew. I wonder if she's pleased, or annoyed, or somehow eager to see us again. At long last, she says: "I'd need to bring more people."

My mood buoys again, even as Yulia stiffens. "How many?"

"Five, in addition to myself. My linguist again, two mechanics, our construction designer, and an astronomer."

"Why an astronomer?"

"She's never seen the stars through an atmosphere," Maddie says, with a smile in her voice. "She's curious."

Yulia turns off her microphone. "I don't like the cost," she says, and it's how quiet she sounds that makes me recognize it. Yulia's afraid, of success or failure I can't be sure.

"It's more people, yes," I concede, even as I wonder at the number, and the combination. "But it's still very few. Between Dmitri's people and mine, we can easily escort them, even if they're here through more than one sunset."

"You don't think their request is unreasonable?"

Irina is next to me, bouncing on her toes, and I keep my eyes off her. "They've been in space for forty years. I have no reason to disbelieve her when she says her astronomer is curious."

Yulia's eyes close. "I don't like having them here." Her voice is subdued. "I don't like people seeing them. I don't like them being normalized."

If I say *death has been normalized* Yulia will throw me summarily out of her office. "You can trust your council," I say instead. "We'll make sure they know the rules, and we'll all watch them—I will coordinate with Dmitri as soon as I leave here. And you know Lev's staff will be cautious."

Even in defeat, Yulia allows herself a small smile. "If Captain Loineau's astronomer is a good listener, that'll go a long way toward making Lev feel better. He does enjoy showing off." She turns the transmitter back on. "Very well, Captain Loineau. You may bring your five people down. And—" she takes a breath, and all of my concerns about her brusqueness vanish— "Thank you, Captain. Your willingness to share information is appreciated."

Together they plan the visit, Yulia suggesting they land near first sunset, so their astronomer will have many hours to look at the stars. I glance down at Irina, who is wide-eyed and vibrating with excitement, and think about how long it's been since I did any stargazing myself.

RECIP: National Earth Space Organization, Vostochny
REPORTER: Loineau, Madeleine, Cmdr. NZKO *Hypatia*
Mission year 40, day 92

With all of those news videos and photographs you sent with us, Vostochny—with all the disparate Earth cultures and alien traditions and exotic locations I'll never see myself—I still could never have imagined anything like Novayarkha.

There's the aesthetic, for one thing. Indoors, it's familiar—in some ways as homey as *Hypatia*. They detached a couple of rings of *Arkhangelsk*—the big one's three kilometers around, so it's a decent ride on their monorail, and a nice long walk—and buried the whole structure sideways, like a doughnut on a plate, under twenty meters of ice. Which would be an impressively deep dig on its own, right? Except they dropped their reactor in first, and covered *that* with ice as well, just in case. I'm thinking their ancestors knew all about spike nukes.

Twenty meters of ice would have been more than enough radiation protection, if they hadn't had to forage for building materials. They mine minerals, which means going outside, and they don't take nearly enough care when they do it. You can't breathe the air for long, but you can expose your skin to the cold for three or four minutes as long as you don't care about the radiation dose. After generations of watching random people die young, you'd think they'd be more careful, but I suppose it's been normalized by now.

Since they *have* to go outside, they pay attention to exterior aesthetics. The stairways leading down are precisely carved in elegant curves, stairs tapering one by one until they end in front of the airlock doors. And every stairway has an integrated ramp, wide and shallow and spiraled with the steps: perfectly utilitarian, perfectly beautiful. The stairway in front of the central administrative building—Anya calls it the Hub—turns in a gentle curve, like a shell from the sea. Maybe they did that for topological reasons, but it's still graceful, lovely, exact.

Along with the architecture, parts of the surface covering the city have etchings in the ice. Actual *art*, as heartfelt and accomplished as anything made on Earth. I confirmed with Anya—those etchings eventually get covered by ice storms, or just eroded away.

So they carve them again. Over and over. Because it's *pretty*.

They liven up the interior more than we do, too. There are ice sculptures everywhere, which of course have to be replaced often. It's warm in there, thanks to the machinery beneath them. There are stone statues as well, people and still lifes and gorgeous, geometric abstracts, all carved to show off the color and vein of the stone.

It's not all rock and ice, of course. Plants are popular, especially big, showy flowers, sturdy variants of chrysanthemums and daisies and lilies. A lot of the lighting is Sol-spectrum LEDs run in strips along the walls, but every ceiling boasts wide, ice-filled tubes leading all the way up to the surface, pulling in as much natural light as possible. I imagine their greenhouses are much more lush than ours. At some point I'll have to ask for a tour, but we ran out of time this visit.

And for a lot of reasons, I'm really, really hoping they'll have us back.

Anya met us alone this time, by the way. Still no gun. I wish I'd asked her why she didn't carry one—if it's a rank thing, or for show, or because she has secret super-spy hand-to-hand combat skills—but whatever the reason, I felt a lot more relaxed. The others all went through the "planetary gravity is very strange" adjustment, and Hina and I strutted around, lording our hand-eye coordination over them while they staggered and called us names.

Anya watched all of this in silence, and I didn't think much about that. But when we got inside and were taking off our helmets, she asked, "Do they always treat you like that?"

"Like what?"

She made an unfamiliar gesture with her hand that vaguely encompassed all of us, and said, "Like you're all the same."

It took me a minute to figure out what she meant, and once I did it was all I could do not to laugh at her. Big Fat Cultural Difference Number One. "Our command structure isn't particularly hierarchical," I told her. "It's more divided along areas of expertise. Ratana and Seung are mech engineers. Divya's the astronomer, and Qara—" I suspected *demolitions expert* was not the sort of phrase that would make Anya comfortable— "Qara's our navigator, and works out location issues for the transceiver."

"And what is *your* area of expertise?" Anya asked me.

I opened my mouth to say *I was a medic*, but I still can't say that out loud. "I don't have one," I told her instead, "so they put me in charge."

She didn't smile at that, but her eyebrows went up.

We started in Orlova's office, where we met the infamous tea-distributing Doctor Halvorsen. I thought Orlova was old, but Halvorsen's got to be creeping toward eighty. Healthy, too, which I'm learning is pretty unusual here for anyone older than me. Halvorsen, unlike Orlova, is a smiling, maternal sort of person, but I suspect that's as much of a front as Orlova's stiff dignity.

"Thank you so much for coming," Orlova said, and I think

there's a possibility she actually meant it. I made the introductions, and Halvorsen was about to spirit away Ratana and Seung to her broken equipment when that Aleksey person came in. He was friendly enough—he seemed a hell of a lot less pompous than he did the first time we came down—which was sort of encouraging until he locked eyes with Hina and I figured it out.

"Are you here to interpret again?" he asked, and damned if she didn't blush like she did last time. She met my eyes, and I swear she hasn't looked so pleading since she was fourteen and asking to stay up late to finish another asteroid assay.

Wasn't I the one who said we needed to make friends?

"We'll probably be okay without a translator," I told her, and was rewarded with a smile. "Aleksey, maybe you can show Hina the layout here. For...research purposes."

Aleksey waited for a nod from Orlova, which was quick enough but decidedly cool, and he and Hina got the hell out of there pretty damn fast. Ratana shot me a look of trepidation that covered pretty much everything I was feeling. Seems Aleksey remembered their little farewell handshake as well as Hina did.

Bad? I don't know. I'm sure it was my imagination that Anya was watching him more closely than she watched Doctor Halvorsen, but she didn't say anything as they left.

Divya and Qara were escorted off to the observatory by the tall, grim-faced woman who'd been part of Anya's guard on our first visit—Katerina, solidly built and absolutely not ill in any way—and Orlova trotted out a few perfunctory words of gratitude before dismissing Anya and me like she was some ancient queen. I swear, Vostochny, if Anya had bowed, it wouldn't have been out of place. No wonder she thinks we're all undisciplined children.

As Anya and I walked down the narrow corridor, I could see the joins on the wall where the sheet metal had been reinforced to hold the weight of the ice. But in addition to the structural changes, there was another obvious addition: a single railing, about five centimeters wide, mounted just below my hip. She followed my eyes. "It's there for the children," she told me, "and anyone who needs some help walking now and then."

I started to notice all the little interior accommodations: marks in the floor indicating a wheelchair lane; frequent benches, edged with flowers and lovely stone sculptures; small cabinets labeled as first aid kits; raised patterns along the walls, symbols and language, for those who couldn't see; tram cars marked in orange with higher rails and wider seats. Not unlike the things we've retrofitted for the Colonel.

"Is it only illness," I asked her, "or do you get injuries as well?"

"Injuries are fairly unusual here," she told me, "beyond the kinds of bruises and scrapes the young people get into when they're brawling."

Brawling. Like her reference to murder. Like it was nothing.

"But people are in and out of illness all the time. It doesn't mean they want to be shut in their homes, and it doesn't mean they always want—or need—to wait for someone to come along and help them."

She was wearing the same thing I'd seen her in before: soft dark fleece trousers, and long-sleeved shirt in an undyed fabric that had to be something like bamboo. Despite her ordinary clothes, she wore an oxygen-generating pack on her back, connected by a small tube to a relatively sophisticated polymer nose-and-mouth seal dangling around her neck like jewelry. We passed a lot of people— still gaping at me, like before, but palpably less afraid, so progress, I guess—and almost all of them were dressed similarly, but with no oxygen pack in sight. Anya, it seems, is one of the only people in the city perpetually prepared to have a wander outside.

"Have you ever been ill?" I asked.

That was apparently an intrusive question, because something about her became abruptly opaque. "No," she said at last, her tone neutral. "My generation has been robust so far. But I'm still young." She looked over at me. "Would you like to see the quarry? We still have an hour or so before we're set to meet the others at the observatory."

The hallway ended in a T at something she called the Outer Rim—capitals implicit—and from there it was a short walk to an airlock that seemed nearly identical to the one we'd entered earlier. She handed me radiation gear—different than hers, with a hard helmet and a built-in shortwave, but with the same lousy seals— and showed me how to fit the flat oxygen pack on my back and wear the seal over my mouth and nose.

It took some practice. "Normally your body doesn't think about breathing," she told me. "You inhale, and the exhaling is automatic. With this system, you have to think about both."

When she was assured I wasn't going to hyperventilate myself into unconsciousness, we stepped out of the airlock and climbed the stairs into another world.

Where their courtyards were polished flat and covered in carvings, this was a factory: low, makeshift buildings—they couldn't have had much radiation shielding, if any—and narrow walkways, opening out onto an enormous hole that was as deep as six levels of *Hypatia*'s labs and habitats. The near side of the hole had a honed, sloped face into which had been carved a narrow pathway zigzagging down to the bottom. The far side was much more rough: layers of rock exposed, revealing the planet's sedimentary past, overhangs and splinters reaching into the gap before them. I've blown enough asteroids to know what they were doing.

"What kind of minerals do you get out of this rock?" I asked Anya.

I didn't take my eyes off the quarry, but I could feel her watching me. "Quartz and muscovite, primarily," she said. "Slate. We use it as a reusable writing material, to make notes for later data transcription. Sometimes for artwork. There are also strains of copper, and iron ore. We get enough trace minerals to make a fairly wide set of alloys." I looked over at her then; I couldn't see her face behind her head covering, but from her eyes I think she was smiling. "Do you want to see our metals lab?"

RECIP: National Earth Space Organization, Vostochny
REPORTER: Loineau, Madeleine, Cmdr. NZKO *Hypatia*
Supplemental

Here's a thing I learned about myself today, Vostochny: I am afraid of heights.

Gravity, you may have noticed, is not a force that's particularly forgiving. *Hypatia*, by virtue of her topology, has minimal gravity in most of our living areas, and no gravity at all in the fuselage where we work. The areas with the most gravity—which is close enough to the gravity on this planet you wouldn't want to fall any great distance in it—don't have hundred-meter drops to a hard rock surface. And they're wider than half a meter.

Actually, I think the quarry path may have been narrower than that.

I clung to the cliffside—or really, I leaned against it, because there was nothing to grab on to—and took tiny, hesitant steps. The path was pitched more steeply than it had looked from the top, and I kept expecting to lose my footing, to slip and fall and plunge into that massive hole. Inside those woefully thin gloves my palms were damp, and the clamminess was spreading. At the first turn, I considered sliding down on my backside, but pride prevailed; I kept determinedly at it, but to be completely honest, by the fourth turn I wasn't moving all that fast.

Ahead of me, Anya strode down the path as if we were traipsing across the courtyard again. "The fabricators aren't active at this time of day," she was saying, and I heard it in my ear over the short-wave because she was too far away for her voice to carry anymore. "We run them unmonitored from time to time, when we're short of materials, but we just finished a run seven sunsets ago, so the quarriers are taking some downtime. We—" She stopped, apparently noticing I wasn't saying anything, and turned around, then looked up. She was two turns past me, too far away for me to read her eyes. "Maddie, are you all right?"

How the hell was I supposed to answer *that* question? "It's been a while since I've been mountain climbing," I said.

There was a pause, and then Anya began climbing back up. "I'm sorry, Maddie," she said, and although I couldn't see, I'm pretty sure she was laughing at me. "I was not thinking." She came up next to me—which was impossible, physics-wise, since that path was only a nanometer wide—and took my arm. "Watch the wall and not the drop," she suggested. "I'll hold on to you on this side."

"If you fall," I felt obligated to point out, "you'll take me down with you."

"I've been climbing in and out of this quarry since I was two years old," she told me. "I'm not going to fall. We'll take it slow. It'll be all right."

"Can't we go back?"

"We're more than halfway," she said, and yeah, she was laughing a little, but there was kindness as well. "If you'd prefer, we can go back up, but at this point down might be easier."

I felt mildly more confident, but I still said, "Don't say 'down'," and then she laughed out loud.

By the time we got to the bottom I was ready to collapse, but I hadn't yet abandoned my pride. I straightened, and breathed, and tried to pretend my heart wasn't trying to thrash its way out of my chest. Anya let me go, and walked ahead of me to a wide double door cut into the stone cliffside. "This is the smelting room," she told me. "Come quickly: there's no airlock here, but the doors are insulated."

She pulled the doors open. I hurried inside, and blinked in the darkness. And any lingering illusion that these people were primitive vanished.

The smelting room was loud, cavernous, and full of massive, automated machinery. All of it was idle, but the environmental coolers sounded just like the exhaust system on *Hypatia*. I wondered, for a moment, where the rest of the heat was going—too much would melt the ice around them in short order—before I remembered they had five kilometers of rings to keep warm. There were six massive, unadorned metal chambers topped with funnels—furnaces, I suspected—and around the perimeter another twelve small trough-like units with a row of hoses suspended over them. There were three doors around the perimeter as well, and I wondered if they led to rooms similarly appointed.

The separation systems and chemical washers were similar to ours, but on a different scale. These were *huge*, far too big to fit even in the fuselage. These were designed not for low-volume refinement of bits of blasted asteroid, but for mass production and precise purification.

You know what I was thinking, Vostochny.

"How much can you move through here?" I asked.

"Seventy or eighty tonnes in a sun cycle," she told me. "About a hundred and fifty a day. That's if we run them constantly; most of the time they're only run when they're staffed. We use the pure metals for very few things, past copper wire for the telephones; most of what we use for building are alloys. The fabrication rooms are through there—" she gestures at a set of battered swinging doors—"down one level, next to the crypt, where we can control the temperature more easily."

That was when I realized I should have brought Kano this time. He knows, off the top of his head, the tensile strength and temperature tolerances we need from our parts. He'd have been able to ask sensible questions about precision and volume and the subtle differences in the behavior of metallic elements. All I could ask was "What kind of alloys can you make?"

"Copper ores," she said, "which are sometimes more stable, especially for kitchenware. Some steel and aluminum. We can set custom concentrations as well. But we get far more graphite and carbon than anything, which is why—" She stopped at that, and looked at me, and whatever else inbreeding has done to them, Vostochny, it hasn't made them stupid. "Maddie. You've said, when you speak of your transceiver, *if* you succeed. Are you short on materials?"

I've made a lot of leaps of faith over the last couple of days, Vostochny. And despite my slagging Kano off, he's not wrong. Anya tweaks all kinds of things in me: curiosity, admiration. Trust. There's no good reason for that at all, except that she's been kind to us. I can't let myself forget that she's an agent of her governor, who I would not trust to remember my name.

But I stood there in that massive room, and I realized I might very possibly be looking at our only viable option.

So I told her. I told her we hadn't known we'd encounter a star system. I told her our transceiver design had to be adapted. I told her Ratana had some ideas, but we were struggling to figure out how to make it all work with the parts we already had.

I hedged. A bit. I didn't tell her about the accident. But I still told her more than I should have.

When I was finished she frowned, staring into the distance. "You're wondering if we could make these parts for you," she concluded.

"Yes."

She stared at the copper smelter for about forty-five seconds before she said, "Maddie, you and I should talk."

RECIP: National Earth Space Organization, Vostochny
REPORTER: Loineau, Madeleine, Cmdr. NZKO *Hypatia*
Supplemental

Yulia Orlova made me wait nearly five full minutes while she scratched notes on a piece of slate on the desk in front of her. I tried, at one point, to read what she was writing, but her lettering is so small I'm not even sure I could read it close up.

It's also possible she was just doing it to annoy me.

Before I went into Orlova's office, Anya fussed over me worse than Kano. "Yulia responds best to respect," she said, more than once. "She'll want to lead the conversation. Don't interrupt her or talk over her—she will listen, but you must wait for your opportunity. And she'll likely say no," Anya concluded. "But if you make your arguments cogently, she'll think about them. I know she appears rigid to you, but Yulia's judgement is sound, and she's not afraid to change her mind."

All of Orlova's behaviors sound like bullying to me, but what's been clear both times we've gone down there is how devoted the public is to this woman. Even Anya, who seems so level-headed, worries about pleasing her. It all reminds me too much of Captain

Lutrell, and how I felt about her, and how guilty I felt when she was killed and I couldn't bring myself to properly grieve.

Anya was telling me *Be respectful and you'll be fine* and I was telling myself *Yulia Orlova is not your past, so get over it.* A lot of voices in my head for this meeting.

Orlova eventually finished writing her little tiny letters, and put the pencil down on her desk. She folded her hands in front of her and looked up at me, smiling. She didn't ask me to sit down, and I have to say, Vostochny, I was pretty impressed that even with me towering over her she was so palpably in charge of the room.

"Anya tells me you have a request, Captain Loineau," she said.

Oh, how much did I want to point out that we'd come down to help *her* out? "Yes, Governor," I said, trying to sound properly Captainly. "Having seen your metals lab, I was hoping you'd be willing to manufacture some parts for us."

Orlova held my gaze, waiting. *That* was a tactic I knew. The Colonel excelled at it, before he was hurt, especially when I was a kid getting lazy during lessons. He'd stare until I was squirming and would have said anything to get him to look somewhere else.

But Orlova's not the Colonel. And I'm not a child in a classroom anymore.

Eventually she looked away, which from another person might have been an admission of defeat. She unfolded her hands and pushed herself upright, moving from behind her desk to a set of wide monitors hanging in line on the wall. They showed images of the full dark on the surface, nothing but dim streams of light stretching upward out of the solar tubes, but the glass reflected the room's light back onto her face, giving her a blue-gray glow.

I couldn't decide if it hid her infirmity or made it look worse.

"You'll recall, Captain," she said, "your promise not to disturb us."

Which wasn't what I'd said at all, but it was a neat semantic trick on her part. "It's my hope fulfilling our request won't be disturbing."

"I'm not at all sure how one manufactures parts without being disturbed."

Respect, dammit. "That's true, Governor. Perhaps I should have said that the information we would be providing in order for the parts to be manufactured might be repurposed in a way that would help your city in addition to our transceiver."

"So you would hold hostage any useful technical information unless we do as you ask."

What sort of people do you suppose she deals with on a daily basis? "I believe we're already providing you with technical information, Governor."

"Indeed you are. But it has nothing to do with fabricating alloys and mechanical parts."

I realized then, Vostochny, that she had me at a disadvantage: I didn't know how badly she needed us, or if she needed us at all. "If you'll allow me to clarify, Governor," I said, "I've no intention of withholding information that could materially stabilize or improve the situation of your citizens."

Which was completely the wrong thing to say. Her eyes snapped back to mine, and damned if she couldn't be impressively flinty when she wanted. "My people are entirely stable without your influence, Captain Loineau," she said. "We have survived two hundred years of space travel, and two hundred on this inhospitable piece of stone. I'll thank you to remember that you're guests here."

And that's when I realized it isn't just Anya, quietly worrying over her people. Orlova is *afraid*, and I'm pretty sure she knows precisely how precarious the situation is in Novayarkha. She's not some despot who insists on worship and only sees what's going well; she's a steel-willed woman hanging on by her fucking teeth, and she's absolutely going to kick the ass of anybody who even hints at threatening her people.

I liked her better after that, Vostochny.

"I apologize, Governor," I said, and I meant it. "I mean no disrespect, now or at any other time." And mindful of Anya's advice, I shut up and waited.

Sure enough, her stiffness slowly eased. "I am sure, Captain, that you are as protective of your people as I am of mine." And damned if I don't think that was a little bit of an apology.

"Of course. And as we're going to be neighbors for a while… it's my desire to be a good neighbor, Governor. That's all I meant."

She turned toward me then, and walked back to her desk. "Anya will have told you why we left the Old World," she said. She lowered herself back into her chair with more care than she'd taken climbing out of it. "I suppose you disagree with our reasoning."

This was beginning to feel too easy. "Not at all, Governor."

She seemed genuinely surprised. "No?"

"All I know of history is what our command chose to send with us," I told her. "But it's clear that society on Earth was…struggling at the time *Archangelsk* chose to leave. It's not a time I would choose to go back to, either."

"Then you understand my concern."

Truth, Anya had said. *As much as you can give her the truth, do so.* "Yes and no," I admitted. "I know the same history you do. Intellectually? Your stance makes sense to me. Emotionally? I know we're not people you need to fear."

"But once your satellite is built—you may be talking to people I need to fear."

Are you, Vostochny? Will you swoop in and take everything away from these people? What is it they have that's worth taking? "I must tell you, Governor," I said, "they're coming with or without our help. *Arkhangelsk* was an early faster-than-light ship. *Hypatia* is newer. When we left Earth, she wasn't common, but neither was she unique. In the decades since we've left, there will have been more, and they will be faster."

I leave the rest unsaid, because she'd figure it out: *They won't take another forty years to get here.*

Now, of course, Vostochny, this could all be bullshit. You might have long ago decided sacrificing generations of families isn't worth the nothing you've had so far from space exploration. Maybe the spirit of the explorer that made you kidnap a bunch of little kids has worn off. Maybe you've regressed back to pre-*Arkhangelsk* days and blown yourselves to little bits.

Maybe we're it: *Hypatia* and these strange, defensive, sick people. But I don't know, and neither does Yulia Orlova.

She sat back, and as circumspect as she is, I could still see the wheels turning. "Let me ask the question this way," she began. "If the others turn out to be the sort of people that *Arkhangelsk* left behind—whose side will you take?"

"*Hypatia*'s, Governor. My people rely on me just as yours do on you."

Another staring contest. This time she didn't look away. Eventually she crossed her legs, folding her hands in her lap, and I wondered how much of her creaking infirmity was performance. "You consider yourself an honorable woman, don't you, Captain Loineau?"

"I've been honest about my loyalties, Governor."

"Just so." She smiled, a little grimly. "I think it's clear that any trust between us must be balanced with caution, don't you agree?"

Hell, yes. "Of course, Governor."

"Your willingness to help Doctor Halvorsen does incline me to grant your request. Having said that," she went on, before I could thank her, "molding and fabricating precise machine parts requires more than just a few hours of consultation. It requires days, perhaps weeks, of testing and configuration, and raw materials that we have labored to bring up from the ground. Would you agree, Captain Loineau, that if we do this for you, you would owe us a favor?"

I felt a prickle at that, a warning tingle on the back of my neck. "Within limits, Governor, yes, I would."

"And what would your limits be?"

I could hear Kano's voice in the back of my head: *careful, Maddie.* "I think that would be impossible to say until I heard what you were asking," I replied.

"An example, then. A lot of our hydraulics are aging, losing lubrication and fluids. In many cases, we have the materials, but we don't have the people to keep up with repairs. Would you be willing to assist with that?"

"Most of my crew are devoted to the build," I said, because I wasn't going to tell her there are only nine of us. "But yes, I could probably spare you some mechanical help now and then."

"And if we needed similar assistance in the future? With building and repairs?"

That sounded like a safe thing to agree to, right? "I'm not able to agree to anything without specifics," I said. "But as a general rule...we'd of course help with building and repairs."

When Orlova shook my hand, Vostochny, I knew she thought she'd won. And here's my big worry: I still don't know what battle she was fighting, or how the hell I'd managed to lose.

RECIP: National Earth Space Organization, Vostochny
REPORTER: Loineau, Madeleine, Cmdr. NZKO *Hypatia*
Supplemental

"I can get you some tea," Anya offered. "They always have some brewing around here."

I looked up at her from my seat on the bench against the wall. I haven't felt so beaten up since the last time I sparred with Seung, and you know how bad an idea it is to spar with Seung. "Don't suppose you have something stronger."

Anya's eyes lightened. "Possibly," she told me. "Let me ask Lev."

She turned and left me, and I leaned my head back against the observatory wall. It's a lovely place, their observatory, as modern and automated as the metals lab, but much more appealing. It's quiet there, except when they shift the telescope, and they keep the lighting low so if they get tired of peering through the eyepiece they can look at the stars through the window. And yeah, they have a real window here—not the rippling ice they use for the tubes in the general habitat. The window is *Arkhangelsk*-salvaged heavy hybrid acrylic, thick and solid, keeping the workspace safe from cold and radiation and anything unpleasant the planet might cough up.

The work tables are almost certainly original *Arkhangelsk* consoles, but the chairs are new: carved stone and inlaid metals, even touches of wood. There are more tables scattered around the perimeter—like where Anya rummaged through a collection of unlabeled jars to scare up something distilled for me—that are also new, and some of them are really ornate. Not so easy to do with stone, but they manage it, because what the hell else are they going to do here?

After greeting me when I arrived, Divya and Qara wisely left me alone. They seemed to be enjoying talking with Lev, who I've learned is the head of the observatory, and he appeared a lot more relaxed than he did when we all ate together. He looked genuinely pleased with their company, which is pretty amazing if you ask me, because when those two start asking questions they don't give up. But he was gamely responding to them, pulling up lines of numbers on old screens and showing them star charts etched on sheets of slate.

The plan was to wait here for Ratana and Seung, who'd meet us when they were finished with Doctor Halvorsen. I was wishing we'd put a time limit on that, and not just because I regretted letting Hina wander off with Aleksey. I needed to get home where it was safe and normal and there weren't any gray-haired governors trying to read my mind.

Anya returned with a small stone cup full of something with a familiar, astringent odor. "It's not as sweet as what Yulia serves," she warned me.

"Fuck sweet," I said. I took a sip; whatever-it-was burned flavorlessly down my throat, and I felt the warmth spreading through my muscles. I leaned back again and closed my eyes. "You guys are careful brewing this, right? I'm not going to go blind or anything?"

"We're more careful with the liquor than we are with the tea."

"Faint praise."

"You're still worried."

I took another sip. She'd poured me quite a bit. "I have been worried," I said, "for the last twenty years." I opened my eyes; the stuff couldn't have been too strong, because I could still see straight. Anya was looking down at me. "You deal with that woman every day?"

"Yulia can be a challenge," she acknowledged, then sat down next to me. The benches are iron lattice, just like the ones on *Hypatia*. You know, Vostochny, you could have at least redesigned the seating over three centuries. "But she's agreed to help you. That's what's important."

She's right, of course. But something about being beholden to Yulia Orlova makes me want to keep drinking.

"Forgive me," Anya said, "but—you must deal with difficult people every day. Is she really so different?"

She did seem genuinely confused. I remembered her remark earlier, about our inappropriate informality. She has no idea she's working for someone so exhausting. "I know how to handle my own people," I told her. "Your governor was something new."

"I forget, sometimes, that not everyone knows how to handle Yulia."

"You coached me pretty well."

"I'm not only thinking of you," she told me, but she didn't elaborate. "I am surprised, a little, that she agreed so easily. She must like you."

I couldn't keep my mouth shut. "Good God. What's she like with people she *doesn't* like?"

"Generally she won't see them at all," Anya said. But she was looking amused again, and I started to feel a little better. If all of this was laughable to Anya, maybe my encounter with Orlova wasn't really so chilling.

I sipped the liquor, and for a while we just sat, watching the others in the room. Qara had completely monopolized Lev, who was showing off the telescope's controls; Divya was chatting with someone very young, a slim girl with big eyes who seemed to struggle getting Divya's questions answered before she asked another. Divya's mind moves so fast, Vostochny, she makes me feel like a slow-witted hamster. The observatory worker looked a little lost, but at least she didn't seem afraid. None of them did, not anymore.

I glanced over at Anya, and found her watching Lev and Qara, a smile on her face. When I raised my eyebrows at her, she said, "Your people are making Lev feel much better. It's nice for him, to have someone enthusiastic to talk to. It's not considered glamorous work, the observatory."

Which was a weird choice of words. "What is considered glamorous work?"

"It varies. When I was young, it was mostly artistry, especially furniture-making. Some of my siblings are still sought after for that. These days, the young people like the radio. They feel it allows them to assert their individuality." She says it like it's a curious thing for someone to want to do.

"I'd have to agree," I told her. "We learned a lot about you, listening to the radio. There was a woman, a couple of weeks back, on that first transmission we heard. She was talking about the tea harvest. She was quite good—interesting and animated. She—"

I stopped talking, Vostochny, because all of Anya's good humor disappeared, and she turned a shade that people tend to turn before they faint. "What's wrong?" I asked.

She shook her head, and regrouped. "That was Tamara." She said the name as if I should know it. "She—" She wouldn't look me in the eye, but I'm pretty sure what I saw on her face was grief. "We lost her a few weeks ago."

Funny, isn't it, Vostochny, how some euphemisms transcend cultures? "I'm sorry," I said.

"Thank you." She was looking down at her hands. "I didn't know her well. But...she's a loss to us." And she sort of sank down into herself, her eyes going out of focus.

Kano says I talk too much. He says I psychoanalyze everyone. But this woman was *sad*. And if there's anything I know about, Vostochny, it's sadness.

"Tell me," I said. After all, if I could be honest with Yulia Orlova, Anya could be honest with me.

"It's always happened," she told me. "Even long before I was born. We think we've left behind the worst parts of ourselves, but they come with us. They come with us, and we never see until it's too late."

Anya had refilled my cup and fetched one for herself. It would be the dinner hour soon, she told me; Doctor Halvorsen would likely release my people then, and we'd be heading home. There was no reason anyone would look askance at us for sitting and having a chat, even though Anya was their chief of police.

Except she's not *police*, I learned. She's a *peace officer*. Which makes me remember that way back when, in *Arkhangelsk*'s era, anyone who wasn't an anarchist was a fascist.

"When I started this job..." She trailed off. "I wanted to be useful to the community, and Yulia told me this was the way to do it. But I was bored a lot of the time. There aren't so many of us that there's a lot for peace officers to do."

I kept my impressions of the fighting reported in their radio broadcasts to myself.

"So I thought, if I couldn't be useful, I could at least be organized. I started going through old crime files, cross-referencing and calibrating. I like math. Order." She smiled a little. "It was satisfying, straightening everything out. Except there were all these cases that had never been solved. Some of them were little things—vandalism, petty theft—I learned to let those go, even though they annoyed me. I was still young myself, and I knew that young people could get irritable and selfish sometimes. If the crimes weren't chronic, I figured whoever was responsible had managed to grow out of whatever was bothering them.

"But they weren't all little things. Some of them were disappearances. People who vanished without a trace. Not many. One every few years, sometimes less. When I'd follow up, it was almost always obvious: someone caught in a storm, or someone who'd withdrawn after a tragedy—a family death, a miscarriage. More rarely, a personal dispute resolved with violence, although those are harder to keep quiet. We're never far from our neighbors. That's not always bad."

She sees that much, Vostochny. Even in this rigid, fixed society, she's not entirely blind to flaws.

"Lately, though, the disappearances have increased. Twelve, just in the five years. Which may seem small to you, but with so few of us—" She was quiet for a moment. "We've grown accustomed to losing people to the ice, but this is different."

I had to wonder how complacent people were here. "Nobody else notices the increase?"

"Oh, they notice," she said, and her smile turned bitter. "We're not so many that people can vanish without the rest of us noticing. Most people assume it's part of an uptick in suicides; those come and go in waves. But others? Even though everybody knows better, some will always say it's the Exiles."

And that, Vostochny, is how I learned Novayarkha isn't the only settlement on this rock.

I assumed, when she started explaining how they blame Exiles for everything from crop failures to winter storms, that they were somehow made up, a bogeyman to frighten little kids, or to keep the population compliant. I could see Orlova doing that, and telling herself it was all for the common good. But it turns out Anya's seen them. And she knows where they came from.

More or less.

"When we first settled here, there was conflict," she told me.

"Some didn't agree with the laws that were made, and wouldn't live within the rules. We tried to persuade them, but those who refused to change were driven from the city. Our ancestors initially believed they'd died on the surface, but some years later they began their attacks."

Two or three times a year—same old Earth years, Vostochny, thanks to all of the automated systems they still use—a bunch of these Exiles storm the town and steal things. Food, and sometimes medicine. Anya says for the last forty years the city has left isolated areas of the food stores and the medical center unlocked. "When I was twelve," she told me, "they killed two of our people during a raid. We killed one of theirs. Yulia was not yet governor, but she was on the council, and she argued that loss of life wasn't worth it when they only stole things we could spare."

"So why not just give them supplies?"

"That's been my argument," she confessed. "But the truth is, we don't know where they're living. They travel on blades or skis over the tundra, but they live in the mountains, and we've found neither equipment nor habitat. I searched myself when I first became a peace officer. I packed a shelter and stayed out for three sunsets. I grew up taking survival training, and even so I nearly died of exposure. Yulia has forbidden anyone from trying again."

I hadn't thought until then how very confined they are in Novayarkha. They have their courtyards, and the surrounding tundra, and even the mountains if they want to climb things—but without proper equipment, they can't explore. *Hypatia* is so much smaller, and she's broken, but she can take us anywhere.

I had so many questions, Vostochny, but none of them were about what I figured she needed to talk about. "Given all of that," I asked, "why do you think they're *not* behind the disappearances?"

She frowned, a thoughtful look. "There are to date twenty-one disappearances still unsolved, dating back thirty years. I've found no evidence—no suggestion at all—that *any* of these people were forcibly taken out of the city. And I've looked very, very hard, Maddie."

I looked up at the window, the stars blinking down at us. "And your Tamara—she's disappeared like the others?"

"I thought so, at first. But it seems her disappearance was more mundane." And she told me about Tamara's paramour, some kid called Rolf, who until he'd been arrested worked at the observatory.

I was right, Vostochny. Humans don't change.

None of this was enough to explain Orlova's skittishness. "When you worry about loss," I said, "you're not just worrying about disappearances, are you?"

She looked straight at me, and said, "You've noticed, I think, we're small for a viable colony."

And here I thought I wasn't being obvious. "I figured you wouldn't have everyone out to meet us," I said, but I know that's not what she meant.

"We must be very careful about our numbers," she told me. "Too many, and our gardens won't sustain us. Too few, and we won't be able to maintain the city, never mind properly mine the quarry. We must be deliberate about diversity, but also about health. People are chosen to bear children based on a history of illness as much as a genetic profile." She's silent for a moment. "Even so. Our doctors recognize a human parent sometimes introduces unpredictability into the process, so we have the incubators for flexibility in the face of miscarriage and stillbirth. We even occasionally use genetic material brought from the Old World, but that's chancier. We can't evaluate what sorts of people they become until they're grown."

What the hell do you suppose *that* means?

"But the most important issues...I'm not a genome scientist, but the balance between cultivating diversity and breeding away from illness requires constant calibration."

We didn't have that problem, of course. We didn't need to

worry about generations. We're all supposed to be home in another forty years, albeit most of us in small boxes. I asked what was probably a horrifically rude question: "Is it so controlled, then? The... way you reproduce?"

Anya seemed to take it in stride. "It's entirely divorced from romantic relationships, if that's what you mean, although there are bonds that are encouraged—or discouraged—because they're seen as more or less suitable for raising children. We have a crèche for incubator births, but we shift children to parental groups as early as we can. Paternity is always anonymous, although sometimes a child's appearance is so close to someone else's everyone knows the truth." She smiles. "There are four children in our school right now that I'm nearly certain are Lev's; we've very few men with those odd cheekbones. But it's considered impolite to speculate."

I looked around the room at all the people, milling around in this reasonably well insulated-but-still-really-fucking-close-to-the-planet's-surface building. I think about that hellish climb down into the quarry. I'm no academic, Vostochny, but I've had some time to think about radiation. "Most of our anti-rads are teratogenic," I tell her.

"Oh, we're careful about radiation while people are pregnant," she tells me. "There's a dormitory close to the Hub; they get much less exposure there. And many of them work here for the duration; that window makes this one of the safest spaces we have. But of course the main goal of Selection is to increase resistance to illness in general. Anti-rads are easy; most of our children, even as infants, handle the medications quite well. Treatment once someone becomes ill..." Her expression closes. "That's more problematic."

You know, Vostochny, despite my background, I don't much worry about the medical stuff. We're healthy. We've got enough antibiotics and antivirals for thirty people for another hundred years. I ran blood on everybody when we came back last time; so far no bugs we've never heard of, although some weird little variants it might be fun to study someday. But cancer treatments? I don't know a ton, but as a general rule they're a pain in the ass. They're designed to kill aggressive cells, and with the rate children grow, it's a much hairier problem. Easier, like Anya says, to prevent cancer to begin with, to select for resistance. Easier to try to keep inherited susceptibilities out of the game.

And at that, I put it all together: Cancer. Environment. Four-hundred-year-old incubators. "*That's* why Yulia is willing to help us."

"She doesn't want your company," Anya agreed, and there was that ghostly smile again, "but she'll take your technology."

"And we'll take yours." I looked down at my cup, which had somehow managed to become empty. "You know, Anya, between Novayarkha and *Hypatia*, there's a lot of messed up people in this neck of the galaxy."

"Indeed." She drained her own cup. "It's a rather good thing we found each other, don't you think?"

It was probably the liquor, Vostochny—or decades of arguing with Kano—but I can't remember ever agreeing with someone so completely before.

CHAPTER TWELVE

THE HUB IS ALWAYS CROWDED AT BREAKFAST, BUT TODAY, IN THE HOURS before the snowstorm, the entire city is moving through, taking advantage of the clear weather while they can. The stones set in the floor, polished and cobbled to a foot-friendly smoothness, are dappled by the ice-diffuse sunlight funneled down via the solar tubes, and the warmth of the glow gives the place an air of home-liness that's often lost in its cavernous ceilings. Costa and I are seated at a table by the wall, somewhat separate from everyone else; still, enough people pass us for Costa to be kept busy with morning greetings. Nobody ever remarks on how much less social than him I am.

"How much more do you think you'll be able to get?" I ask.

He's devouring his food, his usual method of avoiding me. "One more entry's worth," he tells me. "Possibly two, but the media's severely worn. It's not just its age; this kind of storage wasn't meant to be overwritten so many times."

"Useless," I say, half to myself, and he huffs a humorless laugh.

"Deliberate. If it was using the volatile storage they were build-ing back then? It'd have gone to dust by now. This tablet's memory may be unreliable, but the hardware'll outlast both of us."

"Longevity is hardly a virtue if the unit doesn't work."

He looks at me as if I'm the one being impractical. "You can come by later and read what I've got," he says. "But I don't think there's much that'll help."

This doesn't surprise me, as disappointing as it is. Tamara was an inconsistent diarist, and the months when she was working with Lev, she mostly wrote about diction and performance. She had, it seemed, been deeply committed to her new career. But the most important time in her life, the days leading up to her death, should have yielded *something*. "Was there anything at all on Rolf?"

At that Costa finally stops eating, and his eyes meeting mine are troubled. "She wasn't specific. But...it sounded like she was afraid of him."

"She didn't say why?"

"Only that he shouted when he was angry."

"Did Tamara seem to you the sort of person intimidated by a loud voice?"

He gives me an aggrieved look that could have come from Yulia. "With all his lies, Anya, isn't that enough?"

Before I can remind him what circumstantial evidence is, he catches sight of something over my shoulder, and his face changes. There's a flash of something I can't quite identify—apprehension, irritation, *fear*—before his expression blanks and he drops his head back to his breakfast. I turn around to see Maddie by the corridor entrance, with Aleksey standing next to her. Typically, Maddie is gaping at the entire room, taking in the floor and the walls and the solar tubes arranged in rings in the ceiling, palpably delighted by it all.

She's ignoring the crowd parting for them, the way some people are staring. Since coming down regularly with her crew, working with the metals lab on the parts she needs, more and more people have grown used to her presence, but most are still manifestly concerned. Xenophobia, plain and simple.

Irina's nudging at me, trying to keep my attention on Maddie, but Costa has fallen entirely silent. I turn to find him downing his fried greens with businesslike concentration.

"You're afraid of her," I say.

He puts his fork down, chewing and swallowing before looking up at me. "Yes." He's completely calm. "And you're not."

"That's because she's not dangerous."

"You can't possibly know that."

But I do know it, even though I've no way to explain it to him. "I think you should meet her."

At that he looks briefly panicked; but perhaps he remembers that we are friends, that we were infants together, that we shared a foster family and all of life and death. He nods his head.

When I look around again Aleksey is walking toward us. It takes him a moment to notice Maddie isn't following; he turns to call something to her I can't hear. She starts, then flashes him a dazzling grin. Behind me, Costa snorts a laugh. "I suppose she can't be all bad if she knows how to annoy Aleksey."

We stand as they approach, and Aleksey opens his mouth, but before he can say some official words about handing her over to my supervision, Maddie speaks up. "I hadn't noticed the design of those ceiling tubes before. How long do you suppose it took to lay them out like that?"

"I'm sure we have records," I reply. Aleksey looks mildly confused, as if he can't quite believe the interaction has slid from his control. "We can visit the archive later, if you like." More formally, I add, "Thank you, Aleksey. You're relieved of guard duty. And if you'd care to join us for breakfast, you'd be welcome."

My offer isn't entirely sincere, and he probably knows it. But he has left Rolf alone for weeks, and even made an apology of sorts—to me, if not to Rolf—for his overzealousness. He's not without self-awareness, and as I've watched his warming relationship with Hina I've realized where our future is concerned, he and I are in agreement. We should know more of each other than we do.

And he'll outlive me, after all. His training is my duty as much as anything else.

He smiles at my offer, and if he looks distracted and a little disorganized, he also seems genuinely grateful. "Thank you," he tells us, "but I'm behind on my reports. Serafina's been hounding me for days." He flicks his eyes to Costa, and then to Maddie, before he looks back at me. "Another time?"

"Of course." It will mean dining in the crowded Hub again, but perhaps that's something I should be doing more often anyway.

Aleksey leaves, and I make the introductions. Maddie holds her hand out to Costa, and gives him a smile as wide as the first one Hina gave me. Costa, to his credit, manages to shake her hand without flinching, and offers to fetch her something to eat.

Once Maddie and I are alone, she asks, "Am I still smiling?"

I wonder, for a moment, how this could be a thing she doesn't know. "More or less," I tell her. I narrow my eyes. "Your lower lip is trembling a little."

"Ah." She purses her lips and works her jaw. "That would be muscle fatigue. Do you know, Anya, I think tomorrow I'll come down wearing a sign saying DON'T WORRY, I'M NOT HERE TO EAT YOUR CHILDREN."

"Injudicious. You'll have them believing you considered it."

Her next smile is far more relaxed. "I'm sorry if I'm intruding. It just seemed a good time for me to get away from the lab."

There've been what Yulia's calling *communications issues* between Maddie's people and our metals fabricators. Some of it's terminology—*Hypatia*'s parts list was written more than two centuries after we left Earth—but a lot of it, apparently, is a misunderstanding of the severe environment Maddie's satellite will need to withstand. "I have told Damian's people repeatedly," Yulia said to me, frustrated, "that *a bloody cold winter night* is not the same as operating in space. They don't understand why they must be so precise."

Yulia, as always, will get the problem corrected, although my optimism is born mostly of her unexpectedly staunch support of *Hypatia*'s needs. Maddie's friend Seung, who's proven to be cheerfully tireless, has been spending days working with Doctor Halvorsen, and Yulia tells me we may be able to restart a few of the incubators previously decommissioned for parts. Yulia has been more relaxed, more energetic, and her resurgent health has relieved many of my own worries.

"You're not intruding," I say to Maddie, and sip the last of my strong, bitter tea. "Costa was giving me more of Tamara's diary."

Immediately she sobers. "Will it help?"

"I'm not sure what *help* means in this context," I admit. "What I want are answers I'll never get. Even Rolf told me I needed to ask Tamara if I wanted to know the truth."

"What will happen to him?"

"We'll look at the circumstances behind the crime," I explain, "and decide based on that whether to limit his sentence to work supervision, or confine him for the rest of his life. He'll be purged from the genome, of course."

She raises her eyebrows at that, but says nothing, and I wonder, as I often do these days, at the catalogue of oddities accumulating in Maddie's head.

I'm explaining to her what I understand of the tablet storage damage when Costa returns. He's brought her tea sweetened with almond milk, and a plate of lightly grilled grain crisps. Even in fear, Costa is never less than the perfect host.

"Thank you." Maddie picks up a crisp between her graceful fingers, and makes an approving sound when she tastes it. "Maybe when we're done with the technology transfer we can do a food transfer," she says. "Or at least we can get some recipes." She fixes her dark eyes on Costa. "I've got someone on board who might be able to help you with that diary. A storage hardware specialist. Hina. Our daughter. What kind of problems are you having?"

Our daughter. She hasn't used that phrase before for Hina, and a number of strange things turn over in my stomach.

Costa explains to her about Tamara's tablet and the difficulties of piecing together the data surviving around the corrupted areas. Maddie frowns in concentration, and the longer she listens, the more relaxed Costa becomes. "I'll have to ask Hina," she says when he finishes, "but I'm pretty sure we've got some scanners that can assist with retrieval. I don't know if they're in better shape than yours, but they may be more sensitive. And she's very good at piecing together data fragments. It comes from being born on board," she explains, as if she believes Hina's hobby is idiosyncratic. "The only new entertainment we ever get is puzzles we come up with on our own."

And with that, Hina seems as familiar as Maddie. "Do you think she might be able to help, Costa?"

Having Hina help will mean allowing her into his home. It will mean confiding his academic knowledge, acknowledging she might know things he doesn't. I'm giving him an exit, a way to say no that doesn't require him to tell Maddie *I am too afraid to take your help.*

Instead, my old friend seems pleased. "I don't think it'd hurt to try," he says. "If she can piece together even a few words, that's more than we've got now."

They start talking about data storage theories—or rather, Costa starts talking; Maddie keeps an interested look on her face. She may actually be enjoying the lecture. I lean back, letting their chatter wash over me: Costa's familiar voice, animated in a way he only gets when he's talking about something academic; Maddie's with her still-strange accent, expressive and musical and warm. There's something in my heart that it takes me a moment to recognize, although I know it, from long ago: contentment. Perhaps all of Yulia's fears will be proven incorrect. Perhaps *Hypatia* will bring us health and happiness, and we'll all become one family after all.

And then the sirens go off.

CHAPTER THIRTEEN

COSTA GETS TO HIS FEET. "EVERYONE!" HIS VOICE ECHOES DOWN FROM the high ceiling. "Gather around me!" The panicked murmuring quiets as people follow him to the corridor entrance. No matter how many times we practice shelter drills, too many of us know the dangers of raids to react with complete aplomb.

Maddie stands with me. "Stay close to me," I tell her. "Do exactly as I say when I say it. Do you understand?"

Her eyes meet mine, and her eyebrows twitch together, just a little. But she nods.

We head toward the entrance, pushing past Costa and the gathering crowd, and head up the spoke into the main arc of the Inner Rim. There people are running, more than a few in the wrong direction; I stop Karola Boras, who's alone and looking frightened. "Head for your safe room, Karola," I tell her, as calmly as I can. She's only fourteen; why she's alone and out of school I don't know, but I suspect it's not a mistake she'll make again. She nods and runs off, this time with the rest of the crowd. I keep leading Maddie in the opposite direction.

"Is this a bad time," she asks, running next to me, "to ask what the fuck is going on?"

"It's an Exile raid. I need to get to the medical center."

Four minutes if I run, two if I take a tram. I reach the emergency track, and Maddie follows me onto the small platform. I push the throttle forward, urging the tram to its top speed; trams always feel so slow to me, despite the fact that they move faster than I ever could run, even in my youth.

Maddie's too tall for the low handrail to help much, and she's forced to grip my arm. "I thought you said they hadn't hurt anyone in forty years," she says in my ear. Even so close, she has to shout; the sirens are growing louder as we close in on the medical center.

"Would you take the risk?" I ask.

It's been decades since raiders have pushed past the airlock, where we leave containers of generic medical supplies. Officially I attend the medical center during raids to back up Doctor Halvorsen, should she have to move her patients; unofficially, I'm there to hold my life between her staff and the Exiles. Every soul in Novayarkha is irreplaceable, but our medical staff are more irreplaceable than most. Their loss, even to brief incapacity, would affect hundreds of lives.

I jump off the tram before it stops. Maddie lags, but by the time I reach the door to the medical center she's by my side again.

At this hour Doctor Halvorsen should have been in the garden levels, supervising the manual pollinations, but she's here, huddled with Maria behind one of the examination tables. A quick glance reveals no patients, and I'm briefly relieved; but Doctor Halvorsen is looking happier to see me than I'm used to. "Anya," she says, taking a step away from a worried Maria, "I think I may have heard—"

The door to the exterior airlock is yanked open, revealing a solitary figure carrying a long-nosed weapon. She freezes for an instant, and then levels the gun at Maria.

Shock gives me a moment to take in details: her environmental suit, less worn than our quarry suits, hangs off her, far too large; her black eyes, the only thing showing through the balaclava she wears under the hard helmet, are wide and unblinking, as if she didn't expect to make it this far; her gun arm doesn't waver at all.

Doctor Halvorsen makes a small noise and grabs my arm; I shake her off, and she retreats back against the wall. Maria says, "I'm unarmed—take what you need," and no one who doesn't know her well would hear the tremble in her voice. I move slowly, not wanting to alarm the Exile, keeping myself between her gun and Maddie.

The gun doesn't seem to be an energy weapon, at least, but it carries a larger cartridge than our firearms do. Why she needs so much for so few of us is something I don't want to examine too closely.

I open my mouth to repeat Maria's words, but I've somehow lost track of Maddie because she suddenly appears, a tall, kinetic, wild-haired bundle of rage, between Maria and the muzzle of that gun.

"What the fuck are you doing?" she shouts. "You know they'll let you take what you need. Why do you need to threaten them?"

There's half a meter between the gun and Maddie. The Exile hasn't moved, and I keep my eyes on her gun hand, and astonishingly I see her grip loosen, the gun itself waver.

I dive.

Behind the lab table Doctor Halvorsen lets out a shriek. I shove the Exile's arm downward as Maddie hustles Maria to safety. My hand closes over a wrist; the Exile lets out a quiet grunt of surprise, and jerks in an attempt to escape. I hang on, and we both collapse heavily to the ground. I'm not trained for this kind of fighting, but clearly neither is my opponent; she flails at me with the arm I've captured, her other arm reaching helplessly toward the open door. Her gun hand spasms, a finger reaching for the trigger; I shove her again, launching my body weight into her shoulder, and her hand jerks and lets go of the weapon. And then the Exile, suddenly finding her strength, twists out from under me, rolls to her feet, and dashes through the open door.

A moment later I hear the exterior door open—without the usual preliminary cycle; another broken airlock—and the air alarm sounds in the room. I get to my feet and slam the inner door shut, and after a moment the alarm falls silent.

When I turn back, Doctor Halvorsen is peering at me around the lab table, eyes wide, staring at me with something that looks suspiciously like respect. Maddie and Maria emerge from their hiding place unscathed, and adrenaline ignites my relief.

"That was an astonishingly foolish thing to do!" I yell at Maddie. Maria shrinks from my tone.

Maddie does not; instead, she frowns, her eyes focusing on my chin. "You're bleeding," she says, and steps around the table.

I feel it then: a pinpoint of heat on the left side of my jaw. I touch it and find it tender; when I pull my hand away, my fingertips are red. "It's just a scratch." I'm still angry, and the Exile got away, and I've been scratched before.

But Maddie's leaning close, examining my wound. "Where are your antiseptics?"

She's not asking me. Behind her, Doctor Halvorsen is still gaping at me, and it's Maria who opens one of the storage cabinets on the wall. "Sit down," Maddie commands, and points at the examining table. Reluctantly I perch on the edge as Maddie frowns at the floor and shoves the dropped gun out of her way with her foot.

"We need that," I tell her.

"Not right now we don't," she says. Maria, who's reflexively accepted Maddie's authority, hands her a bottle and a cloth. Maddie pulls the stopper out of the bottle and tips the contents onto the cloth, sniffing at it suspiciously before applying it to my chin. It smarts, and I wince.

"Don't be such a baby," she says, but she's distracted. "Do you have some kind of bonding agent? Something to seal the cut?"

Maria heads back to the cabinet, and Maddie dabs gently at my wound. She's focused, her lips tight, and it occurs to me this is what she does after a fight.

I shout; Maddie heals.

Doctor Halvorsen finally manages to move. "Here," she says, reaching toward Maddie. "I can do that."

But Maddie doesn't stop. "I might as well finish what I've started." Her tone is even, and I don't understand what's irritated her.

Doctor Halvorsen retreats, and my annoyance begins to ebb. "Thank you," I say to Maddie quietly, "for looking after Maria."

At that her eyes finally meet mine: she's irate, and possibly scared, and more than a little embarrassed. "You're right. It was a stupid move. I'm not bulletproof."

I close my eyes against the image that phrase conjures in my mind. "Neither is Maria." And then: "You were very brave."

"Kano will agree with you," she says lightly. "Not that I was brave. That I was an ass."

She reaches behind her back, wiggling her fingers, and without being told Maria hands her a small cloth adhesive bandage. Maddie applies it with deft fingers. I wonder why a starship captain would have such facility with wounds, but before I can ask her, the all-clear signal sounds. Yulia's usual announcement comes over the intercom: "The threat is over. You may return to your tasks. Please report any damage or injury to your block mayors."

Maria heaves a palpable sigh of relief. "That's that, then," she says, and returns to the aid cabinet to replace the medicines she's extracted. Doctor Halvorsen pastes on a benevolent smile and approaches us, her eyes on my chin.

"That's not a bad job," she says. "She won't even have a scar." Her smile hasn't quite reached her eyes.

"The wound's not that deep," Maddie tells her absently, but she's frowning at me. "That's all?" she asks, genuinely confused. "Yulia says 'everything's fine now,' and the whole city relaxes?"

"She wouldn't say it if it weren't true," Doctor Halvorsen explains, and turns back to her lab table. But Maddie's face tells me that's not an explanation she understands.

RECIP: National Earth Space Organization, Vostochny
REPORTER: Loineau, Madeleine, Cmdr. NZKO *Hypatia*
Mission year 40, day 106

Turns out the best way to get Yulia Orlova to treat you like an equal is to jump in front of someone else's gun.

The old woman was much more polite this time. She gave me a chair and some of that godawful tea while people milled around her office dealing with the aftermath of the attack. I have to admit, Vostochny: Orlova knows how to direct. Dmitri explained how he would deploy his people during the next attack so they could better defend the med center airlock, while Lev outlined what they'd learned about the Exiles' approach tactics. Anya was on the phone talking to someone about getting the airlock fixed. The whole operation was impressively efficient.

As was Orlova's segue into her interrogation of me. She thanked Lev, gave Dmitri a gracious speech about appreciating his people, and then pitched them both out, leaving Anya on the phone and me wishing some of that rotgut we shared at the observatory was in the damn tea. Anya kept looking at me, and I wondered what she was worried about this time.

Have you noticed how much time Anya spends worrying about Yulia Orlova?

"I'm grateful to you, Captain Loineau," Orlova said when the others were gone. "Maria's very valuable to us. Your selflessness will not go unnoticed."

What an interesting cluster of words that was, Vostochny. In her shoes, I might have stuck with *I owe you one,* but I don't think she likes owing people favors.

"To be fair, Governor," I told her, "I don't think the Exile would have hurt Maria."

She smiled at me, that kind of indulgent smile Captain Lutrell would give me and Seung when we'd ask too many questions. "We have lived with these people for a long time, and I can assure you, they're quite comfortable killing. You very likely saved Maria's life."

But you know, Vostochny, I think Orlova was wrong. First of all, it was Anya who disarmed the invader. And second—look. Some of those movies you sent us with have these amazing fight sequences, and Seung and I spent most of our adolescence trying to re-create them. The trouble is in the movies it's all edits and special effects, and none of the moves have anything to do with properly defending yourself. I've never fought anybody for real, ever.

But that Exile was a really crappy fighter. I mean, they were *terrible.* Not that Anya couldn't have beaten them anyway, but the way they fought back was completely ineffective. They weren't focused on hurting Anya, or on grabbing whatever it was they'd broken in to get. They were focused on getting the hell out. A panic response. Maybe Orlova's not feeding me bullshit, and the Exiles really do have no problems killing. But this one—I have my doubts, Vostochny. And maybe that's just twenty-twenty hindsight and not wanting to believe I was really risking my life.

Because it *was* an impulse. And I was right about Kano yelling at me. Twenty minutes of shouting after I told him, and that was before he heard the rest of it.

"It's unfortunate," Orlova said, apparently finished with the credit-giving part of her speech, "that we don't have sufficient weapons to defend every possible entrance. And their weapons seem to be in much better shape than ours." She gestured at the gun Anya had confiscated, which was sitting on her desk.

The muzzle was pointed at the wall, but I hadn't seen anybody unload it. I don't like guns, Vostochny. I mean, they're not spike nukes, but still: they're not objects I'm keen on getting to know.

"We've worked, over the years, to build up defenses," Orlova went on, "but they seem adept at getting through the cracks."

It took me a minute to figure out she was asking me for advice. "*Hypatia* has never had to worry about self-defense," I told her. "We've never encountered an enemy."

Something in Orlova's eyes flickered, and fuck, I'd told her something I probably didn't want her to know.

"Anya has told me you have archives," she said smoothly. "I imagine some of that information is about defensive weapons."

"I don't know. I've never looked."

Kano's looked. Kano's been fascinated by destruction since he was a kid. But as far as I know he's always been satisfied with academic knowledge and blasting the hell out of asteroids. Orlova's talking about a couple of petty thieves. "Surely, with so few of them—"

"Are you familiar with the concept of guerrilla tactics, Captain Loineau?"

For a person who doesn't like interruption, she sure does a lot of it. "A little."

"We can't truly secure our perimeter. There's no way to do it, not in this terrain, not with our weather. Not without locking ourselves in, which would be unhealthy for a number of reasons."

Full points to her, I suppose, for understanding psychology.

"And the medical center…" She looked away, and I can't always tell, Vostochny, but I think maybe she wasn't acting. "It's been years since they broke in that far. Decades. We've been assuming their predictability, but that seems unwise now. We need weapons, Captain Loineau."

I kept playing dumb. "You *have* weapons, Governor. I've seen them. And surely, with your fabrication methods, you could make more."

She waved the idea aside, irritable. "Yes, yes, we have plenty of handguns. Firepower isn't the issue. We don't need *parity*, Captain Loineau. We need *technology*. Adjustable weapons. Better targeting systems." She leaned forward. "We need something that can destroy with efficiency, something more precise than energy weapons. Something we can use inside without bringing down walls."

There it was: the *quid pro quo*. We want satellite parts, and she wants better killing machines.

And fuck. We really need the parts.

"Most of the information we have with us is history and entertainment." I focused on staying respectful, and not telegraphing how much I wanted to tell her to fuck off. "The technology we have—it's newer than yours, yes; but what I've noticed, walking around your city, is that much of it is just more efficient versions of the same things. Projectile weapons have endured for millennia, and I honestly don't know if Earth weaponry saw the kind of progression you're looking for."

"But you will check," she pressed.

"I can look." I told myself it wasn't a promise to provide anything, but I kind of hate myself for saying it anyway.

She leaned back, wanting me to think she was satisfied, but there was something in the way she looked at me that made me pretty sure she knew I was hedging. How much did I want to bolt out of that fucking office, Vostochny? I am no match for that woman.

"I am also thinking," she said, "that since your ship is in orbit, you can help us locate where the Exiles are. Give us an idea of the size of their camp, what kinds of defenses they have."

Oh, *hell* no. "That I can't help you with."

"Can't?" She'd clearly been waiting to catch me out. "Or won't?"

Anya's stillness was distracting at this point. "Can't, Governor." I think I ruptured organs keeping my tone neutral. "We surveyed this planet when we got here. There's nothing visible from up there."

"You found us."

"We heard your radio signals. Unless the Exiles start transmitting, we've no hope of locating them."

She stared, and I stared back, and I don't think Anya was breathing, and I wondered which of them would be the first to recognize I was lying through my teeth.

Fortunately for me, it wasn't Orlova. "Perhaps—if you could fly closer, listen in on their broadcasts—"

"Anything we could pick up by orbiting closer you'd have already picked up," I pointed out. And no, Vostochny, I didn't work out the physics in my head when I told her that, so that might have been another goddamned lie.

She scowled, but this time, at least, I don't think she was annoyed with me. "Can I trust you, then," she said, as if offering some sort of compromise, "to tell me if you hear anything that might be an Exile broadcast?"

Which was not a compromise, Vostochny. That was a sell-your-soul-to-a-scared-old-woman-for-machine-parts ultimatum.

Fuck.

"I'll let you know if we hear them."

We'd have to listen on purpose, of course. And even if they used some of the frequencies we've been monitoring in Novayarkha, we'd have to triangulate to get a precise location.

But yeah. I'm pretty sure me sticking my nose in because some doctor called Maria who I'd never fucking met before was scared of having a gun pointed at her has escalated an arms race I didn't even know was happening.

After I told him the whole story, Kano stopped speaking to me altogether. And you know what, Vostochny? I wouldn't be speaking to me, either.

RECIP: National Earth Space Organization, Vostochny
REPORTER: Loineau, Madeleine, Cmdr. NZKO *Hypatia*
Supplemental

When we were children, Kano was always the peacemaker, the one who found common ground, who talked us into understanding each other. He always came after me when we'd fought, talked to me until I stopped being a jerk about whatever was bothering me.

After six hours of Kano not coming after me, I went to talk to the Colonel.

Hina was with him, going over data storage and recovery technology with such glee you'd have thought it was her birthday, and I'd have been cheered up by that if I didn't believe at least some of her enthusiasm had to do with another opportunity to see Aleksey the Unimaginative. The second she saw my expression she excused herself to research in her room.

"I'm glad you're all right," the Colonel said on screen.

Why couldn't Kano have opened with that?

I told the Colonel I wasn't scared during the attack, that Anya was the one who took the risks, that I was worried I was misreading everything with Orlova. "Am I being naive?" I asked. "I mean… they're helping us, right? Shouldn't I be gung-ho to help them?"

He thought about that for a while. "They've been living with this threat for a long time," he said at last.

Funny how tone can come through typewritten words. "That's what I thought at the start. That these Exiles made a good excuse for almost everything—power outages, disappearing citizens—hell, a nasty cold. It fits with what I thought about Orlova. Only...I think, Colonel, that she's trying to do good. In a way. I mean, she's still an autocrat and kind of a jerk, but she really seems to care about these people. I think this attack scared her, and made her angry."

"Maybe she needs some time."

"To turn into a pacifist?" I shook my head. "Anya sees future tech and thinks about curing cancer and having healthy children. Orlova sees future tech and thinks about better ways to kill."

"It would have the virtue," he pointed out, "of efficiently and safely removing what she believes is an existential threat to her people."

"I just—that one scared little person was not an existential threat to anybody."

"That one scared little person might have killed you, Maddie. Kano's right about that." He gave me a chance to retort, but I kept quiet. "With the planet as inhospitable as it is, they'd need specialized equipment and aircraft to explore the surface with any efficiency. I suppose my own question would be whether or not it's even possible for them—and if it is possible, why they haven't done it yet."

So many possibilities there, Vostochny: lack of bravery, lack of people, lack of expendable resources. I left the Colonel with no idea of whether or not helping Orlova was the right thing to do. But I keep asking myself the same question:

If *Hypatia* were facing constant threat, how far would I go to keep us all safe?

CHAPTER FOURTEEN

DESPITE COSTA'S CAUTIOUS IMPROVEMENT, I NEVER EXPECTED HE'D welcome Hina and Maddie so easily into his home.

Hina is distinctly different from our young people: more reserved, more measured, less certain of herself. But she's still a young person, still carrying that aura of future and possibility, and here in Costa's home Maddie watches over her like every eagle-eyed crèche worker I've ever known. I wonder if Maddie's over-protectiveness is endemic, or if it's only because Hina's here, in a place Maddie doesn't yet trust.

Maddie and I are in Costa's kitchen, reconstituting lunch while Costa and Hina reconstruct Tamara's diary. Theirs is ghoulish work, but Hina's approaching the project as an academic, and she's brightened Costa's mood considerably. I've chosen a wheat-and-mushroom soup he's fond of, and I'm showing Maddie how to prepare the food packet.

"Don't let it boil," I instruct. "It'll overcook if you put it in too hot."

She seems deeply suspicious of the dried soup mix. "It looks like compost," she says dubiously, and I laugh out loud.

"Taste it," I suggest, "before you condemn it as trash."

Hina and Costa are discussing reference patterns and conduction forces and other terms I know but don't understand, and my old friend seems more engaged than he has in some years. "Why did you train her as an electronics engineer?" I ask.

Maddie seems to think that's a strange question. "We didn't. Not on purpose, at least. Mathematics was one of her earliest aptitudes, along with chemistry. We just let her follow what pleased her."

"That seems very indulgent." *Hypatia*'s not large; I can't imagine they would have enough people to allow children to stray from predefined duties.

"Does it? It keeps her happy." Maddie looks at me, beginning to comprehend my objection. "We did channel her chemistry skills into rocks and mineralogy, which is important when we collect asteroids. And like all of us, she's got enough training to be able to run the ship's critical systems on her own if she has to, including navigation."

"It's difficult for me to understand," I confess. "You're so small, and your resources so limited. To be able to waste an entire mind—" Perhaps they're more crowded up there than I thought.

"Is pursuit of one's own interests considered a waste, then?"

They must have an excess of everything. "Not the way you mean. Costa, for example, is our head teacher, but he's also an artist. Not portraiture, primarily, which is the most popular, but abstracts, and sometimes landscapes." Costa captures the beauty of the distant mountains like no one else. "He was on the list for three years before they registered him."

"He had to *register* to be an artist?"

"Art takes materials. He gets an allocation."

Maddie's clearly still mystified. "What about you?" she asks. "What is it you're interested in?"

It's been nearly fifty years since someone has asked me that question. "Understanding," I tell her at last. "I want to know why the world is the way it is. I'm in the right job, I think."

Before she can answer, Costa looks up at me, his enthusiasm dampened. "You should see this, Anya."

Maddie and I move to the table. Hina is looking apologetic, and a little anxious.

"We can't get all of it," Hina says. "Some of the data is severely faded, and some is actually garbled. Without—" She stops, recognizing my ignorance, and turns to Costa.

"This one," he says, subdued, "was entered the morning before she died."

I lean over the scanner.

He [undecipherable] my mother. Nobody does. Rolf is a crèche baby. He's never loved [undecipherable] says he loves me, and he says I have to teach him [undecipherable] rather teach Lev. At least Lev was kind [undecipherable] never told me that I was too good for everyone else just because I was recessive. When Rolf said that, I pointed out that my mother was recessive and she's dying anyway.

[Undecipherable] fault. How can he understand the loss of what he's never had? I'm never going to tell him, so it doesn't matter.

I'm going to talk to Doctor Halvorsen [undecipherable] twenty-two, and I'm healthy. My mother's sick, but [undecipherable] won't matter. If [undecipherable] to have a baby, I'm [undecipherable] to try. I can't raise a child with Rolf, not the way he is, but he's not the only choice. Lev is sweet, even though [undecipherable] Damian, who's not likely to fall in love with me but is smart and funny and handsome. And he taught Sidela Kjar, of all people, how to draw. That kind of patience has to make a good parent.

I'm telling Rolf later, before we go out. He'll sulk again.

"Rolf kept insinuating despair," I say aloud. "That she would kill herself because she saw no future."

At this point Hina's aware of my distress, and her acute empathy is oppressive. Her dark eyes search my face. "I don't—didn't know her, but it seems to me—if she was talking about children, it doesn't make sense that she wanted to die."

"He'd planned future, and she wanted a future without him." Costa is looking away, his jaw working. He, like me, was hoping against hope that there was some other explanation, some fate for Tamara that was not this hideous betrayal. "Everything he thought they'd planned together—she took it back. Their whole social protest. She decided to be a citizen after all, and he couldn't permit that."

Hina is looking back and forth uneasily between Costa and me, but it's Maddie who speaks. "I'm sorry," she says, to both of us. "I know it's not what you hoped."

"We weren't going to get what we hoped," I say. Costa swallows as he gives me a wan smile. "But this will help us."

We eat, and Maddie's appalled reaction to the reconstituted food restores some of Costa's good mood. Even Hina, who was embarrassed by enjoying a task that had such a grim outcome, begins to laugh and tell jokes, giving me a glimpse of who she is behind her shyness. She's not unlike Maddie: astute, sarcastic, much more informal than what I'm used to, but fundamentally full of optimism and unshakeable good humor. Irina watches her for the whole meal, this young woman who has reached a place in her life Irina was never permitted.

First sunset approaches too soon. Only Léon, *Hypatia*'s taciturn pilot, came down with them this time, and we meet them and their security escort at the Outer Rim airlock. I walk the three of them back out to their ship in the dying light, and Maddie lingers, letting Hina and Léon stride ahead of us, the pilot encouraging Hina's chatter with the occasional monosyllable.

"When will the trial be?" she asks me.

"Unless Rolf says something dramatically different in the face of this—a day or so. No more."

"Would—could I watch the trial?"

Morbid curiosity doesn't seem like Maddie, and it crosses my mind, for a fleeting moment, that she wants to be supportive because she knows it'll be hard for us. For me. But it's more likely part of her cultural study, her attempts to decipher our differences so she can ease the transition for everyone. "Trials aren't public. But we read the verdict and pronounce sentence in the Hub. It will be crowded," I warn. "Tamara was popular, and we haven't had a murder in some years now."

She's quiet for a few steps, and then: "Does it help? Finding out what's happened?"

It won't help Lauren, who's already lost any reason to look to the future. Tamara's friends will be no less brittle and angry, and the public will want only reassurances that law and order, as always, prevail.

And me?

"It's a completed puzzle," I reply. "There's a level of…balance about it, I suppose. But no. It doesn't help."

Maddie stops, looking up at her small ship. "I'm sorry," she says. "Not just for Tamara. But because this is a thing that happens here." She turns toward me, and I can't see her face through the glare. "It shouldn't."

She's right, and I feel, as her ship departs, an unsettling sense of water slipping through my fingers.

MINUTES OF CAPTAIN'S GOVERNING COUNCIL MEETING
SHIP YEAR 147

NOTE TAKER: Liesel Friedrichsen
B. SHIP YEAR 102
D. COLONY YEAR 1

DIRECTIVE 17 GOVERNMENT USE ONLY
SCHOLARLY ACCESS FORBIDDEN

In attendance:

Anna Linden, Captain
Carl Litmanen, Law Enforcement
Golda Shertok, Maintenance and External Defense
Raya Volynov, General Health and Medicine
Liesel Friedrichsen, Secretary

13:01: Meeting called to order by Captain Anna Linden.

Linden: We're currently scheduled to arrive at 87-99-C, lovingly named Morozko by the more mythically-minded of us, in 41 years, 231 days. Golda, what do we know about this rock?

Shertok: Well, it's not paradise. The atmosphere is toxic—I mean, you won't drop dead right away, but there's not enough oxygen to keep you going. The good news is there's a magnetic field. Not a strong one, and it's no substitute for environmental shielding, but we'll be able to use some of the metallic fibers we've been working on to manufacture a lighter-duty protective suit.

Linden: What about refining and transport?

Shertok: We're hoping we can break the materials down with small explosives, which will make it easier to transport minerals back to our refinery on board.

Litmanen: Captain, you know what people—

Linden: I'm aware, Carl. Our destination hasn't changed.

Litmanen: You're going to have to make a statement.

Linden: My successor is going to have to make a statement. But I'm confident once we get there nobody's going to make a serious case for staying on that rock. I don't care if it has a magnetosphere. You can't breathe the air, we'd have to tunnel to build a habitat, and what are we going to build with? It's not practical, and they'll see that as we get closer. We have a mission, and nobody's changing it on my watch.

Litmanen: Captain, I—

Linden: Move on, Carl. Raya? Have you finished the Generation L analysis?

Volynov: I have, Captain. I know you're aware it's…not what we'd hoped. Drug resistance is present in the entire generation.

Linden: Why didn't we see this in the early incubator tests?

Volynov: Respiratory cancers are hard to induce in something that's not breathing the air. The test results were misleading.

Linden: You're recommending we abandon the modification.

Volynov: And prevent those we've modified from breeding. I don't want to see that change recombining with other DNA.

Linden: I'm supposed to tell 200 people they won't be having children.

Litmanen: Is there any reason you need to tell them?

Linden: Fine, fine. But document it. If we can figure out a way around this we may need them back. What's the projected casualty rate on this one?

Volynov: Statistically we're likely to lose another 40. Do you want me say something to them?

Linden: There's no point to that, is there? Just write it up and add the data to the research base. And don't fuck up like this again, Volynov. Our population's already down 30% from when we left Earth.

Volynov: Because of rioting, Captain.

Linden: Exactly. We don't need any help annihilating ourselves. Speaking of - Carl, where are we on the rioting?

Litmanen: Nearly eradicated, Captain. Making an example of Chelnikov was the right thing to do. The rest are worried now.

Linden: Except now I've got Chelnikov's relatives sniping at me about Nielsen's relatives. We are living on a starship, Litmanen. We don't have space for blood feuds.

Litmanen: Original Law states —

Linden: Original Law is eye-for-an-eye bullshit. It was a concession to all the garbage we tried to leave behind. I don't want any more executions, Carl.

Litmanen: Without the potential for execution —

Linden: Executions don't deter shit. We executed one killer and bred half a dozen more, all with one cycle of the airlock.

Litmanen: Respectfully, Captain, if you try to rescind Original Law —

Linden: I'm not rescinding anything, Carl. I didn't wake up stupid. But I still have discretion on when it is and isn't used. You don't like it, take that up with my successor as well. Golda, tell me how much my ship fell apart this week.

Shertok: It's been a good week, actually.

Linden: Finally.

Shertok: We're no closer to microcircuits, but we've been able to machine bearings and balancers to well within tolerance. We should be able to restart Refinery Fifteen within the month.

Linden: I'll be damned. Who's responsible for that?

Shertok: Chernyshevsky's team, Captain.

Linden: I want all their names, and the proper pronunciations. I'll give them credit—and you—in my speech this week. This beast isn't going to live forever, but dammit, we may yet see it outlive us. Anything else?

Litmanen: Captain, I really think we need to —

Linden: Yes, Carl, I know you do. If there's no other business, I'm adjourning the meeting. Thanks for taking notes, Liesel. I'm heading down to the distillery. Who's coming with me?

13:27: Meeting adjourned by Captain Anna Linden.

DISCORD

CHAPTER FIFTEEN

THE STORM HAS ARRIVED, AND THE COUNCIL IS HUDDLED IN YULIA'S office, the public waiting for us outside in the Hub. The crowd is larger than it would have been had the weather been fine; with sunshine, there would've been people on the surface or in the observatory, listening on the radio instead of elbowing their way inside. Under the dark clouds it seems they've nothing better to do than await the verdict in person, and there's more dread in the air than I would expect when anticipating such an obvious answer.

Perhaps the dread's only mine.

"Thank you, Officer Savelova," Yulia says after I finish reading Tamara's final diary entry. She looks terribly sad. Lev, startled at hearing his name, has gone ruddy under his brown skin. Dmitri has his hands folded stoically on the table, but there's a muscle twitching at the base of his jaw.

I'm like Yulia: exhausted and dispirited. I wanted the *why*, and now that I have it, it's changed nothing. We'll vote, and we'll greet the crowd, and Yulia will announce the verdict and Rolf's punishment. I'll take him away to the prison and the small room where he'll spend the rest of his life, and for everyone else Rolf will be the past, along with Tamara.

It seems unconscionable to consign them to history as a pair.

"Shall I call for a vote?" Yulia asks; one by one, we nod. "Very well. First, we must decide: guilty or not guilty?"

We each touch the screen before us, voting privately. The aggregate vote is displayed on the small screen in the center of the table: 0 NOT GUILTY 4 GUILTY.

"Please enter the initial verdict into the public record," Yulia tells Dmitri. She touches a key. "Second: Impulsive, or premeditated?"

Before Tamara's diary entry, I would've given Rolf the benefit of the doubt. I understand crimes of passion, of momentary loss of control. Had he been charged, years ago, with Oksana's death, I might have acknowledged the role of impulsiveness, and argued for treatment for the boiling anger consuming his life. This—I can't comprehend the deliberation it takes to abandon a woman on the tundra, to leave her to suffocate and die.

The system counts for us: 0 IMPULSIVE 4 PREMEDITATED.

Unanimous. No chance for appeal or reduction. Rolf will never see freedom again, and I'm relieved.

Yulia leans back in her chair. This has taken too much out of her; she'll need time off after this trial. Maddie will surely understand if I spend less time with her for a while.

This time it's Dmitri who gets up and fetches water for Yulia. The look he gives me when he places the glass in front of her is full of concern, and I recognize, perhaps for the first time, what awaits us sooner than any of us would like: we are going to have to figure out what we'll do without her. I hold his gaze for several seconds; despite what Yulia has said about him, all I see is a man wanting to do the right thing.

Lev paces, his steps measured, as if he's moving to soothe himself. Would it help if I shared more of Tamara's diary with him? Would it hurt? What would I have done, for one more word from Irina?

Yulia opens her eyes at last, and pushes her chair back; Dmitri hovers, but she waves him away. "I must be on my feet for this," she tells him, but she's kind again. She knows what this has done to all of us. She gets to her feet, then turns and gives Lev a gentle smile. "You were a good friend to Tamara. Take comfort in that."

Lev looks like he's going to weep.

She takes a deep breath and releases the arms of her chair, then strides to the door, quickly and confidently, like a healthy young woman. We fall in behind her, first me, then Lev, then Dmitri; when she opens the door, the loud murmurs echoing through the big room fall rapidly silent.

"Thank you all for coming," Yulia says. There's no need for amplification today. I squint into the crowd; there is Aleksey standing to one side next to Rolf, whose hands are bound behind his back. Ioseph stands on Rolf's other side, official but unarmed, a symbolic escort for a man who has no way to fight. Sofia's further back, standing with Maddie, whose eyes, as always, are skipping restlessly over the crowd. On the other side of the room, Lauren sits in a wheelchair. I haven't seen her in too long: she's thin, all hollows and angles, and her albino skin is a shade of gray I recognize. She has very little time. At least we can give her this much.

I should have been able to save her child.

"We have gone over the evidence," Yulia tells the crowd, "and we have found Rolf Eldaroff guilty of the premeditated murder of Tamara Raskova." No one makes a sound; even Rolf is still, face a mask, eyes fixed on Yulia. "Is there anyone who would speak for Rolf before we pronounce his sentence?"

My eyes search the crowd. They are all attentive, patient, silent. I catch a pair of eyes staring at me: it's Lilith, Tamara's closest friend. There's something in her face I can't decipher.

Yulia waits longer than she needs to. "Very well," she says at last. "Due to the cruel nature of this crime, I am invoking Original Law."

I turn to stare at her. This was not something we discussed. Surely this is an illustration, somehow; a point she's making about justice. She'll take it back. I'm certain. Beyond her, Dmitri is expressionless; Lev still looks broken.

"I offer Tamara's family the right to choose the murderer's punishment, should they so wish." She gestures toward Lauren, who has looked up at her words, the color in her colorless face shifting from gray to stark white.

I risk a glance at Rolf. His eyes have widened, and for the first time since his arrest, I see fear.

He believes her. I believe her.

"Yulia," I say quietly, so the others can't hear, "are you sure this is wise?"

"You of all people should understand about dead children, Anya."

Her response is as quiet as my question, and even stunned by her cruelty, I push on. "I of all people understand that revenge changes nothing. You can't put this on Lauren. It's unfair."

And at that she looks at me, cold fire in those intelligent eyes. "You speak so often of *fairness*, Anya. Fairness to technology. Fairness to the strangers. Fairness to Rolf." She looks away again. "The rule of law—the law that we have all agreed upon—is *fair*, Anya. To *our people*, of whom you are still one. And it's past time you remembered that."

What could she possibly think I've forgotten?

The crowd's eyes have gone to Lauren. Genera, her caretaker, places a hand on Lauren's bony shoulder, but Lauren shrugs it off irritably. Slowly, with as much decisiveness as Yulia, she settles her feet squarely on the floor and pushes herself upright, the blanket covering her lap falling away. Her pale eyes on Yulia's are bright, blazing, furious.

"I want him dead," she says.

The room is silent. There's a rushing in my ears; clearly this is hyperbole, something she's using as a prelude to her real request.

"I want him dead," she repeats, "the way he killed my daughter.

I want him outside on the surface, with no protection, no warmth, no air. I want him left there until he has stopped breathing, until his heart gives out, until the radiation takes him to bones and then to dust. I want no one to find him, no one to speak of him, for the rest of eternity."

"No," I whisper, but nobody hears, because the murmurs have begun, starting close to Lauren and spreading through the crowd. Surely those are protests, admonishments, but that's not the tone. There's anger. There's *approval*. The room takes on a charge I've experienced on a much smaller scale: the spores of violence, the small, isolated discontentments that find each other and explode into life and devour everything before them.

They are going to kill Rolf. *We* are going to kill Rolf.

I look to Yulia, waiting for her to interrupt, to make sense, to talk them down. But that's not what she does. Instead, she nods, and the world collapses in on itself and becomes something unrecognizable.

"Very well. Rolf Eldaroff, you are sentenced to death by exposure, sentence to be carried out immediately."

"No!" I say it louder this time, but the crowd is shouting now, and nobody hears me.

But there is one dissenting voice in the back that I recognize: "Stop this!"

I want to warn her, tell her she can't help, that she needs to run. But Maddie doesn't know Novayarkha. Maddie's innocent. Despite everything that's happened to her, she still believes the universe makes sense.

The crowd, out of curiosity as much as anything, quiets just enough for Maddie's words to be heard. She's still in the corner, struggling to move forward, Sofia, her escort, startled into inaction. There are people grabbing Maddie's arms, even some reaching for her hair, and I remember how disingenuously she took off her helmet the first time she came here. Were it not for the crowd, the distance between the two of us would be ten steps, perhaps twelve; here, now, there is no way for me to get to her in time.

As loudly as I can, I say, "Let her speak!"

The murmurs don't stop, but the hands release her, and Maddie shouts to be heard above the noise. "What kind of government kills its own people? No matter what he did—what do you gain by killing him? Revenge?"

I hear the crowd: *yes* and *yes* and *YES* and they're starting to reach for Maddie again. And in her face, that face that's so familiar to me, there's anguish and anger and realization of what is about to happen.

"You call us barbarians," she says. "You hide here from us—from *us*—and you take the life of a *boy* just because you can, because you think it's balance, and you can't even see what you've become. You think you escaped from Earth? You're fools, every one of you. All you did was bring it with you."

She says this last to me, her eyes burning into mine, but Maddie doesn't understand, and time is running out. I catch Sofia's eye and nod. As Maddie wrenches her arms free, Sofia shoves through the crowd and grabs her, and Maddie struggles and protests as Sofia hauls her off down an auxiliary spoke. I hold my breath for an instant, but no one follows them.

I want to follow them. I want to follow her, and stop her, and tell her she's wrong, that we're not like that, that we're free here.

We're free.

"Governor. She's right." Yulia's already angry with me; I've nothing left to lose. "Revenge is not who we are. It's not *what* we are." Yulia told us all, when she was appointed, that she'd ease the worst abuses of the law. She can't have forgotten. She can't. "End this. We have room in our prison. Rolf can live his life there. He can even be productive."

"Original Law is a part of what we've all agreed to live by, Anya. Part of this community that we carved away from the Old World, that we've fought to preserve." Her tone is one of dismissal; she's done arguing with me. "Am I to unilaterally reverse my invocation of the law because I don't care for how someone's applied it?"

"It's within your power, Governor."

"So is justice." Her eyes on mine are rigid, ruthless. "We are one people, Officer Savelova. Rolf's crime is against all of us. Not the strangers. *Us.*"

"*Please!*" That one word, piercing the chaos, and I meet Rolf's eyes. Rolf, who frightened me, who murdered someone's child, a child like mine; a murderer is staring at me, terrified, because he does not want to die. I look back at Yulia; she's not watching me anymore, nor is she watching Rolf; she's looking over the increasingly out of control crowd, eyes steady, lips thin, approval, disapproval, impossible to tell, but she is doing nothing and she will continue doing nothing. I push my way forward into the crowd, shoving people aside, reaching toward Rolf; but Aleksey already has him by the arm, is already shoving him toward the main Hub airlock, and the crowd buoys them ahead of me and I shout "Aleksey!" and if he hears me he doesn't react. I push and I push but I make no progress; I'm borne forward with the crowd who is pushing their prey to its death. Rolf keeps looking back at me and I think he's shouting my name but I can't hear anything anymore and Aleksey is pushing him and I reach and thread my arms between people and shove and yell but I can't move and it's every nightmare I've ever had only it's real, this is real, and these are my people, my family, and Rolf is going to die.

Aleksey opens the main airlock, and he doesn't have to push Rolf anymore because the crowd shoves him in so hard that Aleksey is jerked after him by the hand he has closed around Rolf's bicep. Rolf's small, thin bicep: why was I afraid of him? I am twelve meters away, then ten, and the inner airlock door closes but the shouts continue, and someone turns on the outdoor monitor, and the screens all around the perimeter of the room show us what is happening outside, and at that everyone grows still, and I start to make progress through the thick crowd. I try to keep my mind on the airlock controls, how quickly I'll have to turn them, how many people I'll have to clear out of the way to get the door open—surely I'll have time, surely I'll be able to do it quickly, go after Aleksey, bring them inside—but my eyes keep getting drawn to the monitors, even as I push forward, centimeter by glacial centimeter, and I won't make it but I have to try.

They appear on the monitor over the door, Aleksey bound up in his environmental coverings so we see nothing but his eyes, his face hidden by his jet-black balaclava, and weren't executioners centuries ago on the Old World dressed in black hoods? But Rolf wears nothing, and he's gasping in the thin, poisonous air, and it must sting, burning his lungs, and radiation on top of all of it although that's not what will kill him, not at all, it will have no time to damage him at all. Aleksey pulls and pulls, and Rolf begins to stagger; Aleksey yanks, his body language expressing annoyance, and Rolf falls to his knees. Aleksey drops him and takes a step back, one hand on the grip of the gun I hadn't realized he was wearing.

Urgency floods my veins, and I push harder, one meter closer, then two; but Rolf is dying, gasping, flailing on the ground with his arms bound and useless, his eyes, so crisp and clear and easy to see on the monitor, full of fear, agony, disbelief. I can't believe it either, and I claw forward, and I'm closer, and any moment my hands will be on the airlock and Rolf will be inside with me and we can do this all over and it will be different and Rolf will be all right.

But I see it, the moment when he dies, when his body, long slack, simply stops, no longer a person but a leftover, an empty container, meaningless meat. I am still pushing toward the airlock, still imagining the feel of the wheel against my palms, and it's too late. I let them kill him. Rolf is gone and Tamara is gone and no matter how I imagine them both safe in my hands they're not, I've failed them, and there's nothing left to do. The crowd relaxes, bloodlust satisfied; I stand five meters away from that elusive airlock as people begin to wander off, back to whatever trivialities were filling up the day before they decided to murder one of their own.

On the monitor Aleksey leans over Rolf's body, then straightens and walks toward the camera and out of the frame. Moments later I hear the outer airlock, and then the inner; Aleksey comes in, tugging off his balaclava, and stops in front of me as if he wants to say something. I keep staring at the monitor, and he turns and walks away.

Behind me I hear metal wheels against the stone floor, along with a step. Genera and Lauren, no doubt, but I don't look around. I can't look away from the shell that was Rolf, its eyes open to the sky. I should turn, say something, what I'm not sure, something comforting, perhaps, to Lauren, who surely didn't mean to kill, except that she did, this woman I've known since I was a child but never seen until today.

"You tried to stop them." Her voice is rough, thin, not like it was when she gave me Tamara's diary.

I say nothing.

There's creaking, and Genera's step; then the shuffle of weaker feet, and Lauren's ragged breath growing closer to me. And then the sound of spitting, and a wet spot through my hair against my neck; more shuffling, and the creak of the chair as Lauren sits. Genera wheels her away, and I stare at the monitor.

Feet recede, doors close. I have no idea how long I stare at that dead thing on the surface. When I finally hear Yulia's familiar step, the sound echoes through the cavernous Hub. The place is empty apart from the two of us.

She stands next to me as I watch Rolf's corpse.

"Lauren is upset, Anya," she says kindly, and it seems I've been forgiven. "Give her some time. She'll come to understand you felt you were doing your duty."

None of the responses I have to those words are things I'd be comfortable saying to Yulia.

"We need balance here," she continues. Approving of me, like a parent. "We need your ability to see the other side of things." Taking away the sting of her earlier words.

Rolf's eyes, staring at the sky. Empty of everything. Like Karl Yasnikoff's, the only thing recognizable in his bloodied face.

Like Irina's, when she left me.

"I know this has been difficult for you." Yulia reaches out and lays her papery fingers over my wrist. "But now we can bury Tamara properly."

Her touch draws my eyes from the empty thing on the monitor. Yulia's skin has faded over time, beyond the sallowness brought on by illness, like she's monochrome, unreal, no more alive than Rolf's corpse. I frown at her fingers. Why is she touching me? She has no standing to touch me. She ordered his death, and I let it happen, and we are two of a kind, but she should not be touching me.

Something dark and gaping blooms in my stomach. I watch Yulia's fingers, and after a moment, they slide off my arm.

"Take the day, Anya," she says. "This has been a taxing investigation, and you need rest." Her voice is still kind, but there's something else in it I haven't heard before: *fear*.

I am glad.

After a few moments her step recedes, and eventually a distant door opens and closes. I look back up at the monitor, and I watch, impotent, the thing that was Rolf.

RECIP: National Earth Space Organization, Vostochny
REPORTER: Loineau, Madeleine, Cmdr. NZKO *Hypatia*
Mission year 40, day 113

Kano spent twenty minutes ranting about how I was never going back to Novayarkha, and for once I let him yell. He says I'm lucky to be alive, which was not a thing he had to argue with me about. Not everybody who was alive when I went down was alive when I left.

That boy. They killed him. *On purpose*. With the full weight of *justice* at their backs, they terrorized and poisoned and suffocated him until he died.

Qara tried the "Well, Maddie, he *was* a murderer" line, but for all that any Deity has ever taught you, Vostochny, do you steal someone's lunch if they've stolen yours? She points out that some of the old texts spout the "eye for an eye" philosophy, and I asked if she wanted to live in that world. She's backed off, but I can see she thinks I'm being unreasonable.

She wasn't there. By your Deities, Vostochny, she wasn't there.

I don't know what I expected to see when I asked if I could watch the trial. Some kind of archaic legal system, I suppose; wigs and robes and gavels or something. Not this. Not the conversion of these polite, nervous people into a fucking mob.

Not that I don't understand the mother's feelings. I've thought some pretty awful things about you, Vostochny, especially after the accident. It's a good thing I didn't have the means to do anything at the time, because I'm kind of vengeful by nature, I think. So Lauren didn't surprise me.

The rest of them did.

You could feel it in the room: an energy, like ozone, like an engine spinning up. It's a word I've seen in books and movies, and I've always thought it was hyperbole, but it's real: *bloodlust*. And that boy—Rolf—he knew it, as soon as Lauren opened her mouth. I saw it in his face, Vostochny. He was terrified. He wanted to deny it. But he knew, even before I could manage to believe it, that they were going to kill him. He lived with these people. They raised him from a baby. And he never doubted they'd follow through.

And of course I opened my big mouth, and Anya at least made sure they heard me, but after that it was chaos. I thought for a while they were going to throw me down and trample me, or even drag me outside as well; but Sofia pulled me away. The crowd let me go, because who the hell was I? Just some stranger they thought was going to corrupt their oh-so-civilized society. Killing me would have meant nothing. So much more important to focus on killing one of their own.

I couldn't have saved him, Vostochny. I know that. Even if I'd been able to pull away from Sofia, even if I'd been able to get to Rolf and pull him to safety, I would have been overwhelmed by everyone else. They were eager for it, all of them: young, old, sick, well.

Is it strange, that I still feel like I should have tried harder?

Sofia's one of the ones who isn't sick, and on top of that she clearly gets her exercise, because her grip on my arm was absolutely unyielding. She's not that big, but I'm pretty sure even my greater bulk wouldn't have worked in my favor for long. So I didn't resist, just kept up with her while she marched me quickly down the main spoke toward the outer airlock where we'd landed.

Except at one point she stopped. "Something wrong?" I asked.

"I want to watch," she explained, and I followed her eyes to a monitor mounted high on the wall.

They broadcast the execution, Vostochny. All over the city. Five kilometers of hallways and homes, and they showed it everywhere. I watched Aleksey—friendly, unimaginative Aleksey—drag that kid along the fucking ice while he choked and gasped for air. I watched Rolf collapse, and watched Aleksey get *annoyed* with him for it. I watched Aleksey stand aside while Rolf called to him for help, and I saw Rolf die, and then I saw Aleksey lean over him, checking for a pulse, and leave the body and walk away. And I swear, Vostochny, Aleksey looked disappointed. I think...I think he thought it went too fast.

Hina's never going down again either, and yeah, there was a lot of screaming over that, and I pulled rank, and it was ugly but even the Colonel backed me up and I don't think Hina's going to speak to any of us again for a decade or two. But at least she'll be here, where's she's safe. She was too easily charmed by that cold-blooded fucking *murderer* Aleksey. They're poison down there, all of them.

"She's not the only one who was charmed," Kano said. And he's right.

Aleksey works for Anya. And Anya stood still, whispering to her governor, while they killed that boy.

I don't know her at all. I just filled in what I needed to see because we're here, Vostochny, we've arrived where we need to be, and this is the purpose of all of our lives, only this, and I wanted there to be more. I wanted to find someone kind and warm who would make me feel less alone.

But it's *all* of them, Vostochny. It's not a pack of horrible people and innocent Anya. It's in their culture, in their blood. Generational awfulness. We're only what we're taught, all of us.

Qara also said that maybe we aren't in any position to judge, because we haven't lived like them. Up to a point, I agree with her. But this is that point, Vostochny. This is it. What they've built down there—it's an abomination. They've bred out any sense of humanity they might have had, and I don't care why. We're not going back there. We've lost too much to risk losing any more.

CHAPTER SIXTEEN

MADDIE WON'T ANSWER.

I can't remember where in our orbit *Hypatia* is. I can't remember if she's even in range. But I need to talk to Maddie, to hear her voice, to have her explain it to me. There's too much I don't understand, and Maddie understands it. Maddie knows.

You think you escaped from Earth? All you did was bring it with you.

I don't know how long I've been on my couch by the radio, or even if I've been transmitting. I remember saying *I'm sorry* over and over, but I'm not sure that was out loud.

It's light again. First or second daylight, I don't know. I don't know what day it is. I think I'm hungry. I know I've missed my daily medications.

Irina's gone.

If she were in the next room, or off somewhere asleep, I would feel her; but the part of me that's connected to her is broken, and I'm alone, and I'm not entirely sure what I'm doing here, except I can't picture being anywhere else. This home is empty. I have kept it empty, generic: dishes, linens, radio. Somewhere—I can't remember where—I have seven drawings of Irina, one done every year of her life except the last, most by Costa, who had a knack for capturing that gleam in her eye, that little-girl bubble of joy that

I somehow never had myself, not when I was small, not now, not ever.

Everything is empty, like Rolf's eyes. If I don't move, don't breathe, I stop feeling anything at all, even my own body, and I can believe I'm a ghost, unreal, like Irina, and if I just wait, as still as I can, I will fade and dissolve and all of the hollowness will vanish.

But it's not hollowness. Not all of it.

My clock chimes: sunset. Rolf has been out there a full sun cycle, alone. Perhaps longer.

Now is the time.

I stand, and my body feels light and heavy all at once, fluid and vaguely out of control, as if I've had too much of Costa's berry vodka, as if I really am nothing but a shade, ready to dissipate into nothingness. When my feet steady I hold out my hands; my fingers are not shaking. All in my mind, then, the insubstantialness, the mist that threatens to stop my brain from making any connections at all. I head for the door, steady enough, but there's a delay, as if each footfall happens too early and the sensation catches up seconds later. I step into the corridor, letting the door swing shut behind me with a solid, hydraulic *thump*. There's no one here. Second sunset, then? With most everyone asleep? Not that it matters, this or anything else. Running into people won't stop me, but this will all be much simpler if no one sees.

I head back up the spoke to the Outer Rim. It's a much longer walk, but it will be dark for seven hours, and there's no hurry, not now. There are people here, but not many; mostly young, absorbed in one another, but not all of them. The few who smile and nod must have missed what happened before, or were standing too far away to understand what I was trying to do. To them, it was another public verdict, another sentencing I went along with, even if I wasn't the one who carried it out.

Vassiliya had cleaned Rolf's cell, changed the linens, made sure there was new soap and reading material and all the things he would need. I thought he would be a troubled inmate, angry and dissatisfied, and I wanted to make it easier for him, to allow him creature comforts. I didn't think he would be dead, that I would have killed him, that soap and linens would be irrelevant. I wonder if Vassiliya has put those things away, stripping the room into impersonality for the next person who'll come to stay. We'll confine them and speak kindly to them and see that they're entertained, and they will be locked up without privacy or agency and they will be *nothing* and is it so different?

What has my life been, to do this to people?

It's a long walk along the Outer Rim, more than an hour from my far-end room to the endcap airlock, and I've passed hundreds of people and nobody has shown surprise or alarm at my presence. Even if they report later that they've seen me, no one will care. It won't matter.

It's never mattered.

I open the inner airlock door, not bothering with subterfuge, and let it snick closed behind me. I reach for the protective clothing: hood, scarf, gloves. I climb into the suit, and then, with those steady fingers that don't feel like my own, I tug the balaclava— *black hood, executioner's hood*—over my face. I wrap the scarf with care, tucking the ends into the collar of the suit, filling in the gaps in the fabric. Comfortable, the radiation clothing. My second skin. There are too many things here to fight, too much of this planet determined to kill us.

Perhaps that's what's happened. After living with its poison for two centuries, perhaps it's seeped into all of us and turned us into everything we fled.

Or maybe Maddie was right. Maybe that's all we've been all along.

I open the outer door, and do what I've never done before: I step outside the city in full dark.

The airlock cycles behind me, and as I climb the stairs to the surface the light fades from dim to almost nonexistent. There are spotlights coming from the solar tubes, from the corridors on the Rims and in the spokes, and a circle from the Hub in the distance. They're so insubstantial, here in the dark, and I'll have to be careful. The only sound is the quiet hiss of the wind, and as my eyes adjust I see a dusting of snow curl up like a living creature and skip over the flat courtyard. The Old World had a moon. I've seen pictures, but I can't imagine, not even a little bit, what it would be like to stand out here and see such a thing.

I turn toward the Hub lights and begin walking.

I've made almost no progress when the cold begins to bite through my protective clothing. I should've prepared better. I should've stopped at the quarry for one of the heavy suits. Someone would have asked me why, perhaps Damian, and I'm not sure he would have given it to me if I'd told him. Although he might not have asked. I'm Anya Savelova, head peace officer, consul of Governor Orlova, our beloved and trusted leader. I could have walked in, fixed a steely eye on whoever was there, and walked out with whatever I liked. Power. I've never wanted to exploit it. I've never seen before how little I really have.

My fingers begin to hurt from the cold, and I swing my arms, stimulating my circulation. I can't fail, not this time, never mind discomfort. I am empty, it's all empty, and my options are finished.

It takes fifteen minutes cutting straight across the arc to get to Rolf's corpse, and by then my hands are entirely numb. That's going to be a problem: Rolf's body is no lighter for being divested of spirit. He's partially covered in snow, and I dust it off, brushing his clothes, his arms, his face. His eyes are fixed open, and the snow and ice have filled them in; he looks almost as if he's wearing protective goggles, like the metallurgists do when they check the refinery output.

I don't touch his eyes, but I shake the snow from his hair, and then I slide my numb hands and under his armpits. I lift his torso, and I pull.

I'm so weak.

I haul him backward, meter by meter. He's stiff, and inflexible, and his heels catch in the ice. A sheet would have helped me, or perhaps rope or cord or even copper wire; my blank and hollow mind has not thought properly ahead. But the cold has become tolerable, even pleasant in an odd way, and it matters less to me how long it takes me to get where I'm going. Doctor Halvorsen takes care of all our dead, young and old, and she'll find me a box for Rolf, not such a small one as she had for that remnant of hope from the incubator, but big enough to hold what is left of him after he's burned. How strange it was, after Irina, to see how many solid pieces were among her ashes. I'd always thought, somehow, that the process would reduce us to sand, but instead there are pieces that are recognizably bones in along with the dry and dusty ash. There was so little with Irina, which didn't make sense; even when she died she was tall for a child, all arms and legs and teeth and wild yellow hair, except she'd lost that, hadn't she?

If I can get Rolf to Doctor Halvorsen, Irina will come back, and I'll remember.

I look up to check my direction. I've angled away from the Hub, away from the Rims. I correct my trajectory, and this time I check at every step, making sure the Hub stays before me and the Inner Rim grows closer instead of farther away. I can see better, and the lights seem brighter, so bright I can see my own shadow; or perhaps that's not a shadow, only Rolf, staring at the stars with his ice-covered eyes. Is Tamara out there somewhere with ice-covered eyes, or did he close her eyes after he killed her? Did he pull her body far enough away that none of us would look or see or have hope of finding her? A heinous crime, and surely Rolf earned his fate, except as I stagger backward, step by step, Tamara's diary replays in my head and I wonder what any of us have beyond that moment where we leave our empty husk behind, why we should run from it, delay it, fight to keep Death at bay. We've died on

Novayarkha over and over again for two hundred years. We died on *Arkhangelsk* before that. We will die today and tomorrow and ever after, and perhaps Rolf did Tamara a favor, a kindness, something we all need, somehow, in order to let go.

I've lost my direction again. Nothing seems to be shaped the way it should be. My arms are numb up to my elbows now, and all I feel of Rolf is the tug of his weight through my shoulders. I take smaller, more careful steps, and Rolf seems to be digging in his heels because I can't pull him quite so easily.

Abruptly I slip, and there's a jolt through my neck, but even that's not severe. I get up, my limbs sluggish and disobedient, and slide my arms under Rolf's again. I pull, and step, and pull, and step, and the light keeps going from bright to dark and I don't know where the Hub is anymore. Doctor Halvorsen will be asleep, but she never minds being wakened to look after someone, has always been practical and cheerful about it, and I don't know how a person stays like that. I don't know how a person becomes like that to begin with. Was I ever cheerful? It was Irina who laughed all the time, and I could feel it, surely I could feel it, I remember feeling it, I remember feeling *something*.

I can't feel anything anymore.

And then there's a step behind me, a voice calling my name, and it's Costa and he says, "By the skies, Anya, what are you doing?"

CHAPTER SEVENTEEN

Costa brings me some analgesic tea, and tells me to sit up.

I'm in his house, wrapped in the heavy quilt from his bed, ensconced on the sofa which is threatening to seduce me back into sleep. I don't want to move at all, but I sit forward, fighting off the torpor that nearly killed me. Irina's still gone, but Costa's things are familiar and his kindness is warm, and it's possible I might still have one foot in the world.

Which means I still have things to do.

The tea is free of alcohol, but it's unexpectedly mild and sweet on my tongue, and it soothes my throat as I swallow. "I need to go back outside," I tell him.

"No, you don't," he says shortly, turning back to the stove. "Maria's taking care of it."

After he brought me back and wrapped me up he disappeared for nearly half an hour, and the only thing keeping me awake was the painful prickle of my limbs as my circulation slowly returned. Apparently he considers Maria, still feeling indebted to me for her rescue during the Exile raid, a safe confidant. I'm only grateful he didn't approach Doctor Halvorsen. Why she seemed like a solution when I was out on the ice I don't know. "What's she doing?"

"She and I brought him in. She's looking after him."

Maria's still young, but she's trained on all the equipment, including the crematorium. "Costa." I want to explain to him, but my mind won't form the words. "How did you find me?"

His shoulders drop, his hands gripping the counter by the stove. "I missed the trial. And then I missed the news. I had all of these assignments to correct, you see, and—" He straightens and turns, and the sorrow on his face makes me dizzy with relief. "Anya. If I'd had any idea that would happen, I would have been there. I would have tried to stop them with you. I'm so sorry."

I take another sip of the tea. It's too soon for it to be working, but the pounding in my head has receded, and it doesn't hurt anymore when I blink. "It wasn't yours to fix, Costa," I tell him, and it's the truth.

"I called you when I finally heard the news. You didn't answer. I figured you needed some time to think. But then I started asking around, and nobody had seen you at all. I went by your house, and when I found you missing I knew what you'd done."

Luck, then, or Costa's sixth sense for trouble. I would have frozen to death. I wouldn't have cared.

"It's not just you," he continues. "There are a lot of people unhappy with how Yulia handled things with Rolf."

"She didn't handle anything," My own vehemence surprises me. "She put Rolf's fate in the hands of a dying, grieving mother. She might as well have suffocated him with her bare hands."

Costa shifts uncomfortably and looks away. "Maria's telling people she saw Exiles behind the Outer Rim this morning. They'll assume that's why Rolf is gone."

"I need to put him in the crypt, Costa."

He smiles, but when he looks at me his eyes are unhappy. He's always been on my side, since we were children, but I've never asked so much of him before. "I'll go with you, Anya, if you want me to."

So it's more than just me now, disregarding Yulia's sentence, the city's laws. I should feel guilt, but the numbness still dominates. Even so, there's a warmth inside of me, an ember burning tenaciously amidst the cold, that might be hope.

The auxiliary lift is small, and I breathe in and out with care, Costa's shoulder pressed into mine. We've come this far without anyone questioning our purpose; we'll do this, and it will be done, and then...then, perhaps, this cold thing inside me will be sated, and I'll find Irina again.

My fear that we'd somehow be stopped—that my culpability would hemorrhage from my skin like an open wound, impossible for anyone to ignore—was unfounded. The post-breakfast crowds largely ignored us; Costa fielded pleasantries, and I, as always, was left alone. It was familiar, and alien, and wrong; but everything is wrong now.

The lift is old and slow, and every lurch and whine jolts my nerves like an electric shock. I close my eyes and begin counting slowly in the back of my mind: prime numbers, a Fibonacci series, anything I can think of, so my brain doesn't think about becoming stuck in this tiny space with my oldest friend, now my co-conspirator. I can add quickly, but patterns take me longer, and by the time I've hit F_{28} the lift has reached the lowest level. I open my eyes and wait for the door to open; those seconds are long enough for me to imagine being trapped here in this small space, suffocated and entombed with Costa, whose only crime has been compassion.

The door opens onto the hallway to the crypt.

This hallway served a different purpose when it was part of *Arkhangelsk*. Doctor Halvorsen says it was an open access corridor, a passage that wasn't insulated or airlocked but left open to the vacuum, allowing people to travel efficiently when wearing the proper suits. I can believe it: the walls are dark and unadorned, and the anemic lights penetrating the dank shadows, unlike the built-in wide fluorescents of the rest of our city, are hanging from the ceiling by hooks manufactured in our own factory. The passage itself is wide but squat, the only place in the city I've ever been where I feel like everything is oriented wrong.

I watch my feet here. The floor is uneven, covered in metal panels secured by rivets. It's been a year since I was down here, escorting the ashes of one of Yulia's sisters. Carlotta, her name was: unusual, even in our city where everyone seems to hunt for unusual names. Carlotta didn't have Yulia's sharp intelligence, but she was kinder, better-humored. I always thought that was in part because she didn't carry Yulia's responsibilities. Her face, at the end, was hollow and skeletal, but she was still inclined to smile.

Something in the back of my throat tastes bitter.

We turn a corner to the small, utilitarian crematorium. Nothing inside but a stack of coffins, nestled neatly against the wall, and the long, shallow furnace.

Maria has left Rolf's coffin on the dais in the center of the room, unmarked as all of them are, and I pick it up. It's light: three kilos, perhaps less. Doctor Halvorsen often frets that our crematorium should be hotter, that it leaves too many bone fragments, but I've never understood why that matters. With Irina, I swept my fingers through the ashes, over and over, and everything I touched that was larger than a speck of dust felt like a jewel, like she had been refracted into it like a ray of sun through a prism. I didn't want to leave her down here, where I could never touch her again.

It was Lauren who came down with me that day, who lifted the box from my hands and tucked my child into the place she would stay for eternity. She was so gentle, so patient, and she never called me mad, and I've lost her daughter, and she will never touch anything of her ever again.

The crypt is divided by age, and, when appropriate, biological connection. Rolf was a crèche baby, like me; he belongs with the others, young and old. His generation was hearty, notably resistant to disease. Out of sixty children born that year, fifty-three of them reached adulthood. With Rolf's death, it's down to fifty-two, which is not a bad number for a generation.

What have we taught them? What will they teach their own?

Costa meets my eyes, raising his eyebrows; offering to carry the small burden. I head back into the hallway, and turn toward the crypt.

Past the crematorium the space opens wide, but the ceiling is still low, and the lights cast the room in deep blue, like the hour before sunrise. The burial hollows dug into the walls are long full; there are free-standing shelves filling the room, like an old-fashioned library. There's a map kept in Novayarkha's central system recording where each person is stacked, but there will be no one to make a record for Rolf.

We reach the crèche shelf, so long it vanishes into the shadows. Our lives are brief, but this shelf, this crypt—it's endless. I'll place Rolf and no one will come to see him or even know he's here, and he'll be lost forever, not just to life, but to the future, as if he'd never been born. Erased, just as Lauren asked.

"Here, I think," Costa says quietly, and his voice sounds flat and strange in the small space.

He points to a spot just above my head, a place where the stack of coffins is shorter than the ones around it, as if someone had, with kindness, left room for this one lost child. I stand on my toes and slot Rolf's coffin into the space; it slides in easily, seamlessly, as if it were intended for that spot all along. I push it until the front of it is flush with the others. I won't remember where it is if I ever come back here.

"Costa."

He takes my hand. "Don't worry. I'll remember."

Before I can tell him it's not his duty, I hear a noise.

I freeze, waiting for the footfall, the voice, something to identify the intruder.

"What is it?" Costa asks. All curiosity, no alarm.

There's nothing, and my anxiety should be eased, but instead that mist settles into my head again, that sense that I'm standing next to the world rather than in it. It's not Irina—I would feel Irina—so it must be imagination. No surprise in this place, with all of its strange memories. I wait, and I breathe, and time passes, and I relax.

And then I hear it again.

It's not a footfall at all: it's a whisper, pushed through someone's lips: a formless string of vowels I can't understand. I make myself say, "Who's there?"

This time, I can hear what the voice says: *Anya.*

It draws my name out, two endless syllables in the dark. "Who are you?" I say, more sharply. This is my job, to get answers. My tone frightens people. They talk to me. They don't play foolish pranks.

Aaaaaaaaaaaaaaaaaanyaaaaaaaaaaaaaaa.

Again, Costa asks me what's wrong, but I can't answer him. There's a sound like coffins sliding against each other, like one is being removed. I scan the shelves up and down: none of the caskets are out of place, not Rolf's half a meter above my head. *Imagination.* But the sound continues, over and over, coffin after coffin sliding free. And more voices joining the first, always saying my name. *Anya. Anya. Anya.* Overlapping. Louder and louder. Rasping so loudly I want to cover my ears.

Costa says something else, but I pull away from him, changing my question. "What do you want?"

One of the voices, louder than the rest, begins to laugh, and then the footsteps start.

Bare feet scrape like sand against the stone floor, some heavy steps, some light, some quick and some slow. Above all of it, pounding in my ears, my own frantic heartbeat. They're between me and the lift, and they're between me and the main stairway up to the Hub, where I would surely be discovered, only I've already been discovered, haven't I? "What do you want?" I ask again, only I'm wailing and they know I'm afraid and they have no reason to answer me because I know what they want and what they'll take and surely I deserve it, the madness of the crypt, and I'll take Rolf to my grave with me and we'll always be spoken of as one.

"Please," I say, and only after the word is out do I remember Rolf's frantic cry, the look on his face telling me he knew it was already far too late.

And then I see them.

Rolf stands at the end of the row, only there are many of him, some younger, brash and confident, the way he was before Oksana, some the bored man I spoke to at the observatory, some the lost-eyed killer blankly telling me he couldn't remember murdering Tamara. But the one in the front is staring at me, his eyes full of hate, his face gray and rotting, skin peeling off, and did he look like that, after only two sunsets on the surface? They all walk closer to me, and I back away, but they seem to move faster, and they're on top of me even as I'm stumbling, and they're behind me and their hands reach out and they're pulling at me, and Rolf says, calmly, "You'll never be alone again, Anya," and something in me breaks and the howl echoing over and over again off the wide, low walls is my own.

RECIP: National Earth Space Organization, Vostochny
REPORTER: Loineau, Madeleine, Cmdr. NZKO *Hypatia*
Mission year 40, day 132

Took us about two weeks to figure out how to handle most of
the parts development nonsense remotely, and another five days
to realize it wasn't going to be enough.

Seung's been shuttling parts up and down all on his own, and
someone—usually Katerina, the tall glowering one always packing some massive piece of weaponry for no useful reason—has
been meeting him at the landing site with a package or a pallet
of whatever they've built for us this time. Everything was going
smoothly, and I was thinking maybe we really could get what we
needed without having to associate with the Murder People again.

Qara saw me write that and said, "For pity's sake, Maddie." But
they *are* murderers. I won't apologize for saying it.

The trouble is...me witnessing a murder hasn't changed our
fundamental dependence on them. And it hasn't changed the fact
that when shit comes up—and shit always comes up, Vostochny—
someone has to deal with it.

A few weeks ago we started seeing fabrication issues again,
stuff we hadn't seen since the early prototypes. Same old problems,

at first: joins we had to re-weld, valves slightly out of spec, alignment issues we could fix with our own equipment. But we can't do anything about tensile strength or liquid metals losing cohesion in a vacuum, and Ratana finally came to me with a mangled fuel vent and said, "This is a waste of time."

I would've sent her down there, with Seung and maybe Léon for gravitas, but Ratana put her foot down.

"They're hierarchical," she reminded me. "I get how you feel, Mads, but this is important, and it has to come from you."

So I radioed Orlova, who made me wait a full fucking hour before answering, as if she didn't have some traumatized lackey constantly monitoring the frequency, and I gritted my teeth and said what I had to. I apologized for troubling her, but we were having some ongoing problems with the fab, and perhaps we could drop by in person to deal with the issues. She was politely magnanimous, and neither one of us mentioned the cold-blooded murder I witnessed last time I was there. The whole conversation was vile and unpleasant and ultimately useful, and the only issue was on my end: Hina.

Seung campaigned relentlessly for her, reminding me how well-trained she was, how easily she'd worked with Costa on their ancient hardware, how her affinity for the people down there made her far better suited to dealing with their metallurgists than an acidic curmudgeon like Léon. He was right about all of it, but I know why she wanted to go down again, and I wasn't having any of it.

And then she came to talk to me.

Hina's always been like Kano: stubborn, argumentative, freezing me out if I don't listen. But I forget, sometimes, how much of the Colonel she has in her, too, and she came to me in my room and sat by the door and waited until I got tired of ignoring her.

"It must have been awful," she said. "Seeing him die."

Do you know, Vostochny? I'd never seen someone die before.

Not up close like that. Everyone here on *Hypatia* died by being torn off the ship. No bodies.

There's a thing that happens, like a circuit break. One instant, and the body's nothing more than residue.

That's all of us. Someday, that's all of us.

"I don't understand it either," she went on, in that same calm voice. "The revenge side—I get that. But revenge should be cold, you know? Long and agonizing. In a way, execution is too quick."

There's my girl.

I still said nothing, and she leaned forward, clasping her hands together, and damned if she didn't get that one from me. "I don't like their justice system, Maddie. But it's theirs. Their laws. Aleksey did his job. You expected him—any of them—to stand up and start a revolution, over a kid who killed someone they loved?"

Fucking logic, Vostochny. I fucking hate it.

"Look," I said to her, "I know. I *know*. I just—it's unstable, Hina, that whole place. They're constantly fighting and people are going missing all the time and it's not safe."

I caught it in her eyes: that Kano flash, that moment of frustration waiting to burst out. But she swallowed it. "We're here inside a broken metal box hanging in a vacuum, eight centimeters between us and a quick freeze. We're breaking ourselves in two to build a communicator, when we don't even know if there's anyone to communicate with on the other side. *Safe* isn't on the table for any of us, Captain. Not in Novayarkha, and not here."

Captain. Damned kid.

"Seung's the best we've got, apart from me. He can do almost all of it. I could go over his information and ask questions and he could do it remotely. But you and I both know any extra step at this point is multiplying the possibility of error, and we don't have time for that."

She sat back and waited.

"You'll see him again, won't you?" I asked at last.

"He's a friend," she told me. "That doesn't change just because he was forced to do something terrible."

Hina's never been among people, never had a chance to learn how to evaluate a real-life situation with strangers.

And neither have I.

So Hina came with us, and I set a blanket rule for both Hina and Seung to check in every twenty minutes if we got separated, and I resigned myself to living with gut-churning worry for my little girl.

RECIP: National Earth Space Organization, Vostochny
REPORTER: Loineau, Madeleine, Cmdr. NZKO *Hypatia*
Supplemental

I wasted a lot of energy working out what I was going to say to Anya. It matters to me a lot that I got her so wrong. I faked politeness talking to Orlova because I had to, but I couldn't have faked anything in front of Anya.

Which turned out to be moot, because she wasn't there.

It was Sofia who greeted us, that horrible child who stopped to watch Rolf's murder on TV like a favorite movie. And Anya wasn't there when we got inside, so I figured she was avoiding us, and of course I was grateful, Vostochny, what do you think?

We took an interior elevator down to the metals lab, which was a relief; I don't think I could have managed that quarry path alone. They have a lot of elevators here, in addition to the ramps at the external airlocks. I remember what Anya told me about people who were less mobile, and the focus on autonomy.

So compassionate in some ways, these murderers.

Orlova met us in the lab, smiling that cool smile of hers. "I'm glad you've made it safely," she shouted over the machines, and dismissed Sofia with a nod. "We'll be able to talk in the monitoring room." She turned her back to us, assuming we'd follow like she was some fucking queen. "It's soundproofed."

We walked through the main chamber, past the automated systems, through the heat and the noise, the thermal radiation from the machinery making the room uncomfortably hot. We passed into a smaller but still spacious room—much cooler, well-lit, filled with tables covered in equipment similar to the archaic hardware in their observatory. The three technicians looked up when Orlova walked in; they nodded to her politely, then returned to work. She'd clearly warned them we were coming, because they ignored us completely.

As soon as she closed the doors I could hear the ventilation systems again, and my own heartbeat. "Now, Captain Loineau," Orlova began briskly. "What exactly has been going wrong?"

I nodded at Seung—his idea, having me give him explicit permission to speak—and he stepped forward, pulling a shard of flaked insulation out of his pocket. "It's mostly the filter alloys and the liquid metals," he explained. "The tensile strength is off. We need a different mix."

We'd agreed, back on *Hypatia*, that we'd take the blame for the whole thing, suggesting our specifications were too vague. Since Orlova's not stupid and she'd know her people fucked up, it'd be down to her to decide how much of the issue to handle in front of a pack of strangers. And for once, Vostochny, we read her right. Orlova took the small chunk of metal and frowned at it, turning it over in her hands, then turned to her technicians.

"Viktor," she said, "didn't you program the generator for this part?"

Viktor—half Orlova's age and twice her height—stood to join us, taking the shard and frowning at it. "I did, Governor. But this isn't the mix I entered. There's too much carbon—see?" He rubbed a bare finger along one of the broken seams, and it left a black smudge on his skin. "It hasn't been heated properly, either." He turned to Seung. "Who gave you this one?"

"I don't remember," Seung said. He did remember: it was a tech named Danna, who I thought was the slim-shouldered squat person facing a monitor in the corner of the room. "This would be fine for light modeling, and we've a need for that sort of thing as well. Someone's just mixed up the manifests."

Viktor kept scowling, and he seemed as disinclined as I was to make excuses for the sloppy mistake, which made me kind of like him. Whether it had been his own error or the error of a minion, I suspected it wouldn't happen again.

"I'll go over the logs later," Viktor said. "For now—are you a metallurgist?"

He was asking Seung, but Hina replied, "I am."

"If I show you how the readout works, do you think you can show me what you need?"

Hina nodded, and she and Seung followed Viktor back to his console.

Left alone with me, Orlova sure as hell didn't beat around the bush.

"I understand you were distressed about what happened the last time you were here," she said.

I didn't say a damn thing. I know Orlova's bait when I hear it. Anya taught me that much.

"I would caution you to remember," she went on, "that you don't know us. You don't know our history, nor the struggles we face. Your judgement is based on a brief and shallow acquaintance. I don't expect you to understand, but I do expect you to mind your own business."

"Even when you're killing someone?"

And here's where she threw me off completely: her face fell, and she looked at the floor, and suddenly she was this tiny, sick old woman. "It was a horrible result, I agree," she told me. "It wouldn't have been my choice. But we have Original Law for a reason, and once invoked, I couldn't take it back. I have no children of my own; Lauren's grief is beyond my own understanding. I would not deny her what she believed would ease it."

See, Vostochny, I *hate* conversations like this, because I start to understand. Hell, I nearly left our metallurgist up on *Hypatia* because she's our only child and I didn't want her flirting with the local cops. The fact that killing a person is *totally and completely wrong* is something I can almost forget.

Almost.

"Has Rolf's death eased her grief, Governor?" I asked, and her eyes froze over again.

"That, like the trial, is entirely none of your business, Captain. And I would thank you to restrict your contact with my people to matters of mutual concern."

Since I'd prefer not to talk to any of them ever, that'll be easy. Let them all vote to kill each other, to throw each other out into the snow, until there's nobody left. "Where's Officer Savelova?" I asked, trying to sound casual.

But I didn't expect Orlova's response. "Officer Savelova is indisposed," she said, and that same chilliness in her voice kept me from asking anything more.

Indisposed.

Indisposed is stupid. It doesn't mean anything. She could have said "on another assignment" or "off duty" or "too pissed off at you to care."

What right does Anya have to be pissed off? *I'm* the one who's mad. And Rolf's the one who's dead. Anya shouldn't be pissed off. She should be on her knees begging someone's forgiveness. Whose, I don't know, but someone in this place must have loved that kid.

I didn't respond, and if Orlova saw something in my face—and really, you know she did, because that damned woman doesn't miss a whole hell of a lot—she let it go. Instead, she decided to make metallurgy small talk. "Viktor is our best technician," she assured me. "He'll get to the bottom of what's been causing trouble, and we'll get you the parts you need."

"I figured you'd be glad to see us failing," I said. I guess I wasn't feeling all that forgiving just yet.

She was silent for a while. "If you're telling us the truth," she said at last, "then if you don't succeed with this station, they'll likely send someone else."

I wondered, then, if it's occurred to her to wonder how, in all of the grand universe, she and I ended up on the same speck of dust.

"I'd like to know what is happening and when," she continued. "I can't keep the Old World from invading. But I can understand, and I can prepare our city."

So here's the frustrating thing, Vostochny. I think Orlova's a bigoted zealot, but I believe she'd lay down her life to protect Novayarkha. By the look of her, she's on her way to doing exactly that: she might make the year, and hear us sending the first messages, but unless you've upped travel speeds by a lot, she's not going to be around to see anyone else drop by. She wants to use us to inoculate her city against Earth, as if *Hypatia*'s a dose of dead virus.

And it's maybe why she didn't stop me from speaking at Rolf's trial. Let them hear me, the crazy woman from the Old World who doesn't believe in killing. See what we're facing? The horror of *mercy*.

I really hate moral relativism, Vostochny. And I hate it most when I kind of understand it.

CHAPTER EIGHTEEN

Lula lula lullaby dream,
Here is my sweet mourning dove.
She sings her music by your bed,
Hush and sleep my precious one.

CHAPTER NINETEEN

"WHERE ARE YOU?" I ASK IRINA.

"I am in the dark," she says.

She looks like herself, small and round-faced and straw-haired, but her voice is Rolf's.

CHAPTER TWENTY

I WAKE.

I've woken before. I was counting days, but I don't know where I left off, and it doesn't matter really because I'm going to stay awake this time.

I know some things I didn't before. I know I'm in Costa's house, and I should've figured it out sooner, because his house smells like no one else's, a mix of pungent umami and ozone. I'm in his bedroom, lying on close-woven sheets on his decadently overstuffed mattress. My own bed is narrower and firmer, and my back aches from this one, and I must have been here for some days.

I open my mouth, afraid I won't be able to do anything but sing, but instead I say "I am tired" with some clarity. My throat is raw, from overuse or under, I'm not sure, and I sound like someone who's been puffing radishweed for years. But my brain and my mouth are connected again.

Slowly I become conscious of my limbs, warm and leaden, and my chest, weighed down by memory. None of it matters. Irina's still gone, and tears trace their way down my temples and into my hair. *Tears mean we are alive,* Costa said to me once, last month or perhaps decades ago. Everything's gone hyper-contrast, black and white, the two sides of my life, before and after Irina, that narrow slice of time where I had her a bright, thready light that vanishes when I reach for it.

I don't want this. I don't want any of this without her. But my alternative is that shapeless darkness with a vicious simulacrum of the only thing that has ever mattered to me, so I blink away the tears and keep my eyes open.

The light brightens and shifts from yellow to bright white as our star moves higher in the sky. It's almost too bright for me to look at before I hear the familiar sound of hydraulics and a door opening, and I can hear them as clearly as if they were in the room with me.

"Did she have a good night?" asks Doctor Halvorsen.

Morning, then. More proof the demon is a liar. But Costa's answer surprises me.

"She was restless," he says. "Calling out a lot."

"The rhyme again?"

"Mostly for Irina."

He sounds miserable, and I would call out to him and tell him I'm better, but that would be a lie.

Doctor Halvorsen makes a frustrated sound. "I'll have to boost the dosage again. Her system is very stubborn."

What is she giving me?

"Isn't there something else you could try?" Costa asks.

"There's an alternative that is supposed to be a more thorough soporific, but I'm short on ingredients for another week, at least. For now, this is all I have." Her voice softens. "I'm sorry, Costa. But at least she's getting some relief. Give it time. She may soon get to the point where she can talk to us, and then we can begin to help her properly."

The day I was born, it was Doctor Halvorsen who opened my incubator, drained the fluids, cleared my airways, held me close while I cried my first cry. She's dedicated her life to bringing each one of us into this world safe and sound. And her words have filled me with as much terror as those creatures in the crypt.

Footsteps grow nearer, and I close my eyes, relaxing every muscle in my face. The mattress shifts as someone sits down, and then Doctor Halvorsen's dry fingers take the pulse at my wrist. She does this with her usual detached gentleness, and everything inside of me wants to snatch my arm away, stand up, run from the room and Costa's house and this doomed city. "Put the tea on, will you, Costa?" she says, tranquil and unconcerned.

Costa's footsteps recede, and Doctor Halvorsen proceeds to give me a thorough physical, throughout which I remain entirely limp. Her hands stay gentle as she prods and rubs, rolls me over to change the sheets and my clothes, including an undergarment keeping the bedding clean. She is kind, patient, unfailingly gentle, and perhaps it's part of what's happened to me that I feel no gratitude for her ministrations, no embarrassment for my impaired state.

I wonder if it means anything that all I can feel is revulsion.

Costa returns after she's finished, long after the tea should have been strong enough. I keep my eyes closed as Doctor Halvorsen gets off the bed, and I hear a stopper pulled out of a bottle, a dribble of liquid upon liquid. "No more than that," she advises Costa. "If she can't sleep with this much, we'll need a different strategy. This will be too hard on the rest of her system if we have to keep it up for long."

Costa sits on the bed, heavier than Doctor Halvorsen, slower to let the mattress take his weight. I take a chance and open my eyes—slowly, so he can allow himself to believe I've only just awakened—and there is Costa, a steaming stone cup in his hand, his familiar face lined, ragged, exhausted. I've worried him, and my revulsion gives way to remorse.

His eyes lock with mine, and he freezes, and for a moment I can't read his expression at all. "Will it hurt her?" he asks Doctor Halvorsen, and I add relief to my spectrum of emotions: Costa is Costa. He won't give me away.

"Not at all," Doctor Halvorsen assures him. "Not at this dosage."

He stays motionless, searching my face for…I'm not sure. "Please." I keep the word inaudible, just between us, between me and the only person in this city I trust.

Costa slides a hand behind my head, cradling the nape of my neck, and lifts my shoulders off the bed. I'm so much weaker than I thought, so close to sleep despite my lucid thoughts, my expanding set of emotions. I want to help him lift me, but I can't, can't do anything but keep my eyes on his and repeat that one word: "Please."

Costa puts the cup to my lips and tips it forward. The liquid hits my tongue, sweet and familiar, and I swallow, trusting him, and he keeps pouring, careful, making sure I don't spill a drop, until the cup is empty in his hand. He settles my head back against the pillow, all gentleness, his familiar eyes so worried, so kind. "Sleep, Anya," he says, and strokes my hair gently, the touch of a loving parent. "You'll feel better tomorrow."

And I feel it, seeping into my veins: the torpor, the miasma, the gateway to hell, and the only companion I'm left with is betrayal.

CHAPTER TWENTY-ONE

I HAVE WOKEN, OVER AND OVER, TO THE SOUND OF THE DOOR, TO DOCTOR Halvorsen coming and going, Costa's gentle hands and the warm drink consigning me back to hell. How many times this has happened I can't know, but this time…this time the formless void is silent, and I am alone, and the peace of it is disorienting and soothing in turns.

I become aware first of my own stillness, and then my breathing, and then the weight of a blanket on my body, the smell of mushroom soup, a thin, horizontal line of light. When I realize I'm able I blink; the light disappears and then reappears. *Door*. It's the line of light under a closed door.

I turn my head, and hear the rustle of the covers around me. I'm still in bed, still at Costa's, but I've come awake on my own this time, stirred by nothing other than my body's belief it needs no more rest. Instinctively I reach for Irina, but the only image I can grasp is that creature in the nightmare, and my mind shies away and chooses solitude.

Twisting toward the nightstand I switch on the lamp. Odd, bright light; Costa has the old lamps, salvaged from the ship, and the spectrum is jarring, but it helps me focus. I inventory my body, turning my head, shifting my arms and legs; I am alarmingly weak, but nothing hurts, not even my head shaking off the tendrils of

Halvorsen's sweet concoction. There's an odor that has to be me, having been confined to this bed for—how long? I glance around the room; there's no calendar, not even a clock. Surely Costa used to keep such things in this room.

When I close my eyes, I see him looking at me as he pours the drug down my throat.

I push the covers away, which takes more effort than I'd have thought, and in one act of will I sit up and swing my feet over the side of the bed. The room spins, and for a moment I think I'll keep rotating and collapse on the floor, but reality stabilizes, leaving only a mild throbbing in my head. Bracing one hand against the wall I get to my feet; this is more difficult, but I shuffle my way to the bathroom.

I have never been an ascetic, have always enjoyed warm water and long baths, but I turn Costa's shower on cold, and strip off my clothes as I wait for the water temperature to drop. My protective undergarment is clean this time; perhaps it was simple biological necessity that woke me.

The water is freezing, bracing, and I gasp involuntarily as I soak my hair and scrub who knows how many days of stink off my skin. I'm working the tangles out of my hair with shaking fingers when I hear a voice.

"Anya?"

It's Costa. I will have to deal with him, but perhaps not just now.

"Are you all right?"

His voice is closer, but he's outside the room, an interesting nod to my modesty.

"Are there any clean clothes?" I ask him.

He's silent for just a moment, but when he says "I'll bring them," I think he sounds relieved.

The act of calling out has exhausted me, and I sit on the floor of the shower, completing the process leaning against the wall. I have to get to my knees to turn off the water, but my mind is clearer, and my weakness seems no worse.

There's a quick knock at the door. "I've left them on the bed," Costa says. And then: "Do you need help?"

He would have been helping me all along, I realize, unless Doctor Halvorsen had come every day. "No," I say. "But I'm hungry."

I'm not, not yet; but he says "I'll make some breakfast" and he sounds almost happy.

I crawl out of the bathroom and pull the clothes off the bed: mine, a stiff sweater knitted from bamboo thread, an old pair of trousers, and clean underwear, which almost cheers me up. I stay on the floor as I dress, slowly; only when I've rested do I lean on the bed to climb to my feet. Stronger than I felt in the shower, but at this stage that means very little.

When I open the bedroom door I'm greeted with the smell of frying onions. He's making something elaborate, but my body responds to the smell with violent hunger pangs, and I wish he'd stuck with soup. This is his home, and he is caring for me, and I have no right to complain. I lower myself shakily into one of his kitchen chairs.

Eventually he prepares two plates and sits across from me. I eat with as much grace as I can manage; my system will likely rebel at the solid food, but the need is irresistible. I finish quickly, and Costa, who's barely touched his, offers me his plate; I shake my head. "I should wait," I tell him. Then: "How am I awake?"

Something crosses his face—shame, frustration—and he looks away. "I started dropping back your dose," he says.

"And Doctor Halvorsen approved this?"

"I didn't tell her."

So he'd listened, if not in the moment. Halvorsen is an authority over all of us; it would have taken a great deal of will for him to defy her, even if he didn't do it to her face. Perhaps I will be grateful for that someday.

Perhaps.

"When she noticed...she had to admit you were doing all right. She's been here every few days to check."

I think of her hands on me and suppress a shudder. "When does she come next?"

"Three sunsets."

"Call her." When he looks uncomfortable, I swallow annoyance, as close to strong emotion as I've felt since I awakened. "I need to go home," I add, as gently as I can. I don't tell him I'd have bolted from the room already if I'd had the strength.

He nods, and looks at his hands; he knows I haven't forgiven him. "I told them we were in the crypt to see Irina," he says. "I didn't tell them about Rolf."

I close my eyes, expecting to see the demon; but instead I see a different face, a different person: light brown hair and deep brown eyes angry and accusing. I open my eyes again. "Thank you," I manage.

He watches me in silence, his expression an unspoken entreaty; but I don't release him. He stands to make the call. He keeps his voice low, and I close my eyes again. I should be thinking of Irina, the one pure thing I carry, but my mind is occupied by those brown curls.

Maddie. Is Maddie all right? Surely Costa would have told me if she wasn't.

He hangs up and turns back to me. "She's on her way," he says, with some surprise, and irritation threatens to flare again. He couldn't possibly misunderstand what she's done to me.

I should ask him what's been happening, what I've missed, but the longer I'm awake the more the apathy washes over me, heavy and gray, a snowstorm trapped forever in the clouds. I can't feel Irina, can't bear the comfort she might bring; Maddie is gone and angry with me and she should be, because I've failed, over and over. I am a stranger in this place, in my home, and I have been since the day I was born, and it doesn't matter and nothing will change.

But something matters. Something must matter somewhere inside of me, because I am resolved Halvorsen will not drug me again.

I'm still at the table when she arrives, and I don't get up, but after she greets Costa I meet her eyes. For an instant those eyes are sharp, shrewish; and then she smiles, that same professional smile, the one she always wears before she pulls out her knives and pricks cheerfully at my heart. "Anya! It's so good to see you up!"

She may not be lying. I would have been a problem, while I was sleeping, something for her to take care of. A time sink. My lucidity will save her some walking. I say nothing, and I watch her face as she realizes I don't intend to answer her.

"Well!" Her voice is still bright, but I can see it in her eyes: she's done with niceties. "Let's examine you, shall we?"

She takes me back to the bedroom, and I insist on standing as she pokes and prods at me. She's taking her time, pushing at my abdomen and having me lift my arms over my head, and just when I think I won't be able to stand anymore she makes me sit so she can take my blood pressure. It's high, I'm sure, and when she says "You need to pace yourself, Anya," I wait for her to produce more medicine for me to take.

But in the end she just steps away from me, sighing. "Well," she says, "It doesn't seem to have hurt you, being weaned off the drug that way."

"Can I go home?" I ask her.

I will go anyway.

Her lips tighten, but she's only thinking. "I'm going to ask Costa to look in on you at every sunrise," she says. "But...yes, I think you're all right on your own."

I should thank her, should manage some level of pleasantry; but I watch in silence as she packs away her instruments and leaves. Costa pokes his head into the room when she's gone. "I don't have to do it if you don't want, An," he offers.

Annoyance, it seems, is the one emotion that won't desert me. "It's probably a good idea for you to keep an eye on me, at least for a few days." I will have to talk to Yulia, and to Aleksey; I will have to find out who's been doing what, if there are complaints backed up, if there's anything in my work that might make me care enough to do it. I look over at him: Costa, who I was raised with, who has been, all of our years together, that same mischief-making boy he was when we were children. He's not young anymore, not at all; healthy, but his hair is gray, and his arms have lost definition, and the lines around his eyes are etched in curves of perpetual unhappiness.

I must look much the same.

When he insists on taking the tram with me, I don't argue. Reality feels sticky, unpleasant, and his presence is no worse than the vibration of the tram or the stale air on my face or the people we pass who look through me, just as they always have. Nothing in Novayarkha has changed; no one has lost anything; I am the only difference here, or perhaps I was always this hollow, lost thing, and I simply didn't know it.

CHAPTER TWENTY-TWO

MATHILDA PEDERSON PLACES HER TEACUP CAREFULLY ON THE TABLE. "WE were just wondering," she says, with uncharacteristic hesitance, "if you could talk with Aleksey for us."

Mathilda's house is small, like mine, but due to an irregularity in pattern, she has an extra solar tube in her living room, giving the space a warm, welcoming light. Even without children, she has long since grown old enough to demand a larger home, but I understand why she hasn't. Light breeds optimism, even here in the conspiracy-laden Third Block, and somewhere in my battered mind I remember optimism makes people live longer, gives them happiness, purpose. I wouldn't take it from her, no matter how futile I think it is.

She began inviting me in for tea three weeks ago, the first time I patrolled there after my illness. At first I thought she was seeking information, gossip, but it was the reverse: she assumed I knew nothing of anything that had happened in my absence. It was from Mathilde I learned that Aleksey had chosen Katerina as his assistant, which was a relief, despite her military-oriented training. Katerina is cold-blooded but unerringly fair, and her interpretation of the rule of law depends less on violence than Aleksey's.

I suspect Dmitri's sorry to lose her. I don't know. I have been suspended from Yulia's council, and from my position as chief peace officer.

"It's only temporary," Yulia told me when she finally made time to see me, the day after I left Costa's. She looked anxious, contrite, as if she didn't want to do this to me, and if I'd been able to feel anything I might have forgiven her. "Doctor Halvorsen needs to monitor you for a while. I'm sure you understand, Anya. It's important that the people have confidence in the ones who keep the peace."

I've been relegated to Third Block patrols for three weeks now, carefully sequestered when Maddie's people are visiting. I was surprised, at first, to learn they were still coming; I'd have expected Maddie to wash her hands of all of us. But it isn't her who comes. Costa says it's usually Seung, and sometimes Kano, and more and more often Hina.

"They seem well," he tells me, although I don't ask. Costa answers all kinds of questions I don't ask, and I can't figure out how to tell him none of it matters anymore.

But from the start Mathilda has been unselfconsciously kind, chatty and patient and demanding nothing of me at all, and even in the gray fog that has become my life I know she's worth my efforts. "I don't get many opportunities to talk to Aleksey," I confess. He is, when not on duty, almost always off on his own somewhere. "What is it you need him to know?"

"We are grateful to have you," she says, which is a polite prevarication she offers without need. "But you can't be here all the time."

I've seen it, in the halls: marks on the walls, missing benches, branches of plants broken. "You're having troubles."

"It's just the children," she tells me hastily, and that's almost certainly a lie. "You come, and you're...reassuring. You calm things. Aleksey comes, or Ioseph, or one of the Turgenev kids from the Outer Rim, and things escalate. They do not listen."

I can't make Aleksey listen, but it's not like him to be so ineffective. However much he believes he can beat the truth out of people, he has always been proactive and surprisingly deft about preventing trouble. A whisper of interest stirs in the back of my head, as if Irina has exhaled into my ear. "What's been happening?"

"It's the strangers." Her lips tighten. "I know you spoke with them. And I trust you when you tell us they're not a threat. But we know nothing of them, Anya. They keep to themselves. They gawk at us as if we're the ones who are strange. And the way they speak—" She shudders. "It's our language. But it sounds—unsettling when they speak it. Eerie."

Bigotry, just like Costa, but here in the Third Block they will fixate on any difference to spin a prediction of coming disaster. They have whispered about disappearances, about the Exiles, about violence and government cover-ups since I was a child. I can't tell them they're paranoid, wrong. I have always been an alien here. I used to think that was bad.

"So you've been arguing?" I prompt. That's an easy guess; the Third Block always argues, and Mathilda is always one of the instigators.

She shrugs, and her skin warms. "We want to feel safe. That's all. But there are different ideas about that." She looks me in the eye. "You know we are passionate here."

Also paranoid, but there has never been any point in saying that. "Meaning things come to blows."

"From time to time, of course. But Aleksey—he does nothing. He sends his people and they break up the fighting and he doesn't listen."

That's the second time she's mentioned listening. "Mathilde. Do you want him to mediate your argument?"

She waves a hand at me. "What does Aleksey know? He's a boy." Mathilde is not ten years older than him. "I want an *exchange*. He spends all his time assigning people here and there and making sure the strangers are kept away from us, and we need information."

Were I my old self, I would suggest they meet one of the strangers. Mathilde would like Léon, I think, Maddie's dour pilot. Even the most innocuous of statements becomes gloomy in Léon's deep, level voice. Léon seems well suited to conspiracy theorists, and quick enough on their feet to keep up with the conversation.

But I am not my old self, and I have no authority, and this is Novayarkha and the end result is not as important as the process. "I'll see if he can give you an audience," I tell her. "But he is very busy, Mathilde. Honestly. I don't believe he's ignoring you on purpose."

She makes a skeptical noise, but she doesn't push the point, and when she starts talking about Tianna Passova's last miscarriage, my mind drifts away again.

Aleksey is away when I return to the Hub, and for the hour it takes me to write out my report onto a well-worn sheet of slate. He has taken to using a desk near Yulia's office; I drop the report there for later input, and head home. Costa has been encouraging me to take meals in the Hub kitchens, so I'm exposed to people even if I won't talk to them, but I'm worn tonight, bleak and overwhelmed, and so much company would serve only to erode me further.

But perhaps there's something useful I can do before I face a solitary meal and the endless night.

Aleksey's home is not precisely on my way, but he lives close to my route through the city center, in the Fourth Block where news travels most quickly. When he was younger, still in Costa's school, we thought he might be a journalist: animated, curious, entirely disinterested in tact. It was Yulia who first saw his leadership potential, the way he could use his blunt charm to influence people against their own interests. She always told me she wanted me to teach him empathy, compassion. I wonder if she's recognized the futility of that.

I have been to Aleksey's home precisely three times before. When he first came to work for me he invited me to dinner; he had a group there, and I knew from the moment I entered the room I would not fit in. To his credit he was a gracious host, and didn't impose on me again; the other times I've visited have been purely work-related, requiring me to stop by on the rare times he was at home. Despite what I said to Mathilda it's curious that he's neglected the Third Block; the bureaucracy of the job isn't especially involved, and Aleksey has had more than enough time to streamline his own process. His behavior is more likely explained by his fundamental dislike of conspiracy theories. Aleksey has always believed himself firmly rooted in reality.

It's not for me, any longer, to tell him how to do his job. But I can relay Mathilda's request, and let Aleksey field it as he sees fit.

I ring his bell, half expecting him to be absent, but he responds over the intercom almost immediately. "Yes?" he says, and he sounds out of breath.

"It's Anya."

"Oh." Surprise, but not overt displeasure; that's something, I suppose. After a moment the door opens. Aleksey looks uncharacteristically unkempt, nervous but not annoyed. When he sees me he actually smiles.

"You're looking well," he says, and I think he means it. But he doesn't invite me inside.

"I'm doing better, thank you." I'm asked so often the lie has become reflexive. "I'm sorry to bother you at home, but I had a request today."

"It's not a bother," he says, but he still doesn't invite me in. "From the Third Block?"

I nod, and his lips thin.

"It's been a struggle," he confesses, and his vulnerability catches me off-guard. "I've tried sending more of my officers, or even different ones, and I can't seem to get them to trust us. It always ends in fighting, and that gets tired. Even for me."

The flash of self-knowledge is a surprise as well. "I'm not sure what will work there," I say. He and I both know the Third Block

has been an issue since long before either of us became peace officers. "But Mathilda Pederson has made a specific request. She'd
like you there, and she'd like you to listen to them."

He frowns, just a little, and I'm reminded of all the things
Aleksey's never been good at. "I'm not sure how that will keep
them from fighting."

"It's not a matter of that." He wants to fix the block, and there's
no way to do that when they don't believe it's broken. I try to
remember how I used to advise him, the lessons I gave him that
he always ignored. "They need another release valve. They argue
with each other until there's nothing left but fists. All you need
to do is answer their questions and let them talk. They won't stop
fighting," I tell him, before he has a chance to point it out, "but it
will distract them. It might distract them long enough to move on
to the next thing."

He looks away at that. "I can't tell them much," he says, and
his voice has grown quiet. "The things they worry about—they're
mad. Still thinking *Hypatia* is alien, half of them. The others thinking they're here to make us all some kind of genetic monsters. And
Yulia—" He stops, and looks back at me. "She feels...strongly...
about the strangers."

I open my mouth to parrot what I know to him, that Yulia is
protective of her people, and that if she sometimes goes too far it's
in aid of keeping us safe. But before I can speak I hear a door close
in the background, and a quick footstep. Instinctively, Aleksey
moves himself into the doorway to block my view.

What an odd thing for him to be modest about. "I'm sorry," I
say. "I should have called first."

"That's all right," he says, and he's looking at me intently, as
if waiting for some response I haven't made yet. "But if you could
be discreet about this, I'd be grateful."

"Of course." Why would he feel the need to ask? His social
life is none of my business, or anyone else's; more often than not,

by the time one of his relationships becomes public enough for gossip, it's over.

And then I remember, and my eyes widen, and he slips into the hallway, pulling the door closed behind him.

"I'll tell Yulia," he says, in a low voice. "Soon. I promise. It's just—Hina doesn't understand about her, not really. I'm sure you found the same with Maddie."

Maddie had been entirely out of her depth with Yulia. Apparently I'd been as well. I wonder if Maddie knows about this, if she approves, if it matters. Their mores are so different from ours. Maddie's anger would be different than Yulia's. Aleksey wouldn't stand a chance against either of them.

"I won't say anything," I promise, and he looks far more relieved than he ought to. "But Aleksey—don't wait. People trust Yulia, and they talk to her. It's one thing for them to know you're smitten. It's another for them to understand it's gone this far."

"Just a few more days," he says. "A week, at the outside. I'll figure out what to say to Yulia."

I leave him and head home. I'm not sure what to think of this bond between by-the-book Aleksey and one of the strangers, a connection so unlikely Yulia wouldn't even have thought to forbid it. I wonder if there is more to it for him than novelty, more for her than hormones. She would be woefully naive. He would know nothing of her world at all.

Somewhere inside myself I feel a glimmer of hope for them, and it glows in my stomach all the way home, a tiny, unlikely light in the heavy fog.

RECIP: National Earth Space Organization, Vostochny
REPORTER: Loineau, Madeleine, Cmdr. NZKO *Hypatia*
Mission year 40, day 140

Swallowing nails in front of Orlova turned out to be worth it. More or less. For the last eight days, the fabrication problems have been minimal.

Kano's outside, building out the orbital adjustment system. Ratana's new design calls for the transceiver to be able to move itself to compensate for the planet's wobble, and to avoid stray solar bursts. We still haven't solved all of the reliability issues, but Ratana's still working on it. She says there's always

That was what Qara calls a glitch, which is her word for when the internal power regulator cuts out in the midst of rerouting the power outside. It doesn't happen every time, and I'm assured it's normal, so, okay, I'm fine with this. Because having the lights and the air and *everything else* abruptly cutting out at random moments, even for a second or two, is somehow not supposed to make me jittery *at all.*

A year of this, Vostochny. There's got to be a way to speed it up.

Kano's been carping at me to talk to Anya. He says I've been irritable. He says if I could have a civilized discussion with Yulia fucking Orlova, I can manage to talk to a woman who was starting to mean something to me. I told him to mind his own fucking business, which is something I do a lot these days.

I haven't told him I've been trying.

A couple of nights ago, I sent a signal at the time we used to talk. Just "are you there" or something equally inane. No response. No sign anybody was even tuned into the same frequency, not that I could tell, because I don't think there's a way to tell, not really, unless she's transmitting. I set up an alarm so *Hypatia* would wake me up if anything at all came over that frequency: nothing. So at least it's not just me she's not talking to.

I started thinking, though, about what Orlova said, and how vague the word *indisposed* really is.

Why am I worried, Vostochny? Not only is she a grown woman, not only was she complicit in that execution, but I haven't known her two months. Why do I feel like I should be taking better care of her, like I shouldn't have frozen her out like I did? What does she care?

What do I?

Kano was right: I was charmed by Anya. I felt, for the first time, like someone might understand how my strange little mind works. There were so many things I didn't feel like I had to explain to her, and that's part of why I was so mad when she did what she did. I assumed, with all the death she'd seen, she'd value life more...but maybe it made her that much less sympathetic to someone like Rolf, who took a life for some ego-driven bullshit reason. Couldn't I have at least listened to her side of it?

Hang on a minute, Vostochny. I have to apologize to Kano.

Bastard made me do it through Qara, of *course*, because even when I'm groveling he has to be a pain in my ass. But after I told her to tell him I'm sorry, and she said he wanted to know for what, and I said for being stubborn and obstructionist, he got on the line and said, "You lack self-awareness, Mads, you know that?" And I told him to fuck off again, but this time he laughed. So I think I'm okay with Kano, at least. I haven't destroyed *every* significant relationship in my life.

She *is* significant.

She was.

RECIP: National Earth Space Organization, Vostochny
REPORTER: Loineau, Madeleine, Cmdr. NZKO *Hypatia*
Mission year 40, day 147

Tell me about iterative fine fabrication, Vostochny. Are these chronic problems always part of the deal? Even after everyone says they're really, for sure, going to fix them?

Seung says it's not so much a problem of quality, but of consistency. "Some of what they send us is absolutely solid," he told me, "but one in ten or one in twenty just falls apart as soon as you put any stress on it, so we have to test all of them."

He wants to take Hina and go down for a couple of days, observe the fab process, see where the weak points might be, advise them on how to improve things. I'd rather send Kano, frankly. Seung's good enough at keeping an eye on Hina, and he tells me she and Aleksey have been spending all their time in public. But he's insufficiently disapproving for my taste, and you're damn right I'm overprotective, Vostochny, what is your point?

Besides that, Kano's much less worried about what people think of him. The Novayarkhans aren't overtly hostile anymore—most of them, anyway—but warmth and friendliness are still hard to come by, and Kano doesn't give a damn about warmth and friendliness.

He's also the one who's been spacewalking—who's out there right now—doing the same job over and over again when we don't get what we need.

I'm getting a lot of practice being polite to Orlova. But it's worth it, Vostochny. Right? Three months ago we had nothing but a pack of rivets and some sheet metal, and a design that wasn't going to work. Now we've got a place that can actually build us precision parts, and I've got no business complaining because they're not perfect.

I don't like how dependent on them we've become.

Hina's been emphasizing, every time, that it doesn't hurt to make friends down there, given everything. Her murderous boyfriend notwithstanding, she's not wrong. I've been thinking Divya should go down again and cultivate her observatory friends. We still get the friendliest reception from Lev and his team, and that's down to her genuine enthusiasm. The astronomers seem to be the sorts of people who do their work because they love it, and I think they enjoy having someone who likes to hear about what they're doing.

If I ever have to raise an army to defend *Hypatia* against Orlova, I'm going to start with the observatory staff. And won't that be a battle, Vostochny? Orlova and her steely-eyed, gun-toting cops throwing people onto the surface, and me with a pack of scientists waving lenses at her and shouting "But Einstein

NZKO *HYPATIA*
CREW DELTA REPORT
================================
UNREGISTERED CREW ABSENCE
TELEMETRY LOST: 1
CREW COMPLEMENT: 25% REDUCTION 4%

CREW COMPLEMENT REDUCTION EXCEEDS TOLERANCE
ERROR EVENT LOGGED
================================

CREW DELTA REPORT COMPLETE

RECIP: National Earth Space Organization, Vostochny
REPORTER: Loineau, Madeleine, Cmdr. NZKO *Hypatia*
Supplemental

NO NO NO NO NO NO NO NO NO NO NO NO NO NO NO
NO IT'S NOT I WON'T NO NO NO NO TAKE IT BACK TAKE
IT BACK TAKE IT FUCK YOU VOSTOCHNY FUCK YOU FUCK
YOU THIS IS YOU THIS IS ALL YOU MONSTERS MONSTERS
MONSTERS FUCK YOU I CAN'T I WON'T NO NO NO NO NO
NO NO

RECIP: National Earth Space Organization, Vostochny
REPORTER: Loineau, Madeleine, Cmdr. NZKO *Hypatia*
Mission year 40, day 148

Kano's dead.
You did this, Vostochny.
I did this.

RECIP: National Earth Space Organization, Vostochny
REPORTER: Loineau, Madeleine, Cmdr. NZKO *Hypatia*
Mission year 40, day 149

The Colonel is watching me write this.

He thinks I have to do it. For my own fucking mental health.

On some level, I know he's right, because I remember. I remember, Vostochny, after the accident twenty years ago, after everyone else died. I remember the importance of rote tasks. I remember that I was the first one who was able to do anything productive. Intellectually, I know all of that helped, that eventually the pain and horror and numbness wore off and I learned how to feel again. I even had some good days, now and then.

I don't think that's going to happen this time.

There's not a lot of wreckage for us to look at, but Ratana says her best guess at cause is the thruster system. That's what she's in the middle of dissecting, but she says it'll take her a few days to scan all the bits she's got left. It had been fussy all week, but nothing that looked dangerous. Kano went out to take it apart so we could retest the pieces. While he was out there...Ratana says it was fast. She saw the red light, and she said to him "Watch it, it's getting hot again," and he said "At least the thing's keeping its thermal mass," and then instead of just heating up it spiked, and the whole section blew.

Kano was holding the main thruster cell in his hand when it happened.

I saw the flare through the window just as the power cut out, and as soon as the generator kicked in Ratana was calling me, frantic. I ran down, thinking about getting into my suit, going out there, bringing him in, taking care of him; I don't have to do much medic stuff anymore, but I remember it, and for Kano, I would do anything, I would bleed for him, I would let myself get blown up in his place. But I got down there, and Léon and Qara were there already, and Léon had their arms around Ratana and she was screaming, and Hina came in behind me and made this...sound. Because there were pieces—his boot, his glove, the shield from his helmet, shards of flesh and bone, although you'd have thought that close he'd have been pulverized into atoms, but he wasn't. And we could all see them, and Kano was dead and I kind of went crazy, Vostochny.

I think I still am.

The bit after that is fuzzy. Léon says I started howling, and I sort of remember that. I had it in my head that if I could shout loud enough and long enough that I could somehow reverse time and undo it all. Force of will: I just needed to demonstrate my sincerity. And they all put their arms around me, and I guess I started struggling, and then I heard the Colonel's voice behind me saying "Let her go, let her go," in that fucking awful cheerful tone, and after that I was just railing at the universe, I think.

We brought in as much debris as we could. They all wanted me to stay away, said they could take care of it; but I'm the closest thing we've got to a doctor. Or a coroner. What good am I if I can't take care of what's left of someone I love? I sorted through everything and separated out what was organic. It was nowhere near all of him, so some of him *was* pulverized into atoms, or is currently flying through space unimpeded in random directions. But there was most of one leg, and fragments of skull, and a lot of pieces of bone I probably could have identified if I'd taken the time.

Nothing that looked like him. Nothing at all. I should have been grateful for that, Vostochny. Shouldn't I?

I weighed and I measured and I made useless notes about his remains, and I entered a cause of death: *precision, contained destruction.* It didn't matter. It doesn't matter. I took everything I had of him and put it in a box, because you prepared us for this, too, Vostochny. The box was made to be a crematory urn, but we didn't have to cremate him to have him fit.

"Where do we bury him?" Hina asked me.

She's been crying since it happened, always quietly, like she doesn't want to bother anybody. She's also been on the radio, and I know what I've said about Aleksey, Vostochny, but I'm not going to cut her off from a sympathetic ear. All the others died when she was five. This is the first loss she's known as an adult, but she remembers. And I don't think it makes it any easier for the rest of us that we'd seen death as adults. This is the first time any of us have lost Kano.

"That asteroid, I think," I told her. "The one he blew up for us after we decided not to destroy the planet."

She smiled at that. "That would make him happy."

Which is ludicrous, of course. Nothing will make him happy, because he's dead, and there's no happiness for him anymore.

We left the wreckage of the transceiver in orbit and flew away from the planet to the last asteroid Kano had spiked. Hina took a piece of the rock he'd given her and put it in the box with him. Ratana put in a small memory stick on which she'd recorded something she wouldn't share with any of us. Léon added a lock of hair. The rest of us took a moment to rest our hands on the top of the box.

And then I suited up, and I carried him outside, and I found a crevice in the asteroid fragments that looked as if it were made for this purpose. And I tucked what was left of Kano into that little space, and I stayed with him until my oxygen ran low and I had to go back to *Hypatia*.

CHAPTER TWENTY-THREE

Costa has been busy composing a new exam for his graduating students, so to humor him I've made myself sit in public in the Hub kitchens over breakfast, huddled mostly undisturbed in a corner. I watch these people, whom I've known all my life, and sometimes familiarity allows me to forget the mob they became. It's soothing, after a fashion, this fantasy of a past that never was, and most mornings I can get through it without the aftertaste of bitterness.

Today something is changed: Aleksey is here, when he should not be. He's been working second shift, retiring well into second daylight; a first sunrise breakfast has not been his routine. And yet here he is, harried and preoccupied in the tea queue, so distracted he doesn't even hear Tomas Karoli's repeated, persistent greetings.

It's none of my business. But I've done the job Aleksey has been doing, and my belief that I should still be doing it has nothing to do with the burden he's been asked to bear.

I reach the tea queue just as Aleksey gets to the front. He's pouring from the oldest pot, the liquid dark, bitter, and close to tasteless: the select brew of the chronically sleep-deprived. Indeed, there are deep circles under his eyes, and I hope it's only lack of sleep that's causing them.

"Aleksey?" I say.

He starts, and his tea sloshes over the top of the cup. I reach for a cloth from the stack, and he says "I'm sorry, Anya," as I wipe off the counter.

"Don't be silly," I tell him. "I'm the one who startled you." I blot up the last of the liquid, then look back at him; he's refilled his cup, and his eyes are darting around the room. I'm reminded of Maddie, but she never looked so nervous, so unhappy. "Are you all right?"

He meets my eyes, but it takes him a moment to focus; and then a version of his typical veneer shrouds his expression, and he offers me a smile. "Just busy," he says. "It'll die down in a few days, I'm sure. Once things have settled out."

Which is absurd, of course, because things won't settle out, not in a few days, not ever. There is nothing but change ahead, and the only way things might settle is if *Hypatia* chooses to abandon us entirely.

There is something in his guarded features, and I wonder if they've done just that.

"What do you mean?" I ask.

Realization comes over his face. "You don't know," he says. "They didn't tell you."

I have missed something. *Maddie.* My stomach instantly becomes a hard knot. "Tell me what? What's happened?"

Aleksey moves away from the tea table, and I follow. He turns back to me, grim. "It's Kano. He's been killed in some kind of accident up there."

I feel a flash of relief, and then shame at that; and then grief, a great sadness for a man I barely knew, whose good-humored eyes were the first I saw when Maddie's people came down, who'd been Maddie's confidant, crewmate, family.

She has lost so much, and now this.

Is she up there alone? Does she have anyone to talk to, to grieve with? Anyone who understands loss?

The urgency takes me all at once, and I pat Aleksey's arm as if he's still a child. "I'm sorry, Aleksey," I say, "but there's something I need to do. Please—" He's been kind, telling me all this, and I need to remember to be kind in return. "If there's anything I can do, for you or for Hina, please just ask me." And I turn and flee the Hub before I hear his response.

When did I last try to call her? For weeks we talked all the time, sometimes daily; turning on the transmitter was muscle memory, brewing tea while I waited for her to pick up the line, saying hello to Ratana or that odd, automated voice that would answer sometimes. It was before Rolf, wasn't it? Or was it after he died, before I went looking for him? Hadn't I tried to call her then, had no response? Or had I been too dazed for that, calling out to her without the radio, somehow expecting my spirit to move her from two hundred kilometers away? I have left it too long, never mind her anger, never mind all the lies I told her, not knowing they were lies. She's suffering up there, and she doesn't need me, I know she doesn't, but I need to let her know she's not abandoned, that I haven't left her to this.

I head across the inner courtyard. We had snow two sunsets ago, and it's firm and dry and crunchy and my feet find easy traction. I run to the Outer Rim airlock in the early first sunrise glow, and I'm home less than ten minutes after my conversation with Aleksey.

My transmitter isn't on the counter. I would have put it away, of course, after Rolf, tucked it back under the sink so I didn't see it every day, have it there reminding me. But it's not there either; there's the wrench I keep for the times the sink leaks, a stone bowl to catch drips, a fine layer of dust from the ore processing vents, and we shouldn't be breathing it, should be worrying as much about that as the radiation. I remove the wrench, the bowl, rummage in the dark corners, and then I head to my bedroom, to the desk drawers that hold nothing but six blank slates and a drawing of Irina that Costa did on a fragile sheet of bamboo paper. I dig in the back of the drawers, finding old pieces of stylus, thin chips of slate knocked off old documents, vestiges of oils used to lubricate my tools. My fingers come out chalky and shiny, but there's nothing, no transmitter, no copper wire, no sign it's ever been here at all.

I was asleep at Costa's house for days.

Costa still has one.

I leave the clutter and head out the door, catching a tram across the arc toward the prison. Ayanna Kassikov and Brae Pasternas are riding as well, sitting behind me on the bench as I peer impatiently into the corridor before us; they're whispering and giggling, maybe about me, maybe about each other; Costa said the other day he thought they might get married, or maybe that was last year and someone else.

I jump off the tram before it stops and run past the prison toward the end of the Outer Rim. I lean on the buzzer; he has to be home, or I could break in, I left my tools at home but I've fixed his door before and that lower left-hand screw never tightens properly, I could probably open it with my fingers. But he opens the door, and he looks harried and worried and he says "Anya?" and I push past him and head for his work table, scanning the detritus around his contraband scanner.

"I need your transmitter, Costa." It's not on the table. Where does he keep it? When was the last time I saw him radio anybody? He listens, mostly, does Costa, but sometimes his students take field trips on the tundra and he needs to monitor them, and it was in his bedroom, I think, probably tucked under the bed, safe from errant feet. I head into the bedroom, the room where I was confined for so long; a lurch of discomfort, but it disappears, because none of that matters and I need to talk to Maddie.

The transmitter isn't under the bed, and I turn to find Costa in the doorway, looking worried. Something's bothering him, but that doesn't matter now, either. "Where is it?" I ask him. "Is it in your kitchen?"

He holds a hand out and I refrain from pushing past him. "An. Wait. Just wait a minute."

Wait? How can I wait? Kano's been dead for...I didn't ask Aleksey. It might have been days.

Costa is my oldest friend, my childhood companion, my brother, and I can give him a moment when he's so clearly upset.

I inhale, then exhale. "I'm sorry," I tell Costa. "I'm being awfully rude. But I can't find my transmitter, and I have to talk to Maddie. I know she's angry with me. I know she won't want to hear it. But I have to." Costa's lost as many people as I have; he knows equally well how important it is to know people are thinking of you.

"You can't, An."

I parse that phrase. *Can't*. Not *shouldn't*. "Why not?"

He looks miserable, the same way he did when I asked him to come to the crypt with me. "If you contact her," he says, and he won't meet my eyes, "Yulia will have Doctor Halvorsen medicate you again."

Something different than urgency begins to burn in my gut. "You'll tell them."

He looks at me then, and how long have I known him without seeing the defeat that lives in his eyes, the chronic addiction to the status quo? "No. I won't tell them anything. I won't have to. Yulia's been monitoring all the radio broadcasts since you became ill. She...she thinks *Hypatia* made you sick, Anya. She thinks Maddie's interfered with the execution of your duties, and it brought back the wrong memories."

Irina. He means Irina. "It didn't bring back anything," I tell him. I'm shouting; I don't know how to do anything else. "Costa. I have to talk to her. It's family she's lost, don't you understand?"

But he's shouting too, and he does understand, and all of this is feeling very much like the madness. "If you try to contact her, Anya, they'll take you away, and me too, and I will not be able to help you and they'll keep you like you were, you understand?" Fear and anguish in his voice; he's telling me the truth. "They are *afraid* for you. I know you don't think they should be, but they are. And they will do what they must to keep you well."

"But they're not keeping me well." I'm crying now, why I'm not sure. "I owe her this, and they're locking me away like some kind of prisoner?"

Costa puts a hand on my arm, warm, gentle, familiar; he's protecting me as best he can, and I can't lose sight of the fact that if I do this, if I violate Yulia's quarantine, he'll be hurt as well. "We're all prisoners here, Anya," he says quietly, and I remember, then, how sharp and insightful he can be sometimes. I look away, and he drops his hand. "It won't be forever," he tells me, but he's trying to give me hope, not offering me fact. "Their transceiver will go up, and we'll adjust, one way or another. Maybe even sooner than that. They'll just be neighbors, not an alien threat. You'll be able to talk to her then."

Months from now. Longer. "This is wrong, Costa," I declare. "This is wrong and you know it."

This time he takes my hands in his, and he holds them tight. "I know," he says softly. I look back at him, and he squeezes. "When they come back I'll give them a message for Maddie, all right?"

It won't be enough. We have food, water, shelter, but nothing in this place has ever been enough and I feel a sharp longing, a pain as if someone has tied a rope around my heart and is tugging with all their might. I want Maddie. I want Irina. All I have is this empty hollow inside of me.

But when I nod to Costa, accepting his offer, an offer forged from reflexive kindness and self-imposed impotence, something in that hollow starts to burn.

RECIP: National Earth Space Organization, Vostochny
REPORTER: Loineau, Madeleine, Cmdr. NZKO *Hypatia*
Mission year 40, day 158

MOTHERFUCKERS DID THIS ON PURPOSE

ARCHIVE #2351

CAPTAIN'S NOTES
SHIP YEAR 53

LOGGED BY: SASCHA LEBED
B. SHIP YEAR 4
D. SHIP YEAR 55

DIRECTIVE 17 GOVERNMENT USE ONLY
SCHOLARLY ACCESS FORBIDDEN

NOTES FOR MELISSA:

- *Miners.* Double-check those medical numbers. The suits should be insulating them nearly as well as being here on the ship. If they're suffering more radiation damage, maybe something else is going on—genetic predisposition, bad/leaky equipment. Follow up. We need to get a handle on this now. If that kind of mortality goes ship-wide, we're fucked.

- *Carla Miskaya*. It's crazy to allow Yuri's father to decide what's done with her. It was an accident, we're all upset, but we can't go killing everybody that fucks up. Get people calmed down, but for fuck's sake, don't shoot at anybody. We all remember what happened when Simo took a shot in West Wing Medical.

- *Zelfira Zelinsky*. Approve her. I know what Piotr said, but her parentage is 100% frozen portable DNA, and we need to keep that in our gene pool. If we don't proactively seek diversity it'll kill us faster than radiation. Also, reproductive decisions are not going political on my watch. You can tell Piotr I said that. If he assassinates me, I forgive you, but for now he can completely fuck off.

- *Treatments*. Look, I know I'm not a doctor, and I know we can't cure everything with the ingredients we've got. The mission founders knew this. We need to focus on drug development, on analysis, and yes, on breeding people who are more resistant to disease. Genetic manipulation sounds like such a lovely idea, but last I fucking checked, Melissa, one reason cancer has stuck with our happy little species since the beginning of time is that it's clever. I don't want to see us birth genmodded babies that die of, I don't know, an allergy to water, just because we thought fucking with DNA was easier than teaching people to wear gloves properly. Our whole purpose is medical research. This isn't an insurmountable problem.

- *Education*. Teach Earth history. Teach why we left. Don't teach kids that a bunch of their ancestors killed a bunch of their friends' ancestors and stole a ship they didn't know what to do with. We don't need those kinds of divisions, and anybody who wants to be an archivist when they grow up can learn it all then. There are only 117 people left who were alive back then, and the kids have no interest in listening to any of them. It literally does not matter who started this shit. We're stuck with each other now, and I'll be damned if I see us split into nations over what a bunch of angry dead people did before most of us were born.

REBELLION

RECIP: National Earth Space Organization, Vostochny
REPORTER: Loineau, Madeleine, Cmdr. NZKO *Hypatia*
Mission year 40, day 164

Apparently my plan to spike nuke that whole fucking city seemed extreme to the others, because they locked me up for a while. Six whole days, in fact.

When I brought it up, they thought at first I wasn't serious. Qara in particular was vehement on that point.

"Can you knock it the fuck off for once, Maddie?" she snapped, and all that trembling anger was turned toward me. "We need to figure out what we're going to *do*."

It wasn't until I'd gone into the munitions storage and come out with an armful of bombs that they realized I meant it. That's when Qara rolled back her declaration that the ignition sensor had been deliberately rigged to spike. Suddenly it wasn't murder, but carelessness; after all, they've been making "mistakes" in the fabrication for *months*, these people who manage to manufacture parts to keep a 400-year-old chunk of hardware functioning and *are not fucking stupid.*

I'm afraid there was yelling, Vostochny. It's possible I asked repeatedly how they could say they loved Kano and propose sitting here like fucking potted plants and dealing with this by *talking*. I mean, nothing personal, but at this point: *fuck* the transceiver. I've had it with death, I've had it with being nice to fucking Yulia Orlova, I've had it with smiling and nodding when that aging monster is plotting behind my back to carve me into pieces.

Novayarkha's doing all this because they thought they were the last of humanity. Now we're here, and they still think they're the last of humanity *that matters*. Fuck *that* across the fucking galaxy. I've witnessed two murders since we've arrived. There's no moral high ground for them to claim.

We're doomed. We're lost. We were never getting home, anyway. The only one of us young enough to survive the trip back doesn't consider Earth her home at all. Those colonists? They fell in love with their own righteousness and couldn't even see it when it started eating them from within. We'd be doing them a favor, really.

Does that sound angry? Vengeful?

Does that make it wrong?

Léon and Divya pinned me while Seung packed the nukes away again and changed the code on munitions locker. I was...not gracious about this. I may have said some genuinely unforgivable things. They actually locked me in my room, and for six days, stuck with nothing but prefab meals from my cabinet, I hated them all.

When they finally sent someone, they sent the Colonel. Of course. Not someone who could force me to stay in the room if I wanted to leave. Just someone thoughtful and perceptive, who'd had a whole life—different friends, different family, different *everything*—before he elected to ally himself with humanity's latest bullshit impossible journey.

I've asked him, now and then, what his life was like before, and he hasn't told me much. But as he sat there in my doorway, not speaking, not typing, it occurred to me that he's probably seen more death than I have. I remember telling Anya about Earth, about everything I've been taught but have never seen.

Why haven't I ever asked him what it was really like?

I'm still not sure what I thought he'd say to me. Maybe some lecture about how killing is never the answer, we need to control our tempers, we still need those fucking parts—some logical fucking bullshit about a duty to the ones we'd left behind.

Not what he did say.

"I miss him."

Three little words on that screen of his, and I fell apart completely, and somehow having him sit with me while I cried was more comforting than having someone actually hug me.

Then we talked for a long time, first about Kano, and then about all of us: his generation, mine, Hina's, everyone we've lost. And eventually I said to him, "I can't do this anymore."

"None of us can," he said. "But we have to anyway."

They let me out after that. They left me in charge, and I don't know why. I'm burned out and hollow. I have no heart left.

None of us do.

We're all shattered, all fragments of what we were. And I don't think we really care about the transceiver anymore, except it's our job and our whole lives and dammit, I'm enough of an idealist to believe that maybe, just maybe, it'll make the future I'll never see a little better than it might otherwise be.

But between you and me, Vostochny—there's still a part of me that wishes they hadn't stopped me, that I'd set those bombs around the city's perimeter, taken them apart the way they took him apart. It's not that I want to kill anyone, not really. I just want them to understand what it is they've done to us.

If vengeance fixes nothing, why is it considered the purview of gods?

RECIP: National Earth Space Organization, Vostochny
REPORTER: Loineau, Madeleine, Cmdr. NZKO *Hypatia*
Supplemental

We all sat together when I called Governor Orlova.

I used the original radio frequency, the one where we'd picked up Tamara's news report. If Orlova asked, I'd tell her distress had made me forget our dedicated channel. She couldn't possibly object to the entire city being able to hear what we had to say to each other.

And I wanted them to hear it. Every one of them.

"I'm sorry to bother you, Governor," My voice caught, just a little; effective, and I hadn't even done it on purpose. "We've had an accident up here."

Orlova immediately went into concerned bystander mode. "I have heard," she said.

I completely avoided looking at Hina. We locked down the radio after Ratana discovered the sabotage, and I know Hina's resented the implication. But even if Aleksey's as pure as the driven snow on this, we couldn't afford him telling his boss what we were suspecting.

Would've loved to see Orlova react to my armful of spike nukes, though.

"I'm so very, very sorry," she continued. "He seemed kind, your Kano. What is it we can we do to help?"

That fucking sincerity again. I looked around at the others, and we all had pretty much the same reaction: if she was acting, she was really good at it. She sounded like a woman who had watched people die—year after year, many of them children—and never let go of the sorrow of it. It would have been so easy to be seduced by that voice, that spontaneous kindness from a stranger.

I thought about putting bits of Kano in a box.

"We'd like to take a closer look at the tolerance testing that's happening for parts," I told her.

"Surely—oh, Captain. Did we cause this death?"

At that I saw Qara's jaw set, and Seung turned away. Sincerity or not, she was pushing it. "A faulty part is an accident, Governor," I told her. We'd agreed on how we'd handle feigned ignorance, but the artificial absolution still stuck in my throat. "We're still trying to figure out the details. Mostly we want to double-check our own notes. Would you object to Hina and Seung spending a few days there?"

"Of course not, Captain." No hesitation at all, but Seung still wouldn't look at me. "I'll have someone meet them."

There was a pause as we waited for her customary perfunctory dismissal, but it didn't come.

"Captain Loineau—I may be overstepping here. But if you wish...we have a place here set aside for our dead, where they rest, side by side, all together. We would be honored to have your dead lie next to ours."

For a moment I was too astonished to speak. "You're very kind, Governor," I told her, and I didn't have to act that time. "But we've made accommodations already."

"Very well. I will await your people. And Captain—please let your crew know that our hearts are with you all. If there is anything we can do to help, you need only ask."

Hina and Seung are flying down now, and I can't get the conversation out of my head. The Colonel is telling me she's just a good actress, that I shouldn't absolve her of anything. But he hasn't met her, Vostochny. He hasn't spoken to her face to face, listened as she spoke of Earth with contempt, of us with mistrust. Offering to bury Kano with her own people—that cost her. For real. I think her shock was genuine. I think her grief is genuine.

I don't know what to think about these people anymore.

RECIP: National Earth Space Organization, Vostochny
REPORTER: Loineau, Madeleine, Cmdr. NZKO *Hypatia*
Mission year 40, day 171

We wouldn't even have known until afterward, but the Colonel was tuned into the radio, waiting for Hina and Seung to check in, when Novayarkha wide-banded a broadcast:

Alert! Alert! Exile incursion in progress! Lock all doors and shelter in place! Do not engage with the enemy! Alert!

After the message looped twice, all of the radio frequencies went dead. Every fucking one of them.

Let me tell you, Vostochny, that made me very, very unhappy.

"How do we get ahold of them?" I asked the Colonel, and I paced in front of him until he told me aloud to knock it off.

"We can't, Maddie," he typed. "With nothing but radio, they can't call us until the city starts broadcasting again."

"That's a completely stupid system," I fumed.

"It's only a stupid system if you need to call a ship in orbit," he pointed out, "and they've never had a need for that."

I swore for a while, and called them barbarians and primitives and regressives, and the Colonel reminded me that waiting was sometimes a thing that had to happen. Fuck waiting, Vostochny. There are things that I'm good at, but waiting is not anywhere close to being on that list, and all I could think of was that clumsy Exile with the gun pointed at Maria and how Hina has no idea how to fight.

It was twenty whole minutes before the radio started broadcasting again, this time with the same all clear I'd heard from Yulia the last time. And then the hourly news report started, just a few minutes late, and the damned incursion wasn't even the top headline. Took them nearly five minutes to get to it.

Not half an hour ago, we were subjected to an attack by the Exiles. Minimal damage has been reported by the medical center, but our internal airlock system was not breached. Please contact your block mayor if you find damage or missing items. In agriculture news—

And that was it.

Anya had said they weren't so frequent—two, maybe three in a year. Nine weeks since the last one seems like way too soon. Given that they hit the medical center again, I figure Anya and I chased them off without something they needed.

When I was down there during the first attack, watching everyone run scared, seeing Maria shaking in the face of someone who certainly seemed determined to kill her, I had a very specific set of sympathies. Now—I wonder, Vostochny, how much of what I've heard of the Exiles is Orlova's one-sided bullshit?

I wonder, if we contacted them—what do you suppose we might learn?

CHAPTER TWENTY-FOUR

WHEN I WAS A CHILD, EXILE RAIDS WERE ALWAYS THE SAME. WE'D BE IN school, or—if they hit during second sunrise—playing games in the Eastern Arc, or even outside in the courtyard if the weather was fine. The alarm would sound, and we'd all rush to one of the big, interior rooms, usually the Hub or Frida Koslova's two-bedroom Inner Rim suite. The adults would huddle in groups, whispering, but we'd all keep playing, albeit more quietly. Costa and I would do codebreaking, trading encrypted messages with each other and seeing if we could stump the other. Sometimes the governor would issue the all-clear before we were finished, and I'd always be disappointed.

I left school at sixteen to dig in the quarry, and after that raids were different. We'd all go to the observation room while guards were put on the explosive stores. When I asked why they weren't guarding the stone, Aleksandra, the blasting coordinator, gave me an incredulous look. "Wherever the Exiles live, they've got their own stone," she said. "We have to make sure we don't make it easier for them to get to it."

At the time, I found her explanation completely logical.

The Third Block, I have learned, handles Exile raids somewhat differently. They do the obligatory counting of heads to report to Dmitri, but once everyone is accounted for, they all adjourn to Anabelle Yeshnikova's single-room house, sitting on the floor and the couch and her perpetually-unmade bed while she keeps the kettle on and produces a suspiciously bottomless supply of fried sugar beets to keep everyone's energy up. Cross-legged on the floor in the corner, I watch them all, letting idle conversation wash over me, wondering why none of them seem frightened. They're all reacting the way Costa and I did: like they've been given a break in the middle of a long day, a time to relax and be idle and socialize if they're so inclined.

They leave me to myself, as people always do, but here I don't feel excluded or isolated Here I feel...still. As close to tranquil as I've felt since my illness.

Five minutes in the all-clear message plays, but while a few people say their goodbyes and leave, most of the crowd remains, sipping tea and watching the younger children milling about the room. Mathilda approaches me, a sleeping infant in her arms, and sits down next to me. I look at the baby; it's dark-skinned and scrunchy-faced, and I don't know whose it is.

"Is that a crèche baby?" I ask.

Mathilda shakes her head. "It's Camina Porokova's little one," she tells me.

Camina recently returned to the quarry, at her own request. Her son was born early, Yulia had told me; healthy, but needy. "He's looking well," I say, and he is: he's little for a child of three months, but his color is good and he has a round face and solid arms. "You're looking after him?"

"Today," she says. "Camina should be sleeping, really, but you know her. The quarry makes her happy, and she does her best to stay happy with him. Which shows, you know. I don't think I've seen such a happy baby in—oh, twenty years?" She gives me a look that makes me wonder if she can read my mind. "Would you like to hold him?"

"I don't want to wake him," I tell her, but I'm already holding out my arms.

He's light, Camina's little one, but he's warm and solid, and he shifts to snuggle against me as I pull him close. "What did she call you again?" I ask him. "Stanislav? A big name for a small one. I think you'll grow into it, though." I'm smiling at him; it's involuntary, but he's a thing of beauty and I can't stop. "What does Doctor Halvorsen say?" I ask Mathilda.

She sniffs. "She says it's too soon to tell. She wants to see how he grows. As if it isn't obvious, how healthy he is. The healthiest preemie I've seen, and you know how many we get in this block. She should mark his genome favored just for that."

"Perhaps he'll be exceptional," I say, rocking him gently, that habit I picked up with Irina and never really lost. "Smart, handsome, good-natured. Perhaps even Doctor Halvorsen will be persuaded to include him for Selection."

"Eh, you're an optimist, Anya," Mathilda says, and I almost laugh out loud.

She sits with me, chattering idly about the children in her block, about the spate of miscarriages that finally seems to be ebbing, until Stanislav wakes up, fussy and starving. Reluctantly I let her take him away. Babies are much like the infrequent weddings we have: a symbol of optimism in a dark and hostile world, and holding him has given me a much-needed break from my bleak thoughts.

We hear the shouts in the corridor before the banging on the door begins, and abruptly everyone is on their feet, alarmed, moving to the far side of the room. I get up as well, instinctively placing myself in front of them, and I hear a familiar voice:

"This is Katerina Eritrova! I am a peace officer! Open the door!"

Did I sound so aggressive, when it was me?

Mathilda is at my right hand, no longer holding the baby. "What is it about, Anya?" she asks, and abruptly I'm the authority in the room. But I don't know what's happening. This protocol is for urgent crimes, pursuit of criminals or stopping something about to happen.

"Katerina," I shout, "it's Anya. I'm going to let you in. No one will harm you."

The others huddle behind me, more silent than I've ever heard them, and I walk to the door and open it. One look at the worry and chagrin on Katerina's face brings relief, and then a gut-clenching anxiety. "What is it?" I ask her.

"I need to search this home," she says, loud enough for the others to hear, but she keeps her eyes on me. "Someone's gone missing."

But she doesn't tell me who, and her expression takes on a silent entreaty. I give her a quiet nod, and turn to the others. "It's all right," I tell them. "She's looking for someone. She won't hurt you or damage your things."

And in fact she doesn't; she's come alone, which is strange as well, and she makes her search with care and efficiency. The others are very still, and belatedly I notice the gun at Katerina's hip, undoubtedly issued for the raid. Under ordinary circumstances, she'd have turned it in by now. She'd have turned it in minutes after the raid was concluded.

Something has gone wrong.

When Katerina finishes she turns to Anabelle, and says "Thank you." Her eyes sweep over the group. "All of you," she adds. "I'm sorry to have bothered you." She catches my eye on the way out, and I follow her through the door.

She stops a few meters down the corridor, where no one in Anabelle's home will be able to hear us. "Were you with them for the whole raid?" she asks.

I nod. "We were locked up tight not three minutes after the alarm went off, and nobody left until well after the all-clear. Katerina. What's happening? Where's Aleksey?"

Her lips tighten. "Getting chewed out by Yulia," she says. "But he'll be out all night doing just this: searching homes. These people...they like you. Do you think you can explain we'll probably have to come back?"

Surely if she was looking for someone, that would be the worst thing she could do. "I'll tell them. But Katerina—who did we lose?"

"We didn't lose anybody," she says grimly. "It was one of the aliens. Yulia's furious; she thinks the woman's in hiding, trying to infiltrate."

It has to be Maddie; none of the others would do anything so foolish. "But you don't think so?" I press.

"I was in the medical center during the raid," Katerina said. "There were witnesses. Three, four people who all saw her taken away by the Exiles."

All of this sounds like madness. "If she was taken by Exiles— Katerina, why are you searching the city?"

"Because," she says, "it was Hina Tadeshi. And Yulia is convinced she's been cozying up to Aleksey to act as a spy."

RECIP: National Earth Space Organization, Vostochny
REPORTER: Loineau, Madeleine, Cmdr. NZKO *Hypatia*
Supplemental

Seung just sent a message just a few minutes ago, on the private frequency I used to use with Anya.

"Maddie. You need to come down. You need to help us. That attack—they took her. They took Hina. She's gone, Maddie, and you need to come down and find her."

Enough's enough, Vostochny.

RECIP: National Earth Space Organization, Vostochny
REPORTER: Loineau, Madeleine, Cmdr. NZKO *Hypatia*
Supplemental

It took far too long to get the story out of Seung. He was with her, he says, when the alarm went off—he'd met up with her and Aleksey after lunch, and they were heading back to the monitoring room—and they followed Aleksey to the med center, the same way I'd followed Anya. Seung got lost in the crowd, and knew nothing until after the all-clear, when Aleksey came to him, frantically looking for Hina. Aleksey says they got separated in the confusion, and he didn't see her after that, but Seung says more than a few people say she was grabbed by the raiders.

They did damage this time, apparently. That med center airlock is a wreck, and the whole area is sealed off. But even so, Seung says Hina's everyone's top priority. Aleksey's been searching the city, and whatever I may think of his imagination, he knows the architecture of the place.

Which doesn't help if she's been taken out of Novayarkha.

Orlova's furious. She keeps accusing Seung of hiding Hina, of infiltrating their pure society and corrupting them, or some such nonsense. She gets very scattershot with the insults when she loses her temper, and that's what's convinced Seung she knows as little as we do about what's happened. He says he had to yell himself to convince her there was no conspiracy here, and that maybe we should stop fighting each other and figure out where Hina's gone.

Interesting that after years of Orlova scapegoating the Exiles, she's so astonished to think they might actually kidnap someone. What her reaction implies I don't have any way of knowing.

But I know someone who does.

I went to the Colonel first, and I did what he'd done for me: I sat with him, silent, until he was ready to speak.

"You need to find her," he typed.

"I will." I promised, even though we both knew I couldn't promise a fucking thing. And then I asked him what I should have asked him months ago: "Colonel. Do you know why we're here, at this star, in this location? Do you remember anything at all?"

"I've tried," he told me. "After the accident—you know about the short-term memory loss. But I lost a lot of what came before that, too. I'm sure Vostochny chose this location for a reason, but I don't remember what it was."

"You may never have known," I pointed out. "You were an accountant."

"Don't make excuses for me. Hina's gone."

"She's *missing*, Colonel."

"We've misunderstood them at every step." This he says out loud.

"*You* haven't," I tell him. "*I* have. I won't anymore."

I looked at him, that expressionless face. About fifteen years ago I realized he was handsome, had probably been strikingly so in his youth, long before I knew him. I wonder if he remembers what led a smart, good-looking, decidedly unmilitary military man to dust off his feet and leave his planet behind. I wonder who he was before we all came to depend on him, before the accident made him depend on us.

"I don't think you've misunderstood all of them, Maddie," he typed.

Oh, Vostochny. I hope to all the Deities you've got that he's right.

CHAPTER TWENTY-FIVE

I FIND ALEKSEY OUTSIDE, IN THE QUARRY, CLIMBING THE PERIMETER SCAF-
folds, his gloved hands probing the rock. I have to call to him twice
before he stops and looks down at me; when he makes his way
down to the quarry floor, I can see enough of his face through the
helmet to guess he hasn't slept since the raid.

"It's been two sunsets, Aleksey," I tell him. "You need rest."

He turns away from me. "I can't. Yulia—" He makes a frustrated sound. "I want to go out on the ice to look for her, but Yulia
won't risk losing anyone. She's got this absurd idea Hina's here,
hiding, so I'm stuck digging through stone for secret rooms and
searching the crypt and the hydroponics level." He shakes his head.
"We're running out of time, Anya."

If Hina's on the ice, we're out of time entirely, have been out of
time since ten minutes after she was lost. "You don't really think
the Exiles have her."

He turns back to me; his eyes are wide, desperate. "She
wouldn't hide from me, Anya. From Yulia? Oh, yes." He sounds as
bitter as I've so often felt. "But not me. It's got to be the Exiles. It
has to be. That's the only answer." And he turns away and climbs
the scaffold again.

It's disorienting, feeling sorry for Aleksey.

Katerina is the one organized enough to give me a grid to cover, and I knock on doors throughout the Inner Rim, apologizing to everyone as I kneel to look under beds and disrupt their closets. The only person who won't let me in is Lauren, and I make a note for Katerina that perhaps someone else would be able to get Lauren to relent.

It's nearly second sunset when I head home, taking far too late the advice I'd given Aleksey. He's right: it's futile to search the city, and it's only Yulia's blindness that makes her insist. But he's wrong, too. The Exiles don't have Hina. It's his inexperience, along with his fear and his love for her, that have made him forget how entrenched rumors of Exile kidnappings are in our lore. He can't admit what's really happened: Hina, caught in the chaos of an unexpected raid, panicked and found herself on the wrong side of an airlock. We teach our children from the moment they can get away from us, but she wouldn't know, has no experience of outside, would so easily become disoriented.

For a moment it's all too much, her and Tamara and Rolf and Irina and Maddie, and I consider, just for a moment, taking a turn to the end of the arc and stepping out the airlock myself. But surely there's work left to do somewhere, and perhaps on the other side of this unrelenting raft of tragedies, I'll find it.

I hear the familiar footfall before he speaks.

"Anya?"

I stop, entirely depleted. "Costa. I'm sorry I can't—" I turn around.

Maddie's with him.

She looks thin and tired and desperate and sad and something sparks in my chest, the cavernous ache of the loss of everything I thought I knew flaring in a blinding flash of longing, regret, sorrow, hope.

I open my mouth, no idea where to begin, but she speaks first. "I'm sorry. I'm so sorry, Anya. I should have answered you. I should have looked for you a long time ago."

Something cold in my veins, some leaden poison I've been carrying, melts into warmth and color, and when I take a breath the tightness that's dominated my chest is entirely gone. "Maddie," I begin, and then something comes out of me, something larger and louder than I could possibly contain, and then I'm sobbing and I move forward and she catches me and it all pours out of me, vast and overwhelming, and I weep and weep and Maddie holds me and endures it and doesn't leave me.

When I'm done crying, she takes a step back, her hands sliding down my arms to take my fingers. "It's not fair of me," she says. "Not like this. But Anya...I need your help. Hina's gone, and nobody will listen to me."

And just like that, my work has found me.

CHAPTER TWENTY-SIX

"I STARTED WITH ORLOVA," MADDIE SAYS. SHE'S HOLDING ONE OF MY old stone cups, and the tea Costa poured her is steaming, but she's not drinking it. "I didn't manage to convince her I hadn't set up Hina as some kind of weird-ass sleeper agent, but I can't object to her having the city thoroughly searched. What I don't understand is why nobody is listening to me about the Exiles."

Somewhere inside I know I'm still exhausted, but Maddie's voice, her face, her presence here on my couch, have given me clarity I've been missing for months. "It's not that nobody's listening, Maddie," I explain. "It's that we've all grown up with them, and kidnapping just isn't something that happens. It's a children's story."

She puts the cup down on the table untouched. "I've heard people," she says, and through her fear I hear a comforting hint of familiar obstinance. "They all talk about kidnappings. The disappearances. You've told me yourself, Anya. People go missing."

"Not often." She needs gentleness now, while she's still grappling with reality. "And the ones I've investigated? I told you. Miscarriages, losing loved ones—they are likely to have been suicides."

"But they're not Hina." She gets to her feet and starts pacing, and I'd forgotten how impossible it is for her to keep still. "Please. Anya. I'm not stupid. I've—" She swallows, and I want to put my arms around her again. "Kano's not the first crew member I've lost," she says, more quietly, and I remember what she said of the children. "I know we're all vulnerable. I know every moment out here—up on *Hypatia*, down here on this frozen nightmare of a planet—every minute we're still breathing is a fucking miracle. And I know you all know this place, and the Exiles, in a way I never will." Her eyes meet mine, and the force of her conviction knocks the air from my lungs. "But you need to *listen to me*, Anya. Can you listen to me? Please?"

There's nothing she can say. But I nod, and she sits down again, elbows on her knees.

"Hina was born up there," she says, her eyes intense on mine. "She grew up with me, on a starship, on a little tin can where there's no wandering in the snow, no nice scenic walks before a storm blows in. At the first sign of alarm, you don't head outside. You head inside, toward the center of the ship. Not in the most blind, irrational panic would Hina run out into the snow. Someone took her, Anya. And if she's not here, that leaves the Exiles."

I open my mouth to tell her she's wrong, that I've seen it all before, that her child is lost, like so many children before her. And I think of Tamara, long lost before I had a chance to save her, and all the others I never found, and Stanislav, warm in my arms, frowning in that earnest way that infants have, small like Hina was once, like Irina, and I turn to Costa. "Tell me about the Exile raid."

He raises an eyebrow at me. "It was the same as always," he starts, and I hold up a hand.

"It wasn't, though. It was too soon. And the weather was clear. Did we have more warning than usual?"

Costa shakes his head. "I don't think anyone was watching, at least not closely. They don't come in clear weather," he explains to Maddie. "They come at the end of a storm, or at the start, so it's harder to see them coming across the tundra."

"They've never hit us so close together before, either." I meet Maddie's eyes; she's thinking what I'm thinking.

"They raided the medical lab," Maddie says.

Costa nods. "It was unstaffed this time. Both Aleksey and Dmitri headed there as soon as we figured out what was happening, but—" He looked away. "We've had to seal if off. Three days, and they haven't been able to fix the airlock yet."

There's something he's been leaving out. "Costa?"

He looks me in the eye. "They broke into the incubator room. Seven of them, shattered. Viktor's still evaluating them, but he's not hopeful."

My stomach turns over. Ten percent of our capacity. "What are people saying?"

"Nothing, yet," he tells me. "Yulia's keeping it quiet. She's been consulting with Doctor Halvorsen. I only found out because Maria told me."

Yulia's always been cagey about our reliance on incubators, even to me, but it's her insistence on secrecy now that's most unsettling. That Yulia could tap more people for Selection isn't the point; if we're so reliant on incubator supply that losing seven alarms her, there's something going on she hasn't shared. I look over at Maddie again. "With this on top of Hina, Yulia isn't going to argue with my priorities anymore. We need to find the Exiles."

"Do you think they'll hurt her?" Maddie asks me.

I see it in her, the same thing I saw in Lauren: *anything, everything, please, just tell me my child isn't dead.* Without a motive, I've no business saying anything at all. "If they wanted her dead, they could have killed her here," I point out. "We can borrow some quarry suits. If we leave at first sunrise, we might be able to cover some ground in the mountains."

Costa interrupts. "You can't, Anya. That's suicide, and I won't let you do it."

"It's not your choice."

"With everything that's happened, you think I'm going to sit here and let you die?"

He's shouting, and he's hurt, and I think he means it, and I try to forget, just for a moment, that he drugged me after I begged him not to. "It's not a matter of looking after me, Costa," I begin, but Maddie puts a hand on my arm.

"I may have a way to help here," she says. She gives Costa a steady look. "But you're not going to like it at all."

CHAPTER TWENTY-SEVEN

I HAVE DECIDED I DO NOT LIKE FLYING.

Maddie explained it to me as best she could before we left, but she grew up in flight. She doesn't understand what it's like for me, never having been anywhere but Novayarkha, walking the Rims, the courtyard, exploring the tundra and sometimes the mountains, ground steady and immovable under my feet. There were swings when I was a child, and the physical sensation is similar as Seung pilots Maddie's little ship off the surface. But a swing eventually returns to equilibrium, which this ship does not.

I grab at the sides of the seat Maddie's strapped me into, fumbling for purchase; utterly unconcerned, Maddie just smiles at me.

"It's more about thrust than aerodynamics," she says. "Don't worry."

I haven't the slightest idea what she's talking about.

The lurching continues as we speed up and climb higher, and I'm suddenly aware I have nothing in my stomach but Costa's tea and whatever remains of a lunch I had long before first sunset. I have a deep need to retch, but I'm not sure anything would come up. My body feels alternately heavier and lighter than it is, and my breathing goes shallow as I try to keep up with the constant shifts. "I'm not entirely sure this is safe," I say at last.

"Of course it is," says Maddie, just as Seung says, "Nothing anywhere is safe." Maddie glares at him, but I'm fairly sure he's the one being honest.

Still, he offers some sympathy. "Qara still can't come down into atmosphere without losing everything she's eaten for the last week. She says it sometimes helps to close her eyes."

I close my eyes, and immediately open them again. "I think that's worse."

I try looking out the window.

There's the familiar horizon, gray and white, and as we climb, the mountains rapidly turn into hills, traces of shadow on a formless surface. I wonder if this view is what drew my ancestors in, if this luminous planet seemed like hope to them. They would have been like Maddie, acclimated to space; and yet here's where they stopped, invested in the future.

There's a bubble in my chest, and the odd sense that my hair is growing lighter, and I grip the armrests again. "We're clearing the gravity field," Maddie tells me. She looks over at me, apologetic. "This may feel a little strange."

My hair lifts off the back of my neck, as if I'm at the peak of an arc on a swing, but instead of settling back against my skin it takes on a life of its own, floating around my face, and the only thing holding my body in place is the harness. Out the window the pale sky has abruptly darkened, and the horizon has become a haloed curve, and when I blink into the darkness there are stars, brighter and whiter and more numerous than I've ever seen at home.

Nausea and fear forgotten, I lean toward the window, blinking away the ambient light from the cabin. *All those stars.* I have never seen anything so astonishing in my life besides Irina.

The stars move, and the bright planet drops away, and I feel briefly dizzy as my brain processes the movement without my body feeling anything beyond a slight centripetal force. "We're coming around to *Hypatia*," Maddie says. "We're going to match her rotation, and then dock. There'll be gravity in the wheel," she adds, finally realizing she's prepared me insufficiently. "There'll be a floor there. It's about the same as being on the planet."

I can feel it as we begin to spin, building our own artificial gravity, and the edge of the starship comes into view. And then, for the first time, I see *Hypatia* up close.

She is broken.

Half of her is not entirely unfamiliar, her form similar to the *Arkhangelsk* I've seen in pictures, although far smaller. But the other half of her, facing away from our planet's surface, is uneven and scarred, as if some giant haphazardly grabbed the ship and pulled it into pieces, then patched over the wound with sheets of mismatched metal.

The ring surrounding the main engine is intact and spinning leisurely, and my body takes on weight again as Seung matches its rotation. By the time we link with *Hypatia*, the gravity has stabilized to a level slightly lower than what I'm used to, and I wonder if that was the cause of Maddie's clumsiness the first time she visited. But when the engines shut down, I realize there's more to it: the gravity is strange, angular, not entirely stable. The difference between rotational gravity and the pull of a planet, I suppose, but it's disorienting, nearly as unpleasant as the turbulence when we took off.

Maddie is watching me with her perceptive eyes. "It took me a few hours to acclimate my first time in Novayarkha," she said. "You'll adjust."

I'm glad one of us is confident.

The door that turns into stairs on the planet opens sideways here on *Hypatia*, and I get my first glimpse of the inside of their ship. Brightness, gray metal, a segment of corridor: nothing interesting, not yet. Seung busies himself with the ship's controls—some kind of check, I suppose, for a system that just brought us from air through nothing—and Maddie helps me release the harness, holding my elbow as I push myself to my feet. The odd gravity knocks me sideways, and I brace my free hand against the side of the small ship; leaning on Maddie I take cautious steps until we emerge in the hallway.

Seung remains behind as Maddie escorts me down the corridor. It's both alien and familiar: the metals are cleaner and newer, and the whole area is better lit, but the curves and angles are like Novayarkha's in miniature. The biggest difference is orientation: where our halls are tall, these are wide, like the crypt, although bright and alive instead of dank and oppressive. Here there are windows—in Novayarkha, we've replaced them with steel ceiling panels and solar tubes. Here I can look sideways and see the stars, and then, slowly rotating into view, the planet of my birth, so small from here, all that grief and misery as far away as another universe.

"Our architecture is a little different than what you're used to," Maddie tells me. She keeps one guiding hand on my elbow, and I gawk, bracing my other hand against the wall step by step. "No big hallways, but there's a lift that takes us up to the body of the ship. The gravity's lower there, though."

My stomach churns in anticipation. "I'm surprised you have lifts."

"There are ladders as well, which are really more like stairs. But the ship is designed for people who'd lose mobility eventually. They planned for us to get old here."

And die, I realize. But also to have families, raise children. It's easy to imagine the corridor overrun by small, enthusiastic feet, the shrieks and laughter of little ones. Maddie was given no choice about becoming a part of *Hypatia*, but her captors spent a great deal of time thinking about both comfort and practicality.

There's a horror to that, but I can no longer feel it with any self-righteousness.

"The room right next to mine is empty," she says, oddly hesitant. "But if you're up to it, I'd like to take you into the medical level first and give you a proper exam. You've never been off-planet in your life—we need to know if you've got physiological limitations we need to watch."

She was so insecure, so unsteady in my world. "I'm up to it," I assure her, and surely their medicine will have the same echoes of familiarity as their home.

We reach the lift door at the end of the curved hallway. To my right is a metal panel, out of place, secured to the wall with rivets. Retrofitted. "What was there?" I ask.

"A stairway," she tells me. "It's still there, but it doesn't lead anywhere now. It's sealed at the other end too. We're big on redundancy around here."

She says it lightly, but my imagination paints a vivid picture anyway.

The lift is a small space, enough for no more than four standing, but it's more spacious than the lift down to the crypt, and Maddie's still holding on to me. She says "Medical" out loud, and the door slides shut with a low chime before we begin to move. I press my free hand against the wall again as I start to feel it, the gradual change in the weight of my body, the creeping substance-lessness. My stomach is still sour, but this time it doesn't worsen. Progress, I suppose.

The lift glides to a gentle stop, and the doors open on a corridor that's much more narrow. "We're in the main body of the ship," Maddie tells me. "The fuselage. The access corridors crisscross, but most of the space is libraries and labs. And our medical facility."

Our steps sound different as we traverse this corridor, just as well-lit but less comfortable, more utilitarian. We are less substantive as well, our feet carrying less weight to the floor beneath us. The sound of my feet is somehow more alien than anything I've yet encountered, and I wonder, then, how long I'll be here.

We turn into a room, and the first thing I notice is a person in a wheelchair.

He looks old, older than anyone I've ever known apart from Halvorsen. His hair, thin on top, is white as ice, and he's emaciated, his arms and legs skeletal in his baggy clothes. His face is not like Maddie's, fine-boned and familiar; he looks instead like Kano, with broad cheekbones and a wide, flat nose. Despite his extreme thinness his pyrite-brown skin has the warmth of health, and his eyes, dark and deep-lidded, fix on me from a relaxed, expressionless face.

Except I realize, as I see a ghostly keyboard projected before his eyes and a screen mounted next to the chair's headrest, that his expressionlessness is not voluntary.

Words appear on the screen: "I think our guest is surprised to see me, Maddie."

Not *quite* expressionless. Something in his eyes definitely looks amused.

"I thought we'd beat you here," Maddie answers easily. "Colonel, this is Anya Savelova. She's going to help us find Hina. Anya, this is the Colonel."

He surely has another name, but neither of them volunteers it. "How do you do?" I say. And then: "I'm sorry to stare."

"That's all right." This time I see his eyes darting over the keyboard, more quickly than I can follow them. "I always stare when I meet new people."

I think he's making a joke.

"Can you help us find Hina, do you think?"

He doesn't need be able to move for me to recognize all the hope and dread in that statement. "I don't know," I tell him truthfully. "But I'll do everything I can."

He's staring at me, and I'm abruptly aware of being unkempt, and probably overly thin myself. But it seems he judges me trustworthy, because the screen says, "Thank you, Anya."

Maddie has moved to the other side of the room and opened a drawer nestled in the wall. "We can learn a lot by asking questions," she says, her back to me as she rummages, "but with your permission I'd like to take some blood. That'll tell us more about what you might be susceptible to up here."

"Of course." The Colonel is still looking at me; I take the chair across from him, and it's only then I notice my leg muscles are shaking. Am I so weak, or is the new environment that much harder on me?

Maddie turns back, holding a familiar capped vial. Still needles, then, but when she places the vial against my arm I feel first a brief cooling, and then nothing as dark red liquid drains into the small tube. She stops when it's less than half as full as I'd expected, and when she removes the needle there's no mark left on my skin at all.

"That's—" I want to ask her how it works, but my eyes have gone to the vial, which she's plugged into a port next to the computer screen that was clearly made for it. The sides of the vial go opaque, and moments later the screen lights up with numbers. The Colonel positions himself before it, his back to me. "Can you analyze it so fast?" I ask.

Maddie leans against the table. "Not all of it," she says. "We can get infection-level data pretty easily—if you're carrying something, or if you're vulnerable to the kinds of microbes we trade around here. More detailed information on nutrition and radiation damage takes a little longer."

"You can get radiation damage from blood?"

"Just trends," she says. "Earlier damage, or unusual cell growth activity. Indicators, rather than anything definitive. Radiation damage is a bitch to diagnose unless you're still hot, or it causes an immediate problem. We mostly rely on preventatives, like you do."

She knows, then, about disease. I remember how easily she navigated our medical center.

The Colonel's screen is pointed away from me, and he must be conscious of that, because this time he speaks: "Your anti-viral regimen is impressive."

I recognize it, that chipper, artificial voice, the one I thought was a computer. "That was you," I say before I can stop myself. "On the radio, all those months ago."

"Yes." I have to remind myself the pleasure in his voice is entirely outside his control. "I've been working on a different design, but I'm afraid the people who invented this particular voice were more clever than I am. New phonemes alone have already taken me twelve years, and I have nothing that sounds nearly this natural."

Natural is overstating it, but we have nothing so sophisticated. "I didn't know," I confess. "I expect I was rude to you back then."

"You weren't, as it happens. But I accept your apology. And now I must ask…you were medicated recently, is that right?"

What could still be in my blood after all these weeks? "Yes. But it's been some time."

"Hm." Even with his cheerful phonemes, I recognize the concern. "How long were you on the drug?"

"Twenty sunsets. About eleven days." Because Costa kept drugging me, even when I asked him to stop.

"And what were the symptoms?"

That isn't the simplest question. "I slept a great deal," I tell him, "only…it wasn't sound sleep. I had vivid dreams."

"Dreams, or nightmares?"

With that bright voice, it sounds like a simple clinical question. "Nightmares," I clarify. "Like I was trapped somewhere, without doors or windows."

"Paranoia," he says, as if it means something. "What about appetite? Nausea?"

There's too much fog around my memories. "I don't remember eating anything, although I must have." I was not malnourished when I awoke. "I remember taking the medicine with tea."

"This would be the tea Seung says tastes like boiled wire?"

Despite myself, I laugh. "Yes, that's the stuff. It's considered a delicacy, but I've always hated it."

"Clearly the drug didn't make you insensible," the Colonel says. "Did the tea taste the same?"

"No." That I remember. "It was sweeter. Maybe a little thicker. More mild. Less...metallic."

"When you would wake, what was it like?"

That was easier to describe. "Like walking into the wind," I tell him. "Like fighting through molasses."

He turns himself away from the screen to face me again; Maddie picks up the keyboard and starts scrolling through the data. "It'll take a bit to isolate everything," he says, in writing again, "but a lot of what I'm seeing are soporifics. They might want to cling to you for a while. You'll have gone through any uncomfortable withdrawal by now, but with something this potent you might see some lingering effects for a few weeks yet."

Which doesn't sound like a tranquilizer at all. "For example?"

"You may find your emotions flattened somewhat," he says. "In extreme situations, there can be hallucinations, but I expect if that was going to happen to you you'd've encountered them already. If you do, though—let someone know right away. There are things we can do that would ease the problem."

And I learn, then, that I wasn't merely medicated for my own good. Maddie and the Colonel believe my friends, well-intentioned or not, were hurting me. I think of Costa's face, full of as much guilt as worry as I followed Maddie and Seung into *Hypatia*'s small ship, and for the first time I begin to recognize what it is I've escaped.

CHAPTER TWENTY-EIGHT

HYPATIA'S FOOD IS FAMILIAR AND EXOTIC ALL AT ONCE: ROOT VEGETABLES and beans, cooked to be just soft enough, but spiced with a subtle floral heat unlike anything I've ever tasted before. The heat is a slow burn, and I should not be eating so much, but I'm hungrier than I thought, and the flavor is lovely. I finish everything Maddie gives me, along with several glasses of entirely familiar water.

"It's our filtration systems," she says, when I remark on it. "Same tech."

They're so different, and yet so many things are the same.

The cafeteria is small, with chairs for no more than forty people. Yulia's guess about their size was close, it seems, but even so Maddie and I are alone for almost the entire meal. Léon stops by at one point, while I'm taking a break to let my tongue cool off, and asks to sit next to me. With a quick glance at Maddie I consent, and the pilot sits, fixing their dark eyes on mine. Léon's face is more lined than Maddie's, although she tells me they're a few years younger; the lines, and the shock of white hair against their deep brown skin, put me in mind of Dmitri.

"Do you think you can help us?" Léon asks.

There's an intensity about Léon, a grave sort of presence that reminds me of being a child in the classroom, warned about telling lies. "I don't know," I tell them honestly. "But I'll do everything I can. And I won't hide anything from you."

Léon stares at me a little longer, and then nods. I exhale; I'd been holding my breath. "Thank you," they say. And then they glance at Maddie, something that might be good humor gleaming in their eyes. "You've been missed here," Léon adds, and then leaves us.

Maddie rolls her eyes. "Léon's the dramatic one," she says, with no sense of irony at all. But she seems amused even though she won't look at me, and I start turning over in my head the possibility she might have felt my absence as I felt hers.

Maddie says they can't start looking for the Exile's camp until the mountains are in darkness. "The spectrometer doesn't care about the temperature," she explains, "but the infrared will be more accurate the colder it is on the surface." I comprehend enough of that to realize she lied to Yulia when she said she needed radio signals to find the Exiles. Before Rolf's death, I'd've been bothered by that.

Waiting for first dark leaves us nearly seven hours, and Maddie has informed me I'm going to sleep.

I'm not entirely sure how she believes this is going to happen. Everything on this ship is new, even the things that are familiar, and I don't want to blink for fear of missing something.

The room she's given me is small, like Costa's kitchen, only there's a window by the bed, and I can watch the stars rotate as much as I like. Maddie is detailing the amenities, but I'm distracted, staring out the window, and when the planet spins leisurely into view, I very nearly jump.

She's asked me something, perhaps about what I might need, but I don't want her to go, I don't want to curl up on this bed, I don't want to sleep. "This is nothing to you, isn't it?" I ask her, gesturing at the view.

She looks out the window, vaguely puzzled. "Not nothing," she says. "Just…I've seen it before. I see it a lot. Not this planet specifically, but star systems. A lot of asteroids, but there were times when we'd wander into a system just to see something new."

"How is it you've traveled so far?"

Maddie seems about as keen as I am on sleep. She settles into an overstuffed chair by the door, and tucks her feet beneath her. "We run five years at a stretch inside a faster-than-light field," she says. More words that mean nothing to me. "And then we come out, and for a year we run sublight, charging our batteries. That's when the time distortion happens. Kano says—" She breaks off and looks away, then continues. "Kano said that we catch it up, sort of, when we're in the field, but I can't get my brain around that. I'm not bad at math, or even basic physics, but the time distortion stuff I have to take on faith."

Her wound is so fresh, and in a way Hina's disappearance has blunted it, given her something she can actually hope for. "I'm sorry about Kano." This place may be strange, but I know how to speak to loss. "He seemed a man of good character."

She inhales, and it catches in her throat. "He knew me," she says simply, and that, more than anything, breaks my heart.

"Did you belong to each other?" I don't know how they think of such things, these people, or if it's even appropriate for me to ask, but she's not offended.

"We all belong to each other," she explains. "Hina's different, of course, because she's our daughter. But the rest of us just kind of...mix." She glances at me. "Is that shocking?"

I wonder what she must think of us. "In Novayarkha, people don't generally formalize their bonds, except around children," I tell her. "Many who bond do so in threes or more, so they can take on more children; but it's not uncommon for bonds to dissolve once the children are grown, and reform in other combinations. We are perhaps less...*mixed*...than you are here, but we have no taboo against it."

She looks relieved, and a little embarrassed, and then she asks: "Who is Irina?" and it's my turn for my breath to catch in my throat.

"Irina's my daughter," I reply. "She was born when I was twenty-two years old. I conceived at the medical center, with an anonymous match pulled from the list of optimal combinations. Doctor Halvorsen said she wanted to be careful with my genes. I remember—" I close my eyes, and I can see Irina, feel the weight of her in my arms, smell the clean, wheat-like odor of infant skin. "She came out, and she was so pale, and her hair was yellow, and I said 'Whose child is this?' and Doctor Halvorsen laughed at me, because she had no way of knowing."

"What happened to her?"

"She died." I can say it now. For a long time, nearly fifteen years, I couldn't. "She was eight years old, and one day she started coughing, and her color went off. It was in her lungs. It took her in three weeks."

Maddie's eyes are bright. "I'm so sorry," she says, but I shake my head.

"Everyone says that to me, do you know? But Irina—she was everything. Every wish, every dream, every hope I've ever had, all bundled into a little body full of energy and joy. And I lost her, and that's altered me, and I've learned to accept that. But without her, Maddie? Without her I'd have no idea what joy looked like. I may never feel it again myself, but without Irina, I'd never recognize it in anyone else. I don't think I'd be able to be compassionate if I'd never had her. I don't think I'd be the sort of person I wanted to be at all."

She's staring at me as if I've said something astonishing, something she's never heard before. "I don't understand you," she says at last. "How you can be so...*whole*."

"Ah." I stretch out on the bed at last, on my side so I can face her. "I'm not whole. Not at all. But I understand the shards." It seems fair enough to ask now. "Tell me how *Hypatia* was broken."

She shifts in the chair and looks away. "I don't remember a lot of it. I was in shock, I think, for a long time."

"Tell me what you do remember."

Her eyes drop closed. Maddie is younger than I am, but sometimes she looks ancient, older than Halvorsen. "We'd done it three times already." Her voice is quiet. "Dropped out of the warp field. The others—most of them didn't think about it at all. It was mostly Seung and me who'd get anxious; he always said he couldn't stop doing the math. Dropping out of the field is a vulnerable point for the ship: you're counting on a whole lot of variables behaving themselves all at the same time. You get caught half-in, half-out, and there's potential for the whole ship to be pulled apart by conflicting gravitational forces, basically shredding any ordinary matter." She smiles a little, eyes still closed. "Not an attractive prospect. But that's not what got us. We fell out of the field just fine, a controlled drop-out, everything nominal. And then there was this huge, deafening sound of something tearing, of metal stress, of screaming alarms, and all the alerts were going and we were climbing into emergency suits." Her eyes open, and she looks at me as if she's apologizing. "We came out in the middle of an asteroid field, you see. When you're in the warp field, you can go through things like that, because they don't really exist where you are."

Which sounds like madness, yet here we both are.

"They'd trained us for this, of course, even while telling us it was astronomically unlikely we'd ever emerge close enough for something to hurt us before we could evade. It wasn't until months afterward that I really understood how lucky we were."

"Lucky?"

"That the impact left us our engines," she explains. "That it left us enough of our living habitat, our nav systems, our information. All it sheared off was the infirmary, the gym, and the classrooms." Her eyes close again. "All of our children, except for Hina. All of the older crew members but the Colonel. He was caught in a corridor; we got him oxygen in time, but his body was too damaged for me to repair."

"You?"

"I was going to take over as the ship's doctor, when Liliana finished training me. She was killed with the rest of them."

"That's a lot of responsibility to take on right after a tragedy." I can feel my eyelids getting heavy, but don't want her to stop talking.

She leans into the corner, relaxing against the wall. "I think that's what got me through, to be honest," she says. "We were all stunned and disoriented, and most people didn't have any idea what to do. I was so busy, looking after wounds, trying to see if I could save the Colonel's life, that there was no time for the loss to paralyze me. And Hina…" She swallows. "It was Kano who came to us all one day and said we had to get our shit together. Hina was five, and that day she'd been sulking in her room because her friends wouldn't play the game she wanted to play, and then suddenly they were dead. She thought she'd killed them. He said 'We *can't* just stop here in the middle of nowhere and let this take us down. She's a child, and she deserves better than that from us.' He's—he was always taking care of the little ones. He took care of us, too, from the beginning."

Something inside of me ripples tentatively, uncertain of its welcome, and around the doorframe, a small hand appears. Irina comes into the room, entirely herself, the apparition of my nightmares forgotten. She looks not at me but at Maddie, and as she climbs onto the chair and curls up against Maddie's stomach, the last small knot in my chest releases and disappears.

"He always said I psychoanalyze people," Maddie says, and Irina turns her dark eyes to mine. "He says I pick everyone else apart, but I don't know myself at all."

It's an astute observation, but it troubles her, and Irina makes it clear I'm not to upset Maddie any further. "You know how to handle a crisis," I point out. "You've taken on your role here, and you've done it well."

Her lips tighten. "I've lost two people in as many weeks. I don't think that's going to get me a medal."

I stare at her until she looks back at me, paying attention. "You did not lose your people, Maddie. You can say it was accident, or you can blame Novayarkha, or the Exiles, or me. But there is no way the loss can be laid at your feet." Kano was right: Maddie doesn't know herself at all. "Forgive me, but you've spent too long looking after other people. You believe everything that happens can be understood, that the injuries of the human body can be quantified and cured, that every problem has an answer. But for Kano, there is only this: you came to us for help because you needed it, and someone in Novayarkha betrayed you. It's at their feet you must place his death, not your own."

Her eyes are growing shiny; Irina curls closer to her, folding her own hands over one of Maddie's. "I wanted to undo it," she says, her voice going husky. "Just back up the clock and keep him inside, or go out myself instead. I couldn't believe he was gone. I *can't* believe it. I still think there has to be some way I can get him back."

In Maddie's lap, Irina closes her eyes. "You can't get him back," I tell Maddie, as gently as I can. "But he will never leave you."

"That's not enough. He's still gone."

"Yes." Hesitantly, I put my own hand out, and cover Irina's, and Maddie's fingers are warm under mine. "But he will never leave you. It isn't enough. It's never enough. It's a cruelty of life that every day we live is behind us and gone forever, lost to eternity. And yet here we are, and we have each other, and on days when we can't live for ourselves, we can live for that."

She turns her hand over, griping my fingers, and in her face there's anguish, raw and unrestrained. "What if I can't find her, Anya? What if Hina's gone as well?"

I hold her hand, not the first hand of a grieving relative that I've held, but the first that pours strength back into me. "Then we will all hold on to each other," I tell her, "and she too will never leave us."

And I'm tired, and I'll succumb to sleep soon, but there's a wonder in realizing that for the first time since Irina, I'm part of an *us*.

RECIP: National Earth Space Organization, Vostochny
REPORTER: Loineau, Madeleine, Cmdr. NZKO *Hypatia*
Mission year 40, day 175

Seung wanted to know if we should wake Anya for our call to Yulia. Truth, Vostochny: I had enough trouble waking myself. Pretty sure she was sleeping when I left, but she's sneaky. She'd've known I was trying to be quiet, even when I clobbered my toe climbing out of bed and swore at the doorframe. So she was probably up, at least a little bit.

I don't know why she thinks she needs to spare my feelings. *I'm* supposed to be taking care of *her*.

The Colonel says I needed the sleep, and he's right. I know the limits of the human body, mine in particular. Kano always told me I was a pain in the ass if I got less than seven hours solid out of twenty-four. But with Hina missing...I keep thinking I'll sleep when we find her, that if I sleep while she's missing, I'm somehow giving up.

I thought the same of Anya, you know. I thought if I could find her, she'd fix this for me. Because she knows that place, those people. She'd know how to get to the truth, how to retrieve Hina from the Exiles.

I always wondered what it was I saw in her when we met, what could possibly be familiar about a woman whose culture splintered off from mine centuries before either of us was born. And I know now, Vostochny. I know.

I sometimes think my selfishness could swallow the universe.

She's not going to fix this for me. And I'm not going to fix this alone. We're all shards, all of us, and the only way for us to give anything substantive to the future, whether it's Hina or Anya's incubators or the fucking transceiver, is to gather ourselves together and make it all whole.

The Colonel says her brain's normal chemical cycle is still disrupted, which is something given how long she's been off the stuff.

Is it churlish of me to wonder about those breakfasts she had with Costa?

The Colonel says their drug refinement is relatively advanced, but their ingredients—by necessity—are mostly organic, compounded from minerals and plants, along with a few more sophisticated elements that must have been brought with *Arkhangelsk*. They had her on benzos, which were definitely plants, and why they'd have sophisticated benzodiazepine manufacturing facilities is an interesting question.

They also had her on Clozapine, and damned if I can figure out why they'd put her on something like that. It's a reliable, old-fashioned standby. For treating fucking *hallucinations*. One panic attack in a graveyard, and Halvorsen goes straight for the sledgehammer.

There were a few other bits in her bloodstream—trace amounts of meds designed to absorb radiation before it can damage cells, which have to be the preventatives they're all taking—but nothing he thinks would have serious long-term effects. More than anything, she needs unmedicated sleep. I don't think the woman's slept more than an hour and a half at a stretch in her life.

And it was long past time I talked to Yulia Orlova without a net.

To her credit, Orlova didn't let my signal hang around unanswered this time. She replied pretty much immediately, and I think she was shouting before the transmitter kicked on.

"You will return Anya at once!"

I have this strange conviction when she's that angry she loses the ability to lie, but that's possibly wishful thinking. "Officer Savelova is here voluntarily," I told her.

Orlova spat something I didn't understand. "Costa told me all of it. How can you imagine, in the aftermath her breakdown, that she knows her own mind?"

"I spoke with her at length before granting her request," I said, and I was pretty calm, Vostochny, for all I wanted to tell that old woman to fuck off. "It's my medical opinion—"

"Your *medical* opinion?"

"Yes." No way I was giving her an explanation. "There was no reason to think the trip would cause her harm."

I braced myself for more yelling, but it was too much to hope Orlova would stay out of control for very long. "I know you care for her," she said more calmly, and fuck her, Vostochny, too little too late. "But you don't know her. Anya's had a difficult life. She's been through a great deal, and we've all looked after her. Whether or not you believe you're doing the right thing—please understand, you don't really know everything she's dealing with."

There was enough truth in that to make me look up at the others, huddled around the radio table in the fuselage.

Ever since my meltdown, there's been a lot more group participation in ship's decisions. A month ago, I'd have resented the hell out of that, feeling like they didn't trust me or were somehow trying to cut me out. Now…it makes me feel stronger, knowing they're all backing me up.

And each of them, when I met their eyes, shook their head at me.

"The instant she tells me she wants to go home," I said, "I'll fly her down myself."

This didn't placate Orlova. "I want to talk to her."

"She's sleeping."

"Wake her up!"

Which was a stupid thing to ask for when she was trying to tell me her big concern was Anya's health. "I'll let her know you'd like to speak to her," I promised. "But I wouldn't expect a call until—" here's where I could've used a clock with local Novayarkha time— "close to second sunrise."

"You ask us to trust you," Orlova said bitterly, "while you're kidnapping our people. How do you expect us to react to this?"

I could have told her I never expected them to change ever, even if we nuked half the tundra, but that might have been counterproductive. "I didn't call to discuss Anya, Governor," I said instead. "I wanted to let you know we'll be trying to find the location of the Exile camp, which will require us to change our position. Since I know some of your people monitor us, we felt we ought to explain before we moved."

I could imagine her face, caught between fury at losing over Anya and wanting to get in on the plan to hunt down her perpetual enemy. "People are going to panic," she said, but she sounded much more measured. "It doesn't matter what I say."

I've learned when Orlova starts the aggrieved noises about what it's going to do to her people, she wants something from me. "We can fly around the other side of the planet and come in over the mountains, but it'll take us longer."

"It wouldn't matter." I can hear it in her voice: the desperate need to have something to trade. Is it bad I felt a little satisfaction at that? "After Anya...whatever the truth may be, people will not trust you."

What's interesting, Vostochny, is how much she was banking on me wanting to be trusted. I'm not entirely sure what she's seen in me to make her think I'm vulnerable to the court of public opinion.

Or maybe she thinks we've got more compassion than she does.

"Let me apologize to you, Governor," I said, "for removing Anya so precipitously. I didn't know, when I visited her, that she would ask me to take her back to *Hypatia* with me." Never lie when you don't have to. "I can only give you my personal assurance that she's safe and well. My priority, at this point, is finding out what's happened to our missing crew member."

There was a long silence after that. "If you find the Exiles, Captain—will you betray us?"

"I'm not at all sure how I could," I said. "They already know where you are."

"They have always, since before I was born, tried to harm us."

You know, Vostochny? I don't know if she was just spouting propaganda, or if she really believes it. And I don't have any idea if she's right or wrong. "Let me promise you this, Governor," I proposed. "There will be no violence—*none*—between the Exiles and Novayarkha. If they try to hurt you, we will defend you."

I didn't make the inverse explicit, but I know she heard it anyway.

"I believe you're a person of your word." She sounded tired, defeated, and hell, maybe I should have felt sorry for her, but every one of us exhaled when she said that. "But they *have* hurt us, Captain. And they will hurt you as well, if you let them."

Even with nothing to bargain with. You've got to be impressed by this woman, Vostochny. She's nothing if not dead consistent.

"Let me reassure you, Governor," I tell her, without looking at the others. "We have no intention of letting them hurt us. We won't be providing any technology to the Exiles, accidentally or otherwise."

Because the whole point of her show of vulnerability, of course, was her fucking arms race. Which I'm still not sure is imaginary.

She lets out a breath. "Thank you, Captain. I'll let our people know you'll be moving, so they won't be alarmed. And—" There was a catch in her voice. "Please tell Anya I'd like to hear from her. And tell her she is loved and missed here, whatever she may think."

We disconnected, and Divya said, "Well *that's* bullshit."

"You don't know that," the Colonel typed. "Horrible people are capable of feeling great love."

"You think Anya will go back?" Seung asked me.

The thing is, Vostochny, I hadn't even questioned it. She's such a creature of that place: obedient, careful. Complacent, at least until recently. Hard to imagine she's sad to be out from under Orlova's thumb, but I remember her laughing as she talked to Lev, her easy camaraderie with Costa, her gentleness with Maria. She loves them. They're as much hers as Hina is mine.

She'd never stay with us, Vostochny. And I'm kind of an ass for wishing she'd want to.

RECIP: National Earth Space Organization, Vostochny
REPORTER: Loineau, Madeleine, Cmdr. NZKO *Hypatia*
Supplemental

Anya must be feeling better, because when she finally got up, she was a huge pain in the ass. Wouldn't let me help her wash or dress; wouldn't even take my arm for balance. I went down to that rock twenty, maybe thirty times, and every time I spent at least fifteen minutes fighting my inner ear for balance. Up here, gravity changes every time you take a step, and she's trying to tell me she doesn't need help.

All this time I've worried about her standing up to Orlova. I'm wondering how any of them ever stood up to Anya.

"I know full well," she said, "the longer I lean on you, the longer it'll take before I'm used to it."

I tried an appeal to her pride. "You won't be able to stay on your feet down that hall."

"Then I'll crawl."

So much for pride.

The way she looked at me, Vostochny, with those calm eyes of hers touched with a little bit of humor, like she's forgiving me for hovering over her, and I'm telling you I haven't felt so irritable about anything in weeks, and so maybe she did it on purpose, I don't know. All I know is being pissed off cleared my head, and it was about fucking time I figured out how to think again.

And of course she stumbled about a thousand times on her way to the lift, but damned if she didn't make it. On the lift she held on to the handrail, which I think was as much about dealing with the dwindling gravity as her still precarious balance, and I tried to think of what she'd need to know to move around more easily.

"Let yourself drift," I suggested. "There's no real up and down in here."

From the look on her face, I could tell that wasn't especially comforting. Just before we stopped, she let go of the rail and started shooting up toward the ceiling. She let out a little noise as I grabbed her elbow, and I couldn't help it: I laughed.

"Come on," I said. "I'll hang on to you for now."

I took her hand and started pushing along the wall toward the fuselage. She's a quick learner, but she kept a death grip on my fingers all he same.

Of all things, it was the fuselage that rendered her speechless. It didn't occur to me until I saw her looking around that she's probably never been anywhere without a defined orientation before. At least the corridors in Novayarkha were familiar to us.

I rambled at her, pointing at the nav and cartographic equipment, all the design simulators that Qara and Léon have been using to test our transceiver redesign. I don't know how much of it means anything to her. With everything I've learned, I know almost nothing about her technical education—or indeed about their technology at all. I've read Seung's reports on their incubators, but things like power generation or engine technologies are all speculation. I suppose I've assumed their engine tech isn't robust enough to repair, or they'd have fled this Deity-forsaken rock long ago.

Everyone was there but the Colonel, who was compounding electrolyte and analgesic patches for Anya. Anya nodded hello to everyone, one at a time, and her eyes took on this calculated look: she was noticing she'd met all of these people before.

Oh, well. No secret is forever.

"Let's find them," I said.

Léon piloted us lower, and even though we reoriented gradually, Anya still kept turning her head. "Your eyes and your inner ear are not used to disagreeing," I told her. "If you get dizzy or nauseated, look at something fixed: the table, me, your own feet."

"But then I'd have to look away," she said, and I swear, Vostochny, her expression was the most remarkable thing: fear and wonder and a longing I'd never seen in her before. I decided if she threw up, we'd manage. It's not like she'd have been the first one to make a nightmarish mess in the fuselage.

We crossed the terminator into night, and Seung brought up the infrared and overlaid it with the spectrometer. Despite everything they mine down there, the planet produces a pretty homogeneous graph. Ice is a stupendously good insulator. To do a proper geologic survey of this place we'd need more than the imaging; we'd want some core samples, probably at least eight of them, from the poles and the equator and some of those intersectional points. Maybe, if the transceiver doesn't work out, we'll take the time.

"What are we looking for?" Anya asked. She was looking from the window to Seung's monitor back to the window again, as if she couldn't take it all in fast enough.

"When we originally scanned the surface," I told her, "we were looking for heat variation. Volcanic structures, mostly; we had no reason to think there'd be life down there. But months of monitoring Novayarkha have given us a pretty good map of what an ice-buried human settlement looks like in terms of outgassing."

"Outgassing," Anya repeated, and just when I thought she was going to make an off-color joke, she said, "You lied to Yulia."

Oh, yeah. That. "I knew she was trying to force my hand. I

just didn't know why. But damned if I was going to promise her anything more than I already had."

When we reached the mountains, Anya kept her eyes on the dark peaks out the window. She wasn't twisting anymore; she was acclimating faster to zero g than I ever did to her planet.

And then she started to cry, sort of quietly. "I'm sorry," she said, when she noticed me noticing.

"Withdrawal is strange," I told her, but we both knew withdrawal had nothing to do with it.

Then Divya said the mountains looked like Guilin, and Anya had no idea what we were talking about, so I went to another monitor and pulled up some of the pictures. Divya's right and wrong, of course; the mountains in Guilin aren't covered in ice, at least in the pictures we have, but the ones outside Novayarkha are spiky the same way.

Karst mountains. Does that even make sense, way out here?

"What is that beside them?" Anya asked me, and it took me a minute to figure out she was talking about the lake. I told her, and she blinked, and her eyes got bright again, and I guess she'd never seen a body of unfrozen water before, had she?

Qara, of course, was staring out the window, focusing on the new. "Porcupine planet," she said, and Ratana chuckled.

"ハリネズミ," Ratana said.

When she was fifteen, Hina made us all learn rudimentary Japanese. She didn't know it any better than we did, but she insisted. "Someday when I'm back on Earth," she told us, "I'll have to be able to speak to my relatives."

"But everybody speaks Russian!" Kano had protested. Hina convinced him in the end, but then, she could always convince Kano of anything.

Léon said, "ハリネズミ doesn't mean *porcupine*. It means *hedgehog*."

"It's the same thing," Ratana insisted, and then they got into one of their arguments-by-habit and I tuned them out.

We found the settlement after about half an hour, the spectrometer strobing over five spots that had to be surface vents, creating a ring around an area where the hills were low to nonexistent. In the center of the circle the spectrometer glowed weakly red: heat. And also, according to our atmospheric detectors, radiation. Much stronger than the radiation leaked by the reactor beneath Novayarkha.

We all stared at Anya while she swore for a while. "About fifteen years ago," she told us at last, "I searched that area of the mountains. I couldn't have been more than half a kilometer away." She seemed annoyed with herself, as if she'd have been better off finding it and then freezing to death.

We're both dosing up on radiation meds—I don't know how long we're going to be outside and I don't think she's built up an immunity to fucking gamma rays—and I'm bringing an extra pack or two with us for when we find Hina. And of course wherever the Exiles are actually living may be perfectly well-insulated against the radiation, and the meds might be unnecessary, which would be lovely, Vostochny, but my recent run of luck hasn't been a good one and I'm not taking any chances.

One other thing before I go.

Anya pointed out that Orlova would undoubtedly be tracking the ECV, so as soon as we land, we've all but given away the Exiles' location. When I asked if Orlova would attack, Anya thought for a long time.

"She's used them for so long," she said, and no lie, I was relieved she could admit that. "I don't know if she'll be able to give up the scapegoat. But when it leaks out that she knows where they are…she'll have to, Maddie. No matter how much they love her, the people will expect something to be done."

So I showed Anya how we'd stop her governor.

She kept her hand in mine until we were far enough into the ring for the floor to become a floor, and then she let me go, stepping carefully so she didn't bounce too much. And I led her to the weapons closet, and I showed her what we have.

"The ones on the top shelf are simple chemical charges," I told her. "They work well in a vacuum; they'll even burn if we need them to. They're our go-to tool for asteroid demolition. Four or five of them and we can take apart a rock six times larger than *Hypatia*." I gestured at the spike nukes, stacked in neat pyramids like fresh citrus, the ones I'd wanted to use to take revenge on her city when Kano died. "Those are easy to target, and can burrow through solid rock as much as four thousand kilometers. We've used them once or twice on very large asteroids." I should have told her then, I suppose, that we—not just me, but all of us—had considered using them, before we knew the planet was inhabited. I think, though, that she already knew. "There were nine of us on *Hypatia* when we got here. Without Kano, we're eight. Our original complement was twenty-three, before we added children. We lost fifteen adults and eight of our children when we were hit by that asteroid. Novayarkha overwhelms us on numbers, Anya, but we've always been able to destroy you."

She looked at the bombs for a long time. I think she was counting them. Or maybe she was just trying to figure out how much of the only world she knew they could demolish.

And then she said: "There's been enough death."

She's right, Vostochny. And I hope to all your Deities that the Exiles feel the same.

CHAPTER TWENTY-NINE

THE TRIP BACK DOWN FEELS MUCH THE SAME AS THE ONE UP, BUT PERhaps because I know what to expect I'm much closer to vomiting than I was before. I don't want to throw up in front of Maddie, and force of will, along with some shallow breathing, keeps me steady enough. But the truth is she's part of the problem. Maddie isn't as good a pilot as Seung, and I've resolved not to ask her how many times she's done this until we've landed safely.

She's cheerful about her bad flying, carefree and relaxed no matter how many air pockets we hit, and Irina stands at her shoulder, eyes widening at every terrifying lurch. The closer we get to the surface, the more I miss the weightlessness of *Hypatia*'s fuselage, and even the odd angular gravity of my room.

Not mine. I know I don't belong there. But I've never slept so well, not since Irina died.

We're landing three hours before second sunset, which will give us time to explore the terrain and hopefully discover the entrance to their habitat. Given the hour, they shouldn't be expecting our arrival: we couldn't have traveled this far from the city unless we'd left in the dark.

The assumption being, of course, that they have no observatory, no patrols, and didn't see *Hypatia*'s flyover or hear the ECV approach. There are more variables than I like, and Maddie's reassurances notwithstanding, my nerves are shaky. These are the demons of my childhood, and I'm dropping in on them as if they are neighbors.

I'm ashamed of how much I'm longing for one of Dmitri's energy weapons.

Our landing site isn't the one *Hypatia* suggested. Once I translated my horizontal knowledge of the mountains to the aerial map, I vetoed the ship's choice. "It's all ice there, and uneven," I told Maddie. "For something the size of the ECV—you'll never get stability, never mind the avalanches." And indeed, as we fly low over the mountains, banks of snow, dislodged by the noise of the engine, careen in graceful waves into the icy valleys below.

My chosen landing site is flatter, but it's also narrower, nestled between deeply sloping hills, and I hold my breath as Maddie does her best to align the ship with the gap. One of the ECV's blunted wings scrapes into a hillside, and we lurch, and Irina glares at me as I let out a little cry of alarm. But Maddie steadies us, and we settle onto the ground, and if the landing wasn't precisely smooth, our placement seems stable enough.

Here, in the gravity I've always known, my nausea finally disappears.

The others wanted to come down with us, but Maddie and I were united in our desire to leave them out of it. Maddie argued that limiting size of the party allowed for more stealth, and made us seem less of a threat. Privately, my reasoning was simpler: taking care of Maddie was going to require all of my attention. I couldn't possibly protect them all, even if I were at my best.

And I'm not. But I'm alive, and perhaps that's something.

In truth, I'm not sure whether or not this is madness. Even in my robust youth, my forays into the mountains were brief and stumbling failures. I hope we can find some evidence of Hina's fate, give Maddie a defined ending to this story, but my priority is making sure she makes it out of this alive.

She descends the stairs first, then moves aside, waiting for me. Irina's standing next to her, unconcerned, watching the snow dance over the landscape. I turn around and climb down backwards, ladder style, one hand on the rail, the other grasping a length of rebar I've claimed as a walking stick. The snow is fresh here, and scattering, and we'll need to be careful.

The first hour's easy: it's an area Aleksey and I mapped out in detail a few years ago during a long sunny spell. I pushed him, I remember. It was full dark that last day before we got back to Novayarkha, and he was displeased. I apologized to him for losing track of time, but privately I took it as a sign of weak character. If keeping our people safe mattered to him, he would have dressed more carefully, made sure he had the ability to get home safely in the dark.

I don't remember why it was so important to spare him my disapproval.

It's the fissure that stops us, a crack nearly eight meters wide: unbreachable with our equipment. Two years ago, it had been a six-centimeter gap in the ice. Under other circumstances I'd suggest we go back, and return with flexible polymer struts to build a makeshift bridge. But if the Exile entrance is near here, they've been able to get past the fissure.

There's a solution I'm not yet seeing.

There's a ridge in the slope of the hill to our right, a little above my head; I gesture toward it, and Maddie nods, but when she reaches up in an attempt to climb, I put my hand on her arm. I point at myself, and she frowns. "I'll do it," I say in my thin voice, but what I want to say is *Unless you've climbed in ice before, you're going to end up in that chasm.*

She may have seen that in my eyes, though, because she frowns at me and mouths a word that I'm pretty sure is *Stubborn.* But she takes my walking stick when I hand it to her, lays it in the snow, and leans down to give me a boost.

She's stronger than I would have thought for someone spending idle days on a starship, and with a little scrambling I make it onto the ledge. The boots I'm wearing are clumsy, and I lean into the rock, my gloved fingers searching for something to hold. I find enough purchase to steady myself, but none of it will save me if I overbalance; I should've pulled the boots off first. As it is, I pull off one glove, and my fingers get a better grip on the side of the hill.

If I glance down, I'm certain I'll see Maddie making wild gestures of objection.

I blink through the snow and scan the crack in the surface. It's uneven, and appears split along staggered fissures: natural, then, probably brought on by a particularly long sunny spell or snow sliding off the mountains and settling between the plates. But there's something else there, something I couldn't see from the ground. With my gloved hand, I fumble for the binoculars brought from *Hypatia*.

There's a bridge half a kilometer away, about three meters down from the surface.

I glance down to catch Maddie's eye and point downward. She holds her hands out; I sit on the ledge and slide down, and she catches me before I can collapse into the snow.

"For your Deity's sake, Anya, put that glove back on," she shouts. I smile, and replace the glove over my chilled fingers, then pick up my stick again.

Half a kilometer takes us twenty minutes in the wind, and we find the bridge set much farther down than it appeared from above. It's a four-meter drop, but the bridge is solid all the way across.

The ropes and carabiners brought from *Hypatia* are less fatigued than the climbing gear we keep in Novayarkha, but the design is essentially the same. I anchor the rope in the ice as Maddie frowns at me again, but I'm not going to let her go down first. I've rappelled down dozens of fissures just like this one. I need to be able to catch her if she falls.

I feed the rappel assembly through my hitch, and I lean into the harness. The anchor holds, and I drop, letting the rope slide slowly through my gloves. The bridge is sturdy and immovable beneath my feet, and I disconnect the assembly and toss it back up. A few minutes later Maddie appears, gripping the rope harder than she needs to, dropping slowly. I brace my feet and hang on to the ends of the rope; she's heavier than I am, but as long as she doesn't let go, I can steady her.

I hang on as she looms closer, bit by bit, and then she's standing next to me and I breathe again.

We turn together and look across the bridge. It's clearly manufactured: no natural ice, no matter how perfectly crystalized, would have such straight edges. The bridge lies low enough to be sheltered from the snow, leaving the icy surface pristine. There's no way to tell how recently it's been crossed. I'm not sure how paranoid the Exiles are—they must understand why we've never been able to do a thorough search of the mountains—but I can't shake the certainty that this whole thing is a trap.

"You should let me go first," I say, but if Maddie can hear me, she ignores me. She takes a step forward, and we walk side by side.

The eight meters to the other side seem like kilometers, and I'm genuinely surprised when we reach it without incident. In the shadow of the cliff there's no glare on Maddie's helmet, and I can see her grinning at me. I have a sneaking suspicion she's enjoying all of this.

There are solid, burnished anchors screwed into the wall on this side; irrelevant if they're not as sturdy as they appear, if this whole bridge is a trap for those who believe they're clever. I tether Maddie and me together, showing her how to clip on to each anchor; I stand beneath her as if I could catch her if she fell instead of plunging along with her. Her progress is slow, clumsy, an artefact of her inexperience, but once her head is at ground level, she makes the rest of the journey with surprising quickness.

She drops the rope down to me, and I thread it through the carabiner and clip it to the first anchor, my feet finding the prominent divots in the ice wall. This is the most physical thing I've done since my breakdown, and about halfway up I start to think I might not make it. My arms are shaking, weak from lack of use; why was I drifting through the city like a spectre, no more real than Irina, when I should have been preparing for what was to happen next? My breathing becomes insistent, rapid; my heart thrums in my ears. I watch my hands on the rope, and it's only the thought of Maddie, who can't do this on her own, who would be lost and freezing and never found, that keeps me moving.

After an eternity the shadows brighten; I've reached the surface. A gloved hand reaches down for me, and it's not until my fingers close around it that I realize it isn't Maddie's.

ARCHIVE #628

PERSONAL TRANSMISSION FROM *ARKHANGELSK* TO EARTH
2200[1]

SENDER: PETRA ILYUSHIN
B. 2184
D. SHIP YEAR 62

DIRECTIVE 17 GOVERNMENT USE ONLY
SCHOLARLY ACCESS FORBIDDEN

Good news: looks like those Arctic Crusader fools didn't end up blowing a hole in the hull after all.

The cease-fire has lasted four days this time, and most of the ACs are under arrest. We're all starting to breathe easier; even some of the crèche children are talking again. I've attached a list[2] of the names I could get so you can tell their families they're all right. Still, there are fourteen little ones nobody can identify, so some of the carers

---

1   Date is interpolated and should not be considered precise.
2   No attachment survives.

are giving them new names. It's good they don't ask me; I'd choose things like Spiky Hair and Big Head and Won't Eat Her Vegetables.

The children are amazing, Mama. Playing in the nursery, bouncing balls in the rings where there's decent gravity, just like we're all still on Earth. I know they're traumatized—we see it mostly at night, when they're trying to sleep—but they're also *kids*, you know?

I laugh, sometimes, playing with them, which is pretty funny, considering most of the time I want to scream.

One advantage to being a child minder is you're invisible to important people, and sometimes they talk when you're right there. The scientists don't want to turn back because the point was for the ship to fly anyway, and on top of that the landing systems weren't finished. They'd have to rebuild some thrusters and some base insulation and a bunch of other technical things I don't understand at all, but the upshot is this: going home would wreck the ship, and nobody wants to do that.

The other thing people say is that we shouldn't be wasting food and medicine on people who stole our ship and killed a bunch of us. I can't disagree, but then I think about what they mean. We can't deport them or throw them into some bottomless gulag. There's only one way to stop using resources on people out here.

Is that the choice? Forgive them or kill them? Did anybody think about things like a justice system when they started this project?

I'm paralyzed, sometimes, by how badly I want to go home. I can't stay here, in this thin metal box. Surely any minute now my shift will end and I'll go outside and I'll pedal home and reheat some of that awful soup you make when we're between produce rations. We'll see if the net is up and watch the news and argue whether it's true or not, and if the air quality is good we'll sit out back with the dogs and watch the stars come out.

There are a lot of stars out here. They say once we start going faster than light we won't see them anymore, which I guess makes sense. But they're so pretty. Not like home; nothing is like home. But they're a comfort, of sorts, and I look at them and imagine Black Nose struggling to climb into my lap like he's still a puppy, and you sitting next to me like everything is fine and the world around us is not on fire.

You always told me you wouldn't live long enough to save the world, but I would.

I think you're going to have to save it without me.

REVELATION

CHAPTER THIRTY

THE HAND HAULS ME UP, AND I SCRAMBLE FOR SOLID GROUND. WHEN I'M released, I look up to see Maddie, standing unnervingly close to the edge of the drop, facing an Exile with a gun. Next to her, Irina stands frozen, protective, radiating energy and calm all at once. Waiting for me to act.

The Exiles wear the same outfit as Maria's attacker from a couple of months ago: the variant of our quarry suits, simultaneously less battered and more worn, balaclavas behind their faceplates concealing their identities. Their weapons, too, are familiar, and not in a way that's comforting. My Exile is carrying a twin of our energy weapons, sleek and sharp-nosed, but it's holstered at her waist, harmless. Maddie's Exile has a mundane handgun, aimed steadily at Maddie's midsection, giving no indication that she won't use it.

No one moves as I push myself unsteadily to my feet. I can see Maddie's eyes through her faceplate, and I'm relieved to find she doesn't look afraid. She does, however, look annoyed, and Irina's eyes widen in warning. I want to tell Maddie to keep still, that now isn't the time for her reflexive self-righteous rage; but she says nothing, and I don't want to speak first. Let them guess what we're thinking.

Despite their balaclavas, we don't have to guess what they're thinking at all. The Exiles are arguing with each other, and even though I can't make out words I can hear the tone of their raised voices. As I stand with Maddie, the two begin gesturing: my rescuer is pointing alternately into the mountains and up at the darkening sky, while the one holding the gun is more agitated. She repeatedly throws her arms in the air, the nose of her weapon sketching a wide arc in more or less the same direction as Maddie and me, and then points at the ground with her free hand. Once—alarmingly—she mimes shoving someone into the chasm.

The gun sweeps toward us again, and Irina flinches while Maddie's still frozen, and this is ludicrous. I yell into the wind and thin air, "Please stop doing that."

Apparently my voice carries well enough, because the Exiles stop arguing to look at me.

"Here or there, stay or go," I shout, channeling Maddie's injudicious tongue. "It's getting dark. If we wait until the cold takes hold, it won't matter if you shove us into the fissure or not."

The Exile who pulled me up takes two steps in my direction. Her eyes are dark—like so many back home—and they narrow as she takes in my face. She turns back to her companion without looking at Maddie at all, and makes a quick gesture with one hand.

The other woman steps toward us, and instinctively I move in front of Maddie; but the Exile is holstering her weapon and reaching into her pocket. When her glove emerges she's clutching two crudely sewed cloth hoods, made of what appear to be old shirts. I meet her eyes and shake my head. If we are to die, I want to see it coming.

But the woman just drops her hand and cocks her head to one side. "I won't hurt you," she says. Her accent doesn't mark her as different from anyone I've ever known.

I wonder how long I'd live, falling down a chasm.

Maddie's blindfolded first, the hood covering her faceplate; and then it's my turn, the cloth concealing everything but a thin band of light toward my feet. I fumble for Maddie's arm, and we lock elbows.

At first I'm supporting Maddie, squeezing her arm so she knows she's not alone. But at some point I realize we're supporting each other: the terrain isn't difficult, but it's unfamiliar, and the Exiles are moving as swiftly as if we were on a flat walkway instead of mountain climbing. Maddie has never walked on anything like this in her life. Her labored breathing is loud enough, even in the thin air, and I remember her panic when I showed her the quarry. Was that only a few months ago?

"We need to slow down," I call to our captors.

"No," Maddie says, but I can hear the tension in her voice. "It'll be dark soon."

She doesn't say the rest: they're not dressed properly for night, and we, despite our more robust suits, would never find our way back in the dark. I straighten, tightening my grip on her arm, and focus on keeping my balance despite the uneven footing.

When the ground begins to slope downward, I feel something like relief. I stumble a little, and Maddie steadies me, and from my other side a hand touches my back and grasps my elbow. From an Exile this kindness is unexpected; her grip is firm but gentle, and she guides me with skill. In these inhospitable mountains, I suppose, they must have their own methods of dealing with the less sure-footed.

It isn't until I hear the familiar airlock mechanism that I realize our methods are likely much the same.

Arkhangelsk, after all, had three rings, not two.

We move on to a metal floor, and from the echo I picture one of the smaller airlocks in Novayarkha's Outer Rim. The Exiles' voices become clear in the oxygenated room, and there's something familiar about one of them. I hear the rustle of fabric, and then Maddie tugs off my hood and the bright light blinds me for a moment as I reach for my helmet. When my head is freed someone pulls the helmet from my hands, and it's Maddie's face in front of me, her hair in its usual mad tangles about her head, and her eyes are studying me anxiously.

"You're all right?" she says.

I have a brief flash of what she must have been like as a child, smart and obstinate and obsessively looking after everyone, even when she was the one in danger. "I'm fine," I say to her, and squeeze her arm with one glove.

Immediately the muzzle of a gun noses between us. "No touching," says one of the Exiles. I look over; her helmet is off, but she's still in her balaclava. Here on the solid floor it's clear how much smaller than us she is, and I wonder if she's a child.

"Let them be, Eleonora."

Eleonora drops the gun, and the other Exile waves a hand at her. "You first," she says. "I'll come after."

We watch as Eleonora strips off her protective clothing, dropping it into a cleaning bin that seems much the worse for wear. Exchanging a glance with Maddie I follow suit; she has no hesitance at all. The decontamination sequence takes longer than it does in Novayarkha, but it smells the same, and when we emerge on the other side I could be home, were it not for the slight woman pointing a rifle at us.

"Why did you come here?"

The other Exile has come through behind us, and her voice sounds weary, and so much older than Eleonora's. Hers is the voice I heard at the pit: she pronounces words like every city dweller I know, and something sparks my memory.

Maddie answers her. "We're looking for someone."

"What does it matter why they came?" Eleonora hasn't dropped the gun, and her voice is spiky, angry. "We should have left her behind. We can't have her here."

I don't have to wonder which of us is *her.*

"It doesn't make a difference." Annoyance, now, from the familiar one. "They've found us, probably from orbit. You think they just stumbled around in the snow?"

"Which is my *point. She* can help us, and—"

Maddie breaks in, sensible enough to speak calmly. "Threatening people isn't going to get me to help you with anything."

"Do you have any idea the threat you've brought to our door, just having her with you?"

"The only threat I've seen so far has been from you."

"That's not—" The familiar voice stops, and her feet shift before she adds, "How long until you're missed?"

Maddie scoffs. "Why would I tell you that?" and I'd argue with her, except I've placed the voice, and in my astonishment I take my eyes off the threat and turn around.

Dark, curly hair, cropped short, shorter than it was when she vanished; those dark Novayarkhan eyes; tawny-beige skin over fine cheekbones and a strong jaw. Vital. Strong. Beautiful. One of Halvorsen's finest genetic achievements.

It's Tamara, entirely alive, entirely healthy, and despite her admonitions to Eleonora none too pleased to see me.

Her eyes on mine are calm, and not at all defensive, and I'm not sure where to begin. Our search-and-rescue expedition has abruptly turned into something entirely different. "Maddie," I say, shocked into social niceties, "this is Tamara."

Maddie's eyes widen, and I see my own feelings reflected there: relief, anger, confusion. "You said they didn't kidnap people."

Exhaustion overtakes me again, but this time it's not entirely physical. The airlock is smaller than ours, cluttered with tools and scraps of safety suits and what smells like old food. There's a stool propped against the wall as well, and I move around Maddie to drop onto it. "I don't think Tamara was kidnapped."

But Maddie doesn't care about the upending of my murder case. "However she got here," she says, turning on Tamara, "obviously they've got experience getting people out of the city without being detected. What have you done with Hina?"

"Who's Hina?"

I can hear it in Tamara's voice: genuine confusion. I'm not surprised, but my heart sinks all the same; I had hoped, despite the hopelessness.

But Maddie doesn't know Tamara, doesn't know Novayarkha, doesn't know that there are things about which we do not lie. "Hina is *my daughter*." There's an unsteadiness in her voice, but somehow it doesn't sound like weakness.

Tamara, unused to such direct challenge, has taken a step back, but Eleonora isn't distracted by Maddie's rage. She's still hanging on to her gun, staring at me, openly hostile, and I stare back. Young, this girl; if we were in Novayarkha I'd be certain she was less than fifteen. She's thin and slight, and already sallow-skinned, those deep telltale circles ringing her eyes.

Why would the Exiles send a sick child to take us in off the snow?

"We didn't take anybody." Tamara's defensive, annoyed that Maddie hasn't deferred to her obvious authority. "Officer Savelova told you the truth. We don't do that."

We.

Maddie crosses her arms. "Why in the hell should I believe you? You *faked your own death* and let them *murder* somebody over it." She's been keeping up after all. "They could have stashed Hina anywhere. You think they'd tell *you* what they did with her?"

I drop Eleonora's glare to look at Tamara. Behind the irritation, there's confusion in her eyes, and just a touch of that fear I saw in so many of my own people when Maddie first arrived. Reluctantly I push myself off the stool; my footing is unsteady, as if my mind is waiting for the floor to become uneven again. "Hina was in the medical center when it was attacked." Out of the corner of my eye I see Eleonora shift in irritation; she dislikes my choice of words. "In the ensuing confusion, she disappeared. Some said they saw her taken."

And Tamara reacts as any Novayarkhan would. Her face changes, first in a flash of understanding, and then into sympathy with a grief we've all endured. "We didn't take her," is all she says, but she says it to me, and not to Maddie.

For my friend, I push the point. "There's nobody new here? Perhaps being treated in your medical center, someone you don't—"

But behind the sadness in Tamara's eyes is just a hint of something else: shame. And I'm blindsided by betrayal again.

"You were there."

"There were only four of us," she explains, her voice full of apology. "We wouldn't have been able to carry a person without being caught, even if we'd wanted to take her." She turns back to Maddie. "I'm sorry, Captain Loineau. Your daughter isn't here."

Captain Loineau. The Exiles, it seems, have a radio of their own.

I expect Maddie to keep raging, to call Tamara a liar, to dredge up a million reasons why what she's hearing is impossible. But perhaps she sees it, too, on Tamara's face: a liar, even one far better than Tamara has ever been, would have been hard-pressed to fake such raw empathy.

Maddie turns away. I reach out a hand, but she flinches, and I let her pass without touching her. She collapses onto the stool I vacated and turns her face to the wall.

Tamara and I exchange a long look, two children of the city who've known too many people lost to the ice. "Eleonora," Tamara says, without turning around, "please let The Elder know we're back."

Eleonora makes an annoyed noise that reinforces her age in my mind, and twists open the inner airlock door. When it clicks shut again, Tamara visibly relaxes. "There are things going on here you don't understand," she begins.

"There's a great deal I don't understand." Despite my anger, despite all the questions fighting for space in my head, half my attention is on Maddie, who still hasn't moved. "Why have you told no one—even your mother—you're alive? Why did you help these people attack us?"

"These people are *us* as well, Officer Savelova."

I open my mouth to reply to that, but Maddie looks up, drawing my attention. She looks a dozen years older, and her lips are thin and gray, but there's still something animated in her eyes behind the dull sorrow. "Strictly speaking," she says, a wraith of her old matter-of-fact self, "she's not wrong, Anya." She shifts in the chair, straightening a little, and I decide to be grateful she's still able to engage with the world. "What made you come here?" she asks Tamara.

At that, Tamara looks away, a flush creeping into her cheeks. "I wanted to do a news story. At first." She looks back at me, defiant, but I catch a hint of the shame again. Whatever else has happened to her here, she's grown up, at least a little. "I used to play tricks on Rolf when we'd walk on the tundra. I'd run and hide from him, make him think I was lost. It was—" She breaks off again, and the blush deepens. "I don't know if I can really explain about Rolf," she says, subdued.

I should say something to let her off the hook, accept my own role in Rolf's murder, in what may very well may have been an utterly botched investigation into Oksana's death years ago. But I find I'm not yet comfortable offering even limited absolution.

"I was over the—one of the hills." It takes me a moment to realize she's deliberately omitting details. Protecting the Exiles. "And I slipped and fell into a crevasse in the ice. I lay there for a few seconds, thinking this was it, I was dead, they'd never find me…and when I sat up I realized I was in a tunnel. I walked into it a few meters, and found a stash of skates and sails, and that's when I knew."

"You told no one."

"I planned to," she insists, but she's looked away again. "Once I got enough evidence to be certain."

"You were going to announce it on the news." Even for Tamara, this is audacious.

One slight lift of the shoulder; she still won't look at me. "I wasn't going to keep it a secret."

I try to picture how Yulia would've reacted to this unvetted breaking news story. The scenario would be comical had it not cost Rolf his life. "What's kept you here?"

At that, she meets my eyes, any hint of apology gone. "We're taught as children," she says, as if I don't know, "that our individual lives aren't important. That we're here to survive, all of us as a whole, and everything we do, everything we *live*, must be in service to that goal."

I shake my head; she's not wrong, not completely, but she's missed so much. "I know it's difficult for the young people," I tell her. "We all know it. We've been trying to—"

"But that's not what I mean." Her eyes have gone bright. "Of course it's oppressive, and impossible to believe all the time. I can see, now, that all of Novayarkha recognizes it; it's just that when you get older it's somehow easier to bear. I *want* to serve, Officer Savelova. We all do. Everyone in Novayarkha, and everyone here, too. We all have the same goal, and I stayed here because here is where I believe I can help."

Maddie coughs out a shadow of a laugh. "See what I mean?" she tells me. "You're all the same. Every one of you as mad as everyone else."

CHAPTER THIRTY-ONE

WHEN I WAS YOUNG—TAMARA'S AGE—YULIA ORLOVA PULLED ME FROM my quarry rotation to make me an apprentice peace officer. I wasn't happy about it. I loved the stone, and the sunshine, and the bitter wind on my hands; but Yulia was offering me meaning, this woman who was not yet governor but certain to be so soon. She praised my temperament and my talent for observation. She told me I could serve my people, bring them peace and consequence, give them a life that built something tangible. She told me I would be a part of a future that mattered.

I hadn't realized how much I needed to hear that until she'd said the words. I hadn't realized how much I'd give away, how much I'd compromise, how much I'd lie to be part of this elusive, consequential future I would never see.

We all become fools for purpose.

Before I can ask Tamara what she thinks our common goal is, Eleonora returns through the inner door, shooting me a glare. "She's ready for us," she says to Tamara, and then sobers. "I don't think—it's going to have to be short."

A look of understanding passes between them, and I turn to Maddie, expecting to see bleak grief, or—at most—exasperation at Tamara's optimism. Instead, she's frowning at Eleonora. I know the look, although I can't understand why she'd be trying to diagnose the young Exile. It's clear what's wrong with her. But Maddie's feeling something besides surrender and hopelessness, and as we follow our captors into the habitat, my stomach unknots a little.

With the airlock so familiar, I shouldn't be surprised by the similarities in the corridor beyond, but in fact the entire effect is profoundly unsettling. The corridor, like our Rims, is taller than it is wide, but it's altogether smaller in scale, clearly built from the auxiliary wheel closest to *Arkhangelsk*'s exhaust system. The arc is tighter, and I can't see far before us, just a few meters past Tamara and Eleonora. Above, the lights are dim, and all artificial—no solar tubes here, no natural light to brighten the bifurcated day and reassure us we haven't been buried alive.

"It's damp in here," Maddie remarks, and she's right. Suddenly the air feels thick and viscous in my throat. What kind of exhaust system do they have? What are they breathing? They can cleanse the environment, obviously—but I'm suddenly claustrophobic and homesick for the sunlit cobblestones in the Hub.

"This area isn't dehumidified," Tamara says, and I wonder how long it took her to ask the question after she arrived. "The system isn't big enough for the whole habitat. It has to go to priority sections."

Maddie takes the opening. "How is it heated?" she asks. Despite the moisture the air is warm, and I wonder if they have something like a quarry themselves.

"The habitat was built on top of *Arkhangelsk*'s auxiliary power core." Tamara sounds like she's reciting notes. "It's not as far down as the core in Novayarkha."

"What do you do for radiation protection?"

"We steal medicine," Tamara says simply.

I wonder if she's thought about the consequences of a long-term stay.

Eleonora ignores this exchange, her fingers skimming the corridor wall with the familiarity of old habit. If she's had any treatment at all, even just a few doses of stolen medicine, she's more ill than I suspected, and I wonder if she knows how little time she has left. I wonder if she's angry. Irina was angry, there at the end: angry and scared, and I held her and held her and still had to let her go.

The arc abruptly opens into a large room, and my anxiety flares. The floor is sheet metal, similar to the ceilings back home, but the walls, apart from support beams, are all exposed stone, veined in gray and layers of iron-red. Old habits have me desperately craving my quarry helmet, or at least my oxygen mask, and I have to hold my breath to calm myself.

There's a touch on my arm. It takes me an instant to realize it's not Irina but Maddie, hesitant, checking in on me. Without looking at her I cover her hand with my own and squeeze, gently. We're not alone, either of us.

But we are entirely outnumbered.

The room is full of people, although my sense of crowd is influenced by the size of the space. A quick count tells me there are not quite two dozen, all dressed alike in undyed woven clothing. They're standing in haphazard lines against the walls, leaving a path through the center of the room. Although I spy a few yellow heads, and skin tones from tundra-pale to hematite, the majority of them share Eleonora's dark hair, dark eyes, copper-brown skin over nondescript cheekbones. No incubators for variety, then; no ability to breed away from genetic defects, either.

At the other end of the makeshift path is an upright chair, outfitted with familiar equipment: a health monitor, an automated intravenous dosage system, a tray holding various pills, patches, and vials. Seated in the chair is a woman, as nondescript as the others; except this woman is far more ill, her hair thin and wiry, as if her deteriorating health has nothing left inside to destroy.

The Elder.

I can see her hands gripping the arms of the chair, but I don't know if that's in response to our presence, or how she keeps herself upright. I've seen enough death to know how close she is, but despite her illness I suspect she's no more than twenty-five years old. I scan the room again. They all range in age from Irina's slight-figured eight to Tamara's twenty-three; but most of them are Eleonora's age: teenagers, give or take a few years.

These can't be all of them. These can't be all the Exiles.

These are *children*.

The Elder lifts one hand, and Tamara turns to us. "Come closer," she says. "Nobody here will hurt you."

Which hadn't crossed my mind at all, but when I look again I notice everyone in the crowd is possessed of a holstered weapon. Yulia's not wrong, then. The Exiles have a solid arsenal. Assuming most of these weapons work, they have us in destructive power if not in numbers.

Maddie's looking at the Elder with that same studied frown she gave Eleonora. When Tamara and Eleonora start moving forward, she follows almost as an afterthought, and I fall into step with her, my eyes searching the faces we pass. Young, younger, youngest. And half of them won't survive until the next tea harvest.

What does Tamara think she—*anyone*—can do to help?

"Thank you for coming, Captain Loineau." The Elder speaks when we're still halfway across the room. Her voice has some strength, but I suspect it would be an effort for her to speak any louder. "And I'm sorry for the way in which you were escorted."

"It's not the escort that's the problem," Maddie says, but her voice is mild. "It's the threats."

The Elder gives Maddie a cool smile, and despite her youth and fragility she puts me squarely in mind of Yulia. "I wouldn't expect you'd understand what we face here," she says, with more than a little condescension. "To bring anyone from Novayarkha here, let alone a member of the Governor's council—we must be vigilant. Our survival is too precarious."

About that, I can't argue.

Maddie's eyes narrow, just a little; for now, she lets the threat lie. "If you don't mind my saying so," she says, "it seems more than precarious." She lets her eyes sweep the small crowd. "How many of the rest of you are ill?"

For the first time the Elder's eyes leave Maddie, and she looks at me. There's intelligence there, and hostility, but also assessment. She's measuring me. I measure her in return.

"There is no 'rest of us,'" she says, still holding my eyes. "We have a few in the nursery, but we don't expect many of them to survive."

Her voice is flinty, and I think the emotion behind the statement is genuine, but I've dealt too long with Yulia to let this Elder see how easily she's gutted me. "How many have you lost?" I ask her.

"Too many to count." But that's a theatrical statement, and she knows it, and after a moment she gives me a thin smile. "In the last twenty years? Forty-seven." There's a whisper off to one side, and the Elder frowns for a moment before saying. "No. Forty-eight."

Forty-eight. Twice what we've lost on the ice in Novayarkha. Twice what is standing here before us.

Is this what Yulia fears from the Exiles? Not their incursions, their violence, but evidence of our fragility? Without Halvorsen's careful order, without Selection and our incubators—how close are we to this fate, too many of us consumed by illness to maintain enough variation, too many lost to maintain our own habitat? Is this the threat Yulia has been fighting all these years—not illness, but fear?

She wouldn't know how they lived here. But with them persisting with us over these centuries, she might guess.

The Elder shifts in her chair and winces, and Maddie steps forward, heedless of Eleonora's hand falling to her gun. "Are you in pain?" Maddie asks.

The Elder nods warily. "All our painkillers make me sleep. I...I would stay awake, as long as I can."

My hand is in my pocket before Maddie reaches out, and I sort the analgesic patches from the electrolytes. This time Eleonora steps forward, alarmed, but Maddie quells her with a glare. "I won't hurt her," she says. Turning back to the Elder, she adds, "I can't even be sure these'll work, given how sick you are. But if you want to try them, they're yours."

A murmur flares up in the room, but the Elder is quick to shut them down. "She's not going to hurt me in front of everyone," she snaps, and I can see from the lines around her lips what raising her voice has cost her.

With the care of long practice, Maddie sweeps the Elder's wiry hair away from her neck and presses the patch against her skin. The Elder's eyes drop closed, just for an instant, and I think everyone in the room is holding their breath. Perhaps it's an illusion, but when she opens her eyes again, she seems more alert, more relaxed. Younger.

"Thank you," she says to Maddie, and her eyes stray to the last three patches. "Are there more?"

"This is all we have with us," Maddie says, and I wonder how many they have on *Hypatia*, how long they take to manufacture. She puts the patches on the table with the little groups of pills, and backs away. "Don't use them more often than once every five hours, or they'll lose their effectiveness." Her eyes scan the room again. "You could shore up these walls a bit," she says.

But the Elder's reply is unexpected. "There used to be more here," she said. "We've cannibalized the walls for the nursery. It's not the rock that's the problem."

Maddie nods, unsurprised; living in space, she would know all about the hazards of radiation. "It's the power core."

"It may have been cracked when they placed it," the Elder tells her, "but we're certain the asteroid that hit fifty years ago accelerated its decay. There was a time here when we were surviving, even comfortable, but the last thirty years our lives have grown very short. We think, sometimes, of trying to excavate and repair it, but..."

She gestures at the room, and I recognize the constraint. Even for the excavation alone this group is small, and losing too many would mean utter failure.

Maddie, having defused the room's hostility, gets to the point. "What is it I can help you with, Elder?"

The Elder's eyes linger for a moment on the medicine, and I see it in her, that pull toward more and greater comfort, resisted because she knows it's artificial, that it can't last. "We want you to send a message for us," she says, finally turning back to Maddie. "We've been fighting to preserve our archive, but our hardware won't last forever. If you could take it with you, transmit it back to Earth with your satellite—none of us live forever, Captain Loineau. But we would be remembered, if nothing else."

I'd forgotten the transceiver, that fragile piece of equipment dependent on Yulia's goodwill. But Maddie doesn't explain to the Elder all the problems she's had, or anything about *Hypatia*'s impaired state. Instead, she's grown still, as she did when she realized Hina's fate, and I can see the tension in her. "Of course, Elder," she says; tension notwithstanding, her voice is still gentle. "We can transmit whatever you'd like. We can even send it now, if you need to preserve a copy, although it'll be traveling the slow way. But—what is it you've got in your archive?"

I have always thought Maddie incapable of subterfuge, but it's clear the Elder doesn't recognize how very closely Maddie is paying attention to her response. "We have some of our own history, of course," the Elder says. "But preserving that...that's for our egos. What's more important are the mission logs."

"From *Arkhangelsk*?"

"Yes."

"How far back do they go?" Still quiet, still unassuming, but the tightness in her voice hums like a wire.

The Elder shifts; still uncomfortable, even with the medicine, and growing tired. "I'm not sure. Some of the earliest entries were damaged—we didn't realize until it was too late that the storage media was deteriorating. A lot was gone before we landed here, we think; but we have most of the data back to about a hundred years before planetfall. We've been trying to be more careful with what's left."

Back in school, when I was as young as Irina, we were taught the history of the Old World: her flora and fauna, the resource-driven politics, the superstition and corruption that led to her destruction. *Arkhangelsk* was our savior, our retreat, our last chance to survive the storm that was to engulf the planet.

Except she hadn't been our last chance at all, and somewhere in the Exiles' archive is the truth

"Why do you hoard this data?" The words are out of my mouth before I consider them.

The Elder looks surprised; I've somehow ceased to be a threat. "We hoard nothing. Novayarkha's got the ship's main logic center. We've never had anything but backups. The originals have always been with you." If she sees the shock in my face, she doesn't react to it. "You're welcome to look at them now," she tells us. "It'll give you something to do while you're waiting."

When I first spoke to Maddie, when she told me of the world my ancestors left, the world I will never see, I went back to Novayarkha's archives, seeking the knowledge I'd thought irrelevant when I was young. What I'd found was rich, tantalizing, spare. There were gaps in the records, especially early, information lost to time. The records were a sliver of the past, a shadow of a shadow, a thin foundation of our civilization. A curiosity. Unimportant, compared to the lessons we had chosen to bring forward with us.

A lie. We'd been shown reality made small, curated and meted out in meager proportions. All of our children—myself, Costa, Tamara, Camina and her new baby—we're all taught the same way, with gaps in our history, everything more out of focus the further back we go.

Hidden from us, all these years, all these centuries.

I don't want to look at the logs. I want to go home, and to Yulia, and find out how much of this she knows.

It's Maddie who asks the more relevant question: "What are we going to be waiting for?"

"There's some time before sunrise," the Elder says. When Maddie shifts with impatience, she adds, "There's no point to risk trying to get back to your ship in the dark. And I want to offer Officer Savelova some entertainment, since she'll be staying with us."

Maddie freezes.

"I'm sorry," she says, her tone brisk and cheerful, and I know her well enough now to hear the danger the Elder will almost certainly miss. "Are you suggesting I leave Anya behind?"

"Maddie," I begin, but she holds up a hand, and any attempt at defusing her is going to be fruitless.

"We can't let her go," the Elder says, composed; but she won't look at me. "She's one of them. She may not harm us from malice, but she'll tell them where we are. It's how she was raised."

Maddie crosses her arms, and I don't know who needs the warning anymore. Whatever traits The Elder shares with Yulia, she has no hope whatsoever of besting Maddie. "Well, then," Maddie tells her, equally composed, "we've got a problem. Because if any of you think I'm leaving her behind, you can head straight to whatever Inferno you might believe in. If you've managed to compose one worse than the here and now."

I have to try again. "Maddie."

But she rounds on me, fiery and furious. "No," she says, and I know that immovable expression. "And if they push the point? We can stand here and out-stubborn each other until the radiation fries every last one of us."

CHAPTER THIRTY-TWO

"THEY WILL *KILL YOU*, ANYA."

Maddie's whispering, but here in these close quarters there is no point, and I don't bother. "Nonsense. They want your help. And they don't know you well enough to know you'll keep your word without a hostage."

We're following Tamara and Eleonora back through the arc, and the familiar insulated walls of the corridor have cleared my head. Tamara's moving with her usual efficient grace, but Eleonora glances back at us every three or four steps, mostly to scowl at me, as if I'm responsible for Maddie's transformation from beatific savior to my avenging warrior.

After Maddie's declaration before The Elder, the crowd began to shift, their lines breaking up; but no one made a sound. Silent protest is cultural, I suppose, but it was unsettling, like a distant vibration in the ice. The Elder gave the kinetic chaos half a minute, then asked Tamara and Eleonora to escort us to the archive room while she decided how she wanted to proceed.

It wasn't an ask, of course, but an order. Even in frailty, The Elder has seasoned, reflexive power. I wonder who, in that room, is positioned to succeed her. I wonder how long they'll live to serve.

"So they're going to lock us in the basement until they get to know me?" Maddie turns away from me; her whole body is tense, twitchy, like a quarrier who's spent the last three hours laying explosives. "Because despite what I just said in there, I don't actually want to stick around long enough for radiation to randomize my DNA. There's a reason nobody here is over twenty-five, or did you miss that part?"

She's picking a fight, possibly the first one we've had, and it's grief, I know it, but her entire history didn't just unravel before her. "You haven't any standing to tell me what to do," I tell her sharply, and this time when Eleonora glances back at me, her face holds some alarm. "We have exactly one asset here, and it's not your ill-timed recalcitrance."

Maddie falls silent, and I should apologize, but just now it wouldn't sound sincere. She steps ahead of me, annoyed, and Tamara takes the opportunity to drop back into her place.

"Officer Savelova. Is my mother all right?"

Her tone is uncertain, part fear, part understanding that I've no incentive to treat her with any kindness at all. "'All right' is relative," I say, but in a few steps I relent. "I spoke to her several days ago. She's unwell. But I believe if she were very close to death, I would've heard."

She glances at me, gratitude in her eyes diluted by sadness. "She doesn't like me very much, you know," she says, with the resignation of someone who long ago recognized an unwelcome truth.

"Parents are complicated." I think of the adoptive family I had, lost to illness when I was still a child, the good and the bad of them. I think of Halvorsen, who will always be the first mother I ever knew. "Love and liking don't always go together."

We walk in silence, and I keep my eyes on Maddie's feet before us. When Tamara speaks again, I can barely hear her. "I didn't think they'd kill him."

I look over at her, studying the woman I'd paid so little attention before she vanished. Under that precise, self-assured beauty I can glimpse, around her eyes and in the set of her lips, the child she used to be, that she still largely is. If she stays healthy, she'll have so many more years to make mistakes. "Neither did I," I admit to her. "We were both wrong." And then, somewhat against my better judgement, I ask, "Did he kill Oksana?"

She considers. "I think he was unspeakably cruel to her," she says at last, and I wonder if she's been thinking about it, if she's trying to excuse her part in Rolf's fate. "He is—was—very good at hiding that part of himself, in the beginning. He may not have physically taken her life, but I've no doubt he made the ice look very attractive."

None of it matters now, and it will not repair anything, but I ask her all the same. "Did he make the ice attractive to you?"

"No." She's candid, trusting, and I wonder what that means. "But I'd started thinking of other things in my life. Things that didn't revolve around him."

"Children."

"Yes." She doesn't ask how I know. "Even before I came here... once you see, really see, how we're all connected, helping feels so natural, doesn't it?"

She's so clear about it, so changed from the woman Rolf spoke of, railing at the restrictions of our carefully balanced lives. I suppose maturity hits some suddenly. I hope she has a chance to live her connected life past this day.

She studies Maddie, several meters ahead of us now, stubbornly trailing at Eleonora's heels. "Your friend. She doesn't know this place. Would it help her to know it was probably peaceful for her daughter, that the cold would have made it painless?"

Tamara has no way of knowing how foolish that suggestion is. Still, when I say "No, I don't think it would help her," my voice is harsher than I intend.

I look up; Irina's by Maddie's side, looking over her shoulder. She's annoyed with me.

Why should Irina feel for Tamara? Tamara's just as guilty as I am.

The archive room is on a lower level, like our fabrication room, and it's both warmer and drier than the rest of the habitat. Tables, chairs, storage bins, cabinets are scattered haphazardly, and there's something in the arrangement that makes me think of *Hypatia*'s fuselage, designed without floor or ceiling. There are multiple screens settled on a neat row of desks, all fronted by the same sturdy keyboards we have in Novayarkha: hardware designed to last centuries, although I'm always shocked to find one without missing keys or frayed connectors.

Maddie has headed immediately for the screens. She's still focused on the archive, and I need to talk to her, to clear the air between us; but I don't want to read the archive, not yet. I don't want to know what lives in the gaps in my knowledge. And yet I've survived the past few days, flying into orbit and places without gravity and learning my friends were drugging me, all because of Maddie. I turn back to Tamara. "Her grief isn't the same as ours," I tell her, granting her absolution. "What she needs is time. Mercy can come later."

Gratitude again, in those young, dark eyes. If only forgiveness was enough.

I wait next to Tamara as Eleonora explains the archive interface to Maddie. Maddie frowns and swipes at the screen, but catches on quickly enough; Eleonora retreats from her and drops into a chair a few tables away, sulking or exhausted, I can't tell. "What do you think The Elder is going to do?" I ask Tamara.

On this point, she knows as little as I do. "I expect she'll promise Captain Loineau whatever she must," Tamara says. "Maybe... maybe you could persuade her to relent."

Tamara, who doesn't know Maddie, has no idea of the absurdity of her idea, but it gives me a pretext to speak with Maddie without Tamara listening in. "I'll try," I tell her.

I pull a chair over to Maddie's desk and sit next to her. She's squinting at the screen, pressing the menu controls with unpracticed clumsiness; I reach to the screen and tap the control labeled *ARKHANGELSK* LOGS, then sit back as the submenu comes up. "Ah," she says, then taps on MISSION MANIFESTS, mimicking my more targeted press. "Not as clunky as I would've thought," she says.

She's still, free hand in her lap, and I want to reach out to her, but I don't know if it's time.

"Kano used to say that about me," she said. "That I was stubborn at all the wrong times."

"He knew you, too."

She turns her head toward me, surprised, and something light flares briefly in her eyes. "Yeah." Her gaze drops to the floor. "None of this is you. None of this is your fault."

"This is why I yelled at you," I explain, but I keep my tone light, and she smiles, just a little. "Maddie. I don't know what's going to happen here. But I know they will not take your life. How we use that knowledge I don't yet understand, but we will use it."

It's Maddie who opens her hand to me, and our fingers intertwine, and there's no need to worry about being overheard because we don't need to speak.

At length she looses my hand and goes back to the screen, and perhaps I make some kind of sound because she stops, turning toward me. "What?"

I don't understand myself, my unsettled stomach, my mind shying away from these mundane records full of missing pieces. "It's too much," I tell her at last.

"It's only history, Anya."

I don't want to say it. I don't want to understand what's happening. "If they've been hiding things from us," I say, "there will be a reason."

"There may be nothing new here at all," she tells me. "And if there is—with all your old hardware, Anya, your people may have genuinely lost what you weren't shown."

I don't think she believes that any more than I do.

She takes my hand again. "That's the thing about history, Anya," she says gently. "What we want to be true doesn't matter. It's the same for me. I don't want to believe any of what's happened. I want reality to be something else." She squeezes my fingers. "The Colonel always taught us that there was power in truth, even in unwelcome truth. And what you know now—it's not a lie. Your life in Novayarkha is not a lie. The only thing you might learn is that the colony didn't become what it is the way you thought it did."

I've always, my whole life, reached for the truth. Now, with it before me—"And what if I've accepted a great many lies, Maddie?"

"Then the truth," she says, "is long overdue. Let's find the truth, Anya."

And we do.

ARCHIVE #13981

INCIDENT REPORT: ATTEMPT BY INSURRECTIONISTS TO STEAL MUNITIONS
DAY 227, COLONY YEAR 22

LOGGED BY: MARGARETE KUZNETSOVA, GOVERNOR
B. SHIP YEAR 172
D. COLONY YEAR 44

That was a clusterfuck.

I should probably add to that. But with two dead? How else am I supposed to put it? At least they took some of the bastards with them. I told fucking Zorah to add more patrols.

Especially because we knew they were coming, although why they told us they needed munitions is beyond me. They couldn't possibly have thought we'd help them, not after what the Insurrectionists did while *Arkhangelsk* was still whole, not after all the lives they took and the damage they did. All those decades— *centuries*—of fine fabrication progress? Gone because of one fatally stupid settlement protest.

There'll never be peace with these people. They'd rather see us all dead, themselves included, before they'll be civilized.

Intel from Civil Defense says they're planning to crash the auxiliary core into the mountains. More destruction. I hope it kills them all. I hope it breaks open and irradiates the whole place. Not even sure I care if it kills us at the same time, as long as it takes care of them.

We've still got the system core, at least. There's no way they can rebuild with the stubs they've been left with. They're stuck on this planet as well, only they have to make do with fewer materials and no manufacturing at all.

I hope they all die. I hope the radiation takes every one of them, and it hurts. For a long time.

Why couldn't they just leave us alone?

ARCHIVE #10001

CONSTRUCTION UPDATE
SHIP YEAR 197, COLONY YEAR 8

LOGGED BY: OLGA TERESHKOVA, DEPARTMENT OF CONSTRUCTION
B. SHIP YEAR 132
D. COLONY YEAR 9

*****
DRAFT
*****

Destruction of the North Medical Facility and severe damage to the engine room and materials fabrication section by Insurrectionist forces have required major modifications to the previously-proposed Settlement Plan. The most significant change is that Settlement will no longer be optional. Given the substantial damage, the Governor's Council has deemed the risk of continued travel to be too high.

Stage One: Location

The original Location Committee specified two possibilities: the Equatorial Crater Plain, which would provide more shelter and easier mining, and the

Polar Tundra, which has a steadier climate but weaker magnetosphere protection.

The loss of Fine Fabrication requires us to focus on the preservation of our current hardware inventory, with an eye toward rebuilding our Fine Fabrication facilities in the ensuing decades. Despite the higher radiation risk, the Polar Tundra is more geologically stable. Therefore, the Location Committee has dropped advocacy for the Equatorial Crater Plain.

All design documents have been altered to assume parts placement in the Polar Tundra, as identified. (Schematic attached.[1])

Risk factors: While the Insurrectionists responsible for the wreckage are currently contained, we have no confidence they're the only outlaws on board.

Proposed mitigation: To preserve what we can of our surviving manufacturing equipment, empower Peace Officers with rapid restraint authority.

Stage Two: Excavation

The stability of the Polar Tundra removes the concern over the surface substrate. Moreover, with the option of remaining aboard *Arkhangelsk* no longer available, power core alterations may safely begin while the excavation is ongoing.

Stage Three: Construction and Migration

Because migration must now be concurrent with construction, the Infrastructure Committee recommends we place the main habitat ring first, modifying the current Secondary Medical Center to be the primary center for the surface habitat.

This will require waiting for the full excavation to be complete, and for a concentric ring of insulation to be placed once the habitat ring is secured.

---

1   See Archive 10,001.s1

Projected time to place and seal the ring is estimated at seven weeks. The ring will be radiation-safe within three weeks. At this point, some individuals will be permanently relocated from *Arkhangelsk*. The outer ring habitat will accommodate 982 people as currently configured; priority will be given to those people on building crews, and with structural and mechanical expertise.

Once the primary ring is structurally sound, the power core will be dropped, and the spokes connected to a central mechanical hub. At this point, the primary ring's environmental structures will be permanent. Placement of the secondary ring will be gated by personnel need.

Crew remaining aboard *Arkhangelsk* will be locking down the tertiary ring to provide accommodation to the Insurrectionists, while also restricting them from sabotaging our efforts.

Risk factors:

1.   There is no backup plan once the primary ring is disconnected. The ship isn't designed to accelerate without the balanced rings, and with the faster-than-light field designed for *Arkhangelsk's* original configuration, attempting ftl travel would be, at best, extraordinarily foolhardy.

2.   Balancing the environment for both plant and human survival is going to be an issue until both rings are placed and sealed. We're going to need to prepare people for real hardship, including food shortages and cold.

3.   No matter how well we seal the rings during construction, we're going to get hit with radiation. We're going to see more illness, and a higher fatality rate.

4.   There is some talk of stranding the Insurrectionists without the secondary power core, or of sabotaging it before we descend. Given the number of Insurrectionists and the relative variety of their genetic backgrounds, this seems an unacceptable waste.

Proposed mitigation:

    1.   N/A.

    2.   The Governor should begin making speeches now, focused on individual sacrifice and the survival of the colony as a whole. The older people won't survive long after we've moved anyway; they should be the primary target of these messages.

    3.   Harvest data from the sick and dying and feed it back into our genome mods. This is the best real-world lab we're going to get. If we play it right, we'll have better data here than from two hundred years of medical trial and error.

    4.   We might consider extracting their genetic material and encoding it with behavioral warnings first; but we're not without citizens who have some sympathy for the Insurrectionists' cause, even if they disagree with their methods. Recommend some case studies here.

MEDICAL OPERATIONS LOG, SHIP-WIDE
DAY 184
SHIP YEAR 165

LOGGED BY: DMITRI CONSTANTIN, DOCTOR
B. SHIP YEAR 122
D. SHIP YEAR 184

Patient Y has developed an intolerance to chlordiazepoxide. Given Patient's response to diazepam, this is unsurprising. Family is unwilling to continue to host Patient without the assistance of some sort of sedative or hypnotic. Referred the case to the Peace Department.

Patient R was sent home Thursday. Nothing left to be done here, and Patient can't tolerate any of the painkillers anymore. Patient's mother asked me for a different solution. I explained about my oath. Patient's mother was unhappy with my response. Private note: We need better pain management, and better end-of-life care. R's just a child and can't understand.

Test run 1,456 completed successfully. It's early to tell much, but mutational effects appear to have been entirely avoided, counteracting the adverse effects of 1,022. I'm calling for more testing, possibly with simultaneous deployment to those modded with 1,022. I'll petition Captain Ossvald for permission to mod some runs in progress as well.

Patient B has fully recovered, although Patient's sight appears permanently impaired. Recommend Patient be returned to horticultural duties with corrective eyewear, with a directive to begin mastering touch-based reading and writing. Also recommend Patient write a text on their experiences. Another accident like that one could kill them, and I'd hate to lose all that knowledge.

ARCHIVE #1244

INTRODUCTORY HISTORY TEXTBOOK, PROPOSED DELETIONS
SHIP YEAR 55

In "Chapter 1: Our Brave Mission," remove the following paragraphs:

But the smooth and hopeful takeoff was not to be. Instead, years before our ship would have been fully prepared to leave, hundreds of riotous, lawless criminals broke in with guns, murdered many scientists, and forced the ship to launch immediately.

After many months of bloody fighting, the criminals were subdued. While some were executed in front of the families of those they had killed, there were those among the scientists who argued another course: unity. The precipitous departure from Earth had left our ship short of essential crew, and many of the criminals had valuable skills. After years of negotiations, compromise was reached, the criminals agreeing to exclude their DNA from our reproductive cache, and to abide by the original regulations formed for Arkhangelsk's mission. The result was our first Consortium Government, dedicated to allowing our mission to proceed once again with safety.

In "Chapter 4: Scientific Advancements," remove the following sentences:

Genome research technology relies on cultured growths that are modded by our senior medical team. New methods and new modifications are constantly under test, used on non- and semi-viable growths hundreds of times before being deployed to the general public.

In "Chapter 17: Government History," remove the listing for Captain Sascha Lebed.

Approved by: Acting Governor Piotr Lubayev

ARCHIVE #94

LAST TRANSMISSION RECEIVED FROM EARTH
SHIP YEAR 11

SENDER: UNKNOWN

Greetings, Starship *Arkhangelsk*.

By our calculations, you should be proceeding to faster-than-light travel shortly after this message reaches you. Thanks to revolution and government interference, we don't know how much we heard of your departure is true. But we wished to send you a message, if we can, before you're out of range forever:

We remember why you were built. We remember why we all worked so hard to get the materials, the correct minds, why so many risked lying to the government and the soldiers in order to keep the project moving. We look at it on our star charts, every night: 974-33, so dim from here. You'll see it, someday, long after all of us are gone, and I hope you find a home there, and are happy.

There's little optimism here these days. The government, as governments often are, is still adept at pitting the wrong people against each other. The few who have amassed great wealth think they've built a fortress, but they don't understand it's seated on rot, on rage, and it'll collapse someday, and they'll have nowhere to run from the wreckage. It's difficult for us to see much of a way forward. We're all trapped, angry, impotent.

But your escape gives us hope beyond reason.

We make you this pledge: we will come after you. We'll reach our hand into the stars just as you've reached, and we'll join you in that star system, build a home with you, and we'll break bread and tell stories until we're all laughing and sobbing and too drunk to stand.

That day may never come. But we promise you, *Arkhangelsk*: we will work for it. We will fight for it. And if Fate has any sense of justice, our children's children will build with you in the light of a new sun.

Be comforted, and be at peace. We are coming.

CHAPTER THIRTY-THREE

WE ARE COMING.

They were always coming after us.

We left the Old World, but they didn't abandon us. They reached after us, mourned us, wished us safe flight. They didn't know the scientists who'd started it all had lost control, had their plans thrown into chaos. They didn't know our mission had shifted, had changed, was upended until internal conflict prevented us from fulfilling it at all. They didn't know we kept warring, kept killing, kept making mistakes. Kept surviving, somehow, through it all.

Dumb luck, Maddie had said.

All of my life, I believed we were alone. I believed there was nothing but us, would be nothing after us. And all of my life, *Hypatia* was on her way here. Maddie was on her way.

The lies should enrage me. All these omissions in what we've been told, what we've been taught—I should be bitter, despairing. And yet here, in this strange and familiar room, among these people who want to kill me, my world finally makes sense.

Maddie, my Maddie, is next to me, her eyes on the screen, oblivious to my bright and brimful heart. She's pulled up the ship's schematic, the plan attached to the construction update we read, the crew's precipitous adaptation after disaster. Of course she would be interested in the logistics of *Arkhangelsk*'s repurposing; they're supposed to be building a satellite after all, a communications device that will bring us more people, *our* people, all of the Old World and all the history we missed.

They've missed our history as well. We will have so much to tell each other.

I blink my eyes clear, and focus on Maddie's work. She's swiping through the Outer Rim—or what became the Outer Rim: *Arkhangelsk*'s massive tertiary ring, home of their scientific work, now home to most of us, to our medical center, to levels of fabrication and mining, to the final home of our dead. The schematic looks like the chiseled maps we've mounted on the Spoke walls, feats of skilled carving and inking, artwork in their own right. Most of us never look at them, never need them; they're useful for small children who are lost, and for those from whom illness or age has taken their ability to orient.

"It seems very like *Hypatia*," I remark to Maddie.

"I guess the centuries between the two ships weren't a renaissance of industrial design." But her tone is distracted. "Anya. What's under the medical center?"

It takes me a moment to realize what she's doing. Curiosity satisfied about our shared history, she's found the closest thing to a map of Novayarkha that exists.

She's doing what Aleksey has been doing for days: searching the city for Hina.

"Maddie," I begin, but she shoots me a glare, and I relent. "There's a lot under the habitat level. There's a birthing room, and a clean room where we can isolate people with radiation exposure. Storage, too. That's where the incubators are kept when they're not in use."

"Show me."

The schematic is for *Arkhangelsk* and not Novayarkha, and it takes me a moment to mentally reorient the space. "Here's the medical center." I tap on a sequence of rooms, then scroll back toward the ring's outer wall. "This, underneath, is where we've set up the birthing room. It's used for incubator births, and if the birthing parent has no other family. And this—" I follow the arc sideways to a small room with no utilities but climate control— "is incubator storage. That's the door Tamara's raid damaged."

But Maddie's not thinking about the raid, or the damage. She's tensed, and her fingers are moving, hands clenching and unclenching. Her mind is racing. "Under that, Anya. What's under that?"

"You mean now?" Fine fabrication takes up most of the Eastern Arc, but because of its specific environmental requirements, it's isolated from the rest of that level. The Crypt requires very little in terms of heat and cooling; all our dead are already burned, and the cold hurts them not at all. "The Crypt, I believe," I tell Maddie; but I haven't been in there often enough, can't picture in my head how far one would have to walk to get under the medical center. "I don't think it's fabrication. There's too much risk of residual chemicals getting into the air, and—what is it?"

"Look at this." She zooms in: walls, one environmental panel, one door, which would be in what's now a floor. "Did you go through the incubator room to do a search, Anya?"

"No, I—" I've been in incubator storage a dozen times in my life. "Maddie. There's no door in there. They'd have sealed it, I suspect, and then—"

"Expanded the crypt?" She looks at me. "Maybe. Maybe. But listen: there's gravity on this planet."

"Yes." We've been here too long, clearly. "There is."

"Up on *Hypatia*? We don't have gravity, except where we spin the ring. *Arkhangelsk* would've been the same. All the ship's structural integrity would've been in the walls and the flooring of the rings. Especially that big ring, which is spinning faster than the others. Steady angular momentum, designed to last for centuries. And then there's gravity, and twelve meters of fucking ice. You tell me they blew out a load-bearing wall to hold some extra coffins,

I'll believe you. But I want to hear you *know* it. You've been there. Because from how this looks, there's a whole unaccounted-for room in that city. And if there is? Hina's there, and we need to leave now, Anya. Not at first sunrise. Now."

She's tapping on the screen, as if it should mean something to me. "Burying the rings changed a lot of things," I point out. "This room—"

She makes an exasperated noise, and across the room I see Tamara look up, frowning. "Look. I've been doing pretty much fuck-all with my life besides studying how to build this fucking satellite we're supposed to build. Yeah, I trained in medicine, but our entire existence is materials science, structural engineering. Mining. All of it. Dammit, Anya, you worked in a quarry for *years*. Think about this. Blocking off an area of the ring is one thing, but they'd've had to shear off and re-seal an entire level to get rid of this space. *Why would they do that?*"

"I—" There's nothing there. There's never been anything there. The lower level of the Inner Rim contains fine fabrication, walled off with temperature-reinforced sheeting, and the crypt, wandering and sinuous rooms, stacks of coffins, small and large, all the ghosts that haunt me at night. Irina appears next to me, unbidden; my stomach is turning over. "Perhaps it was damaged," I suggest. "When they dropped it in."

But she's shaking her head. "No. For it to fit properly—for them to prepare the surface underneath it so it got enough support—it would've had to have happened before they put it in. The damage from their insurrection was in the engine room, an entire kilometer away." She catches Tamara's eye and looks back at me, swearing quietly. "I don't know why nobody knows, I don't know why they've taken her, I don't even know if she's alive. All I know—dammit, Anya, *you do not see that place*. How can you? It's all you've ever known."

She's pleading with me now, and I want to tell her I know Novayarkha like my own heart, and I think of Halvorsen bringing up Irina at every Remembrance and Costa pouring poison down my throat. I remember the view from *Hypatia*'s fuselage of this murderous place and how clean and innocent it looked. I think of all those archives, all kept in secret, and how impossible it would have been to sink the secondary power core in secret.

I think of Yulia's fingers on my arm after Rolf's death.

"All right," I tell Maddie. "We leave now."

She tears up, and even though I'm sure she's only relieved she's convinced me, I reach out and squeeze her hand. She squeezes back, then blinks and straightens in the chair. "Will Tamara shoot us?" she asks.

"I don't know," I tell her honestly. "I imagine it depends on what her alternatives are."

Maddie sets her jaw. "Follow my lead," she says, and gets to her feet.

Not unexpectedly, it's Eleonora that rushes forward, hand on her weapon, but behind her Tamara looks little more than aggravated. Maddie walks around the table toward them, but somehow my transparent friend manages to look relaxed and conciliatory, all the desperation of our conversation concealed. She holds out her hands. "It's all right," she says. "I only have a question."

Eleonora frowns. "I haven't read the archives," she says. "I can't answer any questions."

"It's not about that." Maddie stops a meter away from the girl; I'm watching Eleonora's gun hand, but Tamara's eyes are on me. "The archives refer to people getting sick," Maddie says, and that's at best a stretch of the truth of what we read. "Would you—if you'd permit me to examine you, to see how your illness parallels what was described in the archives…I might be able to help some of you."

It's a brutal and manipulative lie, but it works. Eleonora steps closer, her hand falling from her weapon, and Maddie reaches for the Exile's face. "May I?" she asks, and at Eleonora's nod she probes gently at her throat, feeling for swelling, taking her pulse.

"You're not feverish," Maddie says. "Is that typical?"

"It comes and goes." Eleonora stands passively as Tamara, unengaged, begins looking around the room. "We treat it with willow bark extract. When we can get it." She shoots me a hostile look.

"Do you know where you're sick?"

"Do you mean where the cancer is growing?" Her tone is arch, but she still doesn't tense. "My liver."

"Is that all?"

"So far."

Maddie drops her hands, and I look away from Eleonora's gun long enough to take in the combination of hope and regret on Maddie's face. "Do you mind if I take a look?"

For a moment Eleonora's natural skepticism seems certain to thwart Maddie's plan, but then, astonishingly, the girl nods, and Maddie steps behind her. Eleonora helpfully tugs her shirt out of the waistband of her trousers, and I get a glimpse of the skin of her back, not as anemic as the gray-tan of her face, but covered in purple and green bruises.

"This isn't from the cancer," Maddie says, gently pushing at the wound.

"It's from the raid," Eleonora says. "I took a fall."

"A hard one." At Eleonora's silence, Maddie asks, "Does it hurt?"

"Only when I'm lying down."

"I'm guessing inflammation, or a muscle spasm," Maddie says. "But I'd really like to get one of our medical scanners down here. Salicylic may cut the pain, but I've got better things if inflammation is the big issue."

And then, with the same deft ease with which she'd probed the bruise, Maddie pulls the gun out of the holster at Eleonora's waist. Tamara, finally realizing she needs to be alarmed, pulls the energy weapon, but I can see from her stance she won't use it, not here, not indoors, not where it could destroy everything these people have fought to preserve.

For an instant Eleonora's behavior is age-appropriate, her face reflecting astonishment and hurt; and then she's an Exile again. "You won't kill me," she says to Maddie.

"You're as presumptuous as the rest of them," Maddie says, and I have to remind myself I too want to leave, because I want to tell her she's angry and frightened and I know she doesn't really want to kill anyone. "You tell me my daughter is dead. You show me old maps and messages from your ancestors like they mean a fucking thing. My crew is getting *sniped* by fucking saboteurs, and you're all dying anyway."

"*Maddie.*" I can't keep quiet, and she scowls at me.

"We're *all* dying, Anya. Isn't that what you told me?" She moves the nose of the weapon from Eleonora to Tamara. "I know you won't fire that thing, but please drop it anyway, because I will cheerfully shoot you first."

To her credit, Tamara waits, her arms shaking. "Officer Savelova?"

"Compliance seems prudent," I tell her, and I'm not sure if I'm playing along with Maddie's plot or just trying to stay alive.

Tamara lowers the weapon and puts her hand over the barrel, holding the hilt out toward Maddie. Eleonora wails Tamara's name in frustration as Maddie takes the gun, but I'm most surprised when she holds it out toward me.

"I don't want it," I tell her.

"We can't leave it here," she points out. "Just—put it in your pocket or something. I don't have room in mine."

Gingerly I take it from her; it's close enough to our models that I can at least check the charge. I wonder if I should tell her it wasn't activated. I drop it into my suit pocket.

"Okay." In control, she sounds far more relaxed and cheerful. Tamara moves toward Eleonora, but the young Exile steps away.

"Traitor," she snaps.

"Don't be silly." Maddie scolds her like a parent. "She did the right thing. And I mean it about the anti-inflammatories. Once we find Hina and get her home, I'll bring down enough for all of you, and maybe get some proper medical care into this place. But right now? We need to get back to Novayarkha."

"It's the *middle of the night*," Eleonora says, as if Maddie's stupid. "We don't have the equipment."

"Can we make it back to the ECV?" Maddie asks me.

The idea's mad. The ECV is at least an hour's walk away, and Maddie and I don't know the terrain at all. We'd be at the mercy of two people whose lives we just threatened, whose tenuous trust we've completely violated. "If we wear layers of heavier clothes underneath our suits, we should be able to get that far. If we don't get lost."

"I don't understand," Tamara says. She's unhappy, but she's not frightened, and I'm not sure if that's good or bad. "Why are we rushing? You were going to leave in the morning anyway."

"Hina's back in Novayarkha." At Tamara's look, Maddie makes a dismissive gesture. "I know what you believe. It doesn't matter. She's been gone five days for reasons I don't understand, and I'm not leaving her alone one more second."

I see calculation in Tamara's eyes—the reporter again, or perhaps just a woman making a choice. "Then I'll take you." I'm fairly certain Tamara doesn't believe Maddie's conclusions, but she recognizes the determination of a parent with a lost child. "Leave Officer Savelova here with Eleonora. We'll do exactly what we planned, just sooner."

Eleonora's glaring at me, and I have a sense of exactly how much consideration she'd give before abandoning me outside without my helmet. But if Tamara's a reporter again, I know what I need to say. "There's something wrong in Novayarkha, Tamara," I tell her. "There's something going on in the medical center, and we need to find out what it is."

I expect her to object, to tell me I'm mad, or pandering to

Maddie's delusions. But something flickers across her face, a glimmer of realization, and is gone.

She's not surprised. And I wonder what else I have been missing all these years.

"Your helmets are still in the airlock," she says. "We keep extra thermal clothing there as well. We can change on the way out."

Eleonora says *traitor* again, but all I can see is Maddie's face, grief replaced by energy and optimism, and no matter what Halvorsen's been hiding from all of us, I hope beyond reason we find Hina alive.

CHAPTER THIRTY-FOUR

THE WALK TO THE ECV TAKES US FAR MORE THAN AN HOUR, BUT ALTHOUGH Eleonora has become alarmingly quiet by the time we arrive, she manages to make it up the ladder on her own. Once we're inside, Maddie runs the decontamination sequence and blasts the heat, pulling off her helmet and gloves to show the others it's safe. She's not aiming the gun at anyone anymore; here inside the ECV, we're all at her mercy.

I help Tamara and Eleonora out of their thin protective suits as Maddie fetches emergency blankets for them. The cabin is warming up quickly, but I rub Eleonora's icy fingers between my palms all the same. "That hurts," she says after a few moments.

"That means your nerves aren't damaged," I tell her. She frowns, but in her eyes I see a hint of gratitude. Or perhaps Maddie's optimism is wearing off on me.

Tamara, less chilled than Eleonora, is looking around the cabin, her mouth open. "This—it *flies*?"

Maddie shoots her a grin. "Not gracefully," she admits, "but yeah, it gets us to and from our ship."

"It's not aerodynamic."

"You think big chunks of ring are aerodynamic?"

I catch Tamara's eye and shake my head. "She tried to explain it to me," I confess. "I didn't understand. But it flies nonetheless."

To my surprise it's Eleonora who asks me the question. "You've been up there?"

Her hands are still between mine, and I massage them gently. "It's very much like home," I tell her. "Better lit than what you're used to. But there's a familiarity to it. Although…it smells a lot different."

Eleonora's nose wrinkles, but her eyes have gone wide and full of wonder. "You've seen the planet. From up there."

"I have." I stop rubbing, searching for words. "We are…this place is small. Fragile. Beautiful. You wouldn't think it was deadly."

"Nobody—" She looks away then, and abruptly she becomes young, just another little girl, not a woman at the end of a hard-fought life. "No matter what The Elder says, we all thought like your governor. That they were dead. That they'd never come. And now—" Her features twist back into bitterness. "She'll tell Novayarkha about us, and they'll destroy us. Your governor was right about that, too: they bring destruction."

Maddie crouches down in front of Eleonora, a folded protective suit held out flat before her. "Nobody's destroying anybody," she says. "Now put this on. You'll be less conspicuous."

Puzzled, Eleonora takes the suit, and I stand with Maddie. "She won't, really," I point out. "Yulia knows where we've been. Without Novayarkhan outdoor gear, we're going to stand out regardless."

"As far as Yulia knows," Maddie says, heading for the ship's console, "Eleonora's a member of my crew."

"Nobody on your crew is sick like she is, Maddie. And they all know Tamara. We can't just stroll into the city. We'll be stopped and questioned immediately, and there's no time for any of that. How is it you're planning to get into this mysterious hidden space?"

She fixes me with those determined eyes, and I'm not sure how I've missed that hint of madness behind the intelligence. "Counting on you for that. You know that place inside and out, don't you?"

I've been in the med center a thousand times. I have no idea where anyone could hide a door, never mind a stairway or a lift. "I suppose we could start with incubator storage." Which means we'll be adjacent to the above the crypt, and I clench my fists against a shudder. "Although people are in and out of there all the time."

"Which people?"

"I—" It's a good question. Who have I seen go in there? "It's locked with a senior-level code, although I'd expect most of the medical staff has access. But the only one I've personally seen go in there is Doctor Halvorsen."

"You trust her?"

I have never trusted Halvorsen. "She has no reason to kidnap Hina, never mind without Yulia's permission. But…if Hina's being kept against her will, drugged as I was—we are scrupulous about inventory, because we must be. There will be records, somewhere, of medicines used. These I may be able to access."

Maddie nods. "Okay. So what's the best way in?"

"The quarry," I say immediately. "With the snow due before first sunset, they'll be busy assembling charges and shifting ore. There's a good possibility we can make it past the pit without being detected, and then if we head inside through the metals lab—"

"I have a better idea."

We both turn to Tamara. She's in the vacuum suit from *Hypatia*, her helmet tucked under her arm, and Maddie wasn't wrong: poised, confident, she could pass as a member of the crew. Beside her Eleonora's tugging at the neck of her suit, trying to keep her chin free of the too-large garment.

"I got out of there undetected," Tamara tells us. "I'm pretty sure I can get us back in."

The other end of Tamara's discovered tunnel opens much closer to the Exile habitat, and we have to backtrack. I can see in Maddie's body language her frustration and urgency, but for the moment, like me, she's chosen to trust Tamara. It's Eleonora who's most annoyed, and Maddie has to promise her she'll take her for a flight when this is all finished before the worst of her teenaged excesses vanish. She falls in behind Maddie, and I follow, alert for stumbles. Nothing Maddie had on the ECV fit the child properly; even the boots she's wearing are two sizes too big. I wonder if Maddie can treat her, if she'll grow any more, if her feet will become longer, if she'll lose that hollow look.

Hope is cruel. But I hope all the same.

The tunnel entrance is half a kilometer before the chasm, far east of the ECV, neatly concealed by old runoff and snowdrifts. I'm prepared to pull out our rappelling equipment again, but there are stairs at the entrance, worn but solid. To my surprise the tunnel's tall enough for us all to walk upright, the floor etched for traction. It's very like walking down a corridor at home. I wonder how long ago this was built, an extension of the war that followed us throughout our journey from Earth.

We emerge at the foot of the hill beyond the quarry—out of sight of the city for at least half a kilometer. The hours have given us full daylight, and it's a particularly clear morning, as it often is before a storm. They'll be blasting in the quarry this morning, and with some luck they'll be too busy setting charges and taking readings to notice a few of *Hypatia*'s crew members sauntering over the snow.

But we are noticed as we skirt the quarry. A figure crossing the secondary courtyard raises a hand to us; friendly, casual. Heart in my throat I wave back, and wait for the figure to signal us to wait, or to summon someone else; but she's turned and is walking away from us, toward the Inner Rim, once again absorbed in her own business.

Once we're down the stairs and through the prison airlock I start breathing again. I usher the others in before me; while they start stripping off their helmets and heavy gloves, I peer through the tiny window of the inner door. In the distance, I can see people turning down the west spoke, heading to breakfast, but none of them are headed toward the prison, none of them curious about anyone who's been working outside on this bright morning.

Maddie's idea to have Tamara wear a balaclava seemed sensible in the ECV, but here, in the hallways of my home, I can't believe she could pass as a stranger. Maddie and her people all move differently, never mind their unfamiliar faces. Tamara strides down this hallway as she always has, and even with her face hidden, surely someone will figure out she's one of ours.

"Stop looking so nervous, Anya," Maddie says, her voice low. "They think she's dead, remember? And if anybody asks, she's Hina's backup mineralogist, and she's recovering from windburn on her face."

Why would anyone believe such a flimsy story?

The secondary medical center lift is usually used for prisoners, and most people ignore its existence altogether. When we reach it, I realize I miscalculated; when I was a child, packing into the rarely-used lifts with my giggling friends, we were able to fit far more than four. But in the end we squeeze together, abruptly intimate. Maddie's thigh presses against me, the copious clutter in her pocket pushing against the energy weapon still in mine. I'd forgotten it; I should've left it in the ECV.

"Will anyone be there?" Maddie asks.

I have no idea. "Unlikely, I think. Most of the space is maternity, and there are no live pregnancies right now. There's an incubator due in another two weeks, but it's too early for constant monitoring." Unless something has gone wrong again.

The lift slows and stops, and the door clicks, the hydraulics pulling it open.

It's the smell that hits me first, that familiar combination of human, disinfectant, and ozone. I know this room. I labored here, when Irina was born, and I was hypersensitive to smell as I had been throughout my pregnancy. Halvorsen brought flowers from the garden, lovely fragrant roses, and it helped a little with the odor; but today I'm reminded of the timeless feeling of my body's rhythmic efficiency as I coaxed Irina into the world. There was a moment after they handed her to me, this strange, sticky creature covered in fine white curd, when I couldn't remember who she was, why these people had handed me an infant. And then she made a small noise, more surprised than distressed, and everyone around me was smiling and she was Irina, whole and perfect.

The perimeter of the room is taken up by birthing chairs and a few beds, but the center is devoted to the long table designed to hold a nearly-mature incubator. The incubator is sitting there, lights blinking green, its mechanism clicking quietly every few minutes as the fetus is turned; at the next table is a heated infant bed, and stacks of clean cloths. Everything ready for the birth, despite it not being due for twenty-five sunsets. Halvorsen is never unprepared.

There's a door across the room, opposite the high-backed birthing chairs: incubator storage. The repair to the lock is solid, almost as good as I'd have done myself; Yulia would have insisted that maintenance make it perfect, erasing the insult of the ingress. Which is, under the circumstances, unfortunate; if I enter my access code, assuming it even works anymore, our visit will be on the record, and I can't know for certain that Yulia won't be alerted to our presence. On impulse I enter in an older code—not mine, but Aleksey's, the one I gave him a decade ago during his training. If the code has been rotated it'll be useless, but at least it won't give us away.

The door opens into my hand.

The incubators are neatly lined up, front to back, the rows I remember from the few times I've needed to check this room. One section along the wall to the right of the door is cordoned off, and I can see many of them dark, and more than one dented and missing parts. All lined up carefully, awaiting time and technical skills to fix them. No one would have disturbed them during a search; any further damage would have invited Yulia's ire.

The cordon, intended to warn rather than effectively discourage vandals, is tied loosely to a rivet on the wall. I pull apart the knot and it drops, and I wade into a narrow lane between the rows of damaged incubators. I remember the schematic from *Arkhangelsk*, and I take a few steps away from the door before I look down.

There's a panel in the floor, the seams barely visible.

I crouch down to run my fingers around the edges, but as it turns out I won't need a tool to pry it open; one section of the surrounding floor flexes downward, and my fingers slide easily underneath.

Wordlessly I stand and begin to shift incubators out of the way. The others move to join me. In a few moments there's enough room for all of us to stand around the panel, and they all watch as I lift it easily from the floor.

There's a steel ladder descending into a dark space.

"Let me go first," Maddie says. "I deal with ladders all the time."

Ladders are one thing; what we might find at the bottom is something else. "If I fall," I tell her, "come after me." And I lower myself into the hole in the floor and step, one hesitant foot at a time, onto the ladder.

It's disconcerting, descending into the dark, but at least I have the help of the planet's gravity to keep me oriented. I try to focus on my hands, but the darkness is so complete anything I'm seeing is in my imagination. I close my useless eyes and focus on the position of my body, where my limbs are, how I'm being weighed down, and I don't move a hand until the other has a secure grip.

I count rungs as I descend: forty-nine, fifty. A full level; I'm now at the same level as the crypt. It's still pitch dark as my toe reaches down and touches floor, but the room, unlike the dank crypt, is strangely warm, and my imagination tells me I'm on a narrow ledge surrounding a bottomless pit, a step away from falling down into the power source we buried centuries ago. But when my other foot touches the ground, the room's lights come up, and there's no gaping hole in the center.

Instead, there are people.

Eight of them lie in rows, three-three-two, precisely spaced. Their hospital beds are made up neatly, the blankets folded and tucked under their arms. Each has a band around her bicep connected to an intravenous pump, providing nourishment and possibly medication. Irina wore one in those last days of her life, and I had to wrap the band around her arm twice because they had never been made for such thin limbs. These people are all adults, although a few of them are as emaciated as Irina was. They're not gray and sallow, like victims of the illness, but I've seen enough human decay to know that no amount of intravenous feeding will stave off death once someone begins to look like that.

They're not dead, any of them, not yet. But most of them are visibly pregnant.

CHAPTER THIRTY-FIVE

THE OTHERS DESCEND THE LADDER ONE BY ONE, BUT ANY WORDS THEY'RE saying are lost to the thrumming white noise in my ears. I walk up to the bed closest to me and examine the woman's face. She's thin, her cheekbones hollow, her whole body retreating from her tight, round stomach, but I recognize her: Donatella Yeshinkova, twenty-five when she vanished, thought lost to the ice. Twenty-nine now, her skin paper-thin, any vibrance long lost, and I wonder if her eyes have been closed for all of those four years.

In the next bed is Aerin Ossoff, a Third Block woman even her conspiracy-minded neighbors believed had simply become disoriented outside. Always thin, always weak, she wears a ventilation system across her nose and mouth in addition to the nutrient system in her arm. Dying, then, and from the look of her only four or five months along: the child won't survive either. She's too old for this, not fifteen years younger than I am. She was cheerful, outgoing in a way I never was, and persistently kind in the way some are when they haven't been gifted with much intelligence. She was blithely accepting of me when so many treated me like an alien, and I grieved for her when she disappeared.

The third is Oksana Reikova, too young just as Aerin is too old; and yet here she is, eyes long closed, seven or eight months along with what is certainly not her first. But she's alive, and Halvorsen has known it all along.

I should've asked Rolf so much more. I should've pushed everyone, all these years I believed I was looking for bones.

I want to rip the machines away from them, shake them awake; but I'm ignorant, useless, can do nothing for any of them. They've slept away years of their lives, here in this monstrous crèche of Halvorsen's making, only it can't be just Halvorsen, can it? Eight chronic patients is a full infirmary, and the unconscious require more care than the conscious. Halvorsen has help from someone.

There's a cry I'm sure is not mine, and I turn. Maddie has flung herself at one of the beds, and I leave my own charges behind to join her.

Lying in the center of the middle row is Hina, unconscious like the others, and Maddie's fingers flutter over her, touching her hair, her skin, her arms, desperately seeking reassurance.

"Can we disconnect her?" I ask, hoping Maddie remembers she's the medic here.

"I don't know what she's been given." She turns to me; her face is streaked with tears. "There's got to be information here somewhere."

I scan the room: like our main medical center, there's equipment on tables along the walls. The only exits to the room are the ladder we descended, and a door on the opposite side of the room that must lead to the crypt.

The word *convenient* passes through my mind.

I leave Maddie tethered to Hina, her body curled over her child, and head for one of the monitors along the wall. All the displays are locked, passworded; I enter my default, give the system my fingerprint, but it doesn't respond. I try Aleksey's again, although there'd be no reason for him to be here; his doesn't work either. I need Costa, if he would help, need his contraband machine, his tools that would allow him to shave the fingerprint sensor off to expose the circuitry.

"Here." Tamara's voice is quiet behind me; when I turn to her, she's looking at me steadily. "I can get in."

That same look she had in the Exile's archive room. I step aside, and she enters a code I haven't seen used before. The screen goes briefly blank, and then the records appear.

"How did you do that?" I ask her.

She's quiet for a moment. "Last year," she said. "I needed to see something. A friend told me how to get in."

It had to be Lev. Costa could have done it, and perhaps one or two others, but she had no connection with any of them. "Would you care to tell me what it is you needed to see?"

She makes a small sound, like a laugh. "Am I confessing to a peace officer?"

The patients are all numbered, but there are few enough; I start at the top and begin scanning, looking for distinguishing information. "Not anymore," I tell her, and I realize it's the truth.

"Last year," she told me, "I asked Doctor Halvorsen when I would be Selected. With my mother—" She broke off. "She wasn't sick yet. And I was already twenty-two. I felt like I was just…waiting, unable to look forward, to plan anything. I know it's not done, but I wanted to know how much time I had. She told me I wasn't going to be Selected, that my troublemaking, the company I kept, all of that disqualified me."

I look over at her; that sounds like rubbish. She meets my eyes and gives me a grim smile.

"That's what I thought," she tells me. "Not that I'd put it past Doctor Halvorsen to try to control us that way. But I wanted to see her justification, what she'd put in my medical record to shut me out like that. I broke in expecting to find a peace officer referral, but instead I found out I'm infertile."

It means something, this piece, but I'm still not seeing the whole shape. "She's certain of that."

Tamara nods; if she grieved it, if she's still grieving it, she's showing me none of that at all. "None of my eggs are viable. There's no point even in trying." She exhales. "I was so angry that it was going to be forced on me, and then it was taken away. This thing I never wanted."

"So, the radio."

"I wanted to be in a position where people would listen to me if I found out what else Doctor Halvorsen was lying about. And I thought—" She breaks off, and swallows. "I could raise children, even if I couldn't bear them, just not with Rolf. But there was so much else, and when I found the tunnel?" She shakes her head. "My disappointments seemed less urgent. But it's something to do with this, isn't it? Her lies. It has to be."

"I would have to guess," I tell her.

But I can't begin to guess. None of this makes sense, not with so many Selected waiting to be chosen, not with all those incubators upstairs, operational and waiting. Not with Oksana and Aerin, one too young, one too old. The other sleepers are within Selection range, but there are other disqualifying issues: Donatella carries a genetic blood disorder, Mika Stachevich survived four bouts of cancer as a child, Victoria Mœller had seven arrests before she was fifteen years old. None of these women would ever have been Selected.

How could this possibly be any kind of solution to anything?

"Halvorsen could have told us," I say aloud, but it can't be supply, that makes no sense at all. "She'd have had volunteers to have more children, to try as often as necessary. We'd have complied, or enough of us would have."

For all of my life, Novayarkha has survived on this thin hope, bringing our children into the world one by one, holding our breaths as they grow, waiting to see if they'll be strong and healthy and compliant enough to provide their genetics to future generations. There have always been enough waiting to be Selected, and the incubators always here to give us genetic variance, and balance numbers when generations are thin. Tamara's diary entry, no matter her reasons for writing it, was true: it's always been about the future, about what each of us can give to a world we'll never live to see.

It's been a lie. All of it. But I don't understand why.

"There." Tamara spies the date before I do, and touches the screen, expanding the information. "This record was created last week. It has to be Hina."

Maddie and Eleonora rush over to us and I move aside, watching my friend's eyes scan the data. She swears quietly. "She's pregnant," she says flatly.

"What about the anesthetic?" I ask.

"Similar to what you had in your system," she said, "minus the anti-psychotic." She looks over at me. "A much heavier dose. But if we can get her off it, she might wake up."

She doesn't mention damage or recovery time, and neither do I.

Maddie heads back to Hina's side, and Tamara follows, her eyes on every sleeper she passes. Eleonora reads over my shoulder as I scan Hina's record for details. She's been kept unconscious since her disappearance; I wonder if she had any idea at all what was happening to her. I know enough of basic medicine to recognize the markers of unusually good health, but I know from my own experience how quickly the body surrenders its robustness.

I return to the main list of patients to look through the older records, and I find what must be Aerin's. She's marked TERMINAL, PRE-VIABILITY—and in a line underneath that: HARVEST FIVE MONTHS.

My memory of Halvorsen's tiny coffin twists and darkens.

Behind me, an electronic tone sounds, and I turn to see Maddie carefully unwinding the medical band from Hina's arm, revealing an old-fashioned needle-seated medication port. I flinch. Needles are more primitive, but far less likely than dermal pumps to come loose in a struggle.

Tamara hands Maddie a cloth and a bottle of disinfectant, and Maddie cleans the needle's entry point. Hina's flesh is red and swollen, and I wonder, when we unravel all the others, if we'll see similar sloppiness.

I wonder how practical it would be to airlift them all to *Hypatia*.

With slow precision, Maddie disconnects the tube from the medication port. A tiny bead of blood backs up through the tube, shining in the dim light; Maddie brushes it away. "Hina." She whispers, smoothing Hina's head back from her forehead, gentle and maternal. "Hina, sweetheart, can you hear me?"

It will take days for the drugs to work through Hina's system. Possibly weeks. Possibly forever. But I let Maddie alone.

And then Eleonora, looking up from the computer, says abruptly: "Company."

I hadn't heard it over the sounds of the machines, but her younger ears caught it: footsteps above in the medical center.

Someone is coming.

"Tamara," I whisper, turning to the others, "that door in the back. Take Maddie and Eleonora out of here, through the crypt and up to the main Hub entrance."

"There'll be too many people there," Tamara protests.

"Safety in numbers." They'll be happy to see Tamara home, and in the moment they'll believe Eleonora is one of Maddie's.

"We've come this far, and we're supposed to run away?" That's from Eleonora, looking confused and more than a little frightened.

"Whoever's coming down there is one of my people," I tell her. "You're vulnerable, more than any of us. Maddie can tell you what they'll do if they find an Exile this far into the city."

"I'm not leaving," Maddie says.

She's staring at me with bright, defiant eyes, and I don't think I've really seen her temper before because I can *feel* it, a gravitational wave of will, and if I believed will was enough to defend us I'd back down. "I'll protect Hina. But you need to go."

The footsteps become the sound of hard-soled shoes on the metal rungs of the ladder.

Maddie's still arguing. "You don't know what's coming down."

"I know that this is *my problem*, Madeleine, and I am infinitely more qualified to deal with it."

"She's *my child*."

The footsteps are growing louder, and I curse. "That will not save you. You need to get away from here and let me do what I'm trained to do!"

She takes a step and places herself between me and Hina. "I am *not leaving*," she says, and I wish I was the sort of person who hit people.

"Anya," Tamara says.

I curse again, repeatedly for affect. "Take Eleonora. Keep her safe. We'll follow when we can."

Tamara looks worriedly from me to Maddie, and says "Be careful" before she grabs Eleonora's hand and flees toward the crypt.

On impulse I pull the energy weapon out of my suit pocket. Not useful, not here, but perhaps whoever's coming down will be surprised to find me armed. I move to stand next to Maddie, and together we face the ladder.

"Whatever happens," I tell her, "keep quiet."

"As always," she says, and I wonder if she truly is using this moment to make a joke.

It'll be Halvorsen, checking in on her work. Or Yuri or Katerina or one of her nurses. Not Maria, I hope; Maria's always been so kind. I try to think of who else might have been able to hide an operation like this: Dmitri, perhaps. He's so often thrown by threats he can't control, and this is the sort of thing he might have come up with in the name of civil defense.

I wonder what I'll say to him, to whoever's doing this: people I've known and trusted all my life, my family who has turned out to be monstrous. I move between Maddie and the ladder, the gun strangely steady in my hand.

Feet appear, and I take a breath, and I open my mouth to argue with Halvorsen or Dmitri or anyone else reasonably suspect, except it's none of them.

Instead, the one who drops to the floor and turns to us is Aleksey.

CHAPTER THIRTY-SIX

"Anya! Thank the skies, I was afraid it was Yulia."

He sounds genuinely relieved, and his face is relaxed, but the gun he's carrying is not in its holster but in his hand, pointed at the floor between Maddie and me. He glances at my energy weapon, still aimed at him, and his eyebrows knit in mild confusion.

"I thought we'd checked all of those in after the last raid," he says absently. "Well. I'll take care of it later." He looks past me at Maddie, contrition on his face. "I'm sorry, Captain Loineau. I know you've been worried about her. But as you can see, she's fine."

"Aleksey." My voice is all air and sand, insubstantial. "She's not fine. None of them are fine."

At that, his composure surrenders to worry. He walks past us to the monitor against the wall, ignoring the three rows of women, weapon still in his hand. "That can't be. I checked during Remembrance this morning and everyone was stable." He begins to scroll through the master list, and his expression eases. "I don't know what you saw, Anya, but all the vitals are—Oh! You've disconnected her." Mildly annoyed, he gives Maddie an admonishing look, but his gun is still pointed at the ground. He doesn't know her well enough to read her body language, already simmering, threatening to boil. I drop my own gun hand and step toward him, breaking his line of sight to her.

"Maddie's going to take Hina home," I tell him. My voice still sounds reedy, like it belongs to someone else, and I wonder where Irina's gone, if she's looking after Maddie, if she's going to leave me to handle my choking anger all on my own. "Aleksey. What have you done?"

He's not enraged or surprised or threatened at my question. Instead, his expression holds a touch of embarrassment. "I didn't mean for it to go like this," he says, and he's apologizing to me and I don't understand. "I didn't—the strangers are different, Anya, you were right about that. I didn't think I'd be able to get her pregnant, of course, but your people use nothing." He says this to Maddie, and he looks puzzled.

"That's not entirely true," she says. "But Hina's our daughter. She had no need." I can tell Maddie's composure isn't going to hold much longer. "Why is she here *drugged unconscious* instead of home with us?"

Somehow that's the question that surprises him. "I wanted to tell Doctor Halvorsen," he explained. "I wanted to make sure the baby was healthy. And I wanted her to sequence Hina, so we could have her DNA on record."

And, I suspect, to show Yulia there was no danger in using Maddie's people's DNA. Aleksey has always been frustratingly single-minded. "You brought her here," I said.

"I brought her to the medical center. But then the raid hit. She knows so little of us, even after all these weeks—I locked her in the incubator room, where she'd be safe, but she must have heard the Exiles outside and tried to hide. She found the door in the floor. By the time I caught up with her…" He gestures towards the beds and their silent occupants. "She was horrified. She didn't understand. She kept asking me if they were volunteers." He laughs. *Laughs.* "You must have a great many resources on *Hypatia*," he says to Maddie, and his voice is not without envy. "She doesn't understand what it means to be so resource-constrained, I think."

"So you drugged her to shut her up."

"No. I—" He looks over at me, as if I'll help him explain. "With the raid, I had to get back upstairs before someone came looking for me. So I put her under—gently—until I could have Doctor Halvorsen talk to her. She's so much more persuasive than I am."

He's right, which says nothing good about either of them. "The broken incubators were a diversion."

It's a guess, but he nods at me, sheepish again. "There were so many already non-functional. When I was rushing upstairs I knocked a few over, and that gave me the idea to break the lock and tell people the Exiles had broken in."

"Which they believed."

"They'd already broken through the airlock. Nobody was shocked at one more door. And then—I wasn't sure it would work," he confesses, and he sounds pleased with himself. *Pleased.* "I started asking people frantically if they'd seen Hina, and within five minutes I had half a dozen witnesses swearing they'd seen her dragged off."

People will believe what they want to believe. One of the earliest lessons I'd taught him.

"I figured it would only be a few hours, and I could tell her she'd fainted and let everyone know I'd found her and we'd all be relieved. But...Doctor Halvorsen wants to monitor her. Her unrelated DNA, her lineage centuries separate from ours—she could give us so much information. She could save lives, Captain Loineau. And it wouldn't be forever. Doctor Halvorsen says twenty sunsets, thirty at the outside, and she'll have all the data she needs. Then Hina can go home. I promise you."

Does he really believe that? He turns back to me, apparently aware he's getting nowhere with Maddie. "I know this isn't ideal, Anya, but I know you agree with me. We need them. Hina, *Hypatia*, all the strangers to come. You know Yulia's wrong."

My head is shaking before I speak. "This is not what I meant."

My voice seems to be returning. "You can't kidnap people, Aleksey. You can't keep them drugged and manufacture babies from them. It's utterly inhuman."

He's still sorry, and still confused, and I wonder how much more explicit I need to be. "It's only until we get the incubators fixed," he said. "Or until Doctor Halvorsen figures out the right genes to alter. She's very close."

"To what?" Maddie asks. "Genetic resistance? To *cancer*? Do you people know anything at all about how it works?"

Is *that* what they're trying to manage? But he looks mildly irritated, and it seems I'm not beyond shock after all. He doesn't know what they're doing. He's only guessing, trusting the only hierarchy he's ever known. "Doctor Halvorsen's been making us more robust all her life," he says, regrouping. "This is a temporary issue. Once she's got the right combination of genetic modifications and medicines, we won't need to experiment on anyone anymore, even with the incubators."

The white noise pounding in my ears is beginning to feel like anger. Have we done this all along, here in Novayarkha, before on *Arkhangelsk*, back on the Old World when we told ourselves we were leaving the animals behind? "Five years, Aleksey," I point out. "Oksana disappeared five years ago." And we killed Rolf as much for her as for Tamara. "I don't think Doctor Halvorsen can be particularly close after all this time."

"That's what Hina said," he tells me, and he seems puzzled. "She got angry. Told me she was leaving, that she wasn't coming back, that she was going to get Captain Loineau to make us stop. I didn't want to drug her, but she left me no choice. She'd have destroyed everything."

I feel a rush of affection for Hina, a stranger to me, and the strength that allowed her to stand up to someone she thought she knew, thought she loved. "Why don't you put down the gun," I suggest, as gently as I can, "and we can talk about what we need to do now."

But he knows me, Aleksey, my assistant of a decade, pedantic and inflexible and occasionally, inconveniently observant, and my words change everything. The gun comes up, this time aimed steadily at me. "You didn't know about any of this," he says, and now his expression is flat and unreadable. "Did you?"

Of all the things I've thought were wrong with Aleksey, I never anticipated I would find him a monster. "If I'd known I would've stopped it."

He nods as if he recognizes something. "I thought she was using your naivete to keep other people away," he says. "But I thought you understood, Anya. How else do you think we've been surviving?"

Should I have known? With everything I've seen in my life, the ebb and flow of births, the years when so many died followed by years of robustness—should this have been my conclusion? Should I have known we would cannibalize ourselves in the end? "But we're not." He's still looking at me, still ignoring Maddie, and I should've made her keep the energy weapon, no matter how much she didn't want to take it. "We're killing ourselves. Destroying our people under the pretext of keeping them going. How is this sustainable?"

"We've taken their lives for *all of us*, Anya." He sounds messianic, like the Elder, like Yulia, and if his vision were not so corrupt I might be moved. "They'll sustain us until our technology can catch up again, and then they'll be free."

"They won't be *free*." Maddie's voice is full of a rage even Aleksey can't miss. "Most of them will die, and you know it. The ones who don't will be permanently damaged. You're a murderer." And she has to say it: "Again."

Oh, Maddie.

Aleksey's face shifts in stages, going blank first, the way he looked hauling Rolf out onto the ice. And then his jaw sets and Maddie, brave Maddie, flinches at the look he gives her, and I know at once where this is going.

"Please come away from there, Captain Loineau," Aleksey says, level again.

"If you hurt her," Maddie tells him, "I'll kill you."

Aleksey's response is simple. "How?"

Before Maddie can answer, I turn to face her. "He's not going to hurt her." She's still staring at Aleksey, all rage and fire, and if I could restrain her with a look I would do it. "Maddie. He needs her alive."

I can see her, in my head, releasing her anger, launching herself forward, reaching toward Aleksey, uncaring of the fact that she'd be dropped with a bullet before she got further than a meter. But she chooses wisely, and her chin comes up, and she moves around Hina's table to stand next to me.

And Aleksey looks relaxed again. "Thank you," he says, and moves briskly to Hina's side, gun still on us. He glances down at the sleeping woman, just for a moment, just long enough for me to see real affection in his eyes. He loves her, and that's perhaps more of a horror than what he's done. He looks back up at us and waves the gun toward the computer table. "Please empty your pockets."

Miraculously, Maddie says nothing, just thins her lips and turns toward the computer.

"You too, Anya," he says. "Put that energy weapon on the table and drop your hands to your sides."

I join Maddie and set down my useless weapon. Maddie's unpacking slowly, taking things from her pockets one by one: a small bag of crackers Qara handed her before we left *Hypatia*, three more anti-nausea patches, distributed over three of the pockets of her suit. And then, with her hands still hidden from Aleksey, she reaches out to the energy weapon and touches the power switch, giving me a significant look.

Perhaps she doesn't remember why we can't fire it indoors.

We turn back to Aleksey, and I step ahead of Maddie, just a little, wanting to shield her. She still doesn't understand what he's going to do.

Aleksey nods, satisfied, then takes his eyes off us to look at Hina's arm. "How long ago did you pull her line?"

Maddie's voice is tight, brittle. "Two minutes," she tells him. "Maybe three."

"Oh, good." Relief again, and ease, and everything relaxed but not his gun hand. "Then it won't be much of an interruption." He picks up the dangling intravenous line, and the nose of his gun drops for a moment as he lifts and examines the needle. He rounds the table and for a moment his back is to us as he checks the disconnected line for leaks, and I should have kept my eye on Maddie instead because she lunges at him, and I am slow and clumsy and I lunge after her because there's nothing else I can do.

She grabs for his gun arm, and, startled, he turns, raising the weapon. Maddie clutches at his fingers, and the gun is pointed at her head, and I snatch the used needle out of his other hand and jab it into his neck. He shouts in pain, and Maddie, regrouping, yanks at his arm and twists his hand until the gun clatters to the ground. I keep my hand fisted around the needle, bracing my knuckles against his neck and pushing the needle in, my other arm encircling his shoulders for balance; every time he resists me I cant the needle and he shouts again and I should be appalled that I'm hurting him but it feels like justice.

He wrenches his other arm out of Maddie's grip and swings over his shoulder at me; his fist connects with my face, and my jaw goes numb on one side. I shout "Get the gun!" at Maddie, and she's already diving for it, but he manages to kick it away from her as he's wrestling to get me off of him. I shift my arm to press against his larynx, but my angle is wrong, and he keeps breathing freely. Maddie scrambles for the weapon, but just as her hand closes over the grip, Aleksey twists sharply, loosing my grip and throwing me to the floor. He leaps on top of Maddie and grabs the gun's muzzle, then falls backward, the entire weight of his body jerking it out of her hands. She moves, crouching, to dive at him again, but it's taken her too long, and his gun hand is steady, the weapon pointed at her torso.

At least he's breathing hard.

He pulls the needle out of his neck and throws it across the room; he's not smiling anymore. "You didn't have to do that," he tells me. "We want the same things, Anya. You know this."

"Please." Maddie's entreaty is genuine, but I don't believe for a second she's afraid for herself. "She's my daughter. Let me take her home. We won't bother you again, I promise."

She still doesn't understand. "Aleksey," I begin.

"You've chosen," he says, and for the first time there's menace in his voice. "I can't help you anymore. Come over here and stand in front of me."

He knows the threat to Maddie is enough. I put myself between her and his gun, and he sighs, not without sympathy. "If you must have it like this, Anya, all right. I am sorry, though. I've learned so much from you. And you, Captain Loineau. From what Hina's told me, I'm sorry I won't have a chance to get to know you properly. You have just the kind of sharp mind we need here."

Maddie is genuinely shocked. "You're going to *shoot* us?"

"We've seen," I tell her simply. "He can't let us go."

"Anya taught me practicality," he explains, and how did I not see this before, this hollow shell of his? "She was a good teacher. Our people will be in good hands. Yours, Captain—that's for them to determine, I suppose."

Maddie reaches out, her fingers closing around my arm; she wants to shove me aside, protect me as I'm trying to protect her, and I focus on the touch: her warmth, her kindness, the first time in so long that I've found someone who sees the truth of me, and I look Death in the eye, and I am not afraid.

And then, from behind us, from the door to the crypt, comes a familiar voice. "Aleksey! What do you think you're doing?"

It's Yulia, and I can breathe again.

CHAPTER THIRTY-SEVEN

ALEKSEY SHOULD SHOOT US, ONE AND TWO, QUICK AND EASY; BUT YULIA'S governor, and we're all trained from babyhood to obey. He lowers the gun. "Governor. I—"

Yulia ignores him and storms into the room past the sleepers, Tamara and Eleonora trailing in behind her. She stops before Aleksey, effectively shielding me from him, but somehow I don't think she's under threat. "What have you done?" she demands.

"I—I was—"

"Don't tell me you were going to kill people, Aleksey. Not without a trial, at least." There's acid in her voice, and perhaps since I've spoken with her last she's come to have some regrets about Rolf. She turns to face us, and I see in part why Aleksey's weapon doesn't bother her: she has a gun of her own, tucked into the waistband of her trousers.

Yulia doesn't carry a gun, not ever. The armory is on the other side of the medical center.

"Are you all right, Anya?" she asks, with the solicitousness I've always trusted.

I glance at Tamara and Eleonora, huddled by the door to the crypt, and they appear nothing but relieved to have found us still alive. However Yulia plans to deal with the Exile, she's here to save us now. "Better now, Governor," I say with formality. "If we may—we have a medical situation we must tend to."

Yulia turns, and her eyes light on Hina. A great sadness comes over her face. "Oh," she says. "I'm so sorry, Captain Loineau. This is intolerable."

Why would she take the time to find a weapon?

Maddie, deciding her life is no longer in imminent danger, moves back to Hina's side, her hand on her daughter's forehead. "Hina's lucky," she says, and she doesn't seem sure if she should be outraged or grateful.

"Indeed," Yulia says. And then she turns to Aleksey, and destroys everything. "I told you. No strangers. We've been corrupted by them enough."

Her words hang in my ear, incomprehensible, unparsable, until Aleksey replies, pleading, "It wasn't intentional, Governor. But now that we have her—"

"We'll let Captain Loineau take her home, of course," Yulia interrupts smoothly. "And clearly we need to review our own protective measures. We'll take care of things before Hina leaves. We might even learn something useful from it, given how many generations separate our genomes." She's shaking her head, annoyed and disapproving. "You were right, Anya. He's too short-sighted, too foolish. Why is it that so many young people can't recognize their idealism has a cost?" She doesn't wait for an answer, but holds out her hand. "Give me the weapon."

Aleksey, crestfallen, hands her his gun, hilt-first.

"We'll talk about this later," she tells him, and I know the tone: the promise of future forgiveness easing the sting of admonishment. "Go back to the Hub and wait for me there. I'll help Captain Loineau with Hina."

All recourse exhausted, Aleksey turns and leaves through the door to the crypt, without even a cursory glance back at Hina. His footsteps fade into silence.

I may have gone numb again.

"You knew," I say to Yulia.

There's only kindness in her tone when she turns to me. "I'm sorry, Anya, dear. I've planned to tell you for some time now, especially as the time came for you to take over. I did tell you to leave these poor women to their fates, that I needed you to focus on the rest of the city, those of us that need you. These women never needed you. You can see we take good care of them, as we do all who help us."

Seven here, without Hina. "There were others," I tell her. More names on my list, more young people of childbearing age; not all of them, but more than this.

"Some of your others were here," she confirms, resignation in her tone. "It's difficult, what we ask of them. We learned from them all. Each one was vitally important."

Blood on my hands, all of them. Blood on my hands because I was slow, foolish, believing in an order that never existed. None of it makes sense. "Is this—" What could excuse any of this? "Is it because of the incubators?"

But Yulia looks surprised. "We can't use incubators for this. The environment's too different. They've been an incentive, of course, given how unreliable they've been. They were never built to last forever, after all." She gives Maddie a conciliatory smile. "Even with *Hypatia*'s kind assistance. But we're very close at this point. Once we resolve the issue, we can terminate this experiment and stop overloading them."

"Do you think so?" Maddie's voice sounds strange, stiff, and I want to turn to her but I have to watch Yulia's gun. "You've been doing this for hundreds of years."

"That's—" I shake my head; the roaring is taking over again. "No, Maddie. It's only been five years. Oksana—"

"It's only recently," Maddie fills in, gentle for my benefit, "hiding what they're doing has required kidnapping people."

And I remember the archives. The mentions of test runs, of failures. Of populations not told of consequences, of their own mortality.

Experiments, on ourselves, culminating in this.

This is how we've survived. All along, this is how we've survived.

"What triggered it this time?" Maddie asks. Out of the corner of my eye I see she's moving, just a little, placing herself between Yulia and Hina. "Your incidence of cancers is high, yes; but your survival rate is impressive as well. Has it been getting worse?"

Yulia scoffs at that. "Cancer. We beat that decades ago, in every way that matters. Our life expectancy is up five full years, just in the last two generations. Your people think you bring us progress? We've spent the last four hundred years focused on life-extending medicine. Who on your precious Earth has that kind of perseverance?"

"Oh, I'm sure you could teach us a great deal." Maddie is edging forward, closer to Yulia; I want to tell her to stop, but my tongue is thick and unruly. "But if it's not cancer—why are you doing this?"

And I put it together: all those births after Irina, more children, live and incubator, than I'd ever seen; the current drought, and Halvorsen's tiny casket; some Selected permitted, more often than I can ever recall, to bear more than one child, even as they grow older; the Third Sector miscarriages we've all been told, year after year, were somehow normal because Mathilda's people are odd, insular, not quite part of the rest of us. "It's not cancer," I manage to say. "It's infertility."

Yulia waves a hand at me, dismissive. "It's a temporary setback."

"How bad is it?" I ask, and when her jaw sets, a chill settles in my bones.

"It wouldn't have lasted this long if Magda hadn't been stubborn about it," she says. "You remember, after Irina? That genmod worked so well in the children, and that was all she thought about. You misunderstand her, you know, Anya. Irina was an inspiration to her. She never wanted to lose a child like that again."

My fingers twitch as if they belong to someone else.

"But in her optimism she forgot her science. If we tested for Selection younger, the way I've always told her we ought to, we'd have found the side effects sooner, could have better compensated with the incubators until healthier people come of age. As it stands..." She sighs, annoyed with her old friend. "We treated all the children up to eight years old, then at conception. Fifteen years of births until we learned, five years ago, the therapy had rendered them all infertile. Selection became utterly useless."

Hundreds of people. Confusion, grief, sorrow. Immeasurable loss, because Doctor Halvorsen had refused to heed the past.

Because we had never known it.

"But it's taken us only a third of that time to fix the problem. We're close. Aerin might have had a live birth, if she'd lasted a bit longer. Oksana's given us some extraordinary variants. Camina was our most successful community test—she nearly bore a normal child. We fully expect to have a viable treatment after this yield is complete."

"And if you don't?" Maddie asks her.

"I don't expect you to understand," She's dismissing Maddie, finished with the discussion. "Your people have no future, no vision at all. We do what we must, as we always have."

"You took Oksana." This comes from Tamara, not a reporter this time, but a young woman looking at a leader she once trusted. "Would you have taken me?"

"Goodness no," Yulia snaps. "As Lauren's daughter? Your disappearance would have been far too high profile. Was, indeed, just that. I will admit, though, I did think it a waste, even if that boy didn't kill you." She regroups, straightens; when she smiles at Tamara, it almost seems real. "I'm very glad you're well, though, whatever impulsiveness led you to run away. And thank you," she says to Eleonora, considerably more cool, "for bringing her back to us. We can discuss the rest later."

Just like that, Yulia's recast Eleonora's presence into a diplomatic victory.

My governor looks as she always looks: compact, determined, her frail and aging body held upright with unwavering pride. The kindness in her expression is potentially genuine, the restrained impatience of her body language almost certainly so.

I have known her since I was a child, watched her hair change from brown to white, her skin from tan to sickly gray. I have loved her as mother, sister, protector of us all. I have defied her and confessed, asked questions behind her back but never to her face, and I have never seen her before this moment.

I have never seen any of us before this moment.

"Is Hina all right?" I ask Maddie.

"He didn't hurt her," Maddie confirms.

I keep my voice measured, polite. "Keep an eye on her, if you would." I can't have her impulsiveness, not now. I face Yulia squarely again. "Governor," I say, "I must place you under arrest."

"Oh, come now, Anya," she says, surrendering to her irritability, "you know I had no idea what Aleksey was up to. We'll have a talk with him. You can even lock him up for a few days if it makes you feel better. But we need to move past this."

"Aleksey will answer for Aleksey's crimes," I agree. "And you will answer for yours."

What I'm saying begins to sink in, and she straightens. "I can't imagine what you're talking about, Anya," she says icily.

"You knew Oksana was alive," I say. "You kept me from investigating. You used her to convict Rolf."

"I don't remember coercing your vote on that, Officer Savelova."

She still knows where to hit me, but I can't feel the blows anymore. "And the Exiles. With access to the archives, you had to know where they were."

"What did it matter?" Yulia says. "They were too far away for

Their friends have made other friends, their lovers have found other comforts. And they're here, giving us the most important gift they can give. I suppose I can understand, after Irina, why you may not see it, but that makes it no less true."

"It's worth their lives."

"Of course it is."

"And my life."

A great sadness comes over her face. "That would not be my choice. But yes, your life as well."

"And Tamara's life."

Yulia's lips set. "If she won't see."

All of my anger dissolves in that instant, flooding through and out of me with the heat of so much adrenalin I can feel my hands begin to tremble. Irina huddles close to Maddie; they won't be alone, either of them, and that's as it should be. Irina watches me with the trust of a child, with the knowledge that no one, not even Mother, can make the world what it is not.

And my fingers find what I'm looking for.

"There is something worth all these lives." I'm looking at Yulia, but I'm talking to Maddie, hoping she'll understand, hoping she'll forgive what I have to do. "But it's not your rejection of a history that never was. It's our future. Not Novayarkha's future; everyone's future. Maddie."

"Here," she says, and I can hear it in her voice; she knows.

"How many people were there on Earth when you left it?"

"One billion two hundred and fifty million."

An involuntary gasp escapes me; whatever I imagined, it was nothing like that. "And they can fly."

"They won't come here when you've vanished without a trace," Yulia says.

"Not right away," Maddie acknowledges. "But they will come. Maybe not for a long time, but they will. We explore. We always have. You can't stop that."

I see Yulia's fingers adjust over the trigger of her gun. "I won't allow this, Anya."

"And I won't allow anything else."

I extend the energy weapon toward her.

"Don't be stupid, Anya." Yulia's hand doesn't waver; she's entirely out of patience now. "You'll take out the whole room with that. The med center above us. Half the crypt. Drop this foolishness. It's not too late."

"It is, though." Maddie says this quietly, and I glance at her then, her soft curls wild about her face, this woman who somehow sees all of me, even the parts I've never shown. "It's all right, Anya. Whatever you need to do."

"You'll kill all of us." Yulia's voice is wavering. Anger? Fear? How would I know? "This close to the Hub? The entire infrastructure will collapse."

"Perhaps." This is all so easy now. "But there would be help with repairs. *Hypatia* would help, wouldn't she, Maddie?"

"Yes," Maddie says, and she knows her people, each one of them, as well as she knows me.

"We would, too," Eleonora says. Her voice is thin, reedy; she's overtired, and dying, and perhaps she sees what I see: not death, but a path forward that is, for the first time, not a lie.

"We will not accept help from Exiles!" Yulia's unnerved at the idea, but her gun hand is steady. "We'll die before we put ourselves in your hands."

"I think you're wrong, Yulia," I tell her. I use Tamara's words, words that have been true since before I was born. "We're taught that our individual lives don't matter, that we exist only for each other. And it's true. The Exiles are a part of us, have always been a part of us, the by-product of an old feud that doesn't matter anymore. And Maddie, *Hypatia*—all the Old World is part of us. They'll save us if we let them, Yulia, even though we couldn't save ourselves. I think our people will see that. I think they'll welcome help. And not a one of us in this room makes any difference to that at all."

It's possible, of course, that if Yulia fires I won't be able to fire before I fall. It's possible she'll kill me, and Maddie and Tamara and Eleonora, and all the sleepers will stay imprisoned and everything will be wasted. But my mind is clear, and my reflexes are quick, and even if it's fantasy, even if it's physically impossible for me to retaliate: I would choose death. I would choose to end my journey here, because the people I've lived for are still alive, light years away, bound up in the future of a planet I've never seen.

Yulia can see it in my face. And she doesn't know if she can beat me.

She lowers the gun.

I hear a sob in the corner—not Tamara, but Eleonora, still finding her life precious. I step forward and pull the gun from Yulia's grasp, then take the other gun from her waistband. She looks up at me, and says, almost conversationally, "You've killed us all."

"Perhaps," I say, even though I don't believe it. I feel giddy, weightless, powerful. "But everything dies. Just as everything is forever."

RECIP: National Earth Space Organization, Vostochny
REPORTER: Loineau, Madeleine, Cmdr. NZKO *Hypatia*
Mission year 40, day 205

Yulia Orlova's trial started four weeks to the day after Anya almost blew us the fuck up.

That was after the rioting, though. And the vandalism.

Turns out if you arrest the governor in a place like Novayarkha, people are going to get upset. It's like it's never occurred to them that this peace they've been living with has been at the cost of making too many people swallow their frustrations. Fighting broke out almost immediately, and one afternoon (second sunset, first nightfall—I'll never get it straight, Vostochny, not if we're here a hundred years) almost three hundred people spilled into the Hub shouting and punching each other and breaking more than just furniture and hydraulic doors.

I got a crash course in Novayarkhan medicine working at the med center with Maria. Nearly two hundred patients in a day. I've never been near that many people in my life. Any nerves I might have started with have been etched out of existence.

Maria says she didn't know, by the way. She said Halvorsen was secretive and played favorites, and leaned on Aleksey for a lot of things people didn't tend to lean on peace officers for. Maria says people assumed Halvorsen enjoyed his youth and good looks, and nobody questioned that. I almost believe her.

Almost.

Ratana and Seung came down to do emergency repairs, and I like to think Ratana's pointed warnings about what would happen if they weakened too many of the city's load-bearing structures were responsible for the worst of the violence ending before something exploded.

For her part, Anya made speeches.

Anya's not an orator, Vostochny. But she does this thing where she gets really calm and certain. She wouldn't shout, so they all had to shut up to hear her, and she didn't say anything other than she didn't know what the future held, either. Which actually worked: seems what they really wanted was someone willing to be in charge, even if Anya has no idea what she's doing.

Anya's clear she doesn't *want* to be in charge, but from where I'm standing, she's turning out to be pretty good at it.

After people calmed the fuck down, the politicking began in earnest, and fuck, Vostochny, I don't know how they're going to make it work. We have enough trouble agreeing to anything on *Hypatia*. There are a fair number of people who are just as horrified as Anya to learn what's been going on with the incubators—never mind the kidnap victims—but there's also a pretty loud chorus of "what else were we supposed to do?" And then there are the scientists, or people who like to think of themselves as scientists, who are rooting through the declassified records trying to figure out what sorts of experiments were done, and how they could have more efficiently handled the whole human-experimentation side of it. Like there's a better way to handle vivisection.

So it's really entertaining on the planet right now, Vostochny, and I'm not going to hazard a guess how it's going to come out. Maybe whoever you send after us can help them, or what's left of them. Or maybe they'll be as self-righteous and isolationist with our successors as they were with us.

Aleksey's arrest was pretty straightforward. Not that anybody was particularly protective of Hina, but he openly confessed to kidnapping and drugging her, and deliberately implicating the Exiles in her disappearance. Lies of omission these people roll with; blatant falsehoods, though, seem to bug them a lot. His trial was short and sweet, and although they didn't throw away the key, Anya says he'll be monitored for the rest of his life. Hina spoke up for him, which made my teeth ache, but when they convicted him she looked a little relieved. Or maybe I'm projecting.

Halvorsen waived a trial and admitted guilt. Anya says she'll never practice medicine again. She's past eighty; Anya's probably right. It still doesn't feel like enough.

Orlova's arrest was different. After speaking at length with Lev and Dmitri, Anya charged her publicly with seven counts of kidnapping, one count of conspiracy to deceive the public trust (which is a thing there, although apparently it's mostly been used as a tool for politicians to purge their rivals), and one count of murder: Kano's. I didn't think there was much chance of her being convicted of that, what with all the ways she covered her tracks, but I was grateful to Anya for including it anyway.

Anya reasoned, though, that Orlova's fate would need to be decided a little more democratically. Which makes sense: a beloved governor, charged with some pretty awful stuff? There's a martyr in the making, if you're not careful. But Anya also figured it was past time for Novayarkhans to take charge of their own fate, at least a little. I was less sanguine about the immediate launch into democracy, but for all the times Anya's been wrong about these people, she's been right, too.

And I have to say, the trial was looking pretty decisive, until Orlova's closing statement. Speaking of underestimating. You think I'd've learned, wouldn't you?

Orlova didn't point fingers at Halvorsen, didn't take the role of the impressionable subordinate. She stood before her gathered people, smiling: relaxed, *maternal*, as if she were presenting a toast at the family dinner table. I suppose, in a sense, she was.

"I look at all of you," she began, "and I feel such pride, and such humility. Some of you have known me all my life." She smiled over at Halvorsen, who was watching with an armed guard at her side, and I have to admit, Vostochny, even I felt a pang of admiration. They could've turned on each other, but they didn't.

"The rest of you—I've watched you be born, seen you grow, become lovely children and strong young people. We've all helped each other, experienced joy together, held each other up when our loved ones die." Her smile faded, and the grief in her eyes was, as always, totally fucking sincere. "This has been the reality of our existence, since our ancestors took root here, since we built this place as the last fortress of humanity."

Now, it was never the last fortress of humanity, which you and I both know, Vostochny. But none of *them* would have known. That's a truth as well.

"We all live for each other. Build for each other. Some of you…" Her eyes strayed over the crowd, warm and forgiving. "You've wanted, so much, to give us children. Those of you who've suc- ceeded—I've seen, over and over, your hearts break, stood with you as we slide those tiny boxes into their homes in our crypt."

I couldn't help looking at Anya at this point, but her face had become a mask. She was not missing a fucking word. How often, do you suppose, has she swallowed Orlova's cruelty?

I kind of wanted to punch some people, no joke.

"We've been fighting for the same thing since all of this began." She lifted her clasped hands and began to pace, like a lecturer. "*Survival*. Not for ourselves. Not even for our own small families. For all of us. For each other. For the human race that has worked so hard, century after century, millennium after millen- nium, to destroy itself. Which *still* tries to destroy itself."

She looked at us at that, me and Ratana and Léon and Divya and Qara and Seung, and everybody else turned to stare as well, and for once I took a page from Anya's taciturn book and didn't tell them all to fuck off.

"Humanity dies when we give up hope," she declared.

Hell, who can argue with that?

"Here, in Novayarkha...generation after generation, our hope has always been our children, whether they live to be old, or whether we lose them before they can speak. We subsist on hope today: hope that our children will be stronger, smarter. Healthier. *Better*. What would any of us do, if we believed that looking to tomorrow was fruitless? We would become exactly what we left behind: nihilistic animals determined to destroy our own present."

She stopped pacing and dropped her arms to her side, facing the crowd squarely. "We're too strong, too united, to let despair erode us. We have won so many victories, just coming as far as we have today. When we all choose together to do what we must—there's nothing that can defeat us. Not disease, not radiation, not infertility—not even those who find themselves misguided by good intentions." Her head turned, just a little, and she gave a half-smile to Anya and the tribunal; a few people in the crowd laughed.

"Fighting means we *all* sacrifice. It means we survive, as one community, *together*."

There it was: the damned Collective.

"We have survived on this planet for two hundred years. We survived leaving Earth two centuries before that. Together we are strong. We can defeat any enemy—disease, genetics, even ourselves. We will survive as long as we stand together, with each other. Just as we always have." She gave a slight bow. "Thank you."

There was raucous applause, as if she'd made a campaign speech, and I suppose she had. Anya, Lev, and Dmitri exchanged a look, but they didn't move to quiet the crowd. I thought there might have been some pockets of weaknesses in the applause, but

I figured that was wishful thinking. Orlova had made a hell of a speech for a psychopath.

After the noise died down, there was public comment. I figured we'd be there all night, but the debate was surprisingly brief and civilized, and it wasn't until I was talking to the Colonel later that I remembered this entire style of discussion was new to these people.

The first three speeches were in support of Orlova, but the tone was less *yes, let's continue experimenting on folks somebody somewhere decided were troublemakers* and more *well, you can maybe see some of where she's coming from*, and I started, just a little, to have hope.

Until the fourth speaker, a man roughly Orlova's age, with the same gray hair and insipid complexion. A sick man, unlikely to last a whole lot longer, and I suppose that's the perspective, Vostochny. We think about early death on *Hypatia*—how could we not?—but we're still blindsided by it, pulled to pieces. Here it's *every day*, and it doesn't depend on age or profession or stupid accident. It's random chance and a fact of life, and the man speaking knew a whole lot of his audience didn't expect to make it to his age, never mind Halvorsen's.

"It's so easy to judge them," he began, and he was clearly angry. "It's so easy to say what they did was wrong. But have you thought about it? Truly? Our survival here has always been difficult. Maybe impossible. We all know it. Governor Orlova and Doctor Halvorsen—they've kept us alive. They've given us hope. You'd punish them for that? Really? For *saving your lives?*"

That one got applause, nearly as much as Orlova's speech, but there were more hands coming up, and Anya spoke over the noise. "Please," was all she had to say. The crowd stilled, and she pointed at a young woman standing off to our right: brown hair, brown skin, features that would have been bland had they not been animated by stiff determination. "Yes, Lilith."

Lilith's voice was strong, clear, echoing through the high-ceilinged room. "Our lives have been bought with blood as much as anyone's on the Old World." Rumbles from the crowd again, and this woman got angry. "We're told to look to the future. But why do we think the future is worth deciding whose life is and isn't worth living, taking someone's loves and hopes and dreams, without even asking them? What is the future, anyway, if not a thousand todays yet to come? If this is the only way for us to survive—if we're all just passive, mindless fodder for someone else's use—how can we say we're worth saving at all?"

I like their young people, Vostochny. They remind me of Hina.

The vote, when it came, was not nearly as close as Anya had feared: sixty-four percent voted to convict, and thirty-three percent to acquit. The abstention rate was high, but not high enough to delegitimize the result, and although there was more yelling, nobody started punching people again.

After the trial we figured it'd be best to head home and lay low for a while, at least until the fighting got bad enough for us to help again, and we were almost at the airlock when we heard feet running behind us. It was another young woman—not Lilith, but one who'd been standing next to her, smaller, more animated, her body language brittle and belligerent. "Are you leaving?" she asked when she reached us.

"We weren't planning to stay for the sentencing," I said. "We—"

"No." She took a moment to catch her breath. "I mean are you *leaving*?"

I suppose we could have, Vostochny. We could have guided *Hypatia* to the other side of their world and blocked them out, or just hied our way out of the solar system entirely, saying *screw you* to you as well as them.

"No. We've got a satellite to build."

"Some of us were wondering." Her belligerence fell away, and she looked suddenly shy and awkward, like we all were when we were kids. "Can we help?"

I thought about a lot of things in that moment. I thought about

Kano, about the people who'd followed Orlova's orders to build us bad components. I thought about what they'd done to Hina, to all those other people, how they'd chosen to do their research for centuries, lying and kidnapping and killing. I thought about Anya, and I thought about the thirty-three percent of people who thought what Orlova had done was just fine.

And I thought of the crew of *Arkhangelsk*, so far away from home, and all the worlds they never got to see.

Crossed my mind then, Vostochny, that we can all choose to be something different.

"Yes," I said to her. "I think you can."

CHAPTER THIRTY-EIGHT

"You know if you let them they'll put you in charge," Costa says, fussing over the stove.

We've had little time together lately, but the last week things have quieted, and it seems Novayarkha's routines are taking over again. Dmitri's practicing hypervigilance, sleeping as far as I can tell not at all, but Lev and I have been forcing each other to stand down, just a little, and let the system do what it must.

That none of us have taken on Yulia's former title has escaped no one's notice. I've been talking with Mathilda Pedersen about it; conspiracy theorists or not, all her people are expert at listening to whispers. Costa's not wrong about me, but Mathilda believes it's more habit and familiarity than anything about me in particular.

"Although," she said, "arresting and imprisoning Governor Orlova—that has made you a legend, Anya, and that fate you can't avoid."

"Lev already knows I won't do it," I tell Costa, nibbling on the salted soy nuts he has on his kitchen counter. "And Dmitri doesn't want the job. We should have an election, don't you think?"

He laughs. "There'll be riots."

"You could run."

"And leave my children?" He scoffs. "Pretty sure people would rather I keep teaching, An."

"I still think we should try direct democracy. We might as well change ourselves, before it's forced upon us."

"Life is change," he says. "Isn't that what you always tell me?"

Costa makes soup while I ramble at him about politics. The slate on his wall is blank, the first time I've ever seen it so. Events have eroded our friendship, and I put the distance between us down to that, to my vulnerability, to his betrayal of me that I've forgiven with almost every part of myself. I've missed him, and I've wished, now and then, he would be more willing to reach out to me.

But in the face of his silence it's worth remembering reaching must sometimes go both ways.

"It's a lot of change in a short time," I conclude.

"You seem to be adapting to it well." His back is to me, and I'm not sure what he means.

I shift on the stool. "I think it's more that I've had more time to deal with everything I understood being shattered. I don't expect it'll be so easy for everyone else. How are the children doing?"

He stirs the soup. "The young ones have already forgotten," he says. "To them it's all grown-up games. The older ones…some are scared. But some are hopeful, like you are."

"Are you hopeful, Costa?" And I'm aware, abruptly, how much his answer means to me.

"Sometimes," he says at last. "I suppose…it can't get worse, can it?"

But it's not a joke, that question. "It can always get worse," I allow. "But I don't think it will. Yulia was right about that much: we've survived all of this together, and we'll continue to survive."

And it isn't until my words are out and I see Costa's arm still, the soup spoon left idle, that it all becomes clear to me.

"You voted to acquit," I say, and I want so much for my gut-level certainty to be wrong.

"I abstained."

"You knew." Everything he's cooking suddenly smells foul. "All these years."

"No." He turns to face me, his expression pleading, and I remember the drug poured down my throat, even after I said *please*. "Not all these years. And I never *knew*. But sometimes...I'm a teacher, An. I get all the children, no matter how they're born. I've seen how badly natural births have eroded over the last twenty years. I didn't know why, or even if, but I wondered. That's all."

"You've seen me searching for them, all this time."

"Yes."

"And you never said."

"To what end, Anya?" He begins to get angry, but I don't think he's angry with me. "Even if I thought my suspicions had merit, you couldn't have changed it. And when it started, before we knew the Old World was still out there—what else was Yulia supposed to do? What were we *all* supposed to do? Lie down and fall asleep on the ice?"

"That's a false choice." I keep expecting Irina, but she stays away; my anger, it seems, is my own. "We might as well have been murdering each other for food."

"So you agree with Lilith, then? That we deserved to die?"

"We're not going to die. *Hypatia*—"

"Was *nowhere* when this began." He's just as angry. "You're too used to being right, Anya. You can't put yourself in someone else's place anymore. You can't tell me if you hadn't been governor that you wouldn't have made exactly the same choice as Yulia."

"The hell I can't." He can call it lack of empathy if he wants, but I know, down to my bones, that I would not have condoned what she did. "There are other ways, Costa. There are always other ways."

"I'm not saying it was the best idea," he says. He takes a step closer; he's mollifying me now, but I'm cold all over, and abruptly claustrophobic. "I'm saying I understand why she did it. And I don't think it's fair for us to judge her now, when other answers have appeared. Have you thought about that?"

"We have knowledge," I remind him. "We have expertise. And here, on this planet, we have materials, materials a ship that left the Old World *centuries* after we did didn't have. We should have been told what was happening, no matter how much it would have frightened people. We had the right. And the Exiles—"

"They're a bunch of thieves and killers, An," he says tersely. "That's not even an argument."

I think of Eleonora, rushing through the crypt to get help from people who might just as easily have thrown her out on the tundra. "They're sick and abandoned children, Costa." I get to my feet. "I'm sorry. I'm not terribly hungry tonight."

At that, his anger vanishes. "An—"

"It's all right." I muster something I hope looks like a smile. "We're not fated to agree on everything. I'll see you tomorrow, yes?"

When I leave, we're both allowing ourselves to believe that this will somehow be healed.

At home, I turn on the radio, and Maddie answers right away. "What's wrong?"

I lower myself onto the sofa. I'm so tired, and I need to sleep, and there's so much left to do. "When are you coming back?" I ask.

"Two days," she says. "We're finishing up the scaffolding tomorrow, which is something I can actually help with." She waits for a moment, then says, "Do you need me sooner?"

She would come. She would leave her scaffolding, and her crew, and come down here if I said I needed her, and that's enough on its own. "No. There's nothing to be done here, really. It's just... adjustment."

"For us, too," she says. "It's been the same for so long, and now everything is new."

Irina climbs onto the couch and curls up next to me, her head in my lap. "New is becoming ordinary," I tell Maddie, and she laughs.

"How many people back on Earth," she asks me, "do you suppose get the chance to start all over again?"

I look up at the ceiling where the solar tubes are glowing orange with the light of second sunrise. "All of them," I tell her, and for a little while, my broken heart is made whole.

ORIGINAL MISSION MANIFEST
2200[1]

LOGGED BY: UNKNOWN

DIRECTIVE 17 GOVERNMENT USE ONLY
SCHOLARLY ACCESS FORBIDDEN

INITIAL PROPOSAL FOR LONG-TERM DEEP-SPACE CARRIER
ARKHANGELSK

Primary mission: Research and document long-term medical effects of humans living and reproducing in a deep space environment

Secondary mission: Establish a mining and refinery complex in the vicinity of star system 974-33

Tertiary mission: Establish a maintenance/medical hub for future

---

[1] Date is interpolated and should not be considered precise.

missions exploring star system 974-33
Crew complement: 4,800 (approx.)
Weight tolerance: 450M kg (approx.)
Estimated travel time: 200 years (250 years earth-relative)

Notes:

1.   The mission will be under the jurisdiction of the Unified Nations Consortium. Member states will share development expenses proportionally.

2.   The formal hierarchy on *Arkhangelsk* will parallel current local military/corporate structures.[1]

3.   *Arkhangelsk* will submit regular reports to the Consortium.[2]

4.   Termination of reports from *Arkhangelsk* will not be considered impetus to abandon future exploration of 974-33.

---

1   UNC acknowledges that once *Arkhangelsk* clears the communications bubble, their government will be outside UNC's control.

2   UNC acknowledges the effects of relativity. Reports will be archived throughout the centuries as they arrive and maintained for scholarly purposes.

RESURRECTION

RECIP: National Earth Space Organization, Vostochny
REPORTER: Loineau, Madeleine, Cmdr. NZKO *Hypatia*
Mission year 41, day 32
Final Dispatch

You know, Vostochny, I'm genuinely sorry we'll never meet.

I've had this vision in my head, all these years, of you there on the other end: bored and middle-aged, whiling away the hours at your dead-end job until you receive another scintillating missive from me. Of course, I know it didn't work quite like that. There's been more than one of you, for one thing, and you're a whole different set of people than you were when we left. For another—if the transceiver comes on line properly, you'll get all my messages in a single packet, and you'll probably analyze them heuristically and get irritated with me for all the extemporaneous bullshit I've included.

But I think I'll stick with my fantasy, and picture you on the other end going through it all with me, smiling and laughing and mourning and crying. And maybe even being happy for us all, here at the end.

We left it up to the Colonel. That was Eleonora's idea, but once we heard it, it made the most sense: he's the only one who remembers you. And do you know, Vostochny, when we told him we'd take him back home so he could be put to rest with his family if he wanted, he started to cry, and we had to wait while his ventilator drained his breathing tube. And then he turned on that artificial voice:

"You're my family," he said. "I love you. My home is here, with you, wherever you want to go."

And then we all cried for a while, even Anya, although she'll tell you she didn't.

We spent a couple of months down in the observatory, exploring *Arkhangelsk*'s original trajectory. Turns out 974-33—that little star system *Arkhangelsk* was originally designed to sniff at—is supporting some planets. Divya thinks as many as five of them might be habitable at some level.

So we're going to go and check them out.

I expect you think we're all mad. Except we're not the ones who followed a possibly-lost, potentially mythical generation ship just because our ancestors promised. No matter how you look at it, Vostochny, it's an act of optimism bordering on the insane.

I like you better for that.

It'll be six years to the closest cluster—three out and three back—but we can do most of it at speed, so we figure it'll be a little less than eight here. Aisuru won't even be a teenager yet. I'll still be sorry to miss her babyhood. I liked watching Hina grow up; I was looking forward to watching her daughter. But maybe someday Aisuru will come with us on one of these runs. Who knows? She may be more like us than her mother.

It mystifies me, a little, that Hina has been able to let go of everything that happened to her in Novayarkha. I certainly couldn't live on that planet. My memories of it aren't clean. But she's started calling it home, and she's got friends, and she's got family. That, and her rocks. That world has got plenty of rocks. Hina's happy, and that's all we've ever wanted for her, really.

But my home will always be here, I think. On our odd, broken little ship. Less broken now, with the bits of *Arkhangelsk* pulled from the Exile's abandoned camp.

We had room for them, as it turns out. It took some doing—we had to patch up that part of the lower fuselage we'd left to the vacuum and adapt our food production properly, never mind figuring out a new rotation for our handball tournaments—but we brought up fourteen of them. Five of them chose to stay down in Novayarkha, and three have died, including the Elder, although she held on long enough to see Orlova convicted. Three more I'm fairly sure we'll lose, but the others I've been able to treat with at least temporary success. I can't undo what the planet has done to them, but I've been able to make them feel a little better, for however long it lasts.

It shouldn't feel so huge, Vostochny, to make such a small difference to such a small group of people. But it makes me giddy.

So thanks to our new crew and the pressures of necessity, our ship is nearly whole now, although she'll never be as big as our ancient predecessor. Léon thinks we may even be able to goose more speed out of the engines—we may be home in seven years instead of eight. It's amazing what an engineer's imagination does when you have the proper parts.

She's changed, our ship. She's not yours anymore, not any model that you designed and built. She is herself, made of hope and tragedy and all of our threadbare, determined love. She carries fifty-three now: us, and the Exiles, and Lilith and some others from Novayarkha. And we've got plenty of breathing room. Room for growth. For children. For all of our dreams.

I'm still in charge. You can laugh at that all you want, Vostochny. I hate it, in a way, but I let them choose, and they chose me. Anya says that anyone who wants the job shouldn't have it. I suppose she'd know more about that than I would.

Anya smiles more now. And she laughs. And when we talk about distant stars...she looks young. *Happy.*

Wouldn't that be something? If we all ended up happy?

Anyway, Vostochny. With luck, tomorrow the station will come on line, and I'll be able to say hello and goodbye to you all at once. I've no idea how you're going to take this. I've no idea what you're like, really. I try to believe you're different than the people who sent us here, that while we were learning how to look after one another, you were learning the same. I hope, when we return from our journey, we'll be able to send you all of our notes and pictures and discoveries, and we can talk together like allies, like comrades, all of us excited about what is to come.

Goodbye, Vostochny. I am starting my life now.

CHAPTER THIRTY-NINE

"LEVELS?"

"Holding steady."

I straighten, staring down at the numbers on my console. They've been constant for nearly an hour. We have no excuses anymore. "Very well," I tell Seung. "Initiate the field."

The sounds of our ship have become familiar to me—as familiar as Novayarkha's air handlers and hydraulic doors. I've even grown used to the gravity changes. Maddie tells me I'm as adept in zero g as any of the original crew, but I think she'd say that anyway. Maddie still thinks she needs to pay me compliments to make me like it here.

She doesn't understand I've come home.

On the console, the green bar creeps slowly to the right. I'm alert for the sorts of fluctuations we saw in testing, the ones that meant imminent collapse; but it's been a week since we've seen so much as a vibration.

"Didn't it go faster yesterday?" Maddie says nervously.

"I don't think so." To oblige her, I bring up yesterday's results. "See?" I point at the recorded progress indicator. "It's moving at exactly the same rate."

She doesn't answer, and instead shifts restlessly in front of me until I have to reach out to steady her. I lace my fingers in hers, and she gives me a nervous smile. "I'm not sure about this," she says. "What if I'm saying it wrong? What if they don't understand?"

"You're saying it perfectly." We've been over the message, all of us, again and again, for weeks. "And it doesn't matter if they don't understand. What matters is that they receive it. What matters is that the transceiver works. As long as that happens, we won't matter to them at all."

Hypatia never mattered to them, not beyond her use as a construction vehicle. But the ones who launched *Hypatia* are long dead, like my ancestors, like the crew of *Arkhangelsk* who left Earth with irrational hope for the future. It's possible, of course, that Earth has regressed again, become the hideous place that it was before my people escaped it. But even if they're troubled...a voice from so far away, alive and thriving, will surely mean something to them. Life changes everything, all the time.

"Eighty-nine percent," Seung says, even though we can all see the display. The others are crowding over the control desk, pressed against each other and into the walls, above and around us, overflowing into the hallways outside the fuselage. "Two minutes, Maddie."

I can hear her breath catch. "Someone else should send this," she says, only for my ears.

"No, they shouldn't." I glare at her, the way I used to glare at suspects; but instead of being frightened, she seems to gain strength. Her shoulders square, and her breathing steadies, and she takes a moment to kiss the back of my hand before she releases me.

The indicator reaches one hundred percent, and a quiet cheer goes through the crowd. Maddie inhales, and her eyes survey her crew.

"Are we ready?"

There's a murmur of assent.

As Maddie drifts up to the communications console, I turn toward the window. Irina's there, hands on the sill, bouncing on her toes despite the absent gravity. I would've expected her to be looking down at our old home, blue and white and nearly featureless from this height; but her eyes, bright and excited, are on the stars, and her smile holds all the wonder and delight of the universe.

Maddie turns a switch. "Vostochny Control," she says, her voice steady, "this is the starship *Arkhangelsk Alpha*, formerly *Hypatia*. Do you read?"

And together, we all wait.

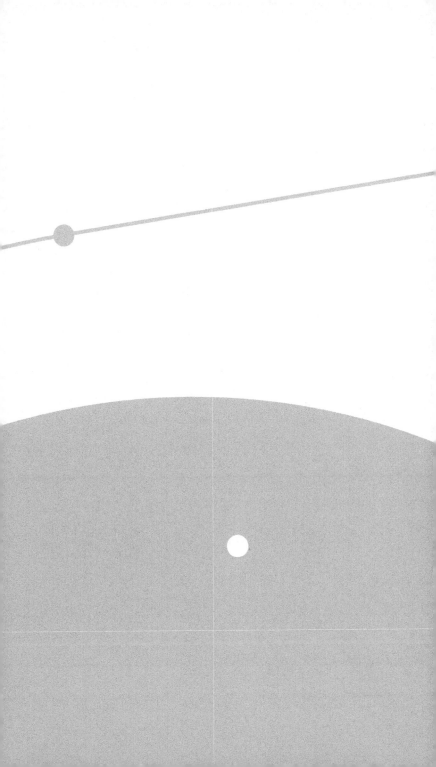

ACKNOWLEDGEMENTS

It's not possible, even in the simplest of situations, to properly remember everyone who's helped with the growth and development of a work of art. *Arkhangelsk* has had a complicated history. There are so many people who kept me going when I didn't think I could move, and I'll thank as many as I can remember.

For tru and Elaine. You both came to this book when it really needed you. Without you, it would never have been written at all.

For Sylvia. My goodness. You make me laugh and cry, but mostly laugh. I know you don't read a lot of spec fic, but I hope you read this.

For Richard and Nancy. I am constantly in awe of your patience, your kindness, and your talents. Thank you for seeing this book in ways I couldn't.

For Lisa, Mac, Ari, and everyone at Absolute Write - you are the backbone of my creativity, the people who are there to shore me up and kick my ass and make me remember why I started doing all this to begin with.

For Lisa and Diana, who gave me excellent, clear-eyed notes. You both helped me grow this book into what it's become, and I will always be grateful.

For Patrick Foster, my book designer, icon designer, branding guy, and friend. Your work brings my work to life, and it's marvelous.

For Seth Rutledge, my cover illustrator - thank you for the beautiful work, and for sticking around even when I dither.

For Theresa, for the psychiatric research, and for confirming that imaginary friends are sometimes a healthy way to cope.

Mostly, and always, for Steve and Emily. I know what I'm like to live with, and y'all do it anyway. I love you both beyond words.

Elizabeth H. Bonesteel began making up stories at the age of five, in an attempt to battle insomnia. Thanks to a family connection to the space program, she has been reading science fiction since she was a child. She currently lives in central Massachusetts with her husband, her daughter, and various cats.

21155828R00260